About the

USA Today bestselling author **Catherine Mann** has books in print in more than twenty countries with Mills & Boon Desire, Mills & Boon Heroes, and other imprints. A six-time *RITA®* finalist, she has won both a *RITA®* and *RT* Reviewer's Choice Award. Mother of four, Catherine lives in South Carolina where she enjoys kayaking, hiking with her dog and volunteering in animal rescue. For more information, visit: catherinemann.com

After years of stifling her writer's muse and acquiring various uninspiring job-titles, **Victoria Parker** finally surrendered to that persistent voice and penned her first Mills & Boon romance. Turns out, creating havoc for feisty heroines and devilish heroes truly *is* the best job in the world. In her spare time, she dabbles in interior design, loves discovering far flung destinations, and getting into mischief with her rather wonderful family.

Carol Marinelli recently filled in a form asking for her job title. Thrilled to be able to put down her answer, she put writer. Then it asked what Carol did for relaxation and she put down the truth – writing. The third question asked for her hobbies. Well, not wanting to look obsessed, she crossed the fingers on her hand and answered swimming but, given that the chlorine in the pool does terrible things to her highlights – I'm sure you can guess the real answer.

Christmas with the Crown

CATHERINE MANN
VICTORIA PARKER
CAROL MARINELLI

MILLS & BOON

First Published in Great Britain 2023
By Mills & Boon, an imprint of HarperCollins*Publishers* Ltd,
1 London Bridge Street, London, SE1 9GF

www.harpercollins.co.uk

HarperCollins*Publishers*
Macken House, 39/40 Mayor Street Upper,
Dublin 1, D01 C9W8, Ireland

ISBN: 978-0-263-32110-4

This book is produced from independently certified FSC™ paper to ensure responsible forest management.

For more information visit: www.harpercollins.co.uk/green

Printed and Bound in the UK using 100% Renewable Electricity
at CPI Group (UK) Ltd, Croydon, CR0 4YY

YULETIDE BABY SURPRISE

CATHERINE MANN

To Savannah

One

Dr. Mariama Mandara had always been the last picked for a team in gym class. With good reason. Athletics? Not her thing. But when it came to spelling bees, debate squads and math competitions, she'd racked up requests by the dozens.

Too bad her academic skills couldn't help her sprint faster down the posh hotel corridor.

More than ever, she needed speed to escape the royal watchers tracking her at the Cape Verde beachside resort off the coast of West Africa, which was like a North Atlantic Hawaii, a horseshoe grouping of ten islands. They were staying on the largest island, Santiago.

No matter where she hid, determined legions were all too eager for a photo with a princess. Why couldn't they accept she was here for a business conference, not socializing?

Panting, Mari braced a hand against the wall as she

stumbled past a potted areca silk palm strung with twinkling Christmas lights. Evading relentless pursuers wasn't as easy as it appeared in the movies, especially if you weren't inclined to blow things up or leap from windows. The nearest stairwell door was blocked by two tourists poring over some sightseeing pamphlet. A cleaning cart blocked another escape route. She could only keep moving forward.

Regaining her balance, she power-walked, since running would draw even more attention or send her tripping over her own feet. Her low-heeled pumps thud-thud-thudded along the plush carpet in time with a polyrhythmic version of "Hark! The Herald Angels Sing" wafting from the sound system. She just wanted to finish this medical conference and return to her research lab, where she could ride out the holiday madness in peace, crunching data rather than candy canes.

For most people, Christmas meant love, joy and family. But for her, the "season to be jolly" brought epic family battles even twenty years after her parents' divorce. If her mom and dad had lived next door to each other—or even on the same continent—the holidays would not have been so painful. But they'd played transcontinental tug-of-war over their only child for decades. Growing up, she'd spent more time in the Atlanta airport and on planes with her nanny than actually celebrating by a fireside with cocoa. She'd even spent one Christmas in a hotel, her connecting flight canceled for snow.

The occasional cart in the hall now reminded her of that year's room-service Christmas meal. Call her crazy, but once she had gained more control over her world, she preferred a simpler Christmas.

Although simple wasn't always possible for someone

born into royalty. Her mother had crumbled under the pressure of the constant spotlight, divorced her Prince Charming in Western Africa and returned to her Atlanta, Georgia, home. Mari, however, couldn't divorce herself from her heritage.

If only her father and his subjects understood she could best serve their small region through her research at the university lab using her clinical brain, rather than smiling endlessly through the status quo of ribbon-cutting ceremonies. She craved her comfy, shapeless clothes, instead of worrying about keeping herself neat as a pin for photo ops.

Finally, she spotted an unguarded stairwell. Peering inside, she found it empty but for the echo of "Hark! The Herald Angels Sing" segueing into "Away in a Manger." She just needed to make it from the ground level to her fifth-floor room, where she could hole up for the night before facing the rest of the week's symposiums. Exhausted from a fourteen-hour day of presentations about her research on antiviral medications, she was a rumpled mess and just didn't have it in her to smile pretty for the camera or field questions that would be captured on video phone. Especially since anything she said could gain a life of its own on the internet in seconds these days.

She grasped the rail and all but hauled herself up step after step. Urgency pumped her pulse in her ears. Gasping, she paused for a second at the third floor to catch her breath before trudging up the last flights. Shoving through the fifth-floor door, she almost slammed into a mother and teenage daughter leaving their room. The teen did a double take and Mari turned away quickly, adrenaline surging through her exhaustion and powering her down the hall. Except now she was going in the opposite direction, damn it.

Simply strolling back into the hall wasn't an option until she could be sure the path was clear. But she couldn't simply stand here indefinitely, either. If only she had a disguise, something to throw people off the scent. Head tucked down, she searched the hall through her eyelashes, taking in a brass luggage rack and monstrously big pots of African feather grass.

Her gaze landed on the perfect answer—a room-service cart. Apparently abandoned. She scanned for anyone in a hotel uniform, but saw only the retreating back of a woman walking away quickly, a cell phone pressed to her ear. Mari chewed her lip for half a second then sprinted forward and stopped just short of the cloth-draped trolley.

She peeked under the silver tray. The mouth-watering scent of saffron-braised karoo lamb made her stomach rumble. And the tiramisu particularly tempted her to find the nearest closet and feast after a long day of talking without a break for more than coffee and water. She shook off indulgent thoughts. The sooner she worked her way back to her room, the sooner she could end this crazy day with a hot shower, her own tray of food and a soft bed.

Delivering the room-service cart now offered her best means of disguise. A hotel jacket was even draped over the handle and a slip of paper clearly listed Suite 5A as the recipient.

The sound of the elevator doors opening spurred her into action.

Mari shrugged the voluminous forest-green jacket over her rumpled black suit. A red Father Christmas hat slipped from underneath the hotel uniform. All the better for extra camouflaging. She yanked on the hat over her upswept hair and started pushing the heavily laden cart toward the suite at the end of the hall, just as voices swelled behind her.

"Do you see her?" a female teen asked in Portuguese, her squeaky tones drifting down the corridor. "I thought you said she ran up the stairs to the fifth floor."

"Are you sure it wasn't the fourth?" another high-pitched girl answered.

"I'm certain," a third voice snapped. "Get your phone ready. We can sell these for a fortune."

Not a chance.

Mari shoved the cart. China rattled and the wheels creaked. Damn, this thing was heavier than it looked. She dug her heels in deeper and pushed harder. Step by step, past carved masks and a pottery elephant planter, she walked closer to suite 5A.

The conspiring trio drew closer. "Maybe we can ask that lady with the cart if she's seen her…"

Apprehension lifted the hair on the back of Mari's neck. The photos would be all the more mortifying if they caught her in this disguise. She needed to get inside suite 5A. Now. The numbered brass plaque told her she was at the right place.

Mari jabbed the buzzer, twice, fast.

"Room service," she called, keeping her head low.

Seconds ticked by. The risk of stepping inside and hiding her identity from one person seemed far less daunting than hanging out here with the determined group and heaven only knew who else.

Just when she started to panic that time would run out, the door opened, thank God. She rushed past, her arms straining at the weight of the cart and her nose catching a whiff of manly soap. Her favorite scent—

clean and crisp rather than cloying and obvious. Her feet tangled for a second.

Tripping over her own feet as she shoved the cart was far from dignified. But she'd always been too gangly to be a glamour girl. She was more of a cerebral type, a proud nerd, much to the frustration of her family's press secretary, who expected her to present herself in a more dignified manner.

Still, even in her rush to get inside, curiosity nipped at her. What type of man would choose such a simple smell while staying in such opulence? But she didn't dare risk a peek at him.

She eyed the suite for other occupants, even though the room-service cart only held one meal. One very weighty meal. She shoved the rattling cart past a teak lion. The room appeared empty, the lighting low. Fat leather sofas and a thick wooden table filled the main space. Floor-to-ceiling shutters had been slid aside to reveal the moonlit beach outside a panoramic window. Lights from stars and yachts dotted the horizon. Palms and fruit trees with lanterns illuminated the shore. On a distant islet, a stone church perched on a hill.

She cleared her throat and started toward the table by the window. "I'll set everything up on the table for you."

"Thanks," rumbled a hauntingly familiar voice that froze her in her tracks. "But you can just leave it there by the fireplace."

Her brain needed less than a second to identify those deep bass tones. Ice trickled down her spine as if snow had hit her African Christmas after all.

She didn't have to turn around to confirm that fate was having a big laugh at her expense. She'd run from an irritation straight into a major frustration. Out of all the hotel suites she could have entered, somehow she'd landed in the room of Dr. Rowan Boothe.

Her professional nemesis.

A physician whose inventions she'd all but ridiculed in public.

What the hell was he doing here? She'd reviewed the entire program of speakers and she could have sworn he wasn't listed on the docket until the end of the week.

The door clicked shut behind her. The tread of his footsteps closed in, steady, deliberate, bringing the scent of him drifting her way. She kept her face down, studying his loafers and the well-washed hem of his faded jeans.

She held on to the hope that he wouldn't recognize her. "I'll leave your meal right here then," she said softly. "Have a nice evening."

His tall, solid body blocked her path. God, she was caught between a rock and a hard place. Her eyes skated to his chest.

A very hard, muscle-bound place encased in a white button-down with the sleeves rolled up and the tail untucked. She remembered well every muscular—annoying—inch of him.

She just prayed he wouldn't recognize her from their last encounter five months ago at a conference in London. Already the heat of embarrassment flamed over her.

Even with her face averted, she didn't need to look further to refresh her memory of that too handsome face of his. Weathered by the sun, his Brad Pitt–level good looks only increased. His sandy blond hair would have been too shaggy for any other medical professional to carry off. But somehow he simply appeared too immersed in philanthropic deeds to be bothered with anything as mundane as a trip to the barber.

The world thought he was Dr. Hot Perfection but she simply couldn't condone the way he circumvented rules.

"Ma'am," he said, ducking his head as if to catch her attention, "is there a problem?"

Just keep calm. There was no way for him to identify her from the back. She would rather brave a few pictures in the press than face this man while she wore a flipping Santa Claus hat.

A broad hand slid into view with cash folded over into a tip. "Merry Christmas."

If she didn't take the money, that would appear suspicious. She pinched the edge of the folded bills, doing her best to avoid touching him. She plucked the cash free and made a mental note to donate the tip to charity. "Thank you for your generosity."

"You're very welcome." His smooth bass was too appealing coming from such an obnoxiously perfect man.

Exhaling hard, she angled past him. Almost home free. Her hand closed around the cool brass door handle.

"Dr. Mandara, are you really going so soon?" he asked with unmistakable sarcasm. He'd recognized her. Damn. He was probably smirking, too, the bastard.

He took a step closer, the heat of his breath caressing her cheek. "And here I thought you'd gone to all this trouble to sneak into my room so you could seduce me."

Dr. Rowan Boothe waited for his words to sink in, the possibility of sparring with the sexy princess/research scientist already pumping excitement through his veins. He didn't know what it was about Mariama Mandara that turned him inside out, but he'd given up analyzing the why of it long ago. His attraction to Mari was simply a fact of life now.

Her disdain for him was an equally undeniable fact, and to be honest, it was quite possibly part of her allure.

He grew weary with the whole notion of the world painting him as some kind of saint just because he'd rejected the offer of a lucrative practice in North Carolina and opened a clinic in Africa. These days, he had money to burn after his invention of a computerized medical diagnostics program—a program Mari missed no opportunity to dismiss as faux, shortcut medicine. Funding the clinic hadn't even put a dent in his portfolio so he didn't see it as worthy of hoopla. Real philanthropy involved sacrifice. And he wasn't particularly adept at denying himself things he wanted.

Right now, he wanted Mari.

Although from the look of horror on her face, his half-joking come-on line hadn't struck gold.

She opened and closed her mouth twice, for once at a loss for words. Fine by him. He was cool with just soaking up the sight of her. He leaned back against the wet bar, taking in her long, elegant lines. Others might miss the fine-boned grace beneath the bulky clothes she wore, but he'd studied her often enough to catch the brush of every subtle curve. He could almost feel her, ached to peel her clothes away and taste every inch of her café-au-lait skin.

Some of the heat must have shown on his face because she snapped out of her shock. "You have got to be joking. You can't honestly believe I would ever make a move on you, much less one so incredibly blatant."

Damn, but her indignation was so sexy and yeah, even cute with the incongruity of that Santa hat perched on her head. He couldn't stop himself from grinning.

She stomped her foot. “Don’t you dare laugh at me.”

He tapped his head lightly. “Nice hat.”

Growling, she flung aside the hat and shrugged out of the hotel jacket. “Believe me, if I’d known you were in here, I wouldn’t have chosen this room to hide out.”

“Hide out?” he said absently, half following her words.

As she pulled her arms free of the jacket to review a rumpled black suit, the tug of her white business shirt against her breasts sent an unwelcome surge of arousal through him. He’d been fighting a damned inconvenient arousal around this woman for more than two years, ever since she’d stepped behind a podium in front of an auditorium full of people and proceeded to shoot holes in his work. She thought his computerized diagnostics tool was too simplistic. She’d accused him of taking the human element out of medicine. His jaw flexed, any urge to smile fading.

If anyone was too impersonal, it was her. And, God, how he ached to rattle her composure, to see her tawny eyes go sleepy with all-consuming passion.

Crap.

He was five seconds away from an obvious erection. He reined himself in and faced the problem at hand—the woman—as a more likely reason for her arrival smoked through his brain. “Is this some sort of professional espionage?”

“What in the hell are you talking about?” She fidgeted with the loose waistband on her tweedy skirt.

Who would have thought tweed would turn him inside out? Yet he found himself fantasizing about pulling those practical clunky shoes off her feet. He would kiss his way up under her skirt, discover the silken inside of her calf…

He cleared his throat and brought his focus up to her heart-shaped face. "Playing dumb does not suit you." He knew full well she had a genius IQ. "But if that's the way you want this to roll, then okay. Were you hoping to obtain insider information on the latest upgrade to my computerized diagnostics tool?"

"Not likely." She smoothed a hand over her swept-back hair. "I never would have pegged you as the conspiracy theorist sort since you're a man of science. Sort of."

He cocked an eyebrow. "So you're not here for information, Mari." If he'd wanted distance he should have called her Dr. Mandara, but too late to go back. "Then why are you sneaking into my suite?"

Sighing, she crossed her arms over her chest. "Fine. I'll tell you, but you have to promise not to laugh."

"Scout's honor." He crossed his heart.

"You were a Boy Scout? Figures."

Before he'd been sent to a military reform school, but he didn't like to talk about those days and the things he'd done. Things he could never atone for even if he opened free clinics on every continent, every year for the rest of his life. But he kept trying, by saving one life at a time, to make up for the past.

"You were going to tell me how you ended up in my suite."

She glanced at the door, then sat gingerly on the arm of the leather sofa. "Royal watchers have been trailing me with their phones to take photos and videos for their five seconds of fame. A group of them followed me out the back exit after my last seminar."

Protective instincts flamed to life inside him. "Doesn't your father provide you with bodyguards?"

"I choose not to use them," she said without explanation, her chin tipping regally in a way that shouted the subject wasn't open for discussion. "My attempt to slip away wasn't going well. The lady pushing this room-service cart was distracted by a phone call. I saw my chance to go incognito and I took it."

The thought of her alone out there had him biting back the urge to chew out someone—namely her father. So what if she rejected guards? Her dad should have insisted.

Mari continued, "I know I should probably just grin for the camera and move on, but the images they capture aren't…professional. I have serious work to do, a reputation to maintain." She tipped her head back, her mouth pursed tight in frustration for a telling moment before she rambled on with a weary shake of her head. "I didn't sign on for this."

Her exhaustion pulled at him, made him want to rest his hands on her drooping shoulders and ease those tense muscles. Except she would likely clobber him with the silver chafing dish on the serving cart. He opted for the surefire way to take her mind off the stress.

Shoving away from the bar, he strode past the cart toward her again. "Poor little rich princess."

Mari's cat eyes narrowed. "You're not very nice."

"You're the only one who seems to think so." He stopped twelve inches shy of touching her.

Slowly, she stood, facing him. "Well, pardon me for not being a member of *your* fan club."

"You genuinely didn't know this was my room?" he asked again, even though he could see the truth in her eyes.

"No. I didn't." She shook her head, the heartbeat throbbing faster in her elegant neck. "The cart only had your room number. Not your name."

"If you'd realized ahead of time that this was my room, my meal—" he scooped up the hotel jacket and Santa hat "—would you have surrendered yourself to the camera-toting brigade out there rather than ask me for help?"

Her lips quivered with the first hint of a smile. "I guess we'll never know the answer to that, will we?" She tugged at the jacket. "Enjoy your supper."

He didn't let go. "There's plenty of food here. You could join me, hide out for a while longer."

"Did you just invite me to dinner?" The light of humor in her eyes animated her face until the air damn near crackled between them. "Or are you secretly trying to poison me?"

She nibbled her bottom lip and he could have sworn she swayed toward him. If he hooked a finger in the vee of her shirt and pulled, she would be in his arms.

Instead, he simply reached out and skimmed back thc stray lock of sleek black hair curving just under her chin. "Mari, there are a lot of things I would like to do to you, but I can assure you that poisoning you is nowhere on that list."

Confusion chased across her face, but she wasn't running from the room or laughing. In fact, he could swear he saw reluctant interest. Enough to make him wonder what might happen if…

A whimper snapped him out of his passion fog.

The sound wasn't coming from Mari. She looked over his shoulder and he turned toward the sound. The cry swelled louder, into a full-out wail, swelling from across the room.

From under the room-service cart?

He glanced at Mari. "What the hell?"

She shook her head, her hands up. “Don’t look at me.”

He charged across the room, sweeping aside the linen cloth covering the service cart to reveal a squalling infant.

Two

The infant's wail echoed in the hotel suite. Shock resounded just as loudly inside of Mari as she stared at thc screaming baby in a plastic carrier wedged inside the room-service trolley. No wonder the cart had felt heavier than normal. If only she'd investigated she might have found the baby right away. Her brain had been tapping her with the logic that something was off, and she'd been too caught up in her own selfish fears about a few photos to notice.

To think that poor little one had been under there all this time. So tiny. So defenseless. The child, maybe two or three months old, wore a diaper and a plain white T-shirt, a green blanket tangled around its tiny, kicking feet.

Mari swallowed hard, her brain not making connections as she was too dumbstruck to think. "Oh, my God, is that a baby?"

"It's not a puppy." Rowan washed his hands at the wet-bar sink then knelt beside the lower rack holding the infant seat. Hc visibly went into doctor mode as he checked the squalling tyke over, sliding his hands under and scooping the child up in his large, confident hands. Chubby little mocha-brown arms and legs flailed before the baby settled against Rowan's chest with a hiccupping sigh.

"What in the world is it doing under there?" She stepped away, clearing a path for him to walk over to the sofa.

"I'm not the one who brought the room service in," he countered offhandedly, sliding a finger into the baby's tiny bow mouth. Checking for a cleft palate perhaps?

"Well, I didn't put the baby there."

A boy or girl? She couldn't tell. The wriggling bundle wore no distinguishing pink or blue. There wasn't even a hair bow in the cap of black curls.

Rowan elbowed aside an animal-print throw pillow and sat on the leather couch, resting the baby on his knees while he continued assessing.

She tucked her hands behind her back. "Is it okay? He or she?"

"Her," he said, closing the cloth diaper. "She's a girl, approximately three months old, but that's just a guess."

"We should call the authorities. What if whoever abandoned her is still in the building?" Unlikely given how long she'd hung out in here flirting with Rowan. "There was a woman walking away from the cart earlier. I assumed she was just taking a cell phone call, but maybe that was the baby's mother?"

"Definitely something to investigate. Hopefully there will be security footage of her. You need to think through what you're going to tell the authorities, review every detail in your mind while it's fresh." He sounded more like a detective than a doctor. "Did you see anyone else around the cart before you took it?"

"Are you blaming this on me?"

"Of course not."

Still, she couldn't help but feel guilty. "What if this is my fault for taking that cart? Maybe the baby wasn't abandoned at all. What if some mother was just trying to bring her child to work? She must be frantic looking for her daughter."

"Or frantic she's going to be in trouble," he replied dryly.

"Or he. The parent could be a father." She reached for the phone on the marble bar. "I really need to ring the front desk now."

"Before you call, could you pass over her seat? It may hold some clues to her family. Or at least some supplies to take care of her while we settle this."

"Sure, hold on."

She eased the battered plastic seat from under the cart, winging a quick prayer of thankfulness that the child hadn't come to some harm out there alone in the hall. The thought that someone would so recklessly care for a precious life made her grind her teeth in frustration. She set the gray carrier beside Rowan on the sofa, the green blanket trailing off the side.

Finally, she could call for help. Without taking her eyes off Rowan and the baby, she dialed the front desk.

The phone rang four times before someone picked up. "Could you hold, please? Thank you," a harried-sounding hotel operator said without giving Mari a chance to shout "No!" The line went straight to Christmas carols, "O Holy Night" lulling in her ear.

Sighing, she sagged a hip against the garland-draped wet bar. "They put me on hold."

Rowan glanced up, his pure blue eyes darkened with an answering frustration. "Whoever decided to schedule a conference at this time of year needs to have his head examined. The hotel was already jam-packed with holiday tourists, now conventioneers, too. Insane."

"For once, you and I agree on something one hundred percent." The music on the phone transitioned to "The Little Drummer Boy" as she watched Rowan cradle the infant in a way that made him even more handsome. Unwilling to get distracted by traveling down that mental path again, she shifted to look out the window at the scenic view. Multicolored lights blinked from the sailboats and ferries.

The Christmas spirit was definitely in full swing on the resort island. Back on the mainland, her father's country included more of a blend of religions than many realized. Christmas wasn't as elaborate as in the States, but still celebrated. Cape Verde had an especially deep-rooted Christmas tradition, having been originally settled by the Portuguese.

Since moving out on her own, she'd been more than happy to downplay the holiday mayhem personally, but she couldn't ignore the importance, the message of hope that should come this time of year. That a parent could abandon a child at the holidays seemed somehow especially tragic.

Her arms suddenly ached to scoop up the baby, but she had no experience and heaven forbid she did something wrong. The little girl was clearly in better hands with Rowan.

He cursed softly and she turned back to face him. He

held the baby in the crook of his arm while he searched the infant seat with the other.

"What?" she asked, covering the phone's mouthpiece. "Is something the matter with the baby?"

"No, something's the matter with the parents. You can stop worrying that some mom or dad brought their baby to work." He held up a slip of paper, baby cradled in the other arm. "I found this note tucked under the liner in the carrier."

He held up a piece of hotel stationary.

Mari rushed to sit beside him on the sofa, phone still in hand. "What does it say?"

"The baby's mother intended for her to be in this cart, in *my* room." He passed the note. "Read this."

> Dr. Boothe, you are known for your charity and generosity. Please look over my baby girl, Issa. My husband died in a border battle and I cannot give Issa what she needs. Tell her I love her and will think of her always.

Mari reread the note in disbelief, barely able to process that someone could give away their child so easily, with no guarantees that she would be safe. "Do people dump babies on your doorstep on a regular basis?"

"It's happened a couple of times at my clinic, but never anything remotely like this." He held out the baby toward her. "Take Issa. I have some contacts I can reach out to with extra resources. They can look into this while we're waiting for the damn hotel operator to take you off hold."

Mari stepped back sharply. "I don't have much experience with babies. No experience actually, other than kissing them on the forehead in crowds during photo ops."

"Didn't you ever babysit in high school?" He cradled the infant in one arm while fishing out his cell phone with his other hand. "Or do princesses not babysit?"

"I skipped secondary education and went straight to college." As a result, her social skills sucked as much as her fashion sense, but that had never mattered much. Until now. Mari smoothed a hand down her wrinkled, baggy skirt. "Looks to me like you have Issa and your phone well in hand."

Competently—enticingly so. No wonder he'd been featured in magazines around the globe as one of the world's most eligible bachelors. Intellectually, she'd understood he was an attractive—albeit irritating—man. But until this moment, she hadn't comprehended the full impact of his appeal.

Her body flamed to life, her senses homing in on this moment, on *him*. Rowan. The last man on the planet she should be swept away by or attracted to.

This must be some sort of primal, hormonal thing. Her ticking biological clock was playing tricks on her mind because he held a baby. She could have felt this way about any man.

Right?

God, she hoped so. Because she couldn't wrap her brain around the notion that she could be this drawn to a man so totally wrong for her.

The music ended on the phone a second before the operator returned. "May I help you?"

Heaven yes, she wanted to shout. She needed Issa safe and settled. She also needed to put space between herself and the increasingly intriguing man in front of her.

She couldn't get out of this suite soon enough.

"Yes, you can help. There's been a baby abandoned just outside Suite 5A, the room of Dr. Rowan Boothe."

Rowan didn't foresee a speedy conclusion to the baby mystery. Not tonight, anyway. The kind of person who threw away their child and trusted her to a man based solely on his professional reputation was probably long gone by now.

Walking the floor with the infant, he patted her back for a burp after the bottle she'd downed. Mari was reading a formula can, her forehead furrowed, her shirt half-untucked. Fresh baby supplies had been sent up by the hotel's concierge since Rowan didn't trust anything in the diaper bag.

There were no reports from hotel security or authorities of a missing child that matched this baby's description. So far security hadn't found any helpful footage, just images of a woman's back as she walked away from the cart as Mari stepped up to take it. Mari had called the police next, but they hadn't seemed to be in any hurry since no one's life was in danger and even the fact that a princess was involved didn't have them moving faster. Delays like this only made it more probable the press would grab hold of information about the situation. He needed to keep this under control. His connections could help him with that, but they couldn't fix the entire system here.

Eventually, the police would make their way over with someone from child services. Thoughts of this baby getting lost in an overburdened, underfunded network tore at him. On a realistic level, he understood he couldn't save everyone who crossed his path, but something about this vulnerable child abandoned at Christmas tore at his heart all the more.

Had to be because the kid was a baby, his weak spot.

He shrugged off distracting thoughts of how badly he'd screwed up as a teenager and focused on the present. Issa burped, then cooed. But Rowan wasn't fooled into thinking she was full. As fast as the kid had downed that first small bottle, he suspected she still needed more. "Issa's ready for the extra couple of ounces if you're ready."

Mari shook the measured powder and distilled water together, her pretty face still stressed. "I think I have it right. But maybe you should double-check."

"Seriously, I'm certain you can handle a two-to-one mixture." He grinned at seeing her flustered for the first time ever. Did she have any idea how cute she looked? Not that she would be happy with the "cute" label. "Just think of it as a lab experiment."

She swiped a wrist over the beads of sweat on her forehead, a simple watch sliding down her slim arm. "If I got the proportions wrong—"

"You didn't." He held out a hand for the fresh bottle. "Trust me."

Reluctantly, she passed it over. "She just looks so fragile."

"Actually, she appears healthy, well fed and clean." Her mother may have dumped her off, but someone had taken good care of the baby before that. Was the woman already regretting her decision? God, he hoped so. There were already far too few homes for orphans here. "There are no signs she's been mistreated."

"She seems cuddly," Mari said with a wistful smile.

"Are you sure you wouldn't like to hold her while I make a call?"

She shook her head quickly, tucking a stray strand of hair back into the loose knot at her neck. “Your special contacts?”

He almost smiled at her weak attempt to distract him from passing over the baby. And he definitely wasn’t in a position to share much of anything about his unorthodox contacts with her. “It would be easier if I didn’t have to juggle the kid and the bottle while I talk.”

“Okay, if you’re sure I won’t break her.” She chewed her bottom lip. “But let me sit down first.”

Seeing Mari unsure of herself was strange, to say the least. She always commanded the room with her confidence and knowledge, even when he didn’t agree with her conclusions. There was something vulnerable, approachable even, about her now.

He set the baby into her arms, catching a whiff of Mari’s perfume, something flowery and surprisingly whimsical for such a practical woman. “Just be careful to support her head and hold the bottle up enough that she isn’t drinking air.”

Mari eyed the bottle skeptically before popping it into Issa’s mouth. “Someone really should invent a more precise way to do this. There’s too much room for human error.”

“But babies like the human touch. Notice how she’s pressing her ear against your heart?” Still leaning in, he could see Mari’s pulse throbbing in her neck. The steady throb made him burn to kiss her right there, to taste her, inhale her scent. “That heartbeat is a constant in a baby’s life in utero. They find comfort in it after birth, as well.”

Her deep golden gaze held his and he could swear something, an awareness, flashed in her eyes as they played out this little family tableau.

"Um, Rowan—" her voice came out a hint breathier than normal "—make your call, please."

Yeah, probably a good idea to retreat and regroup while he figured out what to do about the baby—and about having Mari show up unexpectedly in his suite.

He stepped into his bedroom and opened the French door onto the balcony. The night air was that perfect temperature—not too hot or cold. Decembers in Cape Verde usually maxed out at between seventy-five and eighty degrees Fahrenheit. A hint of salt clung to the air and on a normal night he would find sitting out here with a drink the closest thing to a vacation he'd had in… He'd lost count of the years.

But tonight he had other things on his mind.

Fishing out his phone, he leaned on the balcony rail so he could still see Mari through the picture window in the sitting area. His gaze roved over her lithe body, which was almost completely hidden under her ill-fitting suit. At least she wouldn't be able to hear him. His contacts were out of the normal scale and the fewer people who knew about them, the better. Those ties traced back far, all the way to high school.

After he'd derailed his life in a drunk-driving accident as a teen, he'd landed in a military reform school with a bunch of screwups like himself. He'd formed lifetime friendships there with the group that had dubbed themselves the Alpha Brotherhood. Years later after college graduation, they'd all been stunned to learn their headmaster had connections with Interpol. He'd recruited a handful of them as freelance agents. Their troubled pasts—and large bank accounts—gave them a cover story to move freely in powerful and sometimes seedy circles.

Rowan was only tapped for missions maybe once

a year, but it felt damn good to help clean up underworld crime. He saw the fallout too often in the battles between warlords that erupted in regions neighboring his clinic.

The phone stopped ringing and a familiar voice said, "Speak to me, Boothe."

"Colonel, I need your help."

The Colonel laughed softly. "Tell me something new. Which one of your patients is in trouble? Or is it another cause you've taken on? Or—"

"Sir, it's a baby."

The sound of a chair squeaking echoed over the phone lines and Rowan could envision his old headmaster sitting up straighter, his full attention on the moment. "You have a baby?"

"Not *my* baby. *A* baby." He didn't expect to ever have children. His life was too consumed with his work, his mission. It wouldn't be fair to a child to have to compete with third-world problems for his father's attention. Still, Rowan's eyes locked in on Mari holding Issa so fiercely, as if still afraid she might drop her. "Someone abandoned an infant in my suite along with a note asking me to care for her."

"A little girl. I always wanted a little girl." The nostalgia in the Colonel's voice was at odds with the stern exterior he presented to the world. Even his clothes said stark long after he'd stopped wearing a uniform. These days, in his Interpol life, Salvatore wore nothing but gray suits with a red tie. "But back to your problem at hand. What do the authorities say?"

"No one has reported a child missing to the hotel security or to local authorities. Surveillance footage hasn't shown anything, but there are reports of a woman walking away from the cart where the baby was abandoned. The police are dragging their feet on showing up here to investigate further. So I need to get ahead of the curve here."

"In what way?"

"You and I both know the child welfare system here is overburdened to the crumbling point." Rowan found a plan forming in his mind, a crazy plan, but one that felt somehow right. Hell, there wasn't any option that sat completely right with his conscience. "I want to have temporary custody of the child while the authorities look into finding the mother or placing her in a home."

He might not be the best parental candidate for the baby, but he was a helluva lot better than an overflowing orphanage. If he had help…

His gaze zeroed in on the endearing tableau in his hotel sitting room. The plan came into sharper focus as he thought of spending more time with Mari.

Yet as soon as he considered the idea, obstacles piled in his path. How would he sell her on such an unconventional solution? She freaked out over feeding the kid a bottle.

"Excuse me for asking the obvious, Boothe, but how in the hell do you intend to play papa and save the world at the same time?"

"It's only temporary." He definitely couldn't see himself doing the family gig long-term. Even thinking of growing up with his own family sent his stomach roiling. Mari made it clear her work consumed her, as well. So a temporary arrangement could suit them both well. "And I'll have help…from someone."

"Ah, now I understand."

"How do you understand from a continent away?" Rowan hated to think he was that transparent.

"After my wife wised up and left me, when I had our

son for the weekend, I always had trouble matching up outfits for him to wear. So she would send everything paired up for me." He paused, the sound of clinking ice carrying over the phone line.

Where was Salvatore going with this story? Rowan wasn't sure, but he'd learned long ago that the man had more wisdom in one thumb that most people had in their entire brain. God knows, he'd saved and redirected dozens of misfit teenagers at the military high school.

Salvatore continued, "This one time, my son flipped his suitcase and mixed his clothes up. I did the best I could, but apparently, green plaid shorts, an orange striped shirt and cowboy boots don't match."

"You don't say." The image of Salvatore in his uniform or one of those generic suits of his, walking beside a mismatched kid, made Rowan grin. Salvatore didn't offer personal insights often. This was a golden moment and Rowan just let him keep talking.

"Sure, I knew the outfit didn't match, although I didn't know how to fix it. In the end, I learned a valuable lesson. When you're in the grocery store with the kid, that outfit shouts 'single dad' to a bevy of interested women."

"You used your son to pick up women?"

"Not intentionally. But that's what happened. Sounds to me like you may be partaking of the same strategy with this 'someone' who's helping you."

Busted. Although he felt compelled to defend himself. "I would be asking for help with the kid even if Mari wasn't here."

"Mariama Mandara?" Salvatore's stunned voice reverberated. "You have a thing for a local princess?"

Funny how Rowan sometimes forgot about the princess part. He thought of her as a research scientist. A professional colleague—and sometimes adversary. But most of all, he thought of her as a desirable woman, someone he suddenly didn't feel comfortable discussing with Salvatore. "Could we get back on topic here? Can you help me investigate the baby's parents or not?"

"Of course I can handle that." The Colonel's tone returned to all business, story time over.

"Thank you, sir. I can't tell you how much I appreciate this." Regardless of his attraction to Mari, Rowan couldn't lose sight of the fact that a defenseless child's future hung in the balance here.

"Just send me photos, fingerprints, footprints and any other data you've picked up."

"Roger. I know the drill."

"And good luck with the princess," Salvatore said, chuckling softly before he hung up.

Rowan drew in a deep breath of salty sea air before returning to the suite. He hated being confined. He missed his clinic, the wide-open spaces around it and the people he helped in a tangible way rather than by giving speeches.

Except once he returned home in a week to prepare for Christmas, his window of time with Mari would be done. Back to business.

He walked across the balcony and entered the door by the picture window, stepping into the sitting room. Mari didn't look up, her focus totally on the baby.

Seeing Mari in an unguarded moment was rare. The woman kept major walls up, giving off a prickly air. Right now, she sat on the sofa with her arms cradling the baby—even her body seemed to wrap inward protectively around this child. Mari might think she knew nothing about children, but her instincts were good. He'd watched enough new moms in his career to identify the ones who would have trouble versus the ones who sensed the kid's needs.

The tableau had a Madonna-and-child air. Maybe it was just the holidays messing with his head. If he wanted his half-baked plan to work, he needed to keep his head on straight and figure out how to get her on board with helping him.

"How's Issa doing?"

Mari looked up quickly, as if startled. She held up the empty bottle. "All done with her feeding."

"I'm surprised you're still sticking around. Your fans must have given up by now. The coast will be clear back to your room."

Saying that, he realized he should have mentioned those overzealous royal watchers to Salvatore. Perhaps some private security might be in order. There was a time he didn't have the funds for things like that, back in the days when he was buried in the debt of school loans, before he'd gone into partnership with a computer-whiz classmate of his.

"Mari? Are you going back to your room?" he repeated.

"I still feel responsible for her." Mari smoothed a finger along the baby's chubby cheek. "And the police will want to speak to me. If I'm here, it will move things along faster."

"You do realize the odds are low that her parents will be found tonight," he said, laying the groundwork for getting her to stick around.

"Of course, I understand." She thumbed aside a hint of milk in the corner of the infant's mouth. "That doesn't stop me from hoping she'll have good news soon."

"You sure seem like a natural with her. Earlier, you said you never babysat."

She shrugged self-consciously. "I was always busy studying."

"There were no children in your world at all?" He sat beside her, drawing in the scent of her flowery perfume. Curiosity consumed him, a desperate need to know exactly what flower she smelled like, what she preferred.

"My mother and father don't have siblings. I'm the only child of only children."

This was the closest to a real conversation they'd ever exchanged, talk that didn't involve work or bickering. He couldn't make a move on her, not with the baby right here in the room. But he could feel her relaxing around him. He wanted more of that, more of her, this exciting woman who kept him on his toes.

What would she do if he casually stretched his arm along the back of the sofa? Her eyes held his and instead of moving, he stayed stock-still, looking back at her, unwilling to risk breaking the connection—

The phone jangled harshly across the room.

Mari jolted. The baby squawked.

And Rowan smiled. This particular moment to get closer to Mari may have ended. But make no mistake, he wasn't giving up. He finally had a chance to explore the tenacious desire that had been dogging him since he'd first seen her.

Anticipation ramped through him at the thought of persuading her to see this connection through to its natural—and satisfying—conclusion.

Three

Pacing in front of the sitting room window, Mari cradled the baby against her shoulder as Rowan talked with the local police. Sure, the infant had seemed three months old when she'd looked at her, but holding her? Little Issa felt younger, more fragile.

Helpless.

So much about this evening didn't add up. The child had been abandoned yet she seemed well cared for. Beyond her chubby arms and legs, she had neatly trimmed fingernails and toenails. Her clothes were simple, but clean. She smelled freshly bathed. Could she have been kidnapped as revenge on someone? Growing up, Mari had been constantly warned of the dangers of people who would try to hurt her to get back at her father, as well as people would use her to get *close* to her father. Trusting anyone had been all but impossible.

She shook off the paranoid thoughts and focused on

the little life in her arms. Mari stroked the baby's impossibly soft cheeks, tapped the dimple in her chin. Did she look like her mother or father? Was she missed? Round chocolate-brown eyes blinked up at her trustingly.

Her heart squeezed tight in her chest in a totally illogical way. She'd only just met the child, for heaven's sake, and she ached to press a kiss to her forehead.

Mari glanced to the side to see if Rowan had observed her weak moment, but he was in the middle of finishing up his phone conversation with the police.

Did he practice looking so hot? Even in jeans, he owned the room. Her eyes were drawn to the breadth of his shoulders, the flex of muscles in his legs as he shuffled from foot to foot, his loafers expensive but well worn. He exuded power and wealth without waste or conspicuous consumption. How could he be such a good man and so annoying at the same time?

Rowan hung up the phone and turned, catching her studying him. He cocked an eyebrow. She forced herself to stare back innocently, her chin tipping even as her body tingled with awareness.

"What did the police say?" she asked casually, swaying from side to side in a way she'd found the baby liked.

"They're just arriving outside the hotel." He closed the three feet between them. "They're on their way up to take her."

"That's it?" Her arms tightened around Issa. "She'll be gone minutes from now? Did they say where they will be sending her? I have connections of my own. Maybe I can help."

His blue eyes were compassionate, weary. "You and I both already know what will happen to her. She will be sent to a local orphanage while the police use their limited resources to look into her past, along with all the other cases and other abandoned kids they have in their stacks of files to investigate. Tough to hear, I realize. But that's how it is. We do what we can, when we can."

"I understand." That didn't stop the frustration or the need to change things for this innocent child in her arms and all the children living in poverty in her country.

He scooped the baby from her before she could protest. "But that's not how it has to be today. We *can* do something this time."

"What do you mean?" She crossed her empty arms over her chest, hope niggling at her that Rowan had a reasonable solution.

"We only have a few more minutes before they arrive so I need to make this quick." He hefted the baby onto his shoulder and rubbed her back in small, hypnotic circles. "I think we should offer to watch Issa."

Thank heaven he was holding the child because he'd stunned Mari numb. She watched his hand smoothing along the baby's back and tried to gather her thoughts. "Um, what did you say?"

"We're both clearly qualified and capable adults." His voice reverberated in soothing waves. "It would be in the best interest of the child, a great Christmas message of goodwill, for us to keep her."

Keep her?

Mari's legs folded out from under her and she sank to the edge of the leather sofa. She couldn't have heard him right. She'd let her attraction to him distract her. "What did you say?"

He sat beside her, his thigh pressing warm and solid against hers. "We can have temporary custody of her, just for a couple of weeks to give the police a chance to find out if she has biological relatives able to care for her."

"Have you lost your mind?" Or maybe she had lost hers because she was actually tempted by his crazy plan.

"Not that I know of."

She pressed the back of her wrist to her forehead, stunned that he was serious. Concerns cycled through her head about work and the hoopla of a media circus. "This is a big decision for both of us, something that should be thought over carefully."

"In medicine I have to think fast. I don't always have the luxury of a slow and steady scientific exam," he said, with a wry twist to his lips. "Years of going with my gut have honed my instincts, and my instincts say this is the right thing to do."

Her mind settled on his words and while she never would have gotten to that point on her own, the thought of this baby staying with him rather than in some institution was appealing. "So you'll be her temporary guardian?"

"Our case is more powerful if we offer to do this as a partnership. Both of us." His deep bass and logic drew her in. "Think of the positive PR you'll receive. Your father's press corps will be all over this philanthropic act of yours, which should take some pressure off you at the holidays," he offered, so logically she could almost believe him.

"It isn't as simple as that. The press can twist things, rumors will start about both of us." What if they thought it was *her* baby? She squeezed her eyes closed and bolted off the sofa. "I need more time."

The buzzer rang at the door. Her heart went into her throat.

She heard Rowan follow her. Felt the heat of him at her back. Felt the urgency.

"Issa doesn't have time, Mari. You need to decide if you'll do this. Decide to commit now."

She turned sharply to find him standing so close the three of them made a little family circle. "But you could take her on your own—"

"Maybe the authorities would accept that. But maybe not. We should lead with our strongest case. For her." He cradled the baby's head. "We didn't ask for this, but we're here." Fine lines fanned from the corners of his eyes, attesting to years of worry and long hours in the sun. "We may disagree on a lot of things, but we're people who help."

"You're guilt-tripping me," she accused in the small space between them, her words crackling like small snaps of electricity. And the guilt was working. Her concerns about gossip felt absolutely pathetic in light of the plight of this baby.

As much as she gave Rowan hell about his computer inventions, she knew all about his humanitarian work at the charity clinic. He devoted his life to helping others. He had good qualities underneath that arrogant charm.

"Well, people like us who help in high-stakes situations learn to use whatever means are at our disposal." He half smiled, creasing the lines deeper. "Is it working?"

Those lines from worry and work were real. She might disapprove of his methods, but she couldn't question his motivations, his altruistic spirit. Seeing him deftly rock the baby to sleep ended any argument. For this one time at least, she was on his team.

For Issa.

"Open the door and you'll find out."

* * *

Three hours later, Mari watched Rowan close the hotel door after the police. Stacks of paperwork rested on the table, making it official. She and Rowan had temporary custody of the baby while the police investigated further and tried to track down the employee who'd walked away from the cart.

Issa slept in her infant seat, secure for now.

Mari sighed in relief, slumping in exhaustion back onto the sofa. She'd done it. She'd played the princess card and all but demanded the police obey her "request" to care for the baby until Christmas—less than two weeks away—or until more information could be found about Issa's parents. She'd agreed to care for the child with Rowan Boothe, a doctor who'd saved countless young lives. The police had seemed relieved to have the problem resolved so easily. They'd taken photos of the baby and prints. They would look into the matter, but their faces said they didn't hold out much hope of finding answers.

Maybe she should hire a private detective to look deeper than the police. Except it was almost midnight now. Any other plans would have to wait until morning.

Rowan rested a hand on Mari's shoulder. "Would you get my medical bag so I can do a more thorough checkup? It's in the bedroom by my shaving kit. I'd like to listen to her heart."

He squeezed her shoulder once, deliciously so, until her mouth dried right up from that simple touch.

"Medical bag." She shot to her feet. "Right, of course."

She was too tired and too unsettled to fight off the sensual allure of him right now. She stepped into Rowan's bedroom, her eyes drawn to the hints of him everywhere. A suit was draped over the back of a rattan rocker by sliding doors that led out to a balcony. She didn't consider herself a romantic by any stretch but the thought of sitting out there under the stars with someone…

God, what was the matter with her? This man had driven her bat crazy for years. Now she was daydreaming about an under-the-stars make-out session that would lead back into the bedroom. His bedroom.

Her eyes skated to the sprawling four-poster draped with gauzy netting, a dangerous place to look with his provocative glances still steaming up her memories. An e-reader rested on the bedside table, his computer laptop tucked underneath. Her mind filled with images of him sprawled in that massive bed—working, reading—details about a man she'd done her best to avoid. She pulled her eyes away.

The bathroom was only a few feet away. She charged across the plush carpet, pushing the door wide. The scent of him was stronger in here, and she couldn't resist breathing in the soapy aroma clinging to the air—patchouli, perhaps. She swallowed hard as goose bumps of awareness rose on her skin, her senses on overload.

A whimpering baby cry from the main room reminded her of her mission here. She shook off frivolous thoughts and snagged the medical bag from the marble vanity. She wrapped her hands around the well-worn leather with his name on a scratched brass plate. The dichotomy of a man this wealthy carrying such a battered bag added layers to her previously clear-cut image of him.

Clutching the bag to her stomach, she returned to the sitting room. Rowan set aside a bottle and settled the baby girl against his shoulder, his broad palm patting her back.

How exactly were they going to work this baby bargain? She had absolutely no idea.

For the first time in her life, she'd done something completely irrational. The notion that Rowan Boothe had that much power over her behavior rattled her to her toes.

She really was losing it. She needed to finish this day, get some sleep and find some clarity.

From this point forward, she would keep a firmer grip on herself. And that meant no more drooling over the sexy doc, and definitely no more sniffing his tempting aftershave.

Rowan tapped through the images on his laptop, reviewing the file on the baby, including the note he'd scanned in before passing it over to the police. He'd sent a copy of everything to Colonel Salvatore. Even though it was too early to expect results, he still hoped for some news, for the child's sake.

Meanwhile, though, he'd accomplished a freaking miracle in buying himself time with Mari. A week or so at the most, likely more, but possibly less since her staying rested solely on the child. If relatives were found quickly, she'd be headed home. He didn't doubt his decision, even if part of his motivation was selfish. This baby provided the perfect opportunity to spend more time with Mari, to learn more about her and figure out what made her tick. Then, hopefully, she would no longer be a thorn in his side—or a pain in his libido.

He tapped the screen back to the scanned image of the note that had been left with the baby.

Dr. Boothe, you are known for your charity and generosity. Please look over my baby girl, Issa.

My husband died in a border battle and I cannot give Issa what she needs. Tell her I love her and will think of her always.

His ears tuned in to the sound of Mari walking toward him, then the floral scent of her wrapped around him. She stood behind him without speaking and he realized she was reading over his shoulder, taking in the note.

"Loves her?" Mari sighed heavily. "The woman abandoned her to a stranger based on that person's reputation in the press."

"I take it your heart isn't tugged." He closed the laptop and turned to face her.

"My heart is broken for this child—" she waved toward the sleeping infant in the baby seat "—and what's in store for her if we don't find answers, along with a truly loving and responsible family."

"I'm hopeful that my contacts will have some information sooner than the police." A reminder that he needed to make the most of his time with Mari. What if Salvatore called with concrete news tomorrow? He looked over at Mari, imagining being with her, drawing her into his bedroom, so close to where they were now. "Let's talk about how we'll look after the baby here during the conference."

"Now?" She jolted in surprise. "It's past midnight."

"There are things to take care of, like ordering more baby gear, meeting with the hotel's babysitting service." He ticked off each point on his fingers. "Just trying to fill in the details on our plan."

"You actually want to plan?" Her kissable lips twitched with a smile.

"No need to be insulting," he bantered right back, enjoying the way she never treated him like some freaking saint just because of where he chose to work. He wasn't the good guy the press painted him to be just because he'd reformed. The past didn't simply go away. He still had debts that could never be made right.

"I'm being careful—finally. Like I should have been earlier." Mari fidgeted with the hem of her untucked shirt, weariness straining her face, dark circles under her eyes. "She's a child. A human being. We can't just fly by the seat of our pants."

He wanted to haul Mari into his arms and let her sleep against his chest, tell her she didn't have to be so serious, she didn't have to take the weight of the world on her shoulders. She could share the load with him.

Instead, he dragged a chair from the tiny teak table by the window and gestured for her to sit, to rest. "I'm not exactly without the means or ability to care for a child. It's only for a short time until we figure out more about her past so we don't have to fly by the seat of our pants." He dragged over a chair for himself as well and sat across from her.

"How is it so easy for you to disregard the rules?" She slumped back.

"You're free to go if you wish."

She shook her head. "I brought her in here. She's my responsibility."

Ah, so she wasn't in a rush to run out the door. "Do you intend to personally watch over her while details are sorted out?"

"I can hire someone."

"Ah, that's right. You're a princess with endless resources," he teased, taking her hands in his.

She pulled back. "Are you calling me spoiled?"

He squeezed her fingers, holding on, liking the feel

of her hands in his. "I would never dare insult you, Princess. You should know that well enough from the provocative things I said to you five minutes ago."

"Oh. Okay." She nibbled on her bottom lip, surprise flickering through her eyes.

"First things first." He thumbed the inside of her wrists.

"Your plan?" Her breathing seemed to hitch.

"We pretend to be dating and since we're dating, and we'd be spending this holiday time together anyway, we decided to help with the child. How does that work for a plan?"

"What?" She gasped in surprise. "Do you really think people are going to believe we went from professional adversaries to lovers in a heartbeat?"

He saw her pulse throb faster, ramping up his in response.

"Lovers, huh? I like the sound of that."

"You said—"

"I said dating." He squeezed her hands again. "But I like your plan better."

"This isn't a plan." She pulled free, inching her chair back. "It's insanity."

"A plan that will work. People will believe it. More than that, they will eat it up. Everyone will want to hear more about the aloof princess finding romance and playing Good Samaritan at Christmastime. If they have an actual human interest piece to write about you it will distract them from digging around to create a story."

Her eyes went wide with panic, but she stayed in her seat. She wasn't running. Yet. He'd pushed as far as he could for tonight. Tomorrow would offer up a whole new day for making his case.

He shoved to his feet. "Time for bed."

“Oh, um,” she squeaked, standing, as well. “Bed?”

He could see in her eyes that she’d envisioned them sharing a bed before this moment. He didn’t doubt for a second what he saw and it gave him a surge of victory. Definitely best to bide his time and wait for a moment when she wasn’t skittish. A time when she would be all in, as fully committed as he was to exploring this crazy attraction.

“Yes, Mari, bed. I’ll watch the baby tonight and if you’re comfortable, we can alternate the night shift.”

She blinked in surprise. “Right. The night schedule. Are you sure you can handle a baby at night and still participate in the conference?”

“I’m a doctor. I’ve pulled far longer shifts with no sleep in the hospital. I’ll be fine.”

“Of course. Then I’ll call the front desk to move me to a larger suite so I’ll have enough space for the baby and the daytime sitter.”

“No need to do that. This suite is plenty large enough for all of us.”

Her jaw dropped. “Excuse me?”

“All of us,” he said calmly, holding her with his eyes as fully as he’d held her hand, gauging her every blink. Needing to win her over. “It makes sense if we’re going to watch the baby, we should do it together for efficiency. The concierge already sent someone to pack your things.”

Her chest rose faster and faster, the gentle curves of her breasts pressing against the wrinkled silk of her blouse. “You’ve actually made quite a few plans.”

“Sometimes flying by the seat of your pants works quite well.” Otherwise he never would have had this chance to win her over. “A bellhop will be delivering your luggage shortly along with more baby gear that I ordered."

"Here? The two—three—of us? In one suite?" she asked, although he noticed she didn't say no.

Victory was so close.

"There's plenty of space for the baby. You can have your own room. Unless you want to sleep in mine." He grinned. "You have to know I wouldn't object."

Four

Buttoning up her navy blue power suit the next morning, Mari couldn't believe she'd actually spent the night in Rowan Boothe's hotel suite. Not his room, but a mere wall away. He'd cared for the baby until morning as he'd promised. A good thing, since she needed to learn a lot more before she trusted herself to care for Issa.

She tucked pins into her swept-back hair, but the mirror showed her to be the same slightly rumpled academic she'd always been. While she wasn't a total innocent when it came to men, she wasn't the wild and reckless type who agreed to spend the night in the same suite as a guy she'd never actually dated. She'd expected to toss and turn all night after the confusing turn of events. She couldn't believe she'd agreed.

Yet in spite of all her doubts, she'd slept better than anytime she could remember. Perhaps because the odds of anyone finding her here were next to nil. Her longtime professional feud with him was well-known, and they hadn't yet gone public with this strange idea of joint custody of an abandoned baby. The hotel staff or someone on the police force would likely leak juicy tidbits about the royal family to the press, but it would all be gossip and conjecture until she and Rowan made their official statement verifying the situation.

Soon enough the world would know. Eventually the cameras would start snapping. Her gut clenched at the thought of all those stalkers and the press feeding on the tiniest of details, the least scrap of her life. What if they fed on the innocence of the baby?

Or what if they picked up on the attraction between her and Rowan?

There was still time to back out, write it all off as simple gossip. The urge was strong to put back on that Christmas hat and slip away, to hide in her lab, far, far from the stress of being on show and always falling short. She craved the peace of her laboratory and cubbyhole office, where she truly reigned supreme. Here, in Rowan's suite, she felt so off-kilter, so out of control.

A coo from the other room reminded her she needed to hurry. She stepped away from the mirror and slid her feet into her low, blue pumps. She pulled open her bedroom door, then sagged to rest against the doorjamb. The sight of the little one in a ruffled pink sleeper, resting against Rowan's shoulder, looked like something straight off a greeting card. So perfect.

Except that perfection was an illusion.

Even though Rowan had the baby well in hand, the child was helpless outside their protection. Issa had no one to fight for her, not really, not if Mari and Rowan gave up on her. Even if Mari left and Rowan stayed, he couldn't offer the baby everything Mari could. Her fame—that fame she so resented—could be Issa's salvation.

The baby would get an exposure the police never could have provided. In these days of DNA testing, it wasn't as if fake relatives could step forward to claim a precious infant. So Mari wasn't going anywhere, except to give her presentation at the medical conference, then she'd take the baby for a walk with Rowan.

Looking around the suite strewn with baby paraphernalia, anyone would believe they were truly guardians of the child. Rowan had ordered a veritable nursery set up with top-of-the-line gear. A portable bassinet rested in the corner of the main room, a monitor perched beside it. He'd ordered a swing, a car seat, plus enough clothes, food and diapers for three babies for a month.

He knew what an infant needed, or at least he knew who to call.

Hopefully that call had included a sitter since he was dressed for work as well, in a black Savile Row suit with a Christmas-red tie. God, he was handsome, with his blond hair damp and combed back, his broad hand patting the baby's back. His face wore a perpetual five-o'clock shadow, just enough to be nighttime sexy without sliding over into scruffy.

He filled out the expensive suit with ease. Was there any realm that made this man uncomfortable? He'd taken care of the baby through the night and still looked totally put together.

His eyes searched hers and she shivered, wondering what he saw as he stood there holding Issa so easily. The man was a multitasker. He was also someone with an uncanny knack for getting into a person's mind. He'd found her vulnerable spot in one evening. After all of her tense and bicontinental Christmases, she simply couldn't bear for this child to spend the holidays confused and scared while the system figured out what to do with her—and the other thousands of orphans in their care.

She couldn't replace the child's mother, but she could make sure the child was held, cared for, secure. To do that, she needed to keep her mind off the charismatic man a few feet away.

He looked over at her as if he'd known she was there the whole time. "Good morning. Coffee's ready along with a tray of pastries."

And some sweet, sticky *bouili* dipping sauce.

Her mouth watered for the food almost as much as for the man. She walked to the granite countertop and poured herself a mug of coffee from the silver carafe. She inhaled the rich java fragrance steaming up from the dark roast with hints of fruity overtones. "Did she sleep well?"

"Well enough, just as I would expect from a baby who's experienced so much change," he said, tucking the baby into a swing with expert hands. "The hotel's sending up a sitter for the day. I verified her references and qualifications. They seem solid, so we should be covered through our lecture presentations. Tonight we can take Issa out for dinner and a stroll incognito, kill time while we let the cops finish their initial investigation. If they haven't found out anything by tomorrow, we can go public."

Dinner out? Revealing their plan to the world? Her heart pounded with nerves, but it was too late to go back now. The world would already be buzzing with leaked news. Best to make things official on their own terms.

If Issa's family wasn't found by tomorrow, she would have to call her parents and let them know about her strange partnership with Rowan. First, she had to decide how she wanted to spin it so her parents didn't jump to the wrong conclusions—or try to interfere. This needed to be a good thing for the baby, not just about positive press. She would play it by ear today and call them tonight once she had a firmer idea of what she'd gotten herself into.

Maybe Issa would be back with relatives before supper. A good thing, right?

Rowan started the baby swing in motion. The click-click-click mingled with a low nursery tune.

Mari cleared her throat. "I'll check on Issa during lunch and make sure all's going well with the sitter."

"That's a good idea. Thank you." He cradled a cup in strong hands that could so easily crush the fine china.

She shrugged dismissively. It was no hardship to skip the luncheon. She disliked the idle table chitchat at these sorts of functions anyway. "No big sacrifice. Nobody likes conference lunch food."

Laughing softly, he eyed her over his cup of coffee. "I appreciate your working with me on this."

"You didn't leave me much choice, Dr. Guilt Trip."

His smile creased dimples into his face. "Who'd have thought you'd have a sense of humor?"

"That's not nice." She traced the rim of her cup.

"Neither is saying I coerced you." He tapped the tip of her scrunched nose. "People always have a choice."

Of course he was right. She could always walk, but thinking overlong about her compulsion to stay made her edgy. She sat at the table, the morning sun glistening off the ocean waters outside. "Of course I'm doing this of my own free will, for Issa's sake. It has absolutely nothing to do with you."

"Hello? I thought we weren't going to play games."

She avoided his eyes and sipped her steaming java. "What do you mean, games?"

"Fine. I'll spell it out." He set down his cup on the table and sat beside her, their knees almost touching. "You have made it your life's mission to tear down my research and to keep me at arm's length. Yet you chose to stay here, for the baby, but you and I both know there's more to it than that. There's a chemistry between us, sparks."

"Those sparks—" she proceeded warily "—are just a part of our disagreements."

"Disagreements? You've publically denounced my work. That's a little more than a disagreement."

Of course he wouldn't forget that. "See, sparks. Just like I said."

His eyes narrowed. If only he could understand her point. She only wanted to get past his impulsive, pigheaded mindset and improve his programs.

"Mari, you're damn good at diverting from the topic."

"I'm right on point," she said primly. "This is about our work and you refused to consider that I see things from another angle. You've made it your life's mission to ignore any pertinent input I might have for your technological inventions. I am a scientist."

He scraped a hand over his drying hair. "Then why are you so against my computer program?"

"I thought we were talking about what's best for Issa." She glanced at the baby girl still snoozing in the swing with the lullaby playing.

"Princess, you are making my head spin." He sagged back. "We're here for Issa, but that doesn't mean we can't talk about other things, so quit changing the subject every three seconds. In the interest of getting along better during these next couple of weeks, let's discuss your public disdain for my life's work."

Was he serious? Did he really want to hash that out now? He certainly looked serious, drinking his coffee and downing bites of breakfast. Maybe he was one of those people who wanted to make peace at the holidays in spite of bickering all year round. She knew plenty about that. Which should have taught her well. Problems couldn't be avoided or the resolutions delayed. Best to confront them when given the opening.

"Your program is just too much of a snapshot of a diagnosis, too much of a quick fix. It's like fast-food medicine. It doesn't take into account enough variables." Now she waited for the explosion.

He inhaled a deep breath and tipped back in his chair before answering. "I can see your point. To a degree, I agree. I would welcome the chance to give every patient the hands-on medical treatment of the best clinic in the world. But I'm treating the masses with a skeleton team of medical professionals. That computer program helps us triage in half the time."

"What about people who use your program to cut corners?"

Rowan frowned. "What do you mean?"

"You can't truly believe the world is as altruistic as you? What about the clinics using that program to funnel more patients through just to make more money?"

His chair legs hit the floor, his jaw tightening. "I can't be the conscience for the world," he said in an even tone although a tic had started in the corner of his azure-blue eye. "I can only deal with the problems in front of me. I'm working my tail off to come up with help. Would I prefer more doctors and nurses, PAs and midwives, human hands? Hell, yes. But I make do with what I have and I do what I can so those of us who are here can be as efficient as possible under conditions they didn't come close to teaching us about during my residency."

"So you admit the program isn't optimal?" She couldn't believe he'd admitted to the program's shortcomings.

"Really?" He threw up his hands. "That's your take-away from my whole rambling speech? I'm being practical, and you're being idealistic in your ivory tower of research. I'm sorry if that makes you angry to hear."

"I'm not the volatile sort." She pursed her lips tightly to resist the temptation to snap at him for devaluing her work.

Slowly, he grinned, leaning closer. "That's too bad."

"Pardon me?" she asked, not following his logic at all.

"Because when you get all flustered, you're really hot."

Her eyes shot open wide, surprise skittering through her, followed by skepticism. "Does that line really work for you?"

"I've never tried it before." He angled closer until his mouth almost brushed hers. "You'll have to let me know."

Before she could gasp in half a breath of air, he brushed his mouth over hers. Shock quickly turned to something else entirely as delicious tingles shimmered through her. Her body warmed to the feel of him, the newness of his kiss, their first kiss, a moment already burning itself into her memory, searing through her with liquid heat.

Her hand fluttered to his chest, flattening, feeling the steady, strong beat of his heart under her palm matching the thrumming heartbeat in her ears. His kiss was nothing like she would have imagined. She'd expected him to be out of control, wild. Instead, he held her like spun glass. He touched her with deft, sensitive hands, surgeon's hands that knew just the right places to graze, stroke, tease for maximum payoff. Her body thrilled at the caress down her spine that cupped her bottom, bringing her closer.

Already she could feel herself sinking into a spiral of lush sensation. Her limbs went languid with desire. She wanted more of this, more of him, but they were a heartbeat away from tossing away their clothes and inhibitions. Too risky for a multitude of reasons, not the least of which was the possibility of someone discovering them.

Those sorts of exposé photos she absolutely did not want circulating on the internet or anywhere else.

Then, too soon he pulled away. How embarrassing that he was the one to stop since she already knew the kiss had to end. Never had she lost control this quickly.

Cool air and embarrassment washed over her as she sat stunned in her chair. He'd completely knocked the world out from under her with one simple kiss. Had he even been half as affected as she was by the moment? She looked quickly at him, but his back was to her already and she realized he was walking toward the door.

"Rowan?"

He glanced over his shoulder. "The buzzer—" Was that a hint of hoarseness in his voice? "The baby sitter has arrived."

Mari pressed her fingers to her still tingling lips, wondering if a day apart would be enough time to shore up her defenses again before their evening out.

* * *

That evening, Rowan pushed the baby stroller along the marketplace road. Vendors lined the street, and he eyed the place for potential trouble spots. Even with bodyguards trailing them, he kept watch. The baby in the stroller depended on him.

And so did the woman beside him. Mari wore her business suit, without the jacket, just the skirt and blouse, a scarf wrapped over her head and large sunglasses on for disguise, looking like a leggy 1940s movie star.

She strolled beside him, her hand trailing along stalls that overflowed with handwoven cloths and colorful beads. Bins of fresh fruits and vegetables sat out, the scent of roasting turkey and goat carrying on the salty beach breeze. Waves crashed in the distance, adding to the rhythmic percussion of a local band playing Christmas tunes while children danced. Locals and tourists angled past in a crush, multiple languages coming at him in stereo—Cape Verdean Creole, Portuguese, French, English…and heaven knew how many others.

Tonight, he finally had Mari out of the work world and alone with him. Okay, alone with him, a baby, bodyguards and a crush of shoppers.

The last rays of the day bathed Mari in a crimson glow. She hadn't referenced their kiss earlier, so he'd followed her lead on that, counting it a victory that she wasn't running. Clearly, she'd been as turned on as he was. But still, she hadn't run.

With the taste of her etched in his memory, there was not a chance in hell he was going anywhere. More than ever, he was determined to get closer to her, to sample a hell of a lot more than her lips.

But he was smart enough to take his time. This

woman was smart—and skittish. He made his living off reading subtle signs, deciphering puzzles, but this woman? She was the most complex individual he'd ever met.

Could that be a part of her appeal? The mysterious element? The puzzle?

The "why" of it didn't matter so much to him right now. He just wanted to make the most of this evening out and hopefully gain some traction in identifying Issa's family. While they'd gotten a few curious looks from people and a few surreptitiously snapped photos, so far, no one had openly approached them.

He checked left and right again, reconfirming their unobtrusive security detail, ensuring the men were close enough to intervene if needed. Colonel Salvatore had been very accommodating about rounding up the best in the business ASAP, although he still had no answers on the baby's identity. Issa's footprints hadn't come up in any databases, but then the child could have been a home birth, unregistered. Salvatore had insisted he hadn't come close to exhausting all their investigative options yet.

For now, their best lead would come from controlled press exposure, getting the child seen and praying some legit relative stepped up to claim her.

Meanwhile, Rowan finally had his chance to be with Mari, to romance her, and what better place than in this country he loved, with holiday festivities lightening the air. He would have cared for the baby even if Mari had opted out, so he didn't feel guilty about using the child to persuade Mari to stay. He was just surprised she'd agreed so easily.

That gave him pause—and encouragement.

She hesitated at a stall of clay bowls painted with

scenes of everyday life. She trailed her fingers along a piece before moving on to the jewelry, where she stopped for the longest time yet. He'd found her weakness. He wouldn't have pegged her as the type to enjoy those sorts of baubles, but her face lit up as she sifted through beads, necklaces. She seemed to lean more toward practical clothes and loose-fitting suits or dresses. Tonight she wore a long jean jumper and thick leather sandals.

Her hand lingered on the bracelets before she stepped back, the wistfulness disappearing from her golden eyes. "We should find somewhere to eat dinner. The conference food has left me starving for something substantial."

"Point the way. Ladies choice tonight," he said, curious to know what she would choose, what she liked, the way he'd just learned her preferences on the bracelets. Shoppers bustled past, cloth sacks bulging with purchases, everything from souvenirs to groceries.

Instinctively, she moved between the baby stroller and the hurrying masses. "How about we eat at a streetside café while we watch the performances?"

"Sounds good to me." He could keep watch better that way, but then he always kept his guard up. His work with Interpol showed him too well that crime didn't always lurk in the expected places.

He glanced down the street, taking in the carolers playing drums and pipes. Farther down, a group of children acted out the nativity in simple costumes. The sun hadn't gone down yet, so there was less worry about crime.

Rowan pointed to the nearby café with blue tables and fresh fish. "What about there?"

"Perfect, I'll be able to see royal watchers coming."

"Although your fan club seems to have taken a break." He wheeled the stroller toward the restaurant where the waitress instructed them to seat themselves. Issa still slept hard, sucking on a fist and looking too cute for words in a red Christmas sleeper.

Mari laughed, the scarf sliding down off her head, hanging loosely around her neck. "Funny how I couldn't escape photo-happy sorts at the hotel—" she tugged at either end of the silky scarf "—and yet now no one seems to notice me when some notoriety could serve some good."

"Issa's photo has already been released to law enforcement. If nothing comes of it by tomorrow morning, the story will break about our involvement and add an extra push. For now, anyway, the baby and I make good camouflage for you to savor your dinner."

"Mama-flage," she said as he held out her chair for her.

"Nice! I'm enjoying your sense of humor more and more." And he was enjoying a lot more about her as well this evening. He caught the sweet floral scent on her neck as he eased her chair into place.

His mind filled with images of her wearing only perfume and an assortment of the colorful beads from the marketplace. Damn, and now he would be awake all night thinking about the lithe figure she hid under her shapeless suits.

Mari glanced back at him, peering over her sunglasses, her amber eyes reflecting the setting sun. "Is something the matter?"

"Of course not." He took his seat across from her, his foot firmly on the stroller even knowing there were a half-dozen highly trained bodyguards stationed anonymously around them. She might not use them, but he'd made sure to hire a crew for the safety of both Mari and Issa.

The waitress brought glasses and a pitcher of fruit juice—guava and mango—not showing the least sign of recognizing the royal customer she served. This was a good dry run for when they would announce their joint custody publicly.

"What a cute baby," the waitress cooed without even looking at them. "I just love her little red Christmas outfit. She looks like an adorable elf." She toyed with toes in tiny green booties.

"Thank you," Mari said, then mouthed at Rowan, "Mama-flage."

After they'd placed their order for swordfish with *cachupa*—a mixture of corn and beans—Mari leaned back in her chair, appearing far more relaxed than the woman who'd taken refuge in his suite the night before. She eased the sunglasses up to rest on top of her head.

"You look like you've had a couple of servings of grogue." Grogue was a sugar cane liquor drunk with honey that flowed freely here.

"No alcohol for me tonight, thank you." She lifted a hand. "My turn to watch the baby."

"I don't mind taking the night shift if you're not comfortable."

She raised a delicately arched dark eyebrow. "Somewhere in the world, a couple dozen new moms just swooned and they don't know why."

"I'm just trying to be helpful. You have the heavier presentation load."

She stirred sugar into her coffee. "Are you trying to coerce me into kissing you again?"

"As I recall, I kissed you and you didn't object."

She set her spoon down with a decisive clink. "Well, you shouldn't count on doing it again."

"Request duly noted," he replied, not daunted in the least. He saw the speeding of her pulse, the flush of awareness along her dusky skin.

He started to reach for her, just to brush his knuckles along that pulse under the pretense of brushing something aside—except a movement just out of the corner of his eye snagged his attention. Alert, he turned to see an older touristy-looking couple moving toward them.

Mari sat back abruptly, her hand fluttering to her throat. Rowan assessed the pair. Trouble could come in any form, at any age. The bodyguards' attention ramped up as they stalked along the perimeter, closing the circle of protection. Mari reached for her sunglasses. Rowan didn't see any signs of concealed weapons, but he slid his hand inside his jacket, resting his palm on his 9 mm, just in case.

The elderly husband, wearing a camera and a man-purse over his shoulder, stopped beside Mari.

"Excuse us, but would you mind answering a question?" he asked with a thick New Jersey accent.

Was their cover busted? If so, did it really matter that they went public a few hours early? Not for him or the baby, but because he didn't want Mari upset, bolting away from the press, terrified, like the night before.

She tipped her head regally, her shoulders braced as she placed the sunglasses on the table. "Go ahead."

The wife angled in eagerly. "Are the two of you from around here?"

Rowan's mouth twitched. Not busted at all. "Not from the island, ma'am. We both live on the mainland."

"Oh, all right, I see." She furrowed her brow. "Maybe

you can still help me. Where's the Kwanzaa celebration?"

Mari's eyes went wide with surprise, then a hint of humor glinted before her face went politely neutral. "Ma'am, that's an American tradition."

"Oh, I didn't realize." Her forehead furrowed as she adjusted her fanny pack. "I just didn't expect so much Christmas celebration."

Mari glanced at the children finishing up their nativity play and accepting donations for their church. "Africa has a varied cultural and religious heritage. How much of each you find depends on which portion of the continent you're visiting. This area was settled by the Portuguese," she explained patiently, "which accounts for the larger influence of Christian traditions than you might find in other regions."

"Thank you for being so patient in explaining." The wife pulled out a travel guide and passed it to her husband, her eyes staying on Mari. "You look very familiar, dear. Have I seen you somewhere before?"

Pausing for a second, Mari eyed them, then said, "People say I look like the Princess Mariama Mandara. Sometimes I even let folks believe that."

She winked, grinning mischievously.

The older woman laughed. "What a wicked thing to do, young lady. But then I imagine people deserve what they get if they like to sneak photos for the internet."

"Would you like a photo of me with the baby on your phone?" Mari leaned closer to the stroller, sweeping back the cover so baby Issa's face was in clear view. "I'll put on my best princess smile."

"Oh, I wouldn't even know how to work the camera on that new phone our kids gave us for our fiftieth anniversary." She elbowed her husband. "We just use our old Polaroid, isn't that right, Nils?"

"I'm getting it out, Meg, hold on a minute." He fished around inside his man-purse.

Mari extended her arm. "Meg, why don't you get in the photo, too?"

"Oh, yes, thank you. The grandkids will love it." She fluffed her bobbed gray hair with her fingers then leaned in to smile while her husband's old Polaroid spit out picture after picture. "Now you and your husband lean in to pose for one with your daughter."

Daughter? Rowan jolted, the fun of the moment suddenly taking on a different spin. He liked kids and he sure as hell wanted Mari, but the notion of a pretend marriage? That threatened to give him hives. He swallowed down the bite of bile over the family he'd wrecked so many years ago and pretended for the moment life could be normal for him. He kneeled beside Mari and the baby, forcing his face into the requisite smile. He was a good actor.

He'd had lots of practice.

The couple finished their photo shoot, doling out thanks and leaving an extra Polaroid shot behind for them. The image developed in front of him, blurry shapes coming into focus, much like his thoughts, his need to have Mari.

Rowan sank back into his chair as the waitress brought their food. Once she left, he asked Mari, "Why didn't you tell that couple the truth about us, about yourself? It was the perfect opening."

"There were so many people around. If I had, they would have been mobbed out of the photo. When the official story about us fostering the baby hits the news in the morning, they'll realize their photo of a princess is real and they'll have a great story to tell their grandchildren. We still get what we want and they get their cool story."

"That was nice of you to do for them." He draped a napkin over his knee. "I know how much you hate the notoriety of being royalty."

She twisted her napkin between her fingers before dropping it on her lap. "I'm not an awful person."

Had he hurt her feelings? He'd never imagined this boldly confident woman might be insecure. "I never said you were. I think your research is admirable."

"Really? I seem to recall a particular magazine interview where you accused me of trying to sabotage your work. In fact, when I came into your suite with the room-service cart, you accused me of espionage."

"My word choices may have been a bit harsh. The stakes were high." And yeah, he liked seeing her riled up with fire in her eyes. "My work world just doesn't give me the luxury of the time you have in yours."

"I simply prefer life to be on my terms when possible. So much in this world is beyond anyone's control."

Her eyes took on a faraway look that made him burn to reel her back into the moment, to finish the thought out loud so he could keep learning more about what made this woman tick. But she'd already distanced herself from him, deep in thought, looking off down the road at the musicians.

He needed those insights if he expected to get a second kiss—and more from her. But he was beginning to realize that if he wanted more, he was going to have to pony up some confidences of his own. An uncomfortable prospect.

As he looked at Mari swaying absently in time with the music, her lithe body at ease and graceful, he knew having her would be well worth any cost.

Five

Mari soaked in the sound of street music mellowing the warm evening air. The steady beat of the *bougarabou* drum with the players' jangling bracelets enriching the percussion reminded her of childhood days. Back when her parents were still together and she lived in Africa full-time, other than visits to the States to see her maternal grandparents.

Those first seven years of her life had been idyllic—or so she'd thought. She hadn't known anything about the painful undercurrents already rippling through her parents' marriage. She hadn't sensed the tension in their voices over royal pressures and her mother's homesickness.

For a genius, she'd missed all the obvious signs. But then, she'd never had the same skill reading people that she had for reading data. She'd barely registered that her mother was traveling to Atlanta more and more frequently. Her first clue had come near the end when she'd overheard her mom talking about buying a home in the States during their Christmas vacation. They wouldn't be staying with her grandparents any longer during U.S. visits. They would have their own place, not a room with family. Her parents had officially split up and filed for divorce over the holidays.

Christmas music never sounded quite the same to her again, on either continent.

The sway melted away from her shoulders and Mari stilled in her wrought-iron seat. The wind still wound around her as they sat at the patio dining area, but her senses moved on from the music to the air of roasting meat from the kitchen and the sound of laughing children. All of it was almost strong enough to distract her from the weight of Rowan's gaze.

Almost.

She glanced over at him self-consciously. "Why are you staring at me? I must be a mess." She touched her hair, tucking a stray strand back into the twist, then smoothed her rumpled suit shirt and adjusted the silver scarf draped around her neck. "It's been a long day and the breeze is strong tonight."

Since when had shc cared about her appearance for more than the sake of photos? She forced her hands back to her lap.

Rowan's tanned face creased with his confident grin. "Your smile is radiant." He waved a broad hand to encompass the festivities playing out around them. "The way you're taking in everything, appreciating the joy of the smallest details, your pleasure in it all is… mesmerizing."

His blue eyes downright twinkled like the stars in the night sky.

Was he flirting with her? She studied him suspiciously. The restaurant window behind him filled with the movement of diners and waiters, the edges blurred by the spray of fake snow. She'd always been entranced by those pretend snowy displays in the middle of a warm island Christmas.

"Joy? It's December, Rowan. The Christmas season of *joy*. Of course I'm happy." She thought fast, desperate to defer conversation about her. Talking about Rowan's past felt a lot more comfortable than worrying about tucking in her shirt, for God's sake. "What kind of traditions did you enjoy with your family growing up?"

He leaned back in his chair, his gaze still homed in solely on Mari in spite of the festivities going on around them. "We did the regular holiday stuff like a tree, carols, lots of food."

"What kind of food?" she asked just as Issa squirmed in the stroller.

He shrugged, adjusting the baby's pacifier until the infant settled back to sleep. "Regular Christmas stuff."

His ease with the baby was admirable—and heart-tugging. "Come on," Mari persisted, "fill in the blanks for me. There are lots of ways to celebrate Christmas and regular food here isn't the same as regular food somewhere else. Besides, I grew up with chefs. Cooking is still a fascinating mystery to me."

He forked up a bite of swordfish. "It's just like following the steps in a chemistry experiment."

"Maybe in theory." She sipped her fruit juice, the blend bursting along her taste buds with a hint of coconut, her senses hyperaware since Rowan kissed her. "Suffice it to say I'm a better scientist than a cook. But back to you. What was your favorite Christmas treat?"

He set his fork aside, his foot gently tapping the

stroller back and forth. “My mom liked to decorate sugar cookies, but my brother, Dylan, and I weren't all that into it. We ate more of the frosting than went on the cookies.”

The image wrapped around her like a comfortable blanket. “That sounds perfect. I always wanted a sibling to share moments like that with. Tell me more. Details… Trains or dump trucks? Bikes or ugly sweaters?”

“We didn't have a lot of money, so my folks saved and tucked away gifts all year long. They always seemed a bit embarrassed that they couldn't give us more, but we were happy. And God knows, it's more than most of the kids I work with will ever have.”

“You sound like you had a close family. That's a priceless gift.”

Something flickered through his eyes that she couldn't quite identify, like gray clouds over a blue sky, but then they cleared so fast she figured she must have been mistaken. She focused on his words, more curious about this man than any she'd ever known.

“At around three-thirty on Christmas morning, Dylan and I would slip out of our bunk beds and sneak downstairs to see what Santa brought.” He shared the memory, but the gray had slipped into his tone of voice now, darkening the lightness of his story. “We would play with everything for about an hour, then put it back like we found it, even if the toy was in a box. We would tiptoe back into our room and wait for our parents to wake us up. We always pretended like we were completely surprised by the gifts.”

What was she missing here? Setting aside her napkin, she leaned closer. “Sounds like you and your brother share a special bond.”

“Shared,” he said flatly. “Dylan's dead.”

She couldn't hold back the gasp of shock or the empathetic stab of pain for his loss. For an awkward moment, the chorus of "Silver Bells" seemed to blare louder, the happy music at odds with this sudden revelation. "I'm so sorry, Rowan. I didn't know that."

"You had no reason to know. He died in a car accident when he was twenty."

She searched for something appropriate to say. Her lack of social skills had never bothered her before now. "How old were you when he died?"

"Eighteen." He fidgeted with her sunglasses on the table.

"That had to be so horrible for you and for your parents."

"It was," he said simply, still toying with her wide-rimmed shades.

An awkward silence fell, the echoes of Christmas ringing hollow now. She chewed her lip and pulled the first question from her brain that she could scavenge. "Were you still at the military reform school?"

"It was graduation week."

Her heart squeezed tightly at the thought of him losing so much, especially at a time when he should have been celebrating completing his sentence in that school.

Without thinking or hesitating, she pushed aside her sunglasses and covered Rowan's hand. "Rowan, I don't even know what to say."

"There's nothing to say." He flipped his hand, skimming his thumb along the inside of her wrist. "I just wanted you to know I'm trusting you with a part of my past here."

Heat seeped through her veins at each stroke of his thumb across her pulse. "You're telling me about yourself to…?"

His eyes were completely readable now, sensual and steaming over her. “To get closer to you. To let you know that kiss wasn’t just an accident. I’m nowhere near the saint the press likes to paint me.”

Heat warmed to full-out sparks of electricity arcing along her every nerve ending. She wasn’t imagining or exaggerating anything. Rowan Boothe *wanted* her.

And she wanted to sleep with him.

The inescapable truth of that rocked the ground underneath her.

The noise of a backfiring truck snapped Rowan back into the moment. Mari jolted, blinking quickly before making a huge deal out of attacking her plate of swordfish and *cachupa,* gulping coffee between bites.

The sputtering engine still ringing in his ears, Rowan scanned the marketplace, checking the position of their bodyguards. He took in the honeymooners settling in at the next table. The elderly couple that had photographed them earlier was paying their bill. A family of vacationers filled a long stretch of table.

The place was as safe as anywhere out in public.

He knew he couldn’t keep Mari and the baby under lock and key. He had the security detail and he hoped Mari would find peace in being out in public with the proper protection. The thought of her being chased down hallways for the rest of her life made him grind his teeth in frustration. She deserved better than to live in the shadows.

He owed little Issa a lot for how she’d brought them together. He was moved by the sensitive side of Mari he’d never known she had, the sweetly awkward humanity beneath the brilliant scientific brain and regal royal heritage.

Leaning toward the stroller, Rowan adjusted the baby's bib, reassured by the steady beat of her little heart. He'd given her a thorough physical and thank God she was healthy, but she was still a helpless, fragile infant. He needed to take care of her future. And he would. He felt confident he could, with the help of Salvatore either finding the baby's family or lining up a solid adoption.

The outcome of his situation with Mari, however, was less certain. There was no mistaking the desire in her golden eyes. Desire mixed with wariness.

A tactical retreat was in order while he waited for the appropriate moment to resume his advances. He hadn't meant to reveal Dylan's death to her, but their talk about the past had lulled him into old memories. He wouldn't let that happen again.

He poured coffee from the earthen pot into his mug and hers. "You must have seen some lavish Christmas celebrations with your father."

Her eyes were shielded, but her hand trembled slightly as she reached for her mug. "My father keeps things fairly scaled back. The country's economy is stabilizing thanks to an increase in cocoa export, but the national treasury isn't flush with cash, by any means. I was brought up to appreciate my responsibilities to my people."

"You don't have a sibling to share the responsibility."

The words fell out of his mouth before he thought them through, probably because of all those memories of his brother knocking around in his gut. All the ways he'd failed to save Dylan's life. If only he'd made different decisions… He forced his attention back into the present, on Mari.

"Both of my parents remarried other people, divorced again, no more kids, though." She spread her hands, sunglasses dangling from her fingers. "So I'm it. The future of my country."

"You don't sound enthusiastic."

"I just think there has to be someone better equipped." She tossed aside the glasses again and picked up her coffee. "What? Why the surprised look? You can't think I'm the best bet for my people. I would rather lock myself in a research lab with the coffeemaker maxed out than deal with the day-to-day events of leading people."

"I think you will succeed at anything life puts in your path." Who had torn down this woman's confidence? If only she saw—believed in—her magnificence. "When you walk in a room, you damn near light up the place. You own the space with your presence, lady."

She blew into her mug of coffee, eyeing him. "Thanks for the vote of confidence. But people and all their intangibles like 'magnificence' arc beyond me. I like concrete facts."

"I would say some people would appreciate logic in a leader."

She looked away quickly, busying herself with adjusting the netting around the baby's stroller. "I wasn't always this way."

"What do you mean?"

"So precise." She darted a quick glance at him out of the corner of her eye. "I was actually a very scatterbrained child. I lost my hair ribbons in hotels, left my doll or book on the airplane. I was always oversleeping or sluggish in the morning, running late for important events. The staff was given instructions to wake me up a half hour ahead of time."

His mom had woken him and Dylan up through elementary school, then bought them an alarm clock—a really obnoxious clock that clanged like a cowbell. No one overslept. "Did this happen in your mother's or your father's home?"

"Both places. My internal clock just wasn't impressed by alarms or schedules."

She was a kid juggling a bicontinental lifestyle, the pressures of royal scrutiny along with the social awkwardness of being at least five grades ahead of her peers.

When did she ever get to relax? "Sounds to me like you traveled quite a bit in your life. I'm sure you know that losing things during travel is as common as jet lag, even for adults."

"You're kind to make excuses." She brushed aside his explanation. "I just learned to make lists and structure my world more carefully."

"Such as?" he asked, suddenly finding the need to learn more about what shaped her life every bit as important as tasting her lips again.

"Always sitting in the same seat on an airplane. Creating a routine for the transatlantic trips, traveling at the same time." She shrugged her elegant shoulders. "The world seemed less confusing that way."

"Confusing?" he repeated.

She chewed her bottom lip, which was still glistening from a sip of coffee. "Forget I said anything."

"Too late. I remember everything you say." And what a time to realize how true that was.

"Ah, you're one of those photographic-memory sorts. I imagine that helps with your work."

"Hmm..." Not a photographic memory, except when it came to her. But she didn't need to know that.

"I'm sure my routines sound a bit overboard to you. But my life feels crazy most of the time. I'm a princess.

There's no escaping that fact." She set her mug down carefully. "I have to accept that no matter how many lists I make, my world will never be predictable."

"Sometimes unpredictable has its advantages, as well." He ached to trace the lines of her heart-shaped face and finish with a tap to her chin.

Her throat moved in a long swallow. "Is this where you surprise me with another kiss?"

He leaned in, a breath away, and said, "I was thinking this time you could surprise me."

She stared back at him so long he was sure she would laugh at him for suggesting such a thing, especially out in public. Not that the public problem bothered the honeymooners at the next table. Just when Rowan was certain she would tell him to go to hell—

Mari kissed him. She closed those last two inches between them and pressed her lips to his. Closemouthed but steady. He felt drunk even though he hadn't had anything but coffee and fruit juice all evening. The same drinks he tasted on Mari's lips. Her hands, soft and smooth, covered his on the table. Need, hard and insistent, coursed through his body over an essentially simple kiss with a table between them.

And just that fast, she let go, pushing on his chest and dropping back into her chair.

A flush spread from her face down the vee of her blouse. "That was not… I didn't mean…"

"Shhh." He pressed a finger to her lips, confidence singing through him along with the hammering pulse of desire. "Some things don't need to be analyzed. Some things simply are. Let's finish supper so we can turn in early."

"Are you propositioning me?" Her lips moved under his finger.

Deliberately seductive? Either way, an extra jolt of want shot through him, a want he saw echoed in her eyes.

He spread his arms wide. "Why would you think that?" he asked with a hint of the devil in his voice. "I want to turn in early. It's your night with the baby."

The tension eased from her shoulders and she smiled back, an ease settling between them as they bantered. God, she was incredible, smart and lithe, earnest and exotic all at once. He covered her hand with his—

A squeal from the next table split the air. "Oh, my God, it's her." The honeymooner at the next table tapped her husband's arm insistently. "That princess… Mariama! I want a picture with her. Get me a photo, pretty please, pookie."

Apparently the mama-flage had stopped working. They didn't have until the morning for Mari to become comfortable with the renewed public attention. The story about them taking care of a baby—*together*—was about to leak.

Big-time.

Two hours later, Mari patted Issa's back in the bassinet to be sure she was deeply asleep then flopped onto the bed in the hotel suite she shared with Rowan.

Alone in her bedroom.

Once that woman shouted to the whole restaurant that a princess sat at the next table, the camera phones started snapping before her head could stop reeling from that impulsive kiss. A kiss that still tingled all the way to the roots of her hair.

Rowan had handled the curious masses with a simple explanation that they were watching a baby in foster care. More information would be forthcoming at a morning press conference. Easy as pie.

Although she was still curious as to where all the bodyguards had come from. She intended to confront her father about that later and find out why he'd decided to disregard her wishes now of all times.

Granted, she could see the wisdom in a bit more protection for Issa's sake and she liked to think she would have arranged for something tomorrow…on a smaller scale. The guards had discreetly escorted her from the restaurant, along with Rowan and the baby, and all the way back to the hotel. No ducking into bathrooms or racing down hallways. Just a wall of protection around her as Rowan continued to repeat with a smile and a firm tone, "No further comment tonight."

Without question, the papers would be buzzing by morning. That press conference would be packed. Her father's promo guru couldn't have planned it better.… Had Rowan known that when they kissed? Did he have an agenda? She couldn't help but wonder since most people in her life had their own agendas—with extras to spare.

This was not the first time the thought had come to her. By the time she'd exited the elevator, she was already second-guessing the kiss, the flirting, the whole crazy plan. She knew that Rowan wanted her. She just couldn't figure out why.

Until she had more answers, she couldn't even consider taking things further.

She sat up again, swinging her legs off the side of the bed. Besides, she had a baby to take care of and a phone call to make. Since Issa still slept blissfully in the lacy bassinet after her bottle, Mari could get to that other pressing concern.

Her father.

She swiped her cell phone off the teak end table and thumbed auto-dial…two rings later, a familiar voice answered and Mari blurted out, “Papa, we need to talk….”

Her father’s booming laugh filled the earpiece. “About the boyfriend and the baby you’ve been hiding from me?”

Mari squeezed her eyes shut, envisioning her lanky father sprawled in his favorite leather chair on the lanai, where he preferred to work. He vowed he felt closer to nature out there, closer to his country, even though three barriers of walls and guards protected him.

Sighing, she pressed two fingers to her head and massaged her temples. “How did you hear about Rowan and Issa? Have you had spies watching me? And why did you assign bodyguards without consulting me?”

“One question at a time, daughter dear. First, I heard about your affiliation with Dr. Boothe and the baby on the internet. Second, I do not spy on my family—not often, anyway. And third, whatever bodyguards you’re referring to, they’re not mine. I assume they’re on your boyfriend’s payroll.”

Her head throbbed over Rowan hiring bodyguards without consulting her. Her life was snowballing out of control.

“He’s not my boyfriend—” even though they’d kissed and she’d enjoyed the hell out of it “—and Issa is not our baby. She’s a foster child, just like Rowan said at the restaurant.”

Even though her heart was already moved beyond measure by the chubby bundle sleeping in the frilly bassinet next to her bed.

“I know the baby’s not yours, Mariama.”

“The internet strikes again?” She flopped back, rolling to her side and holding a pillow to her stomach as she monitored the steady rise and fall of Issa's chest as she slept.

"I keep tabs on you, daughter dear. You haven't been pregnant and you've never been a fan of Rowan Boothe."

An image flashed in her mind of Rowan pacing the sitting room with Issa in his arms. "The baby was abandoned in Dr. Boothe's hotel room and we are both watching over her while the authorities try to find her relatives. You know how overburdened Africa is with orphans. We just couldn't let her go into the system when we had the power to help her."

"Hmm..." The sound of him clicking computer keys filtered through the phone line—her father never rested, always worked. He took his position as leader seriously, no puppet leadership role for him. "And why are you working with a man you can't stand to help a child you've never met? He could have taken care of this on his own."

"I'm a philanthropist?"

"True," her dad conceded. "But you're also a poor liar. How did the child become your responsibility?"

She'd never been able to get anything past her wily father. "I was trying to get away from a group of tourists trying to steal a photo of me at the end of a very long day. I grabbed a room-service tray and delivered it." The whole crazy night rolled through her mind again and she wondered what had possessed her to act so rashly. Never, though, could she have foreseen how it would end. "Turns out it was for Rowan Boothe and there was an abandoned baby inside. There's nothing going on between us."

A squawk from Issa sent her jolting upright again to

pat the baby's back. An instant later, a tap sounded on the door from the suite beyond. She covered the mouthpiece on the phone. "We're okay."

Still, the bedroom door opened, a quizzical look on Rowan's face. "Everything all right?"

"I've got it." She uncovered the phone. "Dad, I need to go."

Rowan lounged against the doorjamb, his eyes questioning. Pressing the phone against her shoulder to hold it to her ear, she tugged her skirt over her knees, curling her bare toes.

"Mari, dear," her father said, "I do believe you have gotten better at lying after all. Seems like there's a lot going on in your life I don't know about."

Her pulse sped up, affirming her father was indeed right. This wasn't just about Issa. She was lying to herself in thinking there was nothing more going on with Rowan. His eyes enticed her from across the room, like a blue-hot flame drawing a moth.

But her father waited on the other end of the line. Best to deflect the conversation, especially while the object of her current hormonal turmoil stood a few feet away. "You should be thrilled about this whole setup. It will make for great publicity, a wonderful story for your press people to spin over the holidays. Papa, for once I'm not a disappointment."

Rowan scowled and Mari wished she could call back the words that had somehow slipped free. But she felt the weight of the knowledge all the same. The frustration of never measuring up to her parents' expectations.

"Mari, dear," her father said, his voice hoarse, "you have never been a disappointment."

A bittersweet smile welled from the inside out.

"You're worse at lying than I am. But I love you anyway. Good night, Papa."

She thumped the off button and swung her bare feet to the floor. Her nerves were a jangled mess from the emotions stirred up by talking to her dad…not to mention the smoldering embers from kissing Rowan. The stroke of his eyes over her told her they were a simple step, a simple word away from far more than a kiss.

But those tangled nerves and mixed-up feelings also told her this was not the time to make such a momentous decision. Too much was at stake, the well-being of the infant in their care…

And Mari's peace of mind. Because it would be far too easy to lose complete control when it came to this man.

Six

Refusing to back down from Rowan's heated gaze, Mari stiffened her spine and her resolve, closing the last three feet between them. "Why did you order bodyguards without consulting me?"

He frowned. "Where did you think they'd come from?"

"My father."

"I just did what he should have. I made sure to look after your safety," he said smoothly, arrogantly.

Her chin tipped defiantly. He might have been right about them needing bodyguards—for Issa's sake—but she wasn't backing down on everything. "Just because I kissed you at the restaurant does *not* mean I intend to invite you into my bed."

Grinning wickedly, he clamped a hand over his heart. "Damn. My spirit is crushed."

"You're joking, of course." She stopped just shy of

touching him, the banter sparkling through her like champagne bubbles.

"Possibly. But make no mistake, I do want to sleep with you and every day I wait is…torture." The barely restrained passion in his voice sent those intoxicating bubbles straight to her head. "I'm just reasonable enough to accept it isn't going to happen tonight."

"And if it never happens?" she asked, unwilling to let him know how deeply he affected her.

"Ah, you said 'if.'" He flicked a loose strand of hair over her shoulder, just barely skimming his knuckles across her skin. "Princess, that means we're already halfway to naked."

Before she could find air to breathe, he backed away, slowly, deliberately closing the door after him.

And she'd thought her nerves were a tangled, jangled mess before. Her legs folded under her as she dropped to sit on the edge of the bed.

A suddenly very cold and empty bed.

Rowan walked through the hotel sliding doors that led out to the sprawling shoreline. The cool night breeze did little to ease the heat pumping through his body. Leaving Mari alone in her hotel room had been one of the toughest things he'd ever done, but he'd had no choice for two reasons.

First, it was too soon to make his move. He didn't want to risk Mari changing her mind about staying with him. She had to be sure—very sure—when they made love.

Second reason he'd needed to put some distance between himself and her right now? He had an important meeting scheduled with an Interpol contact outside the hotel. An old school friend of his and the person responsible for their security detail tonight.

Rowan jogged down the long steps from the pool area to the beach. Late-night vacationers splashed under the fake waterfall, others floated, some sprawled in deck loungers with drinks, the party running deep into the night.

His appointment would take place in cabana number two, away from prying eyes and with the sound of the roaring surf to cover conversation. His loafers sank into the gritty sand, the teak shelter a dozen yards away, with a grassy roof and canvas walls flapping lightly in the wind. Ships bobbed on the horizon, lights echoing the stars overhead.

Rowan swept aside the fabric and stepped inside. "Sorry I'm late, my friend."

His old school pal Elliot Starc lounged in a recliner under the cabana in their designated meeting spot as planned, both loungers overlooking the endless stretch of ocean. "Nothing better to do."

Strictly speaking that couldn't be true. The freelance Interpol agent used his job as a world-renowned Formula One race-car driver to slip in and out of countries without question. He ran in high-powered circles. But then that very lifestyle was the sort their handler, Colonel Salvatore, capitalized on—using the tarnished reputations of his old students to gain access to underworld types.

Of course, Salvatore gave Rowan hell periodically for being a do-gooder. Rowan winced. The label pinched, a poor fit at best. "Well, thanks all the same for dropping everything to come to Cape Verde."

Elliot scratched his hand over his buzzed short hair. "I'm made of time since my fiancée dumped me."

"Sorry about that." Talk about headline news. Elliot's past—his vast past—with women, filled headlines across multiple continents. The world thought that's what had broken up the engagement, but Rowan suspected the truth. Elliot's fiancée had been freaked out by the Interpol work. The job had risked more than one relationship for the Brotherhood.

What would Mari think if she knew?

"Crap happens." Elliot tipped back a drink, draining half of the amber liquid before setting the cut crystal glass on the table between them. "I'd cleared my schedule for the honeymoon. When we split I gave her the tickets since the whole thing was my fault anyway. She and her 'BFF' are skiing in the Alps as we speak. I might as well be doing something productive with my time off."

Clearly, Elliot wouldn't want sympathy. Another drink maybe. He looked like hell, dark circles under his eyes. From lack of sleep most likely. But that didn't explain the nearly shaved head.

"Dude, what happened to you?" Rowan asked, pointing to the short cut.

Elliot's curly mop had become a signature with his fans who collected magazine covers. There were even billboards and posters.... All their pals from the military academy—the ones who'd dubbed themselves the Alpha Brotherhood—never passed up an opportunity to rib Elliot about the underwear ad.

Elliot scratched a hand over his shorn hair. "I had a wreck during a training run. Bit of a fire involved. Singed my hair."

Holy hell. "You caught on fire?"

Elliot grinned. "Just my hair."

"How did I miss hearing about that?"

"No need. It's not a big deal."

Rowan shook his head. "You are one seriously messed-up dude."

But then all his former classmates were messed up in some form. Came with the territory. The things that had landed them in that reform school left them with baggage long after graduation.

"You're the one who hangs out in war-torn villages passing out vaccinations and blankets for fun."

"I'm not trailed by groupies." He shuddered.

"They're harmless most of the time."

Except when they weren't. The very reason he'd consulted with Elliot about the best way to protect Mari and Issa. "I can't thank you enough, brother, for overseeing the security detail. They earned their pay tonight."

"Child's play. So to speak." Elliot lifted his glass again, draining the rest with a wince. "What's up with your papa-and-the-princess deal?"

"The kid needed my help. So I helped."

"You've always been the saint. But that doesn't explain the princess."

Rowan ignored the last part of Elliot's question. "What's so saintly about helping out a kid when I have unlimited funds and Interpol agents at my disposal? Saintly is when something's difficult to do."

"And the woman—the princess?" his half-drunk buddy persisted. "She had a reputation for being very difficult on the subject of Dr. Rowan Boothe."

Like the time she'd written an entire journal piece pointing out potential flaws in his diagnostics program. Sure, he'd made adjustments after reading the piece, but holy hell, it would have been nice—and more expedient—if she'd come to him first. "Mari needs my help, too. That's all it is."

Elliot laughed. “You are so damn delusional.”

A truth. And an uncomfortable one.

Beyond their cabana tent, a couple strolled arm-in-arm along the shoreline, sidestepping as a jogger sprinted past with a loping dog.

“If you were a good friend you would let me continue with my denial.”

“Maybe I’m wrong.” Elliot lifted the decanter and refilled his glass. “It’s not denial if you acknowledge said problem.”

“I am aware of that fact.” His unrelenting desire for Mari was a longtime, ongoing issue he was doing his damnedest to address.

“What do you intend to do about your crush on the princess?”

“Crush? Good God, man. I’m not in junior high.”

“Glad you know that. What’s your plan?”

“I’m figuring that out as I go.” And even if he had one, he wasn’t comfortable discussing details of his—feelings?—his attraction.

“What happens if this relationship goes south? Her father has a lot of influence. Even though you’re not in his country, his region still neighbors your backyard. That could be…uncomfortable.”

Rowan hadn’t considered that angle and he should have. Which said a lot for how much Mari messed with his mind. “Let me get this straight, Starc. *You* are doling out relationship advice?”

“I’m a top-notch source when it comes to all the wrong things to do in a long-term relationship.” He lifted his glass in toast. “Here’s to three broken engagements and counting.”

“Who said I’m looking for long-term?”

Elliot leveled an entirely sober stare his way, holding for three crashes of the waves before he said, "You truly are delusional, dude."

"That's not advice."

"It is if you really think about it."

He'd had enough of this discussion about Mari and the possibility of a train wreck of epic proportions. Rowan shoved off the lounger, his shoes sinking in the sand. "Good night."

"Hit a sore spot, did I?" Still, Starc pushed.

"I appreciate your…concern. And your help." He clapped Elliot on the shoulder before sweeping aside the canvas curtain. "I need to return to the hotel."

He'd been gone long enough. As much as he trusted Elliot's choice of guards, he still preferred to keep close.

Wind rolled in off the water, tearing at his open shirt collar as he made his way back up the beach toward the resort. Lights winked from trees. Fake snow speckled windows. Less than two weeks left until Christmas. He would spend the day at his house by the clinic, working any emergency-room walk-ins as he did every year. What plans did Mari have? Would she go to her family?

His parents holed up on Christmas, and frankly, he preferred it that way. Too many painful memories for all of them.

He shut off those thoughts as he entered the resort again. Better to focus on the present. One day at a time. That's the way he'd learned to deal with the crap that had gone down. And right now, his present was filled with Mari and Issa.

Potted palms, carved masks and mounted animal heads passed in a blur as he made his way back to his suite. He nodded to the pair of guards outside the door before stepping inside.

Dimmed lights from the wet bar bathed the sitting

area in an amber glow. Silence echoed as he padded his way to Mari's room. No sounds came from her room this time, no conversation with her royal dad.

The door to Mari's room was ajar and he nudged it open slowly, pushing back thoughts of invading her privacy. This was about safety and checking on the baby.

Not an insane desire to see what Mari looked like sleeping.

To appease his conscience, he checked the baby first and found the chubby infant sleeping, sucking on her tiny fist as she dreamed. Whatever came of his situation with Mari, they'd done right by this baby. They'd kept at least one child safe.

One day at a time. One life saved at a time. It's how he lived. How he atoned for the unforgivable in his past.

Did Issa's mother regret abandoning her child? The note said she wanted her baby in the care of someone like him. But there was no way she could have known the full extent of the resources he had at his disposal with Interpol. If so, she wouldn't have been as quick to abandon her child to him because he could and would find the mother. It wasn't a matter of if. Only a matter of when.

He wouldn't give up. This child's future depended on finding answers.

All the more reason to tread carefully with Mari. He knew what he wanted, but he'd failed to take into consideration how much of a help she would be. How much it would touch his soul seeing her care for the baby. From her initial reaction to the baby, he'd expected her to be awkward with the child, all technical and analytical. But she had an instinct for children, a tenderness in her heart that overcame any awkwardness. A softness that crept over her features.

Watching her sleep now, he could almost forget the way Mari had cut him down to size on more than one occasion in the past. Her hair was down and loose on her pillow, black satin against the white Egyptian cotton pillowcase. Moonlight kissed the curve of her neck, her chest rising and falling slowly.

He could see a strap of creamy satin along her shoulder. Her nightgown? His body tightened and he considered scooping her up and carrying her to his room. To hell with waiting. He could persuade her.

But just as he started to reach for her, his mind snagged on the memory of her talking about how she felt like she'd been a disappointment to her family. The notion that anyone would think this woman less than amazing floored him. He might not agree with her on everything, but he sure as hell saw her value.

Her brilliance of mind and spirit.

He definitely needed to stick to his original plan. He would wait. He couldn't stop thinking about that snippet of her phone conversation with her father. He understood that feeling of inadequacy all too well. She deserved better.

Rather than some half-assed seduction, he needed a plan. A magnificent plan to romance a magnificent woman. The work would be well worth the payoff for both of them.

He backed away from her bed and reached for his cell phone to check in with Salvatore. Pausing at the door, he took in the sight of her, imprinting on his brain the image of Mari sleeping even though that vision ensured *he* wouldn't be sleeping tonight.

Mari's dreams filled with Rowan, filled with his blue eyes stroking her. With his hands caressing her as they floated together in the surf, away from work and responsibilities. She'd never felt so free, so languid, his kisses and touches melting her bones. Her mind filled with his husky whispers of how much he wanted her. Even the sound of his voice stoked her passion higher, hotter, until she ached to wrap her legs around his waist and be filled with his strength.

She couldn't get enough of him. Years of sparring over their work, and even the weather if the subject came up… Now all those frustrating encounters exploded into a deep need, an explosive passion for a man she could have vowed she didn't even like.

Although like had nothing to do with this raw arousal—she felt a need that left her hot and moist between the legs until she squirmed in her bed.

Her bed.

Slowly, her dream world faded as reality interjected itself with tiny details, like the slither of sheets against her skin. The give of the pillow as her head thrashed back and forth. The sound of the ocean outside the window—and the faint rumble of Rowan's voice beyond her door.

She sat upright quickly.

Rowan.

No wonder she'd been dreaming of him. His voice had been filtering into her dream until he took it over. She clutched the puffy comforter to her chest and listened, although the words were indistinguishable. From the periodic silences, he must be talking to someone on the phone.

Mari eased from the bed, careful not to wake the baby. She pulled her robe from over a cane rocking chair and slipped her arms into the cool satin. Her one decadent pleasure—sexy peignoir sets. They made her feel like a silver-screen star from the forties, complete with furry kitten-heel slippers, not so high as to trip her up, but still ultrafeminine.

Would Rowan think them sexy or silly if he noticed them? God, he was filling up her mind and making her care about things—superficial things—that shouldn't matter. Even more distressing, he made her want to climb back into that dream world and forget about everything else.

Her entire focus should be on securing Issa's future. Mari leaned over the lace bassinet to check the infant's breathing. She pressed a kiss to two fingers and skimmed them over Issa's brow, affection clutching her heart. How could one little scrap of humanity become so precious so fast?

Rowan's voice filtered through the door again and piqued her curiosity. Who could he be talking with so late at night? Common sense said it had to be important, maybe even about the baby.

Her throat tightened at the thought of news about Issa's family, and she wasn't sure if the prospect made her happy or sad. She grasped the baby monitor receiver in her hand.

Quietly, she opened the door, careful not to disturb his phone conversation. And yes, she welcomed the opportunity to look at Rowan for a moment, a double-edged pleasure with the heat of her dream still so fresh in her mind. He stood with his back to her, phone pressed to his ear as he faced the picture window, shutters open to reveal the moonlit shoreline.

She couldn't have stopped herself if she tried. And she didn't try. Her gaze skated straight down to his butt. A fine butt, the kind that filled out jeans just right and begged a woman to tuck her hand into his back pocket.

Why hadn't she noticed that about him before? Perhaps because he usually wore his doctor's coat or a suit.

The rest of him, though, was wonderfully familiar. What a time to realize she'd stored so much more about him in her memory than just the sexy glide of his blond hair swept back from his face, his piercing blue eyes, his strong body.

Her fingers itched to scale the expanse of his chest, hard muscled in a way that spoke of real work more than gym time with a personal trainer. Her body responded with a will of its own, her breasts beading in response to just the sight of him, the promise of pleasure in that strong, big body of his.

Were the calluses on his hand imagined in her dream or real? Right now it seemed the most important thing in the world to know, to find out from the ultimate test—his hands on her bare flesh.

His back still to her, he nodded and hmmed at something in the conversation, the broad column of his neck exposed, then he disconnected his call.

Anticipation coursed through her, but she schooled her face to show nothing as he turned.

He showed no surprise at seeing her, his moves smooth and confident. He placed his phone on the wet bar, his eyes sweeping over all of her. His gaze lingered on her shoes and he smiled, then his gaze stroked back up to her face again. "Mari, how long have you been awake?"

"Only a few minutes. Just long enough to hear you 'hmm' and 'uh-huh' a couple of times." She wrapped her arms around her waist, hugging the robe closed and making sure her tingling breasts didn't advertise her arousal. "If I may ask, who were you talking to so late?"

"Checking on our security and following up a lead on the baby."

She stood up straighter and joined him by the window, her heart hammering in her ears. "Did you find her family?"

"Sorry." He cupped her shoulder in a warm grasp, squeezing comfortingly. "Not yet. But we're working on it."

She forced herself to swallow and moisten her suddenly dry mouth. "Who is this 'we' you keep mentioning?"

"I'm a wealthy man now. Wealthy people have connections. I'm using them." His hand slid away, calluses snagging on her satin robe.

Calluses.

The thought of those fingers rasping along her skin made her shiver with want. God, she wasn't used to being this controlled by her body. She was a cerebral person, a thinker, a scientist. She needed to find level ground again, although it was a struggle.

Reining herself in, she eyed Rowan, assessing him. Her instincts told her he was holding something back about his conversation, but she couldn't decipher what that might be. She searched his face, really searched, and what a time to realize she'd never looked deeper than the surface of Rowan before. She'd known his history—a reformed bad boy, the saintly doctor saving the world and soaking up glory like a halo, while she was a person who preferred the shadows.

She'd only stepped into the spotlight now for the baby. And that made her wonder if his halo time had another purpose for him—using that notoriety for his causes. The possibility that she could have been mistaken about his ego, his swagger, gave her pause.

Of course she could just be seeking justification for how his kisses turned her inside out.

Then his hand slid down her arm until he linked fingers with her and tugged her toward the sofa. Her stomach leaped into her throat, but she didn't stop him, curious to see where this would lead. And reluctant to let go of his hand.

He sat, drawing her to sit beside him. Silently. Just staring back at her, his thumb stroking across the inside of her wrist.

Did he expect her to jump him? She'd already told him she wouldn't make the leap into bed with him. Had a part of her secretly hoped he would argue?

Still, he didn't speak or move.

She searched for something to say, anything to fill the empty space between them—and take her mind off the tantalizing feel of his callused thumb rubbing along her speeding pulse. "Do you really think Issa's family will be found?"

"I believe that every possible resource is being devoted to finding out who she is and where she came from."

The clean fresh scent of his aftershave rode every breath she took. She needed to focus on Issa first and foremost.

"Tomorrow—or rather, later this morning—we need to get serious about going public with the press. No more playing at dinner, pretend photos and controlled press releases. I need to use my notoriety to help her."

He squeezed her wrist lightly. "You don't have to put yourself in the line of fire so aggressively."

"Isn't that why you asked me to help you? To add oomph to the search?" His answer became too important to her.

"I could have handled the baby alone." He held her gaze, with undeniable truthfulness in his eyes. "If we're honest here, I wanted to spend more time with you."

Her tummy flipped and another of those tempting Rowan-scented breaths filled her. "You used the baby for selfish reasons? To get closer to me?"

"When you put it like that, it sounds so harsh."

"What *did* you mean then?"

He linked their fingers again, lifting their twined grasp and resting it against his chest. "Having you here does help with the baby's care and with finding the baby's family. But it also helps me get to know you better."

"Do you want to know me better or kiss me?"

His heart thudded against her hand as he leaned even closer, just shy of their lips touching. "Is there a problem with my wanting both?"

"You do understand that nothing is simple with me." Her breath mingled with his.

"Because of who you are? Yes, I realize exactly who you are."

And just that fast, reality iced over her. She could never forget who she was…her father's daughter. A princess. The next in the royal line since she had no siblings, no aunts or uncles. As much as she wanted to believe Rowan's interest in her was genuine, she'd been used and misunderstood too many times in the past.

She angled away from him. "I know you think I'm a spoiled princess."

"Sometimes we say things in anger that we don't mean. I apologize for that." He stretched his arm along the back of the sofa without touching her this time.

"What *do* you think of me?" The opinion of others hadn't mattered to her before…. Okay, that was a lie.

Her parents' opinion mattered. She'd cared what her first lover thought of her only to find he'd used her to get into her father's inner circle.

"Mari, I think you're smart and beautiful."

She grinned. "Organized and uptight."

He smiled back. "Productive, with restrained passions."

"I *am* a spoiled princess," she admitted, unable to resist the draw of his smile, wanting to believe what she saw in his eyes. "I've had every luxury, security, opportunity imaginable. I've had all the things this baby needs, things her mother is so desperate to give her she would give her away to a stranger. I feel awful and guilty for just wanting to be normal."

"Normal life?" He shook his head, the leather sofa creaking as he leaned back and away. "I had that so-called normal life and I still screwed up."

She'd read the press about him, the way he'd turned his life around after a drunk-driving accident as a teen. He was the poster boy for second chances, devoting his life to making amends.

Her negative reports on his program weren't always popular. Some cynics in the medical community had even suggested she had an ax to grind, insinuating he might have spurned her at some point. That assumption stung her pride more than a little.

Still, she couldn't deny the good he'd done with his clinic. The world needed more people like Dr. Rowan Boothe.

"You screwed up as a teenager, but you set yourself on the right path again once you went to that military high school."

"That doesn't erase my mistake. Nothing can." He plowed a hand through his hair. "It frustrates the hell out of me that the press wants to spin it into some kind of feel-good story. So yeah, I get your irritation with the whole media spin."

"But your story gives people hope that they can turn their lives around."

He mumbled a curse.

"What? Don't just go Grinchy on me." She tapped his elbow. "Talk. Like you did at dinner."

"Go Grinchy?" He cocked an eyebrow. "Is that really a word?"

"Of course it is. I loved that movie as a child. I watched a lot of Christmas movies flying across the ocean to spend Christmas with one parent or the other. So, back to the whole Grinchy face. What gives?"

"If you want to change my mood, then let's talk about something else." His arm slid from the back of the sofa until his hand cupped her shoulder. "What else did you enjoy about Christmas when you were a kid?"

"You're not going to distract me." With his words or his touch.

"Says who?" Subtly but deliberately, he pulled her closer.

And angled his mouth over hers.

Seven

Stunned still, Mari froze for an instant. Then all the simmering passion from her dream earlier came roaring to the surface. She looped her arms around Rowan's neck and inched closer to him on the sofa. The satin of her peignoir set made her glide across the leather smoother, easier, until she melted against him, opened her mouth and took him as boldly as he took her.

The sweep of his tongue carried the minty taste of toothpaste, the intoxicating warmth of pure him. His hands roved along her back, up and down her spine in a hypnotizing seduction. He teased his fingers up into her hair, massaging her scalp until her body relaxed, muscle by tense muscle, releasing tensions she hadn't even realized existed. Then he stirred a different sort of tension, a coiling of desire in her belly that pulled tighter and tighter until she arched against him.

Her breasts pressed to his chest, the hard wall of him

putting delicious pressure against her tender, oversensitized flesh.

He reclined with her onto the couch, tucking her beneath him with a possessive growl. She nipped his bottom lip and purred right back. The contrast of cool butter-soft leather beneath her and hot, hard male over her sent her senses on overload.

The feel of his muscled body stretching out over her, blanketing her, made her blood pulse faster, thicker, through her veins. She plucked at the leather string holding back his hair, pulled it loose and glory, glory, his hair slipped free around her fingers. She combed her hands through the coarse strands, just long enough to tickle her face as he kissed.

And this man sure did know how to kiss.

Not just with his mouth and his bold tongue, but he used his hands to stroke her, his body molding to hers. His knee slid between her legs. The thick pressure of his thigh against the core of her sent delicious shivers sparkling upward. All those sensations circled and tightened in her belly with a new intensity.

Her hands learned the planes and lines of him, along his broad shoulders, down his back to the firm butt she'd been checking out not too long ago. Every nerve ending tingled to life, urging her to take more—more of him and more of the moment.

She wanted all of him. Now.

Hooking a leg around his calf, she linked them, bringing him closer still. Her hips rocked against his, the thick length of his arousal pressing against her stomach with delicious promise of what they could have together. Soon. Although not soon enough. Urgency throbbed through her, pulsing into a delicious ache between her legs.

He swept aside her hair and kissed along the sensitive curve of her neck, nipping ever so lightly against her pulse. She hummed her approval and scratched gently over his back, along his shoulders, then down again to yank at his shirt. She couldn't get rid of their clothes fast enough. If she gave herself too long to think, too many practical reasons to stop would start marching through her mind—

A cool whoosh of air swept over her. She opened her eyes to see Rowan standing beside the sofa. Well, not standing exactly, but halfway bent over, his hands on his legs as he hauled in ragged breath after breath. His arousal was unmistakable, so why was he pulling away?

"What? Where?" She tried again to form a coherent sentence. "Where are you going?"

He stared at her in the moonlight, his chest rising and falling hard, like he'd run for miles. His expression was closed. His eyes inscrutable.

"Good night, Mariama."

Her brain couldn't make his words match up with what she was feeling. Something didn't add up. "Good night? That's it?"

"I need to stop now." He tucked his shirt in as he backed away. "Things are getting too intense."

She refused to acknowledge the twinge of hurt she felt at his words. She wasn't opening her emotions to this man.

"Yeah, I noticed." She brazened it out, still committed to re-creating the amazing feelings from her dream. "That intensity we were experiencing about twenty seconds ago was a good thing."

"It will be good, Mari. When you're ready."

Damn, but he confused her. She hated feeling like

the student in need of remedial help. The one who didn't "get" it.

"Um, hello, Rowan. I'm ready now."

"I just need for you to be sure." He backed away another step, his hair tousled from her hungry fingers. "See if you feel the same in the morning. Good night, Mariama."

He pivoted into his room and closed the door behind him.

Mari sagged back on the sofa, befuddled as hell. What was his game here? He bound her to him by enlisting her help with the baby. He clearly wanted her. Yet, he'd walked away.

She wasn't innocent. She'd been with men—two. The first was a one-night stand that had her clamping her legs shut for years to come after she'd learned he'd only wanted access to her family. Then one long-term deal with a man who'd been as introverted as her. Their relationship had dissolved for lack of attention, fading into nothing more than convenient sex. And then not so convenient. Still, the breakup had been messy, her former lover not taking well to having his ego stung over being dumped. He'd been a real jerk.

Whereas Rowan was being a total gentleman. Not pushing. Not taking advantage.

And he was driving her absolutely batty.

Holding back had threatened to drive Rowan over the edge all night long.

At least now he could move forward with the day. The salty morning breeze drifted through the open shutters as he tucked his polo shirt into his jeans, already anticipating seeing Mari. Soon. He'd never wanted a woman this much. Walking away from her last night had been almost impossible. But he was making progress. She wanted him and he needed this to be very, very reciprocal.

So he needed to move on with his plan to romance her. Neither of them had a presentation at the conference today. He suspected it wouldn't take much persuasion to convince her to skip out on sitting through boring slide presentations and rubber chicken.

During his sleepless night, he'd racked his brain for the best way to sweep her off her feet. She wasn't the most conventional of women. He'd decided to hedge his bets by going all out. He'd started off with the traditional stuff, a flower left on her pillow while she'd been in the shower. He'd also ordered her favorite breakfast delivered to her room. He planned to end the day with a beachside dinner and concert.

All traditional "dating" fare.

The afternoon's agenda, however, was a bit of a long shot. But then he figured it was best to hedge his bets with her. She'd seemed surprised by the breakfast, and he could have sworn she was at least a little charmed by his invitation to spend the day together. Although he still detected a hint of wariness.

But reminding her of how they could appease the press into leaving her alone by feeding them a story persuaded her. For now, at least. He just prayed the press conference went smoothly.

Rowan opened his bedroom door and found Mari already waiting for him in the sitting area with Issa cradled in her arms. She stood by the stroller, cooing to the baby and adjusting a pink bootie, her face softening with affection.

Mari wore a long silky sheath dress that glided across subtle curves as she swayed back and forth. And the pink tropical flower he'd left on her pillow was now tucked behind her ear. He stood captivated by her grace as she soothed the infant to sleep. Minutes—or maybe more—later, she leaned to place the baby in the stroller.

She glanced to the side, meeting his gaze with a smile. "Where are we going?"

Had she known he was there the whole time? Did she also know how damn difficult it had been to walk away from her last night? "It's a surprise."

"That makes me a little nervous." She straightened, gripping the stroller. "I'm not good at pulling off anything impetuous."

"We have a baby with us." He rested a hand on top of hers. "How dangerous could my plan be?"

Her pupils widened in response before her gaze skittered away. "Okay, fair enough." She pulled her hand from his and touched the exotic bloom tucked in her hair. "And thank you for the flower."

Ducking his head, he kissed her ear, right beside the flower, breathing in the heady perfume of her, even more tantalizing than the petals. "I'll be thinking of how you taste all day long."

He sketched a quick kiss along her regally high cheekbone before pulling back. Gesturing toward the private elevator, he followed her, taking in the swish of her curls spiraling just past her shoulders. What a time to realize how rarely he saw her with her hair down. She usually kept it pulled back in a reserved bun.

Except for last night when she'd gone to bed. And now.

It was all he could do to keep himself from walking up behind her, sliding his arms around her and pulling her flush against him. The thought of her bottom nestled against him, his face in the sweet curve of her neck… damn. He swallowed hard. Just damn.

He followed her into the elevator and thankfully the glide down went quickly, before he had too much time in the cubicle breathing in the scent of her. The elevator doors opened with a whoosh as hefty as his exhale.

His relief was short-lived. A pack of reporters waited just outside the resort entrance, ready for them to give their first official press conference. He'd expected it, of course. He'd even set this particular one up. But having Mari and the baby here put him on edge. Even knowing Elliot Starc's detail of bodyguards were strategically placed didn't give him total peace. He wondered what would.

Mari pushed the stroller while he palmed her back, guiding her through the lobby. Camera phones snap-snap-snapped as he ushered Mari and Issa across the marble floor. Gawkers whispered as they watched from beside towering columns and sprawling potted ferns.

The doorman waved them through the electric doors and out into chaos. Rowan felt Mari's spine stiffen. Protectiveness pumped through him anew.

He ducked his head toward her. "Are you sure you're okay with this? We can go back to the suite, dine on the balcony, spend our day off in a decadent haze of food and sunshine."

She shook her head tightly. "We proceed as planned. For Issa, I will do anything to get the word out about her story, whatever it takes to be sure she has a real family who loves her and appreciates what a gift she is."

Her ferocity couldn't be denied—and it stirred the hell out of him. Before he did something crazy like kiss her until they both couldn't think, he turned to the reporters gathered on the resort's stone steps.

"No questions today, just a statement," he said firmly with a smile. "Dr. Mandara and I have had our disagreements in the past, but we share a common goal in our desire…to help people in need. This is the holiday season and a defenseless child landed in our radar, this little girl. How could we look away? We're working together to care for this baby until her family can be found. If even Mari and I can work together, then maybe there's hope…."

He winked wryly and laughter rippled through the crowd.

Once they quieted, he continued, "That's all for now. We have a baby, a conference agenda and holiday shopping to juggle. Thank you and Merry Christmas, everyone."

Their bodyguards emerged from the crowd on cue and created a circular wall around them as they walked from the resort to the shopping strip.

Mari glanced up at him, her sandals slapping the wooden boardwalk leading to the stores and stalls of the shoreline marketplace. "Are we truly going shopping? I thought men hated shopping."

"It's better than hanging out inside eating conference food. I hope you don't mind. If you'd rather go back…"

"Bite your tongue." She hip-bumped him as he strode beside her.

"Onward then." He slipped his arm around her shoulders, tucking her to him as they walked.

She glanced up at him. "Thank you."

If he dipped his head, he could kiss her, but even though he'd set up this press coverage, he balked at that much exposure. "Thanks for what?"

"For the press conference, and taking the weight of that worry off me. You handled the media so perfectly.

I'm envious of your ease, though." She scrunched her elegant nose. "I wish I had that skill. Running from them hasn't worked out that well for me."

"I just hope the statement and all of those photos will help Issa."

"Why wouldn't it?"

Helping Interpol gain access to crooks around the world had given him insights into just how selfish, how Machiavellian, people could be. "Think of all the crackpots who will call claiming to know something just to attach themselves to a high-profile happening or hoping to gain access to you even for a short while knowing that DNA tests will later prove them to be frauds."

"God, I never thought of that," she gasped, her eyes wide and horrified.

He squeezed her shoulder reassuringly, all too aware of how perfectly she fit to his side. "The police are going to be busy sifting through the false leads that come through."

"That's why you wanted to wait a day to officially announce we're fostering her…." she whispered softly to herself as they passed a cluster of street carolers.

"Why did you think I waited?" He saw a whisper of chagrin shimmer in her golden eyes. "Did you think I was buying time to hit on you?"

She lifted a dark eyebrow. "Were you?"

"Maybe." Definitely.

She looked away, sighing. "Honestly, I'm not sure what I thought. Since I stumbled into your suite with that room-service cart, things have been…crazy. I've barely had time to think, things are happening so fast. I just hate to believe anyone would take advantage of this precious baby's situation for attention or reward money."

The reality of just how far people would go made his

jaw flex. "We'll wade through them. No one gains access to this child or you until they've been completely vetted. We will weed through the false claims and selfish agendas. Meanwhile, she's safe with us. She turns toward your voice already."

"You're nice to say that, but she's probably just in search of her next bottle."

"Believe what you want. I know differently." He'd seen scores of mothers and children file through his clinic—biological and adoptive. Bonds formed with or without a blood connection.

"Are you arguing with me? I thought we were supposed to be getting along now. Isn't that what you said at the press conference?"

"I'm teasing you. Flirting. There's a difference." Unable to resist, he pressed a kiss to her forehead.

"Oh."

"Relax. I'm not going to hit on you here." There were far too many cameras for him to be too overt. "Although a longer kiss would certainly give the press something to go wild about. Feed them tidbits and they'll quit digging for other items."

Furrows dug into her forehead. "But it feels too much like letting them win."

"I consider it controlling the PR rather than letting it control me." He guided her by her shoulders, turning toward a reporter with a smile before walking on. "Think about all the positive publicity you're racking up for your father."

"This may have started out to be about keeping the press off my back, but now it's more about the baby."

He agreed with her on that account. But the worry on her face reminded him to stay on track with his plan.

"This conversation is getting entirely too serious for a day of fun and relaxation."

"Of course…" She swiped her hand over her forehead, squeezing her eyes closed for an instant before opening them again and smiling. "Who are you shopping for today? For your family?"

"In a sense."

He stopped in front of a toy store.

Her grin widened, her kissable lips glistening with a hint of gloss. "Are we shopping for Issa?"

"For the kids at my clinic."

Toy shopping with Rowan and Issa, like they were a family, tore at Mari's heart throughout the day. The man who'd left a flower on her pillow and chosen her favorite breakfast was charming. But the man who went shopping for the little patients at his free clinic?

That man was damn near irresistible.

Riding the elevator back up to their suite, she grabbed the brass bar for balance. Her unsteady feet had nothing to do with exhaustion or the jerk of the elevator—and everything to do with the man standing beside her.

Her mind swirled with memories of their utterly carefree day. The outing had been everything she could have hoped for and more. Sure, the paparazzi had followed them, lurking, but Rowan had controlled them, fielding their questions while feeding them enough tidbits to keep them from working themselves into a frenzy. Best of all, Issa had gotten her press coverage. Hopefully the right people would see it.

As much as Mari's stomach clenched at the thought of saying goodbye to the baby, she wanted what was best for the child. She wanted Issa to feel—and be—loved unreservedly. Every child deserved that. And

Rowan was doing everything possible to help this child he'd never met, just like he did the patients at his clinic, even down to the smallest detail.

Such as their shopping spree.

It would have been easier to write it off as a show for the press or a trick to win her over. But he had a list of children's names with notes beside them. Not that she could read his stereotypically wretched doctor's scrawl. But from the way he consulted the list and made choices, he'd clearly made a list of kids' names and preferences. The bodyguards had been kept busy stowing packages in the back of a limo trailing them from store to store.

And he hadn't left Issa off his list. The baby now had a new toy in her stroller, a plush zebra, the black-and-white stripes captivating the infant. The vendor had stitched the baby's name in pink on the toy.

Issa.

The one part of her prior life the little one carried with her—a name. Used for both boys and girls, meaning savior. Appropriate this time of year… Her feet kicked. Could the name be too coincidental? Could whoever left the baby have made up the name to go with the season—while leading authorities astray?

She leaned in to stroke the baby's impossibly soft cheek. Issa's lashes swept open and she stared up at Mari for a frozen moment, wide dark eyes looking up with such complete trust Mari melted. What happened if family came forward and they didn't love her as she deserved?

Those thoughts threatened to steal Mari's joy and she shoved them aside as the elevator doors whooshed open. She refused to let anything rob her of this perfect day and the promise of more. More time with Issa. More time with Rowan.

More kisses?

More of everything?

He'd walked away last night because he thought she wasn't ready. Maybe he was right. Although the fact that he cared about her needs, her well-being, made it all the more difficult to keep him at arm's length. And she couldn't even begin to imagine how his plans for seducing her fit into this whole charade with the baby.

Questions churned in her mind, threatening to steal the joy from the day. In a rare impulsive move, she decided to simply go with the flow. She would quit worrying about when or if they would sleep together and just enjoy being with Rowan. Enjoy the flirting.

Revel in the chemistry they shared rather than wearing herself out denying its existence.

Butterflies stirred in her stomach. She pushed the stroller into their suite just as Rowan's arm shot out to stop her.

"Someone's here," he warned a second before a woman shot up from the sofa.

A woman?

The butterflies slowed and something cold settled in her stomach. Dread?

A redhead with a freckled nose and chic clothes squealed, "Rowan!"

The farm-fresh bombshell sprinted across the room and wrapped her arms around Rowan's neck.

Dread quickly shifted to something darker.

Jealousy.

Eight

Rowan braced his feet as the auburn-haired whirlwind hit him full force. He'd spoken with his business partner and thc partner's wife, Hillary, about the current situation. But he'd assured them Elliot Starc had things under control. Apparently his friends weren't taking him at his word.

Who else was waiting in the suite to blindside him? So much for romance tonight.

"Hillary." Rowan hugged his friend fast before pulling away. "Not that I'm unhappy to see you, but what are you doing here tonight?"

She patted his face. "You should know that word spreads fast among the Brotherhood and everyone available is eager to help." She glanced over her shoulder at Mari and the baby. "And of course, we're insanely curious about your new situation."

Mari looked back and forth between them, a look of confusion on her face. "The Brotherhood?"

"A nickname for some of my high school classmates," Rowan explained. "We used to call ourselves the Alpha Brotherhood."

They still did, actually, after a few drinks over a game of cards. The name had started as a joke between them, a way of thumbing their noses at the frat-boy types, and after a while, the label stuck.

Hillary thrust a hand toward Mari. "Hi, I'm Hillary Donavan. I'm married to Rowan's former classmate and present business partner, Troy."

Mari's eyebrows arched upward. "Oh, your husband is the computer mogul."

Hillary took over pushing the stroller and preceded them into the suite as if it was her hotel penthouse. "You can go ahead and say it. My husband is the Robin Hood Hacker."

"I wasn't…" Mari stuttered, following the baby buggy deeper into the room. "I wouldn't…uh…"

"It's okay," Hillary said with a calm smile that had smoothed awkward moments in her days as an event planner for high-powered D.C. gatherings. "You can relax. Everyone knows my husband's history."

Mari smiled apologetically, leaning into the stroller to pull the sleeping baby out and cradle her protectively in her arms. "I'm not particularly good with chitchat."

"That's all right. I talk plenty for two people." She cupped the back of the infant's head. "What an adorable baby. Issa, right?"

"Yes." Rowan pushed the stroller to a corner, lightweight gauzy pink blanket trailing out the side. "Did you see the gossip rags or did the Brotherhood tell you that, too?"

Hillary made herself at home on the leather sofa. "Actually, I'm here to help. Troy and Rowan are more than just business partners on that computer diagnostics project you so disapprove of—" Hillary winked to take the sting out the dig "—they're also longtime friends. I have some last-minute Christmas shopping to do for those tough-to-buy-for people in my life, and voilà. Coming here seemed the perfect thing to do."

The pieces came together in Rowan's mind, Hillary's appearance now making perfect sense. While the Brotherhood kept their Interpol work under wraps, Hillary knew about her husband's freelance agent work and Salvatore had even taken her into the fold for occasional missions. Now she was here. He should have thought of it himself, if his brain hadn't been scrambled by a certain sexy research scientist.

Hillary would make the perfect bodyguard for Mari and Issa. No one would question her presence and she added a layer of protection to this high-profile situation.

Although sometimes the whole Interpol connection also came with dangers. God, he was in the middle of an impossible juggling act.

The baby started fussing and Rowan extended his arms to take her. Mari hesitated, tucking the baby closer. Rowan lifted an eyebrow in surprise.

"Mari? I can take her." He lifted the baby from Mari's arms. "You two keep talking."

"Wow." Hillary laughed. "You sure handle that tiny tyke well. No wonder you're dubbed one of the world's hottest bachelors. Snap a photo of you now and you'll need your own bodyguard."

Mari's smile went tight and Rowan wondered… Holy hell, she couldn't be jealous. Could she? Was that the same look he'd seen drifting through her eyes when Hillary had hugged him earlier? He wanted her to desire him, but he also wanted—needed—for her to trust him.

"Enough, Hillary. You were talking about Troy's computer search...."

"Right—" she turned back to Mari "—and you're taking care of the baby, Rowan. So vamoose. Go fill out your list for Santa. I've got this."

Rowan cocked an eyebrow over being so summarily dismissed. And putting Issa in the bassinet in another room would give him the perfect excuse to slip away and call Troy.

Not to mention time to regroup for the next phase of winning over Mari. He'd made progress with her today.

Now he just had to figure out how to persuade his friends to give him enough space to take that romancing to the next level.

Mari sank to the edge of the sofa. Her head was spinning at how fast things were changing around her. Not to mention how fast this woman was talking.

"Hold on a moment, please." Mari raised a hand. "What were you saying about computer searches into Issa's past?"

Hillary dropped into the wide rattan chair beside her. "No worries. It's all totally legal computer work. I promise. Troy walks on the right side of the law these days. And yes, it's okay to talk about it. I know about my husband's past, and I assume you know about Rowan's. But they've both changed. They're genuinely trying to make amends in more ways than most could imagine."

Mari blinked in the wake of Hurricane Hillary, confused. Why would Rowan have needed to make amends for anything? Sure, he'd led a troubled life as a teen, but his entire adult life had been a walking advertisement for charity work. Even if she disputed some of his methods, she couldn't deny his philanthropic spirit. "I've read the stories of his good deeds."

"There's so much more to Rowan than those stories."

She knew that already. The press adored him and his work, and she had to admit his clinic had helped many. She just wished they could come to an agreement on how to make his work—the computerized side and even the personal side—more effective. If she could solve that problem, who knew how many more small clinics in stretched-thin outposts of the world would benefit from Rowan's model of aid?

"Hillary, why are you telling me this?"

"The competitive animosity between the two of you is not a secret." She tipped her head to the side, twirling a strand of red hair contemplatively. "So I find it strange that you're here."

"I'm here for the baby."

"Really?" Hillary crossed her legs, her eyes glimmering with humor and skepticism. No getting anything past this woman. "There are a million ways the two of you could care for this child other than sharing a suite."

Mari bristled, already feeling overwhelmed by this confident whirlwind who looked like a Ralph Lauren model in skinny jeans and a poet's shirt.

Smoothing her hands over her sack dress, Mari sat up stiffly, channeling every regal cell in her body. "This is quite a personal conversation to be having with someone I only just met."

"You're right. I apologize if I've overstepped." She held up a hand, diamond wedding band set winking in the sunlight. "I've become much more extroverted since marrying Troy. I just wanted you to know Rowan's a better man than people think. A better man than he knows."

Great. Someone else pointing out the perfection of Dr. Rowan Boothe. As if Mari didn't already know. God, how she resented the feelings of insecurity pumping through her. She wanted to be the siren in the peignoir, the confident woman certain that Rowan wanted her with every fiber of his soul. And yes, she knew that was melodramatic and totally unscientific.

Forcing her thoughts to slow and line up logically, she realized that Rowan's eyes had followed her all day long—no skinny jeans needed. And Hillary was right. He and Mari both could have figured out a dozen different ways to care for this baby and stir publicity without sharing a suite. She was here because she wanted to be and Rowan wanted her here, as well.

No more flirting. No more games. No more holding back. She burned to sleep with Rowan.

The next time she had him alone, she intended to see the seduction through to its full, satisfying conclusion.

Finally, Rowan closed his suite door after dinner with Hillary, Troy and Elliot. He plowed his hands through his hair as Mari settled the baby for the night in his room.

He appreciated the help of his friends—but by the end of supper he had never been happier to see them all head to their own suites. Troy and Hillary were staying in the suite across the hall. Elliot Starc was a floor below, monitoring the surveillance vans outside the resort.

Rowan was more than a little surprised that his friends felt such a need to rally around him just because another orphan had landed on his doorstep. Issa wasn't the first—and she certainly wouldn't be the last—child in need of his patronage.

He suspected his friends' increased interest had something to do with Mari's involvement. No doubt he hadn't been as successful as he would have liked at hiding his attraction to her all these years. They were here out of curiosity as well as genuine caring, stepping up on a personal level, even if Mari didn't know the full weight of what they brought to the table for security and he wasn't in a position to tell her.

Now that a story had broken about an orphan at Christmastime, the attention was swelling by the second. Holiday mayhem made it tougher than ever to record all the comings and goings at the resort. Bogus leads were also coming in by the hundreds. So far no sign of a valid tip. Hillary and Troy were rechecking the police work through computer traces, using Interpol databases.

Intellectually, he understood these things took time and persistence, but thinking about the kid's future, worrying about her, made this more personal than analytical.

Somewhere out there, the baby's family had to be seeing the news reports. Even if they didn't want to claim her, surely someone would step forward with information. Even if the answer came in the form of official surrender of parental rights, at least they would know.

He understood full well how family ties didn't always turn out to be as ideal as one would hope. Memories of his brother's death, of his parents' grief and denial burned through him. He charged across the sitting area to the bar. He started to reach for the scotch and stopped himself. After the way his brother died…

Hell, no.

He opted for a mug of fresh local ginger tea and

one of the Christmas sugar cookies instead and leaned against the bar, staring out over the water as he bit the frosted tree cookie in half. Tomorrow, he and Mari both had conference presentations, then this weekend, the closing dinner and ball. Time was ticking away for all of them. He had to make the most of every moment. Tomorrow, he'd arranged for a spa appointment for Mari after her last presentation. Surely she would appreciate some privacy after all the scrutiny….

The door from Rowan's room opened. Mari slid through and closed it quietly after her. "Baby's sleeping soundly. I would have taken her tonight, you know."

"Fair is fair," he said. "We struck a bargain."

"You're a stubborn man. But then I understand that trait well."

Walking toward him, her silvery-gray sheath dress gliding over her sleek figure, she set the nursery monitor on the edge of the bar. Christmas tunes played softly over the airwaves—jazz versions, soft and soothing. Mari had fallen into the habit of setting her iPhone beside the monitor and using the music to reassure herself the listening device was still on.

She poured herself a mug of steaming ginger tea as well, adding milk and honcy. Cupping the thick pottery in both hands, she drank half then cradled the mug to her with a sigh.

He skimmed his knuckles along her patrician cheekbones. "Are you okay?"

Nodding, she set aside her glass. "I just didn't expect the press coverage to be so…comprehensive."

Was it his imagination or did she lean into his touch.

"You're a princess. What you do makes the news." Although even he was surprised at just how intense the media attention had become.

The hotel staff had closed off access to their floor aside from them and the Donavans, a measure taken after a reporter was injured on a window-washing unit trying to get a bonus photo. Rowan rubbed at a kink in the back of his neck, stress-induced from worrying his tail off about all the possible holes in the security. He wasn't sure he felt comfortable taking Mari and Issa out of the hotel again, even with guards.

"But I wanted to bring positive coverage for Issa. Not all of these cranks..."

And she didn't know the half of it. Troy had informed him about a handful of the more colorful leads the police hadn't bothered mentioning. A woman claiming to be Mari's illegitimate half sister had called to say the baby belonged to her. Another call had come from an area prison with someone saying their infant daughter resembled Issa and she thought it was her twin, whom they'd thought died at birth.

All of which turned out to be false, but there was no need to make Mari more upset by sharing the details. "My contacts will sift through them."

"Who are these contacts you keep talking about? Like Hillary and her husband?" She picked up the glass again and sipped carefully.

His glass.

His body tightened as her lips pressed to the edge.

He cleared his throat. "I went to a military high school. Makes sense that some of them would end up in law enforcement positions."

"It was a military *reform* school." She eyed him over the rim of the tumbler through long lashes.

"Actually, about half were there because they wanted a future in the military or law enforcement." He rattled off the details, anything to keep from thinking about how badly he wanted to take that glass from her and kiss her until they both forgot about talking and press conferences. "The rest of us were there because we got into trouble."

"Your Alpha Brotherhood group—you trust these friends with Issa's future?"

"Implicitly."

Shaking her head, she looked away. "I wish I could be as sure about whom to trust."

"You're worried."

"Of course."

"Because you care." Visions of her caring for the baby, insisting Issa stay in her room tonight even though it was his turn, taunted him with how attached she was becoming to the little one already. There was so much more to this woman than he'd known or guessed. She was more emotional than she'd ever let on. Which brought him back to the strange notion that she'd been jealous of Hillary.

A notion he needed to dispel. "What did you think of Hillary?"

"She's outspoken and she's a huge fan of yours." She folded her arms over her chest.

"You can't be jealous."

"At first, when she hugged you…I wondered if she was a girlfriend," she admitted. "Then I realized it might not be my right to ask."

"I kissed you. You have a right to question." He met her gaze full-on, no games or hidden agendas. Just pure honesty. "For the record, I'm the monogamous type. When I'm with a woman, I'm sure as hell not kissing other women."

Her eyes flashed with quick relief before she tipped

her head to the side and touched his chest lightly. "What happened last night—"

"What almost happened—"

"Okay, almost happened, along with the parts that did—"

"I understand." He pressed a hand over hers, wanting to reassure her before she had a chance to start second-guessing things and bolting away. "You want to say it can't happen. Not again."

"Hmm..." She frowned, toying with the simple watch on her wrist. "Have you added mind reader to your list of accomplishments now? If so, please do tell me why I would insist on pushing you away."

"Because we have to take care of the baby." He folded her hand in his and kissed her knuckles, then her wrist. "Your devotion to her is a beautiful thing."

"That's a lovely compliment. Thank you. I would say the same about you."

"A compliment?" he bantered back. "I did *not* expect that."

"Why ever not?" She stepped closer until her breasts almost brushed his chest.

The unmistakably seductive move wasn't lost on him. His pulse kicked up a notch as he wondered just how far she would take this.

And how far he should let it go.

"There is the fact that you haven't missed an opportunity to make it clear how much you don't like me or my work."

"That could be a compelling reason to keep my distance from you." She placed her other hand on his chest, tipping her face up to him until their lips were a whisper apart.

"Be on notice..." He took in the deep amber of her

eyes, the flush spreading across her latte-colored, creamy skin. “I plan to romance you, sweep you off your feet even.”

“You are—” she paused, leaning into him, returning his intense gaze “—a confusing man. I thought I knew you but now I’m finding I don’t understand you at all. But you need to realize that after last night’s kiss…”

“It was more than a kiss,” he said hoarsely.

“You’re absolutely right on that.” Her fingers crawled up his chest until she tapped his bottom lip.

He captured her wrist again just over the thin watch. He thought of the bracelets he’d surreptitiously picked up for her at the marketplace, looking forward to the right moment to give them to her. “But I will not make love to you until you ask me. You have to know that.”

“You’re mighty confident.” Her breath carried heat and a hint of the ginger tea.

Who knew tea could be far more intoxicating than any liquor? “Hopeful.”

“Good.” Her lips moved against his. “Because I’m asking.”

And damn straight he didn’t intend to walk away from her again.

Nine

Mari arched up onto her toes to meet Rowan's mouth sealing over hers. Pure want flooded through her. Each minute had felt like an hour from the moment she'd decided to act on her desire tonight until the second he'd kissed her.

Finally, she would be with him, see this crazy attraction through. Whether they were arguing or working together, the tension crackled between them. She recognized that now. They'd been moving toward this moment for years.

She nipped his bottom lip. "We have to be quiet so we don't wake the baby."

"Hmm..." His growl rumbled his chest against her. "Sounds challenging."

"Just how challenging can we make it?" She grazed her nails down his back, the fabric of his shirt carrying the warmth and scent of him.

"Is that a dare?"

She tucked her hands into the back pockets of his jeans as she'd dreamed of doing more than once. "Most definitely."

Angling his head to the side, he stared into her eyes. "And you're sure you're ready for this?"

She dug her fingers into his amazing tush. "Could you quit being so damn admirable? I'm very clearly propositioning you. I am an adult, a very smart adult, totally sober, and completely turned on by you. If that's not clear enough for you, then how about this? Take me to bed or to the couch, but take me now."

A slow and sexy smile creased dimples into his sun-bronzed face. "How convenient you feel that way since you absolutely mesmerize me."

Her stomach fluttered at the obvious appreciation in his eyes, his voice. His *touch.* He made her feel like the sensuous woman who wore peignoirs. He made her feel sexy. Sexier than any man ever had, and yes, that was a part of his appeal.

But she couldn't deny she'd always found him attractive. Who wouldn't? He took handsome to a whole new level, in a totally unselfconscious way. The blond streaks in his hair came from the sun—his muscles from hard work.

And those magnificent callused hands… She could lose herself in the pure sensation of his caress.

He inched aside the strap of her silvery-gray dress. She'd chosen the silky fabric for the decadent glide along her skin—yes, she usually preferred shapeless clothes, but the appreciation in Rowan's eyes relayed loud and clear he'd never judged her by what she wore. He saw her. The woman. And he wanted her.

That knowledge sent a fresh thrill up her spine.

He kissed along her bared neck, to her shoulder, his teeth lightly snapping her champagne-colored satin bra strap—another of her hidden decadences, beautiful underwear. Her head fell back, giving him fuller access. But she didn't intend to be passive in this encounter. Not by a long shot. Her hands soaked up the play of his muscles flexing in his arms as she stroked down, down, farther still to his waistband.

She tugged his polo shirt free and her fingers crawled up under the warm cotton to find even hotter skin. She palmed his back, scaled the hard planes of his shoulder blades as a jazz rendering of "The First Noel" piped through the satellite radio. He was her latest fantasies come to life.

Unable to wait a second longer, she yanked the shirt over his head even if that meant he had to draw his mouth away from her neck. She flung aside his polo, the red shirt floating to rest on the leather sofa. Fire heated his eyes to the hottest blue flame. He skimmed off the other strap of her dress until the silk slithered down her body, hooking briefly on her hips before she shimmied it the rest of the way off to pool at her feet. She kicked aside her sandals as she stepped out of the dress.

His gaze swept over her as fully as she took in the bared expanse of his broad chest, the swirls of hair, the sun-bronzed skin. He traced down the strap of her bra, along the lace edging the cups of her bra, slowly, deliberately outlining each breast. Her nipples beaded against the satin, tight and needy. She burned to be closer to him, as close as possible.

Her breath hitched in her throat and she stepped into his arms. The heat of his skin seared her as if he'd stored up the African sun inside him and shared it with her now.

"Here," she insisted, "on the sofa or the floor. I don't care. Just hurry."

"Princess, I have waited too damn long to rush this. I intend to have you completely and fully, in a real bed. I would prefer it was my bed, but there's a baby snoozing in the bassinet in my room. So let's go to yours."

"Fine," she agreed frantically. "Anywhere, the sooner the better." She slipped a finger into the waistband of his jeans and tugged.

"I like a lady who knows what she wants. Hell, I just like you."

His hands went to the front clasp of her bra and plucked it open and away with deft hands. She gasped as the overhead fan swooshed air over her bared flesh. Then he palmed both curves, warming her with a heat that spread into a tingling fire.

Through the haze of passion she realized her hand was still on his buckle. Shc fumbled with his belt, then the snap of his jeans, his zipper, until she found his arousal hard and straining against her hand. A growl rumbled low in his throat and she reveled in the sound. Drew in the scent of his soap and his sweat, perspiration already beading his brow from his restraint as she learned the feel of him. Shc stroked the steely length down, up and again.

"We have to be quiet," she reminded him.

"Both of us," he said with a promise in his voice and in his narrowed eyes.

One of his hands slid from her breast down to her panties, dipping inside, gliding between her legs. She was moist and ready for him. If she'd had her way they would be naked and together on the sofa. He was the one who'd insisted on drawing this out, but then they'd always been competitive.

Although right now that competition was delivering a tense and delicious result rather than the frustration of the past. She bit her bottom lip to hold back a whimper of pleasure. He slipped two fingers inside, deeper, stroking and coaxing her into a moist readiness. She gripped his shoulders, her fingernails digging half-moons into his tanned skin. Each glide took her higher until her legs went weak and he locked an arm around her back.

She gasped against his neck, so close to fulfillment. Aching for completion. "Let's take this to the bed."

"Soon, I promise." His late-day beard rasped against her cheek and he whispered in her ear, "But first, I need to protect you."

She gritted her teeth in frustration over the delay. "Rowan, there are guards stationed inside and outside of the hotel. Can we talk about security forces later?"

Cupping her face in his broad palms, he kissed the tip of her nose. "I mean I need to get birth control."

"Oh..." She gasped, surprised that she hadn't thought of it herself. She'd come in here with the intention of seducing him and she hadn't given a thought to the most important element of that union. So much for her genius IQ in the heat of the moment.

"I'll take care of it." He stepped away and disappeared from her room, his jeans slung low on his hips. Lean muscles rippled with every step.

She was an intelligent, modern woman. A scientist. A woman of logic. She liked to believe she would have realized before it was too late.... Before she could complete the thought, Rowan returned. He tossed a box of condoms on the bed.

"My goodness," she said, smiling, "you're an ambitious man."

"I'll take that as another challenge."

"Sounds like one where we're both winners. Now how about getting rid of those jeans."

"Your wish is my command, Princess." He toed off his shoes, no socks on, and peeled down his jeans without once taking his eyes off her.

His erection strained against his boxers and she opened her arms for him to join her. Then he was kissing her again and, oh, my, but that man knew how to kiss. The intensity of him, the way he was so completely focused on her and the moment fulfilled a long-ignored need to be first with a man. How amazing that the man who would view her this way—see only her—would be Rowan.

He reclined with her on the bed, into the thick comforter and stack of tapestry pillows, the crash and recede of the waves outside echoing the throb of her pulse. The sound of the shore, the luxurious suite, the hard-bodied man stretched over her was like a fantasy come true.

Only one thing kept it from being complete—something easily taken care of. She hooked her thumbs into the band of his boxers and inched them down. He smiled against her mouth as his underwear landed on the floor. Finally—thank heavens—finally, they met bare body to bare body, flesh-to-flesh. The rigid length of him pressed against her stomach, heating her with the promise of pleasure to come.

She dragged her foot up the back of his calf, hooking her leg around him, rocking her hips against him. He shifted his attention from her lips to her neck, licking along her collarbone before reaching her breasts—his mouth on one, his hand on the other. He touched and tasted her with an intuition for what she craved and more, finding nuances of sensitive patches of skin she hadn't realized were favored spots.

And she wanted to give him the same bliss.

Her fingers slid between them until her hand found his erection, exploring the length and feel of him. His forehead fell to rest against her collarbone. His husky growl puffed along oversensitized skin as she continued to stroke. Her thumb glided along the tip, smoothing a damp pearl, slickening her caress. Her mind filled with images of all the ways she wanted to love him through the night, with her hands and her mouth, here and in the shower. She whispered those fantasies in his ear and he throbbed in response in her hand.

Groaning, he reached out to snatch up the box of condoms. Rolling to his side, he clasped her wrist and moved her hand away, then sheathed himself. She watched, vowing next time she would do that for him.

Next time? Definitely a next time. And a next night.

Already she was thinking into the future and that was a scary proposition. Better to live in the now and savor this incredible moment. She clasped Rowan's shoulders as he shifted back over her again.

He balanced on his elbows, holding his weight off her. The thick pressure of him between her legs had her wriggling to get closer, draw him in deeper. She swept her other leg up until her ankles hooked around his waist. Her world filled with the sight of his handsome face and broad shoulders blocking out the rest of the world.

He hooked a hand behind her knee. "Your legs drive me crazy. Do you know that?"

"I do now. I also know you're driving me crazy waiting. I want all of you. Now." She dug her heels into his buttocks and urged him to…

Fill her.

Stretch her.

Thrill her.

Her back bowed up to meet him thrust for thrust, hushed sigh for sigh. Perspiration sealed them together, cool sheets slipping and bunching under them. In a smooth sweep, he kicked the comforter and tapestry pillows to the floor.

Tension gathered inside her, tightening in her belly. Her head dug back into the mattress, the scent of them mingling and filling every gasping breath. He touched her with reverence and perception, but she didn't want gentle or reverent. She needed edgy; she needed completion.

She pushed at his shoulder and flipped him to his back, straddling him, taking him faster and harder, his heated gaze and smile of approval all the encouragement she needed. His hands sketched up her stomach to her breasts, circling and plucking at her nipples as she came, intensifying waves of pleasure, harder, straight to the core of her. She rode the sensations, rode him, taking them both to the edge…and into a climax. Mutual. She bit her bottom lip to hold back the sounds swelling inside her as she stayed true to their vow to keep quiet. Rowan's jaw flexed, his groans mingling with her sighs.

Each rolling wave of bliss drew her, pulling her into a whirlpool of total muscle-melting satisfaction. Her arms gave way and she floated to rest on top of him. Rowan's chest pumped beneath her with labored breaths. His arms locked around her, anchoring her to him and to the moment.

Her body trembled in the wake of each aftershock rippling through her.

Exhaustion pulled at her but she knew if she slept, morning would come too fast with too many questions and possibilities that could take this away. So she blinked back sleep, focusing on multicolored lights beyond the window. Yachts, a sailboat, a ferry. She took in the details to stay awake so once her languid body regained strength, she could play out all those fantasies with Rowan.

She wanted everything she could wring from this stolen moment in case this night was all they could have before she retreated to the safety and order of her cold, clinical world.

"Are you asleep?" Mari's soft voice whispered through Rowan's haze as he sprawled beside her.

He'd wanted Mari for years. He'd known they would be good together. But no way in hell could he have predicted just how mind-blowingly incredible making love to this woman would be.

Sleep wasn't even an option with every fiber of him saturated with the satiny feel of her, the floral scent of her, the driving need to have her again and again until…

His mind stopped short of thoughts of the end. "I'm awake. Do you need something?"

Was she about to boot him out of her bed? Out of her life? He knew too well how fast the loyalties of even good people could shift. He grabbed the rumpled sheet free from around his feet and whipped it out until it fanned to rest over them.

She rolled toward him, her fingers toying with the hair on his chest. "I'm good. *This* is good, staying right here, like this. The past couple of days have been so frenzied, it's a relief to be in the moment."

"I hear ya." He kissed the top of her head, thinking of the bracelets he'd bought for her from the market and planning the right time to place them on her elegant arm.

Her fingers slowed and she looked up at him through long sweeping eyelashes. "You're very good with Issa. Have you ever thought about having kids of your own?"

His voice froze in his throat for a second. He'd given up on perfect family life a long time ago when he'd woken in the hospital to learn he and his brother were responsible for a woman losing her baby. Any hope of resurrecting those dreams died the day his brother crashed his truck into the side of a house.

Rowan sketched his fingers along Mari's stomach. He'd built a new kind of family with the Brotherhood and his patients. "I have my kids at the clinic, children that need me and depend on me."

"So you know that it's possible to love children that aren't your blood relation."

Where was she going with this? And then holy hell, it became all too clear. She was thinking about the possibility of keeping Issa beyond this week. "Are you saying that you're becoming attached to the little rug rat?"

"How could I not?" She leaned over him, resting her chin on her folded hands as she looked into his eyes. "I wonder if Issa landed with me for a reason. I've always planned not to get married. I thought that meant no kids for me—I never considered myself very good with them. But with Issa, I know what to do. She even responds to my voice already."

She was right about that. They shared a special bond that had to be reassuring to an infant whose world had been turned upside down by abandonment. But questions about the baby's past *would* be answered soon. He thought of Hillary and Troy working their tails off to find the baby's family. He hated to think of Mari setting herself up for heartache.

She shook her head before he could think of how

to remind her. "I know it's only been a couple of days and she could well have family out there who wants her. Or her mother might change her mind. I just hate the limbo."

He swept her hair from her face and kissed her, hard. "You won't be in limbo for long, I can promise you that." Guilt pinched over how he'd brought her into this, all but forced her to stay with him. "My friends and I won't rest until we find the truth about Issa's past. That's a good thing, you know."

"Of course I do. Let's change the subject." She pulled a wobbly smile. "I think it's amazing the way your friends all came to help you at the drop of a hat."

"It's what we do for each other." Just as he'd done his best to help his buddy Conrad reconcile with his wife earlier this year. He owed Conrad for helping him start the clinic, but he would have helped regardless.

"In spite of your rocky teenage years, you and your friends have all turned into incredible success stories. I may not always agree with some of your projects, but your philanthropic work is undeniable. It's no secret that your other friend, the casino owner—Conrad Hughes—has poured a lot of money into your clinic, as well."

He tensed at her mention of one of his Alpha Brotherhood buddies, wishing he could share more about the other side of his life. Needing to warn her, to ensure she didn't get too close. There weren't many women who could live with the double life he and his friends led with their Interpol work. Mari had enough complicating her life with her heritage. Better to keep the conversation on well-known facts and off anything that could lead to speculation.

"Conrad invested the start-up cash for my clinic. He

deserves the credit. My financial good fortune came later."

"No need to be so modest. Even before your invention of the diagnostics program, you could have had a lucrative practice anywhere and you chose to be here in Africa, earning a fraction of the salary."

He grunted, tunneling his hand under the sheet to cup her butt and hopefully distract her. "I got by then and I get by even better now."

She smiled against his chest. "Right, the billions you made off that diagnostics program we keep arguing about. I could help you make it better."

He smacked her bottom lightly. "Is that really what you want to talk about and risk a heated debate?"

"Why are you so quick to deflect accolades? The press is totally in love with you. You could really spin that, if you wanted."

He grimaced. "No, thanks."

She elbowed up on his chest. "I do understand your reticence. But think about it. You could inspire other kids. Sure you went to a military reform school, but you studied your butt off for scholarships to become a doctor, made a fortune and seem to be doing your level best to give it all away."

"I'm not giving it *all* away," he said gruffly, a sick feeling churning in his gut at the detour this conversation was taking. He avoided that damn press corps for just this reason. He didn't want anyone digging too deeply and he sure as hell didn't want credit for some noble character he didn't possess. "If I donate everything, I'll be broke and no good to anyone. I'm investing wisely."

"While donating heavily of your money and time."

Throwing all his resources into the black hole of guilt

that he'd never fill. Ever. He took a deep breath to keep that dark cavern at bay.

"Stop, okay?" He kissed her to halt her words. "I do what I do because it's the right thing. I have to give back, to make up for my mistakes."

Her forehead furrowed. "For your drunk-driving accident in high school? I would say you've more than made restitution. You could hire other doctors to help you carry the load."

"How can a person ever make restitution for lives lost?" he barked out, more sharply than he'd intended. But now that he'd started, there was no going back. "Do you know why I was sentenced to the military reform school for my last two years of high school?"

"Because you got in a drunk-driving accident and a woman was injured. You made a horrible, horrible mistake, Rowan. No one's denying that. But it's clear to anyone looking that you've turned your life around."

"You've done your homework where my diagnostics model is concerned, but you've obviously never researched the man behind the medicine." He eased Mari off him and sat up, his elbows on his knees as he hung his head, the weight of the memories too damn much. "The woman driving the other car was pregnant. She lost the baby."

"Oh, no, Rowan how tragic for her." Mari's voice filled with sadness and a hint of horror, but her hand fluttered to rest on his back. "And what a heavy burden for you to carry as the driver of the car."

She didn't know the half of it. No one did. To let the full extent of his guilt out would stain his brother's memory. Yet, for some reason he couldn't pinpoint, he found himself confessing all for the first time. To Mari. "But I wasn't driving."

Her hand slid up to rub the back of his neck and she sat up beside him, sheet clasped to her chest. “The news reports all say you were.”

“That’s what we told the police.” He glanced over at her. “My brother and I both filled out formal statements saying I was the driver.”

She stared back at him for two crashes of the waves before her eyes went wide with realization. “Your brother was actually the one behind the wheel that night? And he was drunk?”

Rowan nodded tightly. “We were both injured in the car accident, knocked out and rushed to the nearest hospital. When I woke up from surgery for a punctured lung, my mother was with me. My dad was with my brother, who’d broken his nose and fractured his jaw. They wanted us to get our stories straight before we talked to the police.”

That night came roaring back to him, the confusion, the pain. The guilt that never went away no matter how many lives he saved at the clinic.

“Did your parents actually tell you to lie for your brother?” Her eyes went wider with horror. Clearly her parents would have never considered such a thing.

Most never would. He understood that, not that it made him feel one bit better about his own role in what had happened. She needed to understand the position they’d all been in, how he’d tried to salvage his brother’s life only to make an even bigger mistake. One that cost him…too much.

“We were both drunk that night, but my brother was eighteen years old. I was only sixteen, a minor. The penalty would be less for me, but Dylan could serve hard time in jail. If I confessed to driving the car, Dylan could still have a future, a chance to turn his life around while he was still young."

"So you took the blame for your brother. You allowed yourself to be sentenced to a military reform school because your family pressured you, oh, Rowan…" She swept back his hair, her hands cool against his skin. "I am so sorry."

But he didn't want or deserve her comfort or sympathy. Rather than reject it outright, he linked fingers with her and lowered her arms.

"There was plenty of blame to go around that night. I could have made so many different choices. I could have called a cab at the party or asked someone else to drive us home." The flashing lights outside reminded him of the flash of headlights before the wreck, the blurred cop cars before he'd blacked out, then finally the arrival of the police to arrest him. "I wasn't behind the wheel, but I was guilty of letting my brother have those keys."

His brother had been a charismatic character, everyone believed him when he said he would change, and Rowan had gotten used to following his lead. When Dylan told him he was doing great in rehab, making his meetings, laying off the bottle, Rowan had believed him.

"What about your brother's guilt for what happened that night? Didn't Dylan deserve to pay for what happened to that woman, for you giving up your high school years?"

Trust Mari to see this analytically, to analyze it in clear-cut terms of rights and wrongs. Life didn't work that way. The world was too full of blurred gray territory.

"My brother paid plenty for that night and the decisions I made." If Rowan had made the right choices in the beginning, his brother would still be alive today. "Two years later, Dylan was in another drunk-driving accident. He drove his truck into the side of a house. He died." Rowan drew in a ragged breath, struggling like hell not to shrug off her touch that left him feeling too raw right now. "So you see, my decisions that night cost two lives."

Mari scooted to kneel in front of him, the sheet still clasped to her chest. Her dark hair spiraled around her shoulders in a wild sexy mess, but her amber eyes were no-nonsense. "You were sixteen years old and your parents pressured you to make the wrong decision. They sacrificed you to save your brother. They were wrong to do that."

Memories grated his insides, every word pouring acid on freshly opened wounds. He left the bed, left her, needing to put distance between himself and Mari's insistence.

He stepped over the tapestry pillows and yanked on his boxers. "You're not hearing me, Mari." He snagged his jeans from the floor and jerked them on one leg at a time. "I accept responsibility for my own actions. I wasn't a little kid. Blaming other people for our mistakes is a cop-out."

And the irony of it all, the more he tried to make amends, the more people painted him as some kind of freaking saint. He needed air. Now.

A ringing phone pierced the silence between them.

Not her ringtone. His, piping through the nursery monitor. Damn it. He'd left his cell phone in his room. "I should get that before it wakes the baby."

He hotfooted it out of her room, grateful for the excuse to escape more of her questions. Why the hell couldn't they just make love until the rest of the world faded away?

With each step out the door, he felt the weight of her gaze following him. He would have to give her some kind of closure to her questions, and he would. Once he had himself under control again.

He opened the door leading into his bedroom. His phone rang on the bamboo dresser near the bassinet. He grabbed the cell and took it back into the sitting area, reading the name scrolling across the screen.

Troy Donavan?

Premonition burned over him. His computer pal had to have found something big in order to warrant a call in the middle of the night.

Mari filled the doorway, tan satin sheet wrapped around her, toga-style. "Is something wrong?"

"I don't know yet." He thumbed the talk button on the cell phone. "Yes?"

"Hi, Rowan." Hillary's voice filled his ear. "It's me. Troy's found a trail connecting a worker at the hotel to a hospital record on one of the outlying islands—he's still working the data. But he's certain he's found Issa's mother."

Ten

Mari cradled sleeping Issa in her arms, rocking her for what would be the last time. She stared past the garland-draped minibar to the midday sun marking the passage of the day, sweeping away precious final minutes with this sweet child she'd already grown to love.

Her heart was breaking in two.

She couldn't believe her time with Issa was coming to an end. Before she'd even been able to fully process the fact that she'd actually followed through on the decision to sleep with Rowan, her world had been tossed into utter chaos with one phone call that swept Issa from them forever.

Troy Donavan had tracked various reflections of reflections in surveillance videos, piecing them together with some maze of other cameras in everything from banks to cops' radar to follow a path to a hint of a clue. They'd found the woman who'd walked away from the room-service trolley where Issa had been hidden. They'd gone a step further in the process to be sure. At some point, Mari had lost the thread of how he'd traced the trail back to a midwife on the mainland who'd delivered Issa. She'd been able to identify the mother, proving the baby's identity with footprint records.

The young mother had made her plan meticulously and worked to cover her tracks. She'd uncovered Rowan's schedule to speak at this conference then managed to get hired as a temp in the extra staff brought on for the holiday crowd. That's why she hadn't been on the employee manifest.

It appeared she'd had a mental breakdown shortly after leaving her child and was currently in a hospital. Issa had no grandparents, but she had a great aunt and uncle who wanted her. Deeply. In their fifties, their four sons were all grown but they hadn't hesitated in stepping up to care for their great niece. They owned a small coastal art gallery on the mainland and had plenty of parenting knowledge. They weren't wealthy, but their business and lives were stable.

All signs indicated they could give Issa a wonderful life full of love. Mari should be turning cartwheels over the news. So many orphans in Africa had no one to call their own and here Issa had a great family ready and eager to care for her.

Still, Mari could barely breathe at the prospect of handing over the baby, even though she knew this was the best thing for Issa.

The main door opened and Mari flinched, clutching the tiny girl closer. Rowan entered, lines fanning from his eyes attesting to the sleepless night they'd both endured after the fateful phone call about Issa's identity.

Rowan had scraped his hair back with a thin leather tie, his jeans and button-down shirt still sporting the wrinkles from when she'd tossed them aside in an effort to get him naked. That seemed eons ago now. Those moments after the call when they'd hastily gotten dressed again had passed in a frenzied haze.

"Any news?" she asked, feeling like a wretched person for hoping somehow she could keep Issa. She wasn't in any position to care for a baby. She'd never even given much thought to being a mother. But right now, it was the only thing she could think about. Who knew that a baby could fill a void in her life that she would have never guessed needed filling?

He shook his head and sat on the arm of the sofa near her, his blue eyes locked on the two of them. "Just more verification of what we learned last night. The mother's note was honest. Her husband was a soldier killed in a border dispute. And just more confirmation to what we already knew—she picked up a job doing temp work here, which is why she didn't show up on the initial employee search. The woman you saw that night running from the cart was, in fact, Issa's mother. She has family support back on the mainland. But it appears her husband's death hit her especially hard when she was already suffering from postpartum depression."

That last part hadn't been in the early reports. The whole issue became muddier now that the baby hadn't been left out of selfishness, but rather out of a deep mental illness. "Issa ended up in a room-service cart because of postpartum depression?"

"Approximately one in eight new mothers suffer from it in the States." He pinched the bridge of his nose as if battling a headache. "Even more so here with the rampant poverty and lack of medical care."

Mari's arms twitched protectively around the bundled infant. Would it have made a difference for Issa's mother if the family had been more supportive? Or had they been shut out? So many questions piled on top of each other until she realized she was simply looking for someone to blame, a reason why it would be okay to keep Issa. The scent of baby detergent—specially bought so she could wash the tiny clothes herself—mingled with sweet baby breath. Such a tender, dear bundle…

When Issa squirmed, Mari forced herself to relax—at least outwardly. "I guess I should be grateful she didn't harm her child. What happens now?"

Mari's eyes dropped to the child as Issa fought off sleep, her tiny fingers clenching and unclenching.

"She goes to her family," he said flatly.

"Where were they when Issa's mother felt so desperate?" The question fell from Mari's heart as much as her mouth, the objective scientist part of her nowhere to be found. She had to be certain before she could let go.

Rowan's hand fell to a tiny baby foot encased in a Christmas plaid sleeper. "The aunt and uncle insist they offered help, and that they didn't know how badly their niece was coping."

"Do you believe them?"

"They don't live nearby so it's entirely possible they missed the signs. Issa's only three months old." He patted the baby's chest once before shoving to his feet again, pacing restlessly. "They came for the funeral six weeks ago, left some money, followed up with calls, but she told them she was managing all right."

"And they believed her." How awful did it make her that she was still desperately searching for something to fault them for, some reason why they couldn't be the right people to raise the little angel in her arms.

"From everything our sources can tell, they're good people. Solid income from their tourist shop." He stopped at the window, palming the glass and leaning forward with a weary sigh. "They want custody of Issa and there's no legal or moral reason I can see why they shouldn't have her."

"What about what we want?" she asked quickly, in case she might have second thoughts and hold back the words.

"We don't have any rights to her." He glanced back over his shoulder. "This is the best scenario we could have hoped would play out. That first night when we spoke to the cops, we both never really dreamed this good of a solution could be found for her."

"I realize that… It's just…"

He turned to face her, leaning back and crossing his arms over his chest. "You already love her."

"Of course I care about her."

A sad half smile tipped his mouth. "That's not what I said."

"I've only known her a few days." Mari rolled out the logic as if somehow she could convince herself.

"I've watched enough new mothers in my line of work to know how fast the heart engages."

What did he hope to achieve by this? By stabbing her with his words? "I'm not her mother."

"You have been, though. You've done everything a mother would do to protect her child. It's not surprising you want to keep her."

Mari's throat clogged with emotion. "I'm in no position to take care of a baby. She has relatives who want her and can care for her. I know what I have to do."

"You're giving her the best chance, like a good mother." He cupped the back of her head, comfort in his gaze and in his touch.

She soaked up his supporting strength. "Are you trying to soften me up again?"

"I'm wounded you would think I'm that manipulative." He winked.

"Ha," she choked on a half laugh. "Now you're trying to make me smile so I won't cry."

He massaged her scalp lightly. "It's okay to cry if you need to."

She shook her head. "I think I'll just keep rocking her, maybe sing some Christmas carols until her family arrives. I know she won't remember me, but…"

A buzzer sounded at their suite door a second before Hillary walked in, followed by Troy. Mari sighed in relief over the brief reprieve. The aunt and uncle weren't here yet.

Hillary smiled gently. "The family is on their way up. I thought you would want the warning."

"Thank you for your help tracking them down." Mari could hardly believe she managed to keep her voice flat and unemotional in light of the caldron churning inside her.

Troy sat on the sofa beside his wife, the wiry computer mogul sliding an arm around Hillary's shoulders. "I'm glad we were able to resolve the issue so quickly."

Yet it felt like she'd spent a lifetime with Rowan and the baby.

Hillary settled into her husband's arm. "Mari, did Rowan tell you the tip that helped us put the pieces together came from the press coverage you brought in?"

"No, not that I remember." Although he might have

said something and she missed it. Since she'd heard Issa was leaving, Mari had been in a fog.

"Thanks to the huge interest your name inspired, we were contacted by a nurse whose story sounded legit. We showed her the composite sketch we'd pieced together from the different camera angles." Hillary rambled on, filling the tense silence. "She identified the woman as a patient she'd helped through delivery. From there, the rest of the pieces came together. She never would have heard about this if not for you and Rowan. You orchestrated this perfectly, Mari."

"With your help. Rowan is lucky to have such great friends."

And with those words she realized she didn't have people to reach out to in a crisis. She had work acquaintances, and she had family members she kept at arm's length. She spent her life focused on her lab. She'd sealed herself off from the world, running from meaningful relationships as surely as she ran from the press. Shutting herself away from her parents' disapproval—her father wanting her to assume her role of princess, her mother encouraging her to be a rebellious child embracing a universe beyond. Ultimately she'd disappointed them both. Rowan and this baby were her first deep connections in so long....

And it was tearing her apart to say goodbye to them.

She didn't want this pain. She wanted her safe world back. The quiet and order of her research lab, where she could quantify results and predict outcomes.

The buzzer sounded again and Mari bit her lip to keep from shouting in denial. Damn it, she would stay in control. She would see this through in a calm manner, do nothing to upset Issa.

Even though every cell in her cried out in denial.

* * *

Rowan watched helplessly as Mari passed the baby over to her relatives—a couple he'd made damn sure to investigate to the fullest. He'd relocated orphans countless times in his life and he'd always been careful, felt the weight of responsibility.

Never had that weight felt this heavy on his shoulders.

He studied the couple, in their fifties, the husband in a crisp linen suit, the wife in a colorful dress with a matching headscarf. The aunt took Issa from Mari's arms while the uncle held a diaper bag.

Mari twisted her hands in front of her, clearly resisting the temptation to yank the baby back. "She likes to be held close, but facing outward so she can see what's going on. And you have to burp her after every ounce of formula or she spits up. She likes music—"

Her voice cracked.

The aunt placed a hand on her arm. "Thank you for taking such good care of little Issa, Princess. If we had known about our niece's intentions, we would have volunteered to take Issa immediately. But when a young mother assures you she is fine, who would ever think to step in and offer to take her child? Trust us though, we will shower her with love. We will make sure she always knows you have been her guardian angel…."

With teary eyes, Mari nodded, but said nothing.

Troy stepped into the awkward silence. "My wife and I will escort you to your car through a back entrance to be sure the press doesn't overrun you."

Thank God, Troy quickly ushered them out before this hellish farewell tore them all in half. Rowan stole one last look at the baby's sweet chubby-cheeked face, swallowed hard and turned to Mari. No doubt she needed him more now.

The second the door closed behind the Donavans, Mari's legs folded.

She sank into the rocking chair again, nearly doubled over as she gulped in air. Her lovely face tensed with pain as she bit her lower lip. "Rowan, I don't think," she gasped, "I can't…I can't give my presentation this afternoon."

He understood the feeling. Rowan hooked his arm around her shoulders. "I'll call the conference coordinator. I'll tell them you're sick."

"But I'm never sick." She looked up at him with bemused eyes, bright with unshed tears. "I never bow out at work. What's wrong with me?"

"You're grieving." So was he. Something about this child was different, maybe because of the role she'd played in bringing Mari to him. Maybe because of the Christmas season. Or perhaps simply because the little tyke had slipped past the defenses he worked so hard to keep in place as he faced year after year of treating bone-crushing poverty and sickness. "You're human."

"I only knew her a few days. She's not my child…." Mari pressed a hand to her chest, rubbing a wound no less deep for not being visible. "I shouldn't be this upset."

"You loved her—you still do." He shifted around to kneel in front of her, stroking her face, giving Mari comfort—a welcome distraction when he needed it most. "That's clear to anyone who saw you with her."

"I know, damn it." She blinked back tears. "I don't want to think about it. I don't want to feel any of this. I just need…this."

Mari grabbed his shirt front, twisted her fist in the

fabric and yanked him toward her as she fell into him. Rowan absorbed their fall with his body, his shoulders meeting the thick carpet. Mari blanketed him, her mouth meeting his with a frenzy and intensity there was no denying. She'd found an outlet for her grief and he was damn well ready to help her with that. They both needed this.

Needed an outlet for all the frustrated emotions roaring through the room.

She wriggled her hips erotically against his ready arousal. A moan of pleasure slipped from her lips as she nipped his ear. There was no need to be silent any longer. Their suite was empty. Too empty. Their first encounter had been focused on staying quiet, in control as they discovered each other for the first time.

Tonight, control didn't exist.

He pushed those thoughts away and focused on Mari, on making sure she was every bit as turned on as he was. He gathered the hem of her dress and bunched it until he found the sweet curve of her bottom. He guided her against him, met her with a rolling rhythm of his own, a synchronicity they'd discovered together last night.

Sitting up, increasing the pressure against his erection, she yanked his shirt open, buttons popping free and flying onto the carpet. Her ragged breathing mingled with his. He swept her dress off and away until she wore only a pale green satin bra and underwear. He was quickly realizing her preference for soft, feminine lingerie and he enjoyed peeling it from her. He flung the bra to rest on the bar. Then twisted his fist in her panties until the thin strap along her hip snapped. The last scrap of fabric fell away.

She clasped his head in her hands and drew his face

to her breasts. Her guidance, her demands, made him even harder. He took her in his mouth, enjoying the giving as much as the taking. Her moans and sighs were driving him wild. And yes, he had his own pent-up frustrations to work out, his own regret over seeing Issa leave… He shut down those thoughts, grounding himself in the now.

Arching onto her heels, Mari fumbled with the fly of his pants.

"Condom," he groaned. "In my pocket."

He lifted his butt off the floor and she stroked behind him to pluck the packet free. Thank heaven he'd thought to keep one on him even in a crisis. Because he couldn't stomach the thought of stopping, not even for an instant.

Then he felt her hands on him, soft, stroking. He throbbed at her touch as she sheathed him in the condom, then took him inside her. His head dug back as he linked fingers with her, following the ride where she took him, hard and fast, noisy and needy. The fallout would have to take care of itself, because right now, they were both locked in a desperate drive to block out the pain of loss.

Already, he could feel the building power of his release rolling through him. He gritted his teeth, grinding back the need to come. Reaching between them to ease her over the edge with him. One look at her face, the crescendo of her sweet cries, told him she was meeting him there now. He thrust, again and again until his orgasm throbbed free while hers pulsed around him.

He caught her as she collapsed into his arms. He soaked in the warmth of her skin, the pounding of her heart—hell, everything about her.

The cooling air brought hints of reality slithering

back, the world expanding around them. The roaring in his ears grew louder, threatening this pocket of peace. It was too soon for him to take her again, but that didn't rule out other pleasurable possibilities.

Rowan eased Mari from him and onto her back. He kissed her mouth, her jaw, along her neck, inhaling the floral essence of her. Her hands skimmed up and down his spine as she reclined languidly. Smiling against her skin, he nipped his way lower, nuzzling and stroking one breast then the other.

"Rowan?"

"Shhh..." He blew across her damp nipple. The damp brown tip pebbled even tighter for him and he took her in his mouth, flicking with his tongue.

He sprinkled kisses along the soft underside, then traveled lower, lower still until he parted her legs and stroked between her thighs, drawing a deep sigh from her. He dipped his head and breathed in the essence of her, tasted her. Teased at the tight bundle of nerves until she rambled a litany of need for more. He was more than happy to comply.

A primitive rush of possession surged through him. She was his. He cupped the soft globes of her bottom and brought her closer to him, circled and laved, worked her until her fingers knotted restlessly in his hair. He took her to the edge of completion again, then held back, taking her to the precipice again and again, knowing her orgasm would be all the more powerful with the build.

Her head thrashed against the carpet and she cried out his name as her release gripped her. Her hands flung out, knocking over an end table, sending a lamp crashing to the floor.

He watched the flush of completion spread over her

as he slid back up to lay beside her. The evening breeze drifted over them, threatening to bring reality with it.

There was only one way to make it through the rest of this night. Make love to Mari until they both collapsed with exhaustion. Rolling to his knees, he slid his arms under her, lifting as he stood. He secured her against his chest, the soft give of her body against his stirring him.

Her arm draped around his neck, her head lolling against him as she still breathed heavily in the aftermath of her release. He strode across the suite toward his bedroom, his jeans open and riding low on his hips. Hell, he'd never even gotten his pants off.

He lowered Mari to his bed, the sight of her naked body, long legs and subtle curves stirring him impossibly hard again. Shadows played along her dusky skin, inviting him to explore. To lose himself in the oblivion of her body. To forget for a few hours that the emptiness of their suite was so damn tangible… No baby sighs. No iPhone of Christmas lullabies. Gone.

Just like Issa. Their reason for staying together.

Eleven

Mari had spent a restless night in Rowan's arms. As the morning light pierced through the shutters, he'd suggested they get away from the resort and all the memories of Issa that lurked in their suite. She hadn't even hesitated at jumping on board with his plan.

Literally.

Mari stretched out on the bow of the sailboat and stared up at the cloudless sky, frigate birds gliding overhead with their wide wings extended full-out. Waves slapped against the hull, and lines pinged against the mast. Rowan had leased the thirty-three-foot luxury sailboat for the two of them to escape for the day to a deserted shore. No worries about the press spying on them and no reminders of the baby. Nothing to do but to stare into the azure waters, watching fish and loggerhead turtles.

God, how she needed to get away from the reminders. Her time with the baby had touched her heart and made her realize so many things were missing in her life. Love. Family. She'd buried herself in work, retreating into a world that made sense to her after a lifetime of feeling awkward in her own skin. But holding that sweet little girl had made Mari accept she'd turned her back on far too much.

That didn't mean she had any idea how to fix it. Or herself. She watched Rowan guiding the sailboat, open shirt flapping behind him, sun burnishing his blond hair.

Rowan had made love to her—and she to him—until they'd both fallen into an exhausted sleep. They'd slept, woken only long enough to order room service and made love again. She had the feeling Rowan was as confused and empty as she, but she couldn't quite put her finger on why.

For that matter, maybe she was just too lost in her own hurt to understand his.

In the morning, he'd told her to dress for a day on a boat. She hadn't questioned him, grateful for the distraction. Mari had tossed on a sarong, adding dark glasses and an old-school Greta Garbo scarf to make her escape. He'd surprised her with a gift, bracelets she'd admired at the marketplace their first night out with Issa. She stretched her arm out, watching the sun refract off the silver bangles and colorful beads.

Rowan sailed the boat, handling the lines with ease as the hull chopped through the water toward an empty cove, lush mountains jutting in the distance. They'd followed the coast all morning toward a neighboring island with a private harbor. If only the ache in her heart was as easy to leave behind.

She rolled to her tummy and stretched out along her

towel, her well-loved body languid and a bit stiff. Chin on her hands, she gazed out at the rocks jutting from the water along the secluded coastline. She watched the gannets and petrels swoop and dive for fish. Palm trees clustered along the empty shoreline, creating a thick wall of foliage just beyond the white sandy beaches. Peaceful perfection, all familiar and full of childhood memories of vacationing along similar shores with her parents.

A shadow stretched across her, a broad-shouldered shadow. She flipped to her back again, shading her eyes to look up at Rowan. “Shouldn’t you be at the helm?”

“We’ve dropped anchor.” He crouched beside her, too handsome for his own good in swim trunks and an open shirt, ocean breeze pulling at his loose hair. “Come with me and have something to drink?”

She clasped his outstretched hand and stood, walking with him, careful to duck and weave past the boom and riggings. The warm hardwood deck heated her bare feet. “You didn’t have to be so secretive about our destination.”

“I wanted to surprise you.” He jumped down to the deck level, grasping her waist and lowering her to join him. He gestured to where he’d poured them two glasses of mango juice secured in the molded surface between the seat cushions, the pitcher tucked securely in an open cooler at his bare feet.

“That’s your only reason?”

“I wasn’t sure you would agree, and we both needed to get away from the resort.” He passed her a glass, nudging her toward the captain’s chair behind the wheel. “Besides, my gorgeous, uptight scientist, you need to have fun.”

“I have fun.” Sitting, she sipped her drink. The sweet

natural sugars sent a jolt of energy through her, his words putting her on the defensive. “My work is fun.”

He cocked an eyebrow, shooting just above his sunglasses.

“Okay, my work is rewarding. And I don’t recall being all that uptight when I was sitting on the bar last night.” She eyed him over the glass.

“Fair enough. I’m taking you out because I want you mellow and softened up so when I try to seduce you later you completely succumb to my charm.” He thudded the heel of his palm to his forehead, clearly doing his best to take her mind off things. “Oh, wait, I already seduced you.”

“Maybe I seduced you.” She tossed aside her sunglasses and pulled off his aviator shades, her bracelets chiming with each movement. She leaned in to kiss him, more than willing to be distracted from the questions piling up in her mind.

Like where they would go from here once the conference was over. Since she didn’t have any suggestions in mind, she sure wasn’t going to ask for his opinion.

“Whose turn is it, then, to take the initiative?” He pulled her drink from her and stepped closer.

“I’ve lost count.” She let her eyes sweep over him seductively, immersing herself in this game they both played, delaying the inevitable.

“Princess, you do pay the nicest compliments.” He stroked her face, along the scarf holding back her hair, tugging it free.

“You say the strangest things.” She traced his mouth, the lips that had brought her such pleasure last night.

“We’re here to play, not psychoanalyze.”

Her own lips twitched with a self-deprecating smile. “Glad to know it, because I stink at reading people.”

"Why do you assume that?" His question mingled with the call of birds in the trees and the plop of fish.

"Call it a geek thing."

"You make geek sexy." He nipped her tracing finger, then sucked lightly.

She rolled her eyes. "You are such a..."

"A what?"

"I don't even have words for you."

His eyes went serious for the first time this morning. "Glad to know I mystify you as much as you bemuse me."

"I've always thought of myself as a straightforward person. Some call that boring." She flinched, hating the feeling that word brought, knowing she couldn't—wouldn't—change. "For me, there's comfort in routine."

Those magnificently blue eyes narrowed and darkened. "Tell me who called you boring and I'll—"

She clapped a hand over his mouth, bracelets dangling. "It's okay. But thanks." She pulled her hand away, a rogue wave bobbing the boat beneath her. "I had trouble making friends in school. I didn't fit in for so many reasons—everything from my ridiculous IQ to the whole princess thing. I was either much younger than my classmates or they were sucking up because of my family. There was no sisterhood for me. It was tough for people to see the real me behind all that clutter."

"I wasn't an instant fit at school, either." He shifted to stand beside her, looping an arm around her shoulders bared by the sarong.

She leaned against him, looking out over the azure blue waters. The continent of her birth was such a mixture of lush magnificence and stark poverty. "You don't need to change your history to make me feel better. I'm okay with myself."

"God's honest truth here." He rested his chin on top of her head. "My academy brothers and I were all misfits. The headmaster there did a good job at redirecting us, channeling us, helping us figure out ways to put our lives on the right path again."

"All of you? That's quite a track record."

He went still against her. "Not all of us. Some of us were too far gone to be rehabilitated." His sigh whispered over her, warmer than the sun. "You may have read in the news about Malcolm Douglas's business manager—he was a schoolmate of ours. He lost his way, forgot about rules and integrity. He did some shady stuff to try and wrangle publicity for his client."

"Your friend. Malcolm. Another of your Brotherhood?"

"Malcolm and I aren't as close as I am to the others. But yes, he's a friend." He turned her by her shoulders and stared into her eyes. "We're not perfect, any of us, but the core group of us, we can call on each other for anything, anytime."

"Like how the casino owner friend provided the start-up money for your clinic…"

Rowan had built an incredible support system for himself after his parents failed him. While she'd cut herself off from the world.

"That he did. You wouldn't recognize Conrad from the high school photos. He was gangly and wore glasses back then, but he was a brilliant guy and he knew it. Folks called him Mr. Wall Street, because of his dad and how Conrad used his trust fund to manipulate the stock market to punish sweatshop businesses."

"You all may have been misfits, but it appears you share a need for justice."

"We didn't all get along at first. I was different

from them, though, or so I liked to tell myself. I didn't come from money like most of the guys there—or like you—and I wasn't inordinately talented like Douglas. I thought I was better than those overprivileged brats."

"Yet, Conrad must respect you to have invested so much money to start the clinic."

"If we're going to be honest—" he laughed softly "—I'm where I am today because of a cookie."

"A cookie?" She tipped her head back to the warm sunshine, soaking in the heat of the day and the strength of the man beside her.

"My mom used to send me these care packages full of peanut-butter cookies with M&M's baked into them." His eyes took on a faraway look and a fond smile.

Mari could only think that same mother had sent him to that school in his brother's place. Those cookies must have tasted like dust in light of such a betrayal from the woman who should have protected him. She bit back the urge to call his mother an unflattering name and just listened, ocean wind rustling her hair.

"One day, I was in my bunk, knocking back a couple of those cookies while doing my macro biology homework." He toyed with the end of her scarf. "I looked up to find Conrad staring at those cookies like they were caviar. I knew better than to offer him one. His pride would have made him toss it back in my face."

She linked fingers with him and squeezed as he continued, her cheek against the warm cotton of his shirt, her ear taking in the steady thrum of his heart.

"We were all pretty angry at life in those days. But I had my cookies and letters from Mom to get me through the days when I didn't think I could live with the guilt of what I'd done."

What his family had done. His mother, father and his brother. Why couldn't he see how they'd sacrificed him?

"But back to Conrad. About a week later, I was on my way to the cafeteria and I saw him in the visitation area with his dad. I was jealous as hell since my folks couldn't afford to fly out to visit me—and then I realized he and his dad were fighting."

"About what?" She couldn't help but ask, desperate for this unfiltered look into the teenage Rowan, hungry for insights about what had shaped him into the man he'd become.

"From what Conrad shouted, it was clear his father wanted him to run a scam on Troy's parents and convince them to invest in some bogus company or another. Conrad decked his dad. It took two security guards to pull him off."

Hearing the things that Rowan and his friends had been through as teens, she felt petty for her anger over her own childhood. The grief Rowan and his friends had faced, the storms in their worlds, felt so massive in comparison to her own. She had two parents that loved her, two homes, and yes, she was shuttled back and forth, but in complete luxury.

"And the cookie?"

"I'm getting there." He sketched his fingers up and down her bare arm. "Conrad spent a couple of days in the infirmary—his dad hit him back and dislocated Conrad's shoulder. The cops didn't press charges on the old man because the son threw the first punch. Anyhow, Conrad's first day out of the infirmary, I felt bad for him so I wrapped a cookie in a napkin and put it on his bunk. He didn't say anything, but he didn't toss it back in my face, either." He threw his hands wide. "And here I am today."

Her heart hurt so badly she could barely push words out. "Why are you telling me this?"

"I don't know. I just want you to understand why my work is so important to me, so much so that I couldn't have kept Issa even if her family didn't come through. Because if I start keeping every orphan that tugs at my emotions, I won't be able to sustain all I've fought so hard to build. The clinic…it's everything to me. It helps me fill the hole left by Dylan's death, helps me make up for the lives lost."

She heard him, heard an isolation in his words in spite of all those friends. He'd committed himself to a life of service that left him on a constant, lonely quest. And right then and there, her soul ached for him.

She slid her hand up into his hair, guiding his mouth to hers. He stepped between her knees, and she locked her arms around his neck. Tight. Demanding and taking.

"Now," she whispered against his mouth, fishing in his back pocket for a condom.

He palmed her knees apart and she purred her approval. Her fingers made fast work of his swim trunks, freeing his erection and sheathing him swiftly, surely.

She locked her legs around his waist and drew him in deeper. He drove into her again and again. She angled back, gripping the bar, bracelets sliding down to collect along her hand. He took in the beauty of her, her smooth skin, pert breasts, her head thrown back and hair swaying with every thrust. The boat rocked in a rhythm that matched theirs as his shouts of completion twined and mingled with hers, carried on the breeze.

In that moment she felt connected to him more than physically. She identified with him, overwhelmed by an understanding of him being as alone in the world as her. But also hammered by a powerlessness to change that. His vision and walls were as strong as hers, always had been. Maybe more so.

What a time to figure out she might have sacrificed too much for her work—only realizing that now, as she fell for a man who would sacrifice anything for *his*.

The taste of the sea, sweat and Mari still clinging to his skin, Rowan opened the door to their suite the next morning, praying the return to land and real life wouldn't bring on the crushing sense of loss. He'd hoped to distract her from Issa—and also find some way to carve out a future for them. They were both dedicated to their work. They could share that, even in their disagreements. They could use that as a springboard to work out solutions. Together. His time with her overnight on the sailboat had only affirmed that for him.

He just hoped he'd made a good start in persuading Mari of the same thing.

Guiding her into the suite with a hand low on her spine, he stepped deeper into the room. Only to stop short. His senses went on alert. There was someone here.

Damn it, there was more traffic through this supposedly secure room than through the lobby. Which of course meant it was one of his friends.

Elliot Starc rose from the sofa and from Mari's gasp beside him, clearly she recognized the world-famous race-car driver…and underwear model.

Rowan swallowed a curse. "Good morning, Elliot. Did you get booted out of your own room?"

Laughing, Elliot took Mari's hand lightly and ignored Rowan's question. "Princess, it's an honor to meet you."

"Mr. Starc, you're one of Rowan's Brotherhood friends, I assume."

Elliot's eyebrows shot up. "You told her?"

"We talk." Among other things.

"Well, color me stunned. That baby was lucky to have landed in Rowan's room. Our Interpol connections kept all of you safe while bringing this to a speedy conclusion."

Crap. The mention of Interpol hung in the air, Mari's eyes darting to his.

Oblivious to the gaffe, Elliot continued, "Which brings me to my reason for being here. I've emailed a summary of the existing security detail, but I need to get back to training, get my mind back in the game so I don't set more than my hair on fire."

Rowan pulled a tight smile. "Thanks, buddy."

Mari frowned. "Interpol?"

Elliot turned sharply to Rowan. "You said you told her about the Brotherhood."

"Classmates. I told her we're classmates." He didn't doubt she would keep his secret safe, but knowing wouldn't help her and anything that didn't help was harmful. "You, my friend, made a mighty big assumption for someone who should know better."

"She's a princess. You've been guarding her." Elliot scratched his sheared hair. "I thought… Ah, hell. Just…" Throwing his hands out and swiping the air as if that explained it all, Elliot spun on his heel and walked out the door.

Mari sat hard, sinking like a stone on the edge of the sofa. "You're with Interpol?" She huffed on a long sigh. "Of course you're with Interpol."

"I'm a physician. That's my primary goal, my mission in life." He paused, unable to dodge the truth as he kneeled in front of her. “But yes, I help out Interpol on occasion with freelance work in the area. No one thinks twice about someone like me wandering around wealthy fundraisers or traveling to remote countries.”

He could see her closing down, pulling away.

“Mari?”

“It’s your job. I understand.”

“Are you angry with me for not telling you?”

“Why would you? It’s not my secret to know. Your friend…he assumed more about us than he should. But you know I won’t say a word. I understand well what it’s like to be married to your work.”

Her words came out measured and even, her body still, her spine taking on that regal “back off” air that shouted of generations of royalty. “Mari, this doesn’t have to mean things change between us. If anything we can work together.”

“Work, right…” Her amber eyes flickered with something he couldn’t quite pin down.

“Are you all right?”

“I’ll be fine. It’s all just a lot to process, this today. Issa yesterday.”

He cradled her shoulders in his hands. She eased away.

“Mari, it’s okay to shout at me if you’re mad. Or to cry about Issa. I’m here for you,” he said, searching for the right way to approach her.

“Fine. You want me to talk? To yell? You’ve got it. I would appreciate your acting like we’re equal rather than stepping into your benevolent physician shoes because no one would dare to contradict the man who does so much for the world.” She shrugged free of his grip.

“Excuse me for trying to be a nice guy.” He held up his hands.

"You're always the nice guy." She shot to her feet. "The saint. Giving out comfort, saving the world, using that as a wall between you and other people."

"What the hell are you talking about?" He stood warily, watching her pace.

"There you go. Get mad at me." She stopped in front of him, crossing her arms over her chest. "At least real emotions put us on an even footing. Oh, wait, we're not even. You're the suave doctor/secret agent. I'm the awkward genius who locks herself away in a lab."

"Are we really returning to the old antagonistic back-and-forth way of communicating?" he asked. Her words felt damn unfair when he was working his tail off to help her through a rough time. "I thought we'd moved past that."

"That's not what I'm talking about and you know it. You're a smart man."

"Actually, you're the certified genius here. How about you explain it to me."

"You want me to cry and grieve and open myself up to you." She jabbed his chest with one finger, her voice rising with every word. "But what about you? When do you open up to me? When are you going to give me something besides the saintly work side of your life?"

"I've told you things about my past," he answered defensively.

"To be fair, yes you have," she conceded without backing down. "Some things. Certainly not everything. And when have you let me in? You're fine with things as long as you're the one doling out comfort. But accepting it? No way. Like now. You have every reason to grieve for Issa."

"She's in good hands, well cared for," he said through gritted teeth.

"See? There you go doing just what I said. You want me to cry and be emotional, but you—" she waved a hand "—you're just fine. Did you even allow yourself to grieve for your brother?"

His head snapped back, her words smacking him even as she kept her hands fisted at her sides. "Don't you dare use my brother against me. That has nothing to do with what we're discussing now."

"It has everything to do with what we're talking about. But if I'm mistaken, then explain it to me. Explain what you're feeling."

She waited while he searched for the right words, but everything he'd offered her so far hadn't worked. He didn't have a clue what to say to reassure her. And apparently he waited too long.

"That's what I thought." She shook her head sadly, backing away from him step by step. "I'm returning to my old room. There's no reason for me to be here anymore."

She spun away, the hem of her sarong fluttering as she raced into her room and slammed the door. He could hear her tossing her suitcase on the bed. Heard her muffled sobs. And heard the click of the lock that spoke loud and clear.

He'd blown it. Royally, so to speak. He might be confused about a lot of things. But one was crystal clear.

He was no longer welcome in Mari's life.

Twelve

The conference was over. Her week with Rowan was done.

Mari stood in front of the mirrored vanity and tucked the final pin into her hair, which was swept back in a sleek bun. Tonight's ball signified an official end to their time together. There was no dodging the event without being conspicuous and stirring up more talk in the press.

As if there wasn't enough talk already. At least all reports from the media—and from Rowan's Interpol friends—indicated that Issa was adapting well in her new home after only a couple of days. Something to be eternally grateful for. A blessing in this heartbreaking week.

Her pride demanded she finish with her head held high.

After her confrontation with Rowan, she'd waited the

remainder of her stay, hoping he would fight for her as hard as he fought for his work, for every person who walked through those clinic doors. But she hadn't heard a word from him since she'd stormed from his room and she'd gone back to her simple room a floor below. How easily he'd let her go, and in doing so, broken her heart.

But his ability to disconnect with her also filled her with resolve.

She wouldn't be like him anymore, hiding from the world. She was through staying in the shadows for fear of disappointing people.

Mari smoothed her hands down the shimmering red strapless dress, black swirls through the fabric giving the impression of phantom roses. The dress hugged her upper body, fitted past her hips then swept to the ground with a short train. It was a magnificent gown. She'd never worn anything like it. She would have called it a Cinderella moment except she didn't want to be some delicate princess at the ball. She was a one-day queen, boldly stepping into her own.

Her hands fell to the small tiara, diamonds refracting the vanity lights. Carefully, she tucked the crown—symbolic of so much more—on her head.

Stepping from her room, she checked the halls and, how ironic, for once the corridor was empty. No fans to carefully maneuver. She could make her way to the brass-plated elevator in peace.

Jabbing the elevator button, she curled her toes in her silken ballet slippers. Her stomach churned with nerves over facing the crowd downstairs alone, even more than that, over facing Rowan again. But she powered on, one leather-clad foot at a time. While she was ready to meet the world head-on in her red Vera Wang, she wasn't prepared to do so wearing high heels that would likely send her stumbling down the stairs.

She was bold, but practical.

Finally, the elevator doors slid open, except the elevator wasn't empty. Her stomach dropped in shock faster than a cart on a roller-coaster ride.

"Papa?" She stared at her father, her royal father.

But even more surprising, her mother stood beside him. "Going down, dear?"

Stunned numb, she stepped into the elevator car, brass doors sliding closed behind her.

"Mother, why are you and Papa here? *Together?*" she squeaked as her mom hugged her fast and tight.

The familiar scent of her mom's perfume enveloped her, like a bower of gardenias. And her mom wasn't dressed for a simple visit. Susan Mandara was decked out for the ball in a Christmas-green gown, her blond hair piled on top of her head. Familiar, yet so unusual, since Mari couldn't remember the last time she'd seen Adeen and Susan Mandara standing side by side in anything other than old pictures.

Her father kissed her on the forehead. "Happy Christmas, little princess."

She clutched her daddy's forearms, the same arms that used to toss her high in the air as a child. Always catching her.

Tonight, her father wore a tuxedo with a crimson tribal robe over it, trimmed in gold. As a child, she used to sneak his robes out to wear for dress-up with her parents laughing, her mother affectionately calling him Deen, her nickname for him. She'd forgotten that happy memory until just now.

Her mother smoothed cool hands over her daughter's face. "Your father and I have a child together." She gave

Mari's face a final pat. "Deen and I are bonded for life, *by* life, through you. We came to offer support and help you with all the press scrutiny."

Did they expect her to fail? She couldn't resist saying, "Some of this togetherness would have been welcome when I was younger."

"We've mellowed with age." Susan stroked her daughter's forehead. "I wish we could have given you a simpler path. We certainly wanted to."

If her mother had wanted to keep things simple, marrying a prince was surely a weird way to go about it.

Her father nodded his head. "You look magnificent. You are everything I wanted my princess to grow up to be."

"You're just saying that because I'm decked out in something other than a sack," she teased him, even though her heart ached with the cost of her newfound confidence. "But I can assure you, I still detest ribbon cuttings and state dinners."

"And you still care about the people. You'll make your mark in a different manner than I did. That's good." He held out both elbows as the elevator doors slid open on the ground floor. "Ladies? Shall we?"

Decorations in the hallway had doubled since she went upstairs to change after the final presentation of the day. Mari strode past oil palm trees decorated with bells. Music drifted from the ballroom, a live band played carols on flutes, harps and drums.

The sounds of Christmas. The sounds of home. Tables laden with food. She could almost taste the sweet cookies and the meats marinated in *chakalaka.*

A few steps later, she stood on the marble threshold of the grand ballroom. All eyes turned to her and for a moment her feet stayed rooted to the floor. Cameras clicked and she didn't so much as flinch or cringe. She wasn't sure what to do next as she swept the room with her eyes, taking in the ballroom full of medical professionals decked out in all their finery, with local bigwigs in attendance, as well.

Then her gaze hitched on Rowan, wearing a traditional tuxedo, so handsome he took her breath away.

His hair was swept back, just brushing his collar, his eyes blue flames that singed her even from across the room. She expected him to continue ignoring her. But he surprised her by striding straight toward her. All eyes followed him, and her heart leaped into her throat.

Rowan stopped in front of them and nodded to her father. "Sir, I believe your daughter and I owe the media a dance."

Owe the media?

What about what they owed each other?

And how could he just stand there as if nothing had happened between them, as if they hadn't bared their bodies and souls to each other? She had a gloriously undignified moment of wanting to kick him. But this was her time to shine and she refused to let him wreck it. She stepped into his arms, and he gestured to the band. They segued into a rendition of "Ave Maria," with a soloist singing.

Her heart took hope that he'd chosen the piece for her. He led her to the middle of the dance floor. Other couples melted away and into the crowd, leaving them alone, at the mercy of curious eyes and cameras.

As she allowed herself to be swept into his arms—into the music—she searched for something to say. "I appreciate the lovely song choice."

"It fits," he answered, but his face was still creased in a scowl, his eyes roving over her.

"Don't you like the dress?"

"I like the woman in the dress," he said hoarsely. "If you'd been paying attention, you would have realized my eyes have been saying that for a long time before you changed up your wardrobe."

"So why are you scowling?"

"Because I want this whole farce of a week to be over."

"Oh," she said simply, too aware of his hand on her waist, his other clasping her fingers.

"Do you believe me? About the dress, I mean." His feet moved in synch with hers, their bodies as fluid on the dance floor as they'd been making love.

"We've exchanged jabs in the past, insults even, but you've always been honest."

"Then why are you still sleeping on another floor of the hotel?"

"Oh, Rowan," she said bittersweetly. "Sex isn't the problem between us."

"Remind me what is?"

"The way you close people—me—out. It took me a long time to realize I'm deserving of everything. And so are you."

"I guess there's nothing left to say then."

The music faded away, and with a final sweep across the floor he stopped in front of her parents.

Rowan passed her hand back to her father. "With all due respect, sir, take better care of her."

Her mother smothered a laugh.

Her father arched a royal eyebrow. "I beg your pardon."

"More security detail. She's a princess. She deserves to be cared for and protected like one."

With a final nod, Rowan turned away and melted into the crowd and out of her life.

Five hours later, Mari hugged her pillow to her chest, watching her mom settle into the other double bed in the darkened room. "Mother, aren't we wealthy enough for you to have a suite or at least a room of your own?"

Susan rolled to her side, facing her daughter in the shadowy room lit only by moonlight streaming in. "I honestly thought you would be staying with Dr. Boothe even though this room was still booked in your name. And even with the show of good faith your father and I have given, we're not back to sharing a room."

Curtains rustled with the night ocean breeze and sounds of a steel-drum band playing on the beach for some late-night partiers.

"Rowan and I aren't a couple anymore." Although the haunting beauty of that dance still whispered through her, making her wonder what more she could have done. "It was just a…fling."

The most incredible few days of her life.

"Mari dear, you are not the fling sort," her mother reminded her affectionately. "So why are you walking away from him?"

Tears clogged her throat. "I'm honestly too upset to talk about this." She flipped onto her back, clenching her fists against the memory of his tuxedoed shoulders under her hands.

The covers rustled across the room as her mother sat up. "I made the biggest mistake of my life when I was about your age."

"Marrying my father. Yeah, I got that." Was it in her DNA to fail at relationships? Her parents had both been divorced twice.

"No, marrying the man I loved—your father—was the right move. Thinking I could change him? I screwed up there." She hugged her knees to her chest, her graying blond hair trailing down her back. "Before you think I'm taking all the blame here, he thought I would change, as well. So the divorce truly was a fifty-fifty screw-up on our part. He should have realized my free spirit is what he fell in love with and I should have recognized how drawn I was to his devotion to his country."

What was her mother trying to tell her? She wanted to understand, to step outside of the awkwardness in more ways than just being comfortable in a killer red dress. Except her mom was talking about not changing at all.

"You're going to have to spell it out for me more clearly."

"Your father and I weren't a good couple. We weren't even particularly good at being parents. But, God, you sure turned out amazing," her mother said with an unmistakable pride, soothing years of feeling like a disappointment. "Deen and I did some things right, and maybe if we'd focused more on the things we did right, we might have lasted."

Mari ached to pour out all the details of her fight with Rowan, how she needed him to open up. And how ironic was it that he accused her of not venting her emotions? Her thoughts jumbled together until she blurted out in frustration, "Do you know how difficult it is to love a saint?"

Her mother reached out in the dark, across the divide between their beds. "You love him?"

Mari reached back and clasped her mother's hand.

"Of course I do. I just don't know how to get through to him."

"You two have been a couple for—what?—a week? Seems to me like you're giving up awful fast."

Mari bristled defensively. "I've known him for years. And it's been an intense week."

"And you're giving that up? I'd so hoped you would be smarter than I was." Her mom gave her hand a final squeeze. "Think about it. Good night, Mari."

Long into the night, Mari stared out the window at the shoreline twinkling with lighted palm trees. The rolling waves crashed a steady reminder of her day sailing with Rowan. He'd done so much to comfort her. Not just with words, but with actions, by planning the day away from the hotel and painful memories.

What had she done for him?

Nothing.

She'd simply demanded her expectations for him rather than accepting him as he was. He'd accepted and appreciated her long before a ball gown. Even when he disagreed with her, he'd respected her opinion.

Damn it all, she *was* smarter than this. Of course Rowan had built walls around himself. Every person in his family had let him down—his parents and his brother. None of them had ever put him or his well-being first. Sure, he'd made friends with his schoolmates, but he'd even admitted to feeling different from them.

Now she'd let him down, as well. He'd reached out to her as best he could and she'd told him what he offered wasn't good enough, maybe because she'd been scared of not being enough for him.

But she knew better than that now. A confidence flowed through her like a calming breeze blowing in off the ocean. With that calm came the surety of what to do next.

It was time to fight for the man she loved, a man she loved for his every saintly imperfection.

Rowan had always been glad to return to his clinic on the mainland. He'd spent every Christmas here in surgical scrubs taking care of patients since moving to Africa. He welcomed the work, leaving holiday celebrations to people with families.

Yet, for some reason, the CD of Christmas carols and a pre-lit tree in the corner didn't stir much in the way of festive feelings this year. A few gifts remained for the patients still in the hospital, the other presents having been passed out earlier, each box a reminder of shopping with Mari.

So he buried himself in work.

Phone tucked under his chin, he listened to Elliot's positive update on Issa, followed by a rambling recounting of his Australian Christmas vacation. Rowan cranked back in a chair behind his desk, scanning a computer file record on a new mother and infant due to be discharged first thing in the morning.

One wing of the facility held a thirty-bed hospital unit and the other wing housed a clinic. Not overly large, but all top-of-the-line and designed for efficiency. They doled out anything from vaccinations to prenatal care to HIV/AIDS treatment.

The most gut-wrenching of all? The patients who came for both prenatal care and HIV treatment. There was a desperate need here and he couldn't help everyone, but one at a time, he was doing his damnedest.

The antibacterial scent saturated each breath he took. Two nurses chatted with another doctor at the station across the hall. Other than that, the place was quiet as a church mouse this late at night.

"Elliot, if you've got a point here, make it. I've got a Christmas Eve dinner to eat."

Really, just a plate to warm in the microwave but he wasn't particularly hungry anyhow. Visions of Mari in that red gown, cloaked in total confidence, still haunted his every waking and sleeping thought. He'd meant what he'd said when he told her it didn't matter to him what clothes she wore. But he was damn proud of the peace she seemed to have found with being in the spotlight. Too bad he couldn't really be a part of it.

"Ah, Rowan, I really thought you were smarter than me, brother," Elliot teased over the phone from his Australian holiday. The background echoed with drunken carolers belting out a raucous version of "The Twelve Days of Christmas."

"As I recall, our grades were fairly on par with each other back in the day."

"Sure, but I've had about four concussions since then, not to mention getting set on fire."

A reluctant smile tugged at Rowan. "Your point?"

"Why in the hell did you let that woman go?" Elliot asked, the sounds of laughter and splashing behind him. "You're clearly crazy about her and she's nuts about you. And the chemistry… Every time you looked at each other, it was all I could do not to shout at you two to get a room."

"She doesn't want me in her life." The slice of her rejection still cut so much deeper than any other.

"Did she tell you that?"

"Very clearly," he said tightly, not enjoying in the least reliving the moment. "I think her words were along the lines of 'have a nice life.'"

"You've never been particularly self-aware."

He winced, closing down the computer file on his new maternity patient. "That's what she said."

"So are you going to continue to be a miserable ass or are you going to go out and meet Mari at the clinic gate?"

At the gate? He creaked upright in his chair, swinging his feet to the floor. "What the hell are you talking about? You're in Australia."

But he stormed over to look out his office window anyway.

"Sure, but you tasked me with her security and I figured some follow-up was in order. I've been keeping track of her with a combo of guards and a good old-fashioned GPS on her rental car. If my satellite connection is any good, she should be arriving right about… now."

Rowan spotted an SUV rounding the corner into sight, headlights sweeping the road as the vehicle drove toward the clinic. Could it really be Mari? Here? Suddenly, Elliot's call made perfect sense. He'd been stringing Rowan along on the line until just the right moment.

"And Rowan," Elliot continued, "be sure you're the one to say the whole 'lovc you' part first since she came to you. Merry Christmas, brother."

Love her?

Of course he loved her. Wanted her. Admired her. Desired her. Always had, and why he hadn't thought to tell her before now was incomprehensible to him. Thank God for his friends, who knew him well enough to boot him in the tail when he needed that nudge most.

Thank God for Mari, who hadn't given up on him. She challenged him. Disagreed with him. But yet here she was, for him.

The line disconnected as he was already out the door and sprinting down the hall, hand over his pager to keep it from dislodging from his scrubs in his haste. His gym shoes squeaked against the tiles as he turned the corner and burst out through the front door, into the starlit night. The brisk wind rippled his surgical scrubs.

The tan SUV parked beside the clinic's ambulance under a sprawling shea butter tree. The vehicle's dome light flicked on, and Merry Christmas to him, he saw Mari's beautiful face inside. She stepped out, one incredibly long leg at a time, wearing flowing silk pants and a tunic. The fabric glided along her skin the way his hands ached to do again.

Her appearance here gave him the first hope in nearly a week that he would get to do just that.

"You came," he said simply.

"Of course. It's Christmas." She walked toward him, the African night sky almost as magnificent as his princess. She wore the bracelets he'd given her, the bangles chiming against each other. Toe-to-toe, she stopped in front of him, the sweet scent and heat of her reaching out to him. "Where else would I be but with the man I l—"

He pressed a finger against her lips. "Wait, hold that thought. I have something I need to say first. I love you, Mariama Mandara. I've wanted you and yes, loved you, for longer than I can remember. And I will do whatever it takes to be worthy of your love in return."

"Ah, Rowan, don't you know? You're already exactly what I need and everything I want. God knows, if you get any more saintly you're likely to be raptured and I would miss you so very much. I love you, too."

Relief flooded him, his heart soaking up every word like the parched ground around him absorbing a rain shower. Unable to wait another second, he hauled her to his chest and kissed her, deeply, intensely, hoping she really understood just how much he meant those words. He loved her. The truth of that sang through him as tangibly as the carols carrying gently through an open window.

Ending the kiss with a nip to his bottom lip, Mari smiled up at him. "I had a far more eloquent speech planned. I even practiced saying it on the way over because I wanted the words to be as special as what we've shared together."

"I hope you trust I love you, too." He only wished he had a more romantic way of telling her.

"I do. You showed me." She tugged the ends of the stethoscope draped around his neck, her bracelets sliding along her arm. "I just needed to stop long enough to listen with my heart. And my heart says we're perfect for each other. That we're meant to be together."

"Then why did we give each other such a hard time all these years?"

"We are both smart, dedicated people with a lot to offer, but we should be challenged. It makes us better at what we do." She tugged his face closer, punctuating the words with a quick kiss. "And if I have my way, I'm going to challenge you every day for the rest of my life."

"You have mesmerized me since the moment I first saw you." Desire and love interlocked inside him, each spiking the other to a higher level.

"That's one of the things I love most about you." She toyed with his hair, which just brushed the collar of his scrubs.

"What would that be?" He looped his arms low around her waist.

"You think my baggy, wrinkled wardrobe is sexy."

"Actually, I think peeling the clothes off of you is life's most perfect pleasure." He brought them closer together, grateful to have her in his arms, determined never to let this woman slip away from him again.

"Well, then, Dr. Boothe, let's find somewhere private to go so you can unwrap your Christmas present."

* * * * *

TO CLAIM HIS HEIR BY CHRISTMAS

VICTORIA PARKER

CHAPTER ONE

HE WAS GOING to propose. Any minute now.

It was every little girl's dream. A handsome man, one of the most beautiful she'd ever seen, sat opposite her at an intimate table for two, with a velvet box nestled in his inside pocket. Aristocracy, no less. The suave Savile Row sophisticate who was Viscount Augustus. The man who'd set the scene so superbly.

Dimly lit chandeliers cast a seductive romantic ambience throughout the room of the critically acclaimed restaurant, where Michelin chefs were famous for creating masterpieces of haute cuisine. Open fires crackled and crystal tinkled as exorbitantly priced champagne flowed, poured into flutes in an amber rush of opulent effervescence. And beyond the wide plate-glass windows lay the majestic vista of the Tarentaise Valley—Savoie, bathing in the rose-pink wash of dusk, its white-capped mountains towering from the earth like watchful sentinels over the exclusive lavish ski resort of Pur Luxe.

Stunning. Awe-inspiring. The stage was set.

All that was left were the words.

And Princess Luciana Valentia Thyssen Verbault was paralysed with dread.

Please, God, please get me out of this somehow...

There is no way out, Luce. Not only do you have a duty to your people but a deal is a deal. And you made one with the devil himself.

Lord, she hated her father right now. *'Go to the Alps,'* he'd said. *'Take a few days to think things over, get your head together.'*

Luciana had taken in his seemingly sincere autocratic face, paler since she'd last seen him as his health continued to deteriorate, and thought, yes, a few days to ponder. After all, she'd thought, she had years before her coronation, plenty of room to breathe, to barter for more time. But, as the saying went: Men plan. Fates laugh.

King Henri of Arunthia was being pushed by his doctors to retire. So she'd come to inhale the invigorating crisp air, to infuse her mind with solace. Reassess. Come up with a strategy where matrimony wouldn't equate to losing the only person she lived for. What her father *hadn't* said was that he was dropping her smack-bang in the midst of her worst nightmare by sending Augustus to seal the deal.

She supposed she should have seen it coming. Avoiding the Viscount via any means possible since her return home from China three weeks ago obviously hadn't worked a jot. All she'd done was delay the inevitable.

You can run but you can't hide. Wasn't that what they said?

Truth was, for so long she'd been living on borrowed time, wishing with all her heart that time would miraculously stand still. But time, as she'd soon realised, waited for no man. Let alone a woman as desperate as she was to avoid the ticking clock.

Now she would pay the ultimate price for bartering with her father five too short years ago. Five years of living a normal existence, well hidden in her sanctuary near Hong Kong. Five years of latitude and liberty in exchange for total compliance—starting now.

'Luciana? Is the *filet* not to your liking, *querida*?'

Her eyelashes fluttered as she fought the urge to squeeze them shut. Pretend she was anywhere but here. *Querida…* Lord, she wished he wouldn't call her that. Wished too that she could extinguish the heat banked in his blue eyes. Hadn't he had enough carnal relations for one afternoon? She almost asked him. If he'd enjoyed the brunette in his suite. The one who'd answered his door half naked and ravaged. But the truth was she couldn't care less. It was the endearments she loathed. They hinted at affection and love and there would be none in this marriage. On either side.

He was playing a part, though, wasn't he? She wondered, then, if he was going to get down on one knee. While she sincerely hoped not, he was a virtuoso at playing the press and they'd want the fairy story.

Fairy story. Yeah, right. A fool's dream. Like so many others that taunted her day and night.

'It's wonderful, thank you,' she said, attempting another small mouthful even as her stomach roiled.

It could be the best *filet mignon* in the world and it would still taste like black ash. Though no one would ever know it. Trained by the best, she was the perfect picture of elegant refinement. Graceful to a fault.

'Good. I want tonight to be perfect,' he said softly. Slick and skilful.

Luciana whipped out the serene smile she'd perfected since the cradle—not too bright or flashy, nor too dull. *Just perfect*, as her mother would say. Neglecting to add the tiny detail that it would strip her throat raw every time she faked it.

'I want tonight to be perfect.'

Guilt trickled through the turbulent maelstrom of emotions warring for dominance in her chest. He was trying, wasn't he?

Of course he is—he wants a throne of his own. Of course he's pulling out every weapon in his cultivated arsenal.

Still, it wasn't his fault that the 'arranged marriage' part of her conditioning hadn't quite taken root. It wasn't his fault that she dreamed of another. It wasn't his fault that she had a taste for dark and dangerous.

Yes, and look what trouble that landed you in. Surely you've learned your lesson by now?

And Augustus was good-looking. Very handsome, in fact. Sandy blond hair artfully shorn and midnight-blue eyes. He had women after him in their droves. Yet he was her duty—tall and fair. The man she'd been ordered to wed. And from there to his bed.

A phantom knife sliced through her stomach and instinctively she bowed forward to ease the lancing pain… Then she forced her poise to kick in, reached gingerly for her glass and poured the amber liquid down her throat. Maybe if she got tipsy enough she'd have enough anaesthetic on board to say yes without shattering into a million pieces.

Flute back to the table, Luciana picked up her fork to push the tenderised beef around her gold-rimmed plate on the off-chance that he'd reach for her hand again. Once this evening was more than enough.

Would she ever get used to his touch? It was nothing like when *he'd* touched her. Nothing like the wickedly high jolt of electricity that had surged through her veins, or the blaze of her blood creating a raging inferno inside her.

Stop! For the love of God, Luciana, stop.

Problem was, as always, she found it impossible to halt the flow. The fiery rush of memories. Memories of a man who'd given her a gift to last a lifetime.

Pain and secrecy thumped inside her ribs like a dark heart. Because no one could know. No one could ever, *ever* know.

Princesses of the realm, first in line to the throne, were *not* meant to disgrace themselves by breaking free of their dutiful chains. Not meant to alter their appearance beyond recognition to avoid the paparazzi and go to rock concerts in Zurich dressed like a hippy, doling out false names. Not meant to fall in love…no, *lust* at first sight and have wild, passionate love affairs. They especially weren't supposed to have them with Arunthia's enemy. Not that she'd known exactly who he was when they'd met.

Such an ironic twist of fate. One she would have reduced to a dream if she didn't hold and squeeze and hug and kiss the living proof of her reckless walk on the wild side every single day. Yet, despite it all—despite knowing she'd given her innocence to a treacherous, dangerous man—she could never, *would* never regret it. Because her first and only lover had given her a gift that was the single most brilliant, bright spark of joy in her world…her son.

Discreetly she sneaked a peek at the mobile phone hidden in her lap to see if Natanael's goodnight text had come through. Nothing. She stifled the melancholy of missing him by picturing him playing happily with her sister Claudia and baby Isabelle, while Lucas watched on adoringly, protectively. Possessively.

At times it physically hurt to look at them. The perfect family. So deeply, devotedly in love. Their beautiful marriage was eons away from the unions she was used to. Luciana hadn't known such a thing existed. She would do anything for that. Pay any price.

Envy, thick and poignant, pierced her chest with a sweet, sharp ache and she cursed herself for feeling that way. Wanting what she couldn't have. Plunging lower than the black trench of despair she'd dug beneath her own feet. On the verge of letting loose the scream that was irrevocably bottled up inside her.

Come on, Luce. You know happiness isn't written in the cards for a royal firstborn. Only duty.

Luciana tried to swallow and block the lash of repercussions her trip down the aisle would provoke before anguish swept her mind away on a tide of insanity.

Stop this! You're protecting him—just as you've always done.

But how was she ever going to leave her heart? The person she needed in order to breathe, as if he were the very air itself? Her gorgeous little boy.

Claudia had sworn she'd save him from the oppressive walls of Arunthe Palace, love him as Luciana did until she could figure out a way for them to be together always. As Queen she'd have more power. She would think of something. She *had* to.

In the meantime Luciana would always be near—but what about his tub time, and the way he liked to be tucked tight and snug into bed? Luciana wanted to run his bath with his favourite bubbles that made his tender skin smell sweet. And what about when he called for her in the night when he was having bad dreams? *She* wanted to hold him when he was scared.

The thought of him asking for her and her not being there… It tormented her mind. How she was going to explain it all to him she had no idea. And how was she going to leave Natanael behind if this man dragged her to his family estate in Northern Arunthia?

So tell him. Tell him. He might understand. Support you. Help you.

This man? No. No, she didn't trust him not to betray her confidence. Didn't trust anyone.

You made a deal, Luciana. Now you pay.

Ah, yes, a deal made in naïve, youthful folly. In desperation such as she'd never known. A pact etched in her mind like an effigy on a tombstone. A shiver ghosted over her as she was haunted by the past…

'Please...please, Father. I can't do it. I can't get rid of him.' She knew he was small, so small inside her, but she couldn't take him away, she couldn't give him up. She couldn't.

'Luciana, you are not married. You will bring disgrace on us all. You are the heiress to the throne and the father of the child you carry is an enemy of this nation. Do you

forget his assassination attempt? On me? He is a traitor to the crown.'

'Yes, but I didn't know who he was. I—'

'If this man ever discovered your child's existence he could use him as a pawn to gain power over us. He could take Arunthia. And do you honestly want his Satan of an uncle getting his hands on your son? We have avoided war for sixty years—do you want your people to live in tyranny as those in Galancia do?'

'No, no. But...no one need ever know. I could go away for a while. Please, I'm begging you. Pleading with you... Let me keep him.'

The King's deep sigh filled the oppressive air stifling his office and she teetered on the precipice of throwing her pride to the gale and plunging to her knees.

Then he said, 'Five years, Luciana. Five years of freedom. That is all I will give you. But the world must never know he is yours because Thane must never, ever find him. You will never be able to claim him as your son and heir. Do you understand me?'

'Yes. Yes, I understand,' she said—wild, frenzied, frantic. Unthinking of the consequences of what she was agreeing to. So desperate she would have sold her soul in that moment.

'You will be hidden well in the Far East, and in five years you will return to take the throne and do your duty. You will marry, Luciana, am I clear?'

'Yes—yes, I swear it. I'll do whatever you want. Just let me have him.'

His steely eyes were clouded with disappointment and grief and sorrow. That gaze was telling her she would rue this day, this bargain.

Luciana ignored it. As long as her son got to take his first breath, got to walk upon the earth and live life to the full, without the constraints of duty like a noose around his neck, she would make a deal with the devil himself. And so she did.

* * *

Augustus's voice shattered her bleak reflection and she tuned back in to the chatter that fluttered around them in a hushed din.

All she had to do was remember that her happiness came second to Natanael's safety. And she *would* keep him safe if it was the last thing she did.

'Luciana? Would you like coffee and dessert or…?'

Or…? Lord, not now. Not when she was falling apart at the seams. She wasn't ready to hear those words. Not yet. *Not ever.*

She felt powerless. Completely out of control. Like a puppet on a string.

The room began to spin.

'Yes, thank you, that would be wonderful,' she said, her voice thankfully calm and emotion-free as she plastered a cringe-worthy beatific smile on her face.

Coffee. Crème brulée. That would buy her another twenty minutes, surely.

Panic fisted her heart as the tick of the clock pounded in her ears. Tick-tock. Tick-tock.

The walls loomed, closing in around her, crushing her lungs.

Calm down, Luce. What are you going to do—hyperventilate and pass out? Make a total fool of yourself?

She needed air. She couldn't breathe.

'I'm sorry—please excuse me. I think I need…' To go out on the balcony? No, no, no, he'd follow her and drop to one knee, she knew. 'To visit the restroom. I'll only be a few minutes.'

After all that she realised he wasn't listening. Someone on the other side of the room had caught his eye, and Luciana frowned as his lightly tanned face stained a ghastly shade of grey.

'Augustus? Are you all right? Did you hear what I said?'

Slowly he shook his head. 'I do not believe it. Luciana,

you will never guess who is dining in this very room. I had no idea. Your father will be most displeased. I am so sorry…'

He was *sorry*? Ah, wonderful. One of his women, no doubt. The buxom brunette from earlier, come to ruin his perfect proposal? She didn't want to know. It was her parents' marriage all over again. No doubt she'd be faced with his mistresses most mornings too.

Well, that's better than you warming his bed, isn't it?

Anything was better than that.

'Don't worry about it, Augustus. Your secret is safe with me.' Her father wouldn't care less who the man whored with. There was more likelihood of mutual backslapping. 'I'll be back soon.'

Ignoring her, on he went. 'Of all the places in all the world…'

Luciana bit into her bottom lip, stifling the impulse to run like a world class sprinter. Praying for this evening to be over. Praying someone would rescue her from this nightmare. Before the truth escaped on the scream that was building gradually, inexorably, and she single-handedly destroyed the very life she was trying to protect.

'Of all the places in all the world… What an unpleasant surprise.'

His cousin, Seve, who was seated to his right at the oval dining table, leaned his upper body sideways in an effort to be discreet.

'I can see the sweat beading on his upper lip from here. It's your old pal from that exclusive rich joint you were sent to in Zurich. Viscount Augustus.'

Prince Thane of Galancia deflected the gut-punch the word *Zurich* evoked and sneered. 'He was no *pal* of mine.'

For the one disastrous university term Thane had attended after his father's death the Viscount had caused him no end of trouble—which he'd soon discovered was a horrendously bad idea—and subsequently shaken in his shoes every time he looked Thane's way. Which had pleased Thane no end. It meant he'd generally kept a vast distance.

He couldn't abide the man. Augustus was a wolf in sheep's clothing. Polished until every inch of him gleamed, he was a silver-tongued bureaucrat with sly eyes and a treacherous mind.

Seve smirked as if Thane had said the words out loud and he'd found it highly amusing. 'What's more, he's dining with none other than Princess Luciana of Arunthia. One of Henri's stuck-up brood.'

Thane resisted the urge to growl. 'Then they belong together.' A match made in heaven. 'How do you know it's definitely her? Last I heard, she lived abroad.'

He couldn't remember the last time he'd seen a photograph of *any* of them. Recent intel was off his radar, since he had zero interest in becoming embroiled with his uncle's ongoing bitter feud with the house of Verbault. He'd made that mistake ten years ago, in his father's day. Had the scars and the bitter aftertaste to prove it. Nowadays every time he thought of that varmint Henri a seizure of antagonistic emotion diseased his mind, so the less he heard or saw of the entire family the better. Besides, his every waking moment was spent deflecting blows from the latest fiasco in Galancia.

'I *know* because the two of them having fun on the slopes made the French headlines this morning. Rumour has it she's newly returned from Hong Kong, due to take the crown any day.'

Thane would have predicted a snowball in hell before he felt envy for a Verbault, but right then envy was definitely the evil he was up against. He wanted *his* crown. Taken from the hands of his uncle and placed in his own, where it should be. Before the man caused his people further damage. Four years… It seemed eons away, and his patience was wearing perilously thin.

He thrust his fingers through his hair and tucked some of the long, wayward strands behind his ear. 'It isn't hard to work out what Augustus wants. The vapid Viscount has always been an ambitious sleaze with illusions of grandeur.'

Seve chuckled darkly. 'Very true. Although I will say that marriage to her will be no chore for him. Look at her. By God, she's absolutely stunning.'

Thane couldn't care less if she was Cleopatra. She was still a Verbault. Granted, he refused to get snarled up in that age-old vendetta again, but he wasn't ignorant or blind to the reasoning for it. Verbault greed had once crippled a vulnerable Galancia, and rebuilding its former glory was an ongoing battle. Forgiveness would never be proffered. So the day he aligned with one of them would be the day he rode bareback with the Four Horsemen of the Apocalypse.

Seve, meanwhile, was still staring her way. Smitten. Practically drooling. 'I don't think I've ever seen a more beautiful woman in my life.'

'That's saying something, considering how many you've bedded,' Thane incised sardonically.

His cousin, his second in command, his best friend—the only person he would ever trust—shrugged his wide shoulders. 'Wouldn't do you any harm to get laid either, cousin. Come on—I didn't drag you here just to hurtle down the black slopes all day.'

He knew fine well what Seve had dragged him here for. All work and no play made Thane a dull, arrogant ass, apparently—and for a minute or three he had considered it. But when the redhead sitting to his right had appeared from nowhere he'd turned to stone. Unable even to contemplate getting close to another woman. In fact, if she touched his arm one more time…

Dios, didn't she know he was dangerous? That his blood ran black and his heart was dead? That he was more powerful and more feared than any other man in Europe? Surely his scars were enough to give her a clue?

Maybe he should give the mindless female a lesson in Princes of Galancia. Top of the list: do not touch.

He *hated* being touched. Didn't want anyone close to him. Ever again. While getting beaten to a pulp couldn't possibly hurt him any longer, it was the softer stuff that was more dangerous. One taste and he might very well crave it. Long for more of it. Glut himself on it. Live for it. Every touch. Every caress. Every kiss. Until it was taken away, as it inevitably would be. Leaving him empty. Aching. *Feeling.* Weak. And the dark Prince of Galancia could not afford to be weak. Not again. When he was weak he took his eye off the ball and everything went to hell.

Thane reached for his tumbler of rare single malt, his hand stalling in mid-air as an army of ants marched across his nape. Instinct born from a childhood in the barracks made him turn to peer over his right shoulder. Past the garish pine trees smothered in red ribbons and gold baubles, declaring the onslaught of the festive season. *How quaint. How pointless.*

Ah, yes, there was Augustus. Averting his gaze like an errant schoolboy. No woman with him—not that Thane could see.

But what he *did* see was a striking, statuesque blonde walking in the direction of the hallway that led to the restrooms. No. Not blonde at all. Her rich, decadent shower of loose tousled waves reminded him of a dark bronze. Like new-fallen acorns.

Now, *she* was beautiful. And that thought was so incredulous, so foreign, that he felt a tingle of something suspiciously close to shock.

His avid gaze locked on its target, his usual two-second scan turning into a drawn-out visual seduction, and he trailed his eyes over the low scooped neck of the black sheath that hugged her feminine curves. Lingered on the lapels of her long white dress coat, frisking and teasing all that flawless golden flesh.

A faint frown creased her brow and Thane narrowed his

eyes as she raised one hand and rubbed over the seam of her lips with the pad of her thumb.

A pleasurable shiver of recognition rippled over his skin and his entire body prickled with an unfathomable heat.

Ana used to do that. Stroke her mouth that way. When he'd asked her why, she'd said it likely came from sucking her thumb when she was a little girl. Thane had smiled and cracked some joke about her still liking things in her mouth, and she'd proceeded to prove him right. Many times over…

The brazen fires of lust swirled through his groin, and when the woman inhaled deeply—the action pushing those full, high breasts of surreal temptation to swell against the thin silk of her dress—ferocious heat speared through his veins until he flushed from top to toe.

It couldn't be. Could it? His Ana? Here in the Alps? No, surely not. Ana's hair was sable-black. Her body far more slender.

Look at me, he ordered. *Turn around*, he demanded. *Now.*

And she did. Or rather she spared a glance across the room in his direction, then wrestled with her poise, giving her head a little shake.

Thane's hands balled in frustration. But he kept watching as she reached the slightly secluded archway leading to the restrooms. Alone, doubtless believing she was unseen, she tipped her head back, glancing skyward as if praying to God, and graced him with the elegant curve of her smooth throat.

Another flashback hit with crystalline precision—*his* woman, arching off the bed, back bowed as she seized in rapture beneath him, inarticulate cries pouring from her swollen ruby-red mouth. And for the first time in his life—or maybe the second—his insides started to shake. *Shake.*

Dios, was his mind playing tricks on him? *Months* he had searched for her. For that trail of sable hair, that mesmerising beauty mark above her full lips, those clothes that harked of dark blood, a roaming gypsy. No stone had been unturned in Zurich, since that was where they had met, where she had *claimed* to live. Torturous years of not knowing whether she was dead or alive. Living with the grief. The ferocious anger and self-hate that choked him at the notion that he might not have protected her. That she could have been taken from him because of who he was.

He blinked and she was gone. Disappeared once again. And before he knew it he'd shoved his chair backwards with an emphatic scrape.

'Thane?'

'Restroom,' he said, and followed the dark blonde, his heart stampeding through his chest.

Thane thrust the double doors wide, then took a sharp right down the first corridor—and came to a dead end. A swift turn about and he flung open the double doors to the wraparound balcony. Empty.

Impatience thrummed inside him. The notion of being thwarted tore at his guts. He closed the doors with a quick click, turned and—

Slam.

'Ooof.' He ran straight into another body so hard and fast he had to grab hold of her upper arms to stop her from careening backwards and crashing to the floor.

'I…I'm sorry. I wasn't looking where I was going. Please…'

Just the sound of her voice washed clean rain over him. She was breathless, winded, clutching his lapels as if he was her life raft in the darkest, most turbulent storm.

'Please. I need to…'

That soft, husky whimper flung him back in time, sent electricity sizzling over every inch of his skin. And the way she'd jolted—he would hazard a guess she'd felt it too.

Stumbling back a step, she jacked up her chin and their gazes caught, clashed…

Madre de Dios!

'Ana?'

Brandy-gold eyes flared up at him as bee-stung lips

parted with a gasp. And for the endless moments they stared at one another she seemed to pelt through a tumult of emotions. He could virtually see them flicker over her exquisite face. Fancied each one mirrored his own. She was astounded. Bewildered. Likely in denial. Half convinced she was hallucinating. And all the while Thane drank her in as if he'd been dying of thirst and his pulse-rate tripled to create a sonic boom in his ears.

He wanted to take her in his arms. Bury his fingers into the luxurious fall of her hair. Hold her tightly to him. Despite the internal screech of warning not to touch, not become ensnared in her again.

Thane swallowed around the emotional grenade lodged in his throat. 'Ana, where have you been? I looked for you. What happened? I…'

Unable to wait a second longer, he reached out—but she staggered back another step; her brow pinched with pain.

'No. No! Don't touch me. I'm sorry. You must be mistaking me for someone else. I…'

That pain morphed into something like fear and punched him in the gut.

'Please excuse me,' she said, and she made to duck past him.

His confusion made his cat-like reflexes take a second too long to kick in.

'Ana? What are you talking about?'

Why was she scared of him? He didn't like it. Not one bit. Everyone else? Yes. Her? No.

A man emerged from around the corner and when Thane recognised Augustus he almost swung his fist in the other man's face. Though at the last second he thought better of it. His word, he'd been told, was vehement enough. Consequently he opened his mouth to deliver a curt command but the Viscount beat him to the punch.

'Luciana? Are you all right, *querida*?'

Luciana? Hold on a minute… *Querida*?

What the *hell* was going on?

'Luciana? Is this man bothering you?'

Thane whipped around to face him. 'Back off, Augustus,' he ground out, jabbing his finger at the other man while he tried to think around the incessant clatter in his brain. 'And while you are doing that, if you know what is good for you, turn around and *walk away*.'

Augustus paled beneath his tanned skin, nodded and went to do just that. But not before he motioned to Ana with a jerk of his chin. Or was it Luciana? *Dios*, Thane felt as if his head was splitting in two.

'Why are you beckoning her? How do you know each other?' Thane asked, darkly incredulous.

Augustus straightened to his full height. Thane would give the man points for the gutsy move if he still weren't several inches shorter than him and trying on a smug smirk for size. But what really set Thane's teeth on edge was the way the disturbingly dashing Viscount—who was as suave and golden as Thane was dark and untamed—practically stripped the sheath from Ana's body with his lustful covetous gaze. It made a growl threaten to tear up his throat. He felt as if he could grow fangs.

'Luciana is to be my fiancée, Prince Thane. So I would appreciate it if you…'

The rest of his words were swept away on a tide of realisation and a watery rush sped through his ears, drowning out sound.

'*Fiancée*?' he repeated, black venom oozing from his tone. Because that meant… That meant…

With predator-like grace he pivoted to look back at the woman who had bewitched him so long ago. Invaded his every salacious dream for five years.

Eyes closed, she tucked her lips into her mouth and bit down hard enough to bruise.

'Do I take it I am in the company of Princess Luciana of *Arunthia*?' His voice seethed with distaste, so cold and hard he imagined it could shatter every windowpane within a ten miles radius. '*Am I?*'

His increase in volume snapped her awake and she elevated her chin, stood tall and regal, while she ruthlessly shuttered her expression.

'You certainly are, Prince Thane of *Galancia*,' she said, in a sexy, sassy voice that sent a dark erotic wave of heat rushing down his spine.

Ah, this was his Ana, all right. She looked more fearsome than Augustus could any day of the week, and Thane had the absurd desire to kiss that mulish line right off her lush, sulky mouth. Even *knowing* who she was. A Verbault. Henri's daughter. And didn't *that* fill him with no small amount of self-disgust? This had to be the universe's idea of a sick joke.

Thane crossed his arms over his wide chest and arched one livid brow as they faced off in the hallway.

'Did you know who I was back then?'

Had she known and set out to destroy him by luring him in? Because the Arunthian hussy had almost managed it. Almost driven him to the brink of insanity in the aftermath of her disappearance.

If he'd blinked he would have missed it. The way her smooth throat convulsed. The way she shot a quick glance in Augustus's direction as if to check he was still there. He was. Unfortunately. Soaking up every word.

'I'm afraid I have no idea what you're talking about. I've never met you before in my life. Now, if you gentlemen will excuse me, I suddenly find I'm very tired.'

Stupefied, he rocked back on his heels as she blew past them like a hurricane, leaving her signature trail of destruction in her wake.

A flash fire started in the pit of his gut and his mood took a deadly turn. The voracious heat was exploding to sear through his veins, to fire his blood as pure, undiluted anger blazed through his system.

Had she *actually* denied knowing him? *Him*? Prince Thane of Galancia? Had she *actually* walked away from him? *Again*?

A haze of inky darkness clouded his vision, his mind.

Ah, Princess. Big mistake. *Huge*. Massive, grave error of judgement.

He wanted answers. *Now*. Wanted to know if she'd known his true identity all along. If she'd been toying with him. Why she'd vanished in the middle of the night after she'd promised she would stay. Why she'd plunged him into the pit of Hades for months on end—something he would make her pay dearly for. But most of all he wanted her away from this sleaze-bag. Thane may no longer want to bed her, but he'd be damned if he stood by while Augustus took what was his.

Fact was he wanted her full attention. And, by God, he would get it.

This was not happening. This was just *not* happening.

Luciana shoved her clothes into her suitcase with one hand while she grappled with a cordless phone in the other.

Lord, she was shaking so hard she was likely calling Venezuela. One touch from that man and it was as if she'd been dormant in some cryonic stasis for five years and he'd plugged her into the national grid. Twenty minutes later her body was still burning; incinerator-hot, making her feel like a living, breathing flame.

Dangerous. That was what he was.

Worse still, when she'd literally crashed into him for a split second she'd thought she was dreaming again. That she'd conjured up his memory to save her from the nightmare her return had condemned her to. So often she slept with him in her bed, his fingers a ghost-like touch drifting over her body. Caressing, devouring with a fervour she longed for. And during that breathless moment in that hallway suddenly, shockingly, she'd wanted to cry. Weep in sheer relief that he was here. Holding her once more. Wrapping her in his ferocious unyielding strength.

That body… Such inordinate power that he vibrated with it. She'd met some powerful men in her time but Thane… No comparison. None. His every touch was a jolting shock-wave of acute pleasure and pain. And it had been so long since she'd been touched. She'd almost begged him to crush her against his hard, muscular chest for one blissful second, just so she could live in the illusion that he was here and she was safe.

But that was all it was—a fantasy. A fallacy. She would never be safe in Thane's arms.

So why did a part of her still crave him? Even knowing what and who he was?

Luciana moaned out loud. Her father was right—she was an absolute disgrace.

She'd do well to remember that invariably her dreams turned dark and his hands turned malicious and she woke in a cold, clammy and anguished sweat. That in actuality he was the most lethal, autocratic man in Europe, who co-ruled his country and his people with a merciless iron fist.

And that look in his glorious dark eyes when he'd gazed at her… As if she was his entire world… A lie. Her cruel imagination. If she needed proof to substantiate that theory all she had to do was recall his blistering disgust and anger as he'd ground out her title. Realised her true identity.

His granite-like countenance hadn't broken her heart. Certainly not. The man was rumoured to be a mercenary, for pity's sake.

Imagine that man getting hold of your son and using him as a pawn in his power-play?

Over her dead body.

That hypothesis was akin to someone upending a bucket of cold water over her head and she calmed enough to hit the right keys.

'I need a car outside in five minutes and a private jet waiting at the Altiport to take me to Arunthia. Can you do that?'

'Yes, *madame*.'

'Thank you.'

Depressing the call button, she flipped the lid of her case and yanked the zipper all the way around.

She had to get home. Get Natanael out of the country until she was sure Thane wouldn't come after her. The savage vehemence pouring off him as she'd left had scarred her for eternity. That was *not* a man you messed with.

The tap on her door flung her heart into overdrive and she crept up to the door to peek into the security viewer.

Shoulders slumping, she unlatched the lock and allowed the porter in to collect her bag. 'Thank you. I'll meet you downstairs.' Luciana pulled a two-hundred-euro note from her jacket pocket and conjured up a sweet smile. Feminine wiles and all that.

'The back door, okay?'

His boyish grin told her she was in the clear and she grabbed her handbag and scarpered from the room.

Down in the private elevator she went. Out through the back exit and into a frosty evening that nipped her cheeks.

The door of the limousine was an open invitation and Luciana sank into the plush leather, not wasting one vital moment. 'Can you take me to the Altiport, please? Fast as you can.'

The door slammed shut with a heavy clunk.

The locks clicked into place.

'Sure thing, lady.'

Lady? Frowning, she glanced up into the rearview mirror to see a peculiar pair of deep-set titanium-grey eyes staring back at her.

Luciana's blood curdled in her veins.

Then that voice—as brutal and vicious as the thrash of a whip—sliced through the leather-scented cabin, its deadly effect severing her air supply.

'We meet again, *Princess* of Arunthia.'

Vaulting backwards in her seat, she crushed herself into the corner and scoured the dim recesses of the car, her heart thudding a panicked tempo.

Black sapphire eyes glittering as starkly as the stars in the Courchevel sky, he raised one devilish dark brow and said, scathingly, 'Did you really think I would allow you to turn your back on me a second time, Luciana? Disappear into the night once more? How very foolish of you.'

Dressed from head to foot in a bespoke black Italian suit, he lounged like an insolent predator—a sleek panther perusing his kill.

'Well, let us get one thing perfectly clear right now. *This* time you will *not* walk away from *me*.'

CHAPTER TWO

SHE COULDN'T MOVE. Not one muscle.

'This time you *will* not *walk away from* me.'

What did he mean by that? Did she have to wait until *he* walked away from *her*? How long was that going to take? An hour? A day?

If she didn't start breathing she'd never find out.

Luciana yanked her focus dead ahead in order to stitch up the tattered remnants of her composure. She couldn't do that and look at him at the same time. It was futile. The mere sight of him, dangerous and dominating, skewed her equilibrium and turned her brain to mush.

The privacy glass rose up before her, sending her heart slamming around her ribcage. For a second she toyed with the idea of launching herself from the car, but then remembered the locks had snapped into place. A moment later the limousine began to rock down the steep incline from the lodge and the risk of hyperventilating became a distinct possibility.

Breathe, Luce, for heaven's sake breathe. He probably just wants to talk on the way to the Altiport.

Why, oh, why hadn't she looked at which car she was getting into? She was supposed to be avoiding trouble. Being good. The refined, beyond reproach, virtuous Queen she was born to be. She could already hear her mother… *So reckless, Luciana. So unthinking.*

She let loose a shaky exhalation, then took a deep lungful

of air. And another. Then seriously wished she hadn't. His audacious dark bergamot and amber scent wrapped around her senses like a narcotic, intensely potent and drugging as it swirled up into her brain, making her vision blur. Her entire body wept with want.

How did he still do this to her? After all this time? *How*? It was as if he engulfed her in his power, lured her in with his black magic. Well, any more of his lethal brand of masculinity and she'd be done for.

Clearing her throat, she straightened in her seat. With far more sangfroid and bravado than she felt, she said, 'Why am I here? What *exactly* is it you want from me?'

Seconds ticked by and he didn't so much as murmur. Merely allowed the atmosphere to stretch taut. And, since she was hanging on to the very last fraying threads of her control, it didn't take her long to snap.

Up came her head—*big* mistake as she realised too late it was exactly what he'd been waiting for, what he wanted: her full attention, total control over this…whatever *this* was. His gaze crashed into hers. Unerringly. Mercilessly.

Oh, Lord.

Overwhelming anguish held her in stasis as her every thought fled and she allowed her treacherous heart to devour the dark beauty that was Prince Thane.

Devastating—that was what he was. Bewitching her with that breathtaking aura of danger. Those high, wide slashing cheekbones and obsidian eyes framed with thick decadent inky lashes. That chiselled jaw that was smothered in a seriously sexy short beard. On anyone else it would be labelled designer stubble. But this was Thane and he wasn't vain in the least. Or he hadn't been. In truth, she'd been amazed at just how clueless to his gorgeous looks he was.

His hair was longer, she noticed. *Dishevelled* was a ridiculously romantic word for the mussed-up glossy black hair that fell in a tumble to flick his shoulders, one side swept back and tucked behind his ear. Unkempt, maybe.

Hideously long… But she kind of liked it. Craved to run her fingers through it. Had to fist her hands to stop herself from doing just that.

The dim interior lighting camouflaged his facial scars but she remembered every one. The slash in his top lip, just shy of the full cupid's bow. The second, enhancing the sensuous, kissable divot in his chin. Another slicing into the outer corner of his left eyebrow.

Her throat grew tight, swelling in sadness and hurt for him. Just as it had five years ago. Not that he'd ever talked to her about them. The one time she'd asked he'd shut down so hard it had taken her sitting astride his lap wearing nothing but lace panties to tease him out of it.

Ah, Luce, don't remember. Don't.

His tongue sneaked out and he briefly licked his lips, but otherwise he remained still, watching…waiting…his sensationally dynamic body vibrating with dark power. And she clutched her handbag tighter still, fingers burying into the leather—

Whether it was the feel of her phone poking through the side of her bag or the sudden realisation that the car was at a standstill she wasn't sure, but she crashed back to earth with a thud.

The car had actually stopped!

Luciana shuffled on her bottom to peek out of the window and saw the huge security gates of the lodge swing open in front of the car. Electronic operation. Unmanned. Drat.

Twisting the other way, she grasped the cushioned leather and peeked out of the back window, her eyes widening as she spied her bellboy, still at the top of the drive, waving for her attention, with her case in his hand.

Oh, my life!

Her speech faculties finally deigned to kick in. 'You have to turn around,' she said, with her best do-it-or-else regal intonation. 'You've left my case back there.'

And as soon as they pulled up back at the lodge she was making a run for it.

'Really?' he drawled, mock astonishment lifting his brows high above his vivid eyes. 'How unfortunate.'

Luciana narrowed her gaze on him. That was it? *Unfortunate?*

'Well? Aren't you going to go back for it?' she asked, her tone pitched to an ear-splitting squeak.

'And give you the opportunity to run again? I think not, *princesa*. Consider yourself under lock and key.'

The limo turned right onto the main road and picked up speed. But not nearly as fast as her temper.

Anger sparked. Revving up to be free of its leash. And she let it take hold. Uncoil deep inside her. Unravel at a breakneck pace. It was wonderful. Glorious. Just what she'd hankered for all day. *All day?* No. Since she'd stepped off the plane from Hong Kong, thoroughly powerless, with her façade firmly in place.

'Just *who* do you think you are? You can't just *take* me like this.'

Cool as you like, he simply said, 'Watch me.'

She sucked in air through her nose. 'Are you playing with me? You're taking me to the Altiport, right? I have a plane to catch.'

'We *are* going to the Altiport, *si*.'

'Good. That's good.'

Though he hadn't really said what was happening when they got there, had he?

Warily, she ventured, 'And you'll let me get on my own plane to Arunthia, yes?'

'No.'

Mouth falling agape, she coughed out an incredulous laugh. 'Are you *serious*?'

'Deadly,' he said, as sharp as a blade.

His eyes were as cold and hard as steel. Where once they'd been tender and warm. Had she known him at all?

she wondered, fighting a miserable flare of anguish. Even a little bit? Or had the last few years killed any ounce of decency and compassion he'd possessed?

Icy fingers of dread curled around her throat. 'So where *are* you taking me?'

'Galancia.'

The world tilted as if the car had skidded down an embankment with a five-score gradient and she went woozy. *Galancia?* No, no, *no*!

Luciana scoured his expression, desperate to find even a flicker of his dry humour, and came up blank. Galancia… She shuddered in her own skin.

'No way. You haven't got a hope in hell of getting me to that place. I have to go home.'

He pursed his lips and cocked his head in faux contemplation. 'Not today. Today you will go where I ordain.'

'But…but that's tantamount to abduction!'

'I suppose technically it is. Yet during the several minutes we've been in this car I haven't heard you call for assistance once.'

It didn't bode well that he was right. But, honest to God, the man was so distracting. Still, why *wasn't* she petrified out of her mind, screeching her head off?

'Give me a second and I'll scream blue murder. Though let's face it,' she said, gesturing to the luxurious car. 'There's no one to hear me, is there?'

'Not now, no. You are seven minutes too late, *princesa*. Though Seve may help you.'

'Who on earth is Seve?'

'The driver.'

She almost shuffled to the edge of the bench seat and raised her fist to knock on the glass partition. Almost. Frankly, she knew better.

'Friend?'

'Cousin,' he drawled, a flicker of a devilish smile playing about his mouth.

It was obscene how relieved she was to see that tiny flirtation with humour—that hint of the man she'd fallen for on a raucous, cluttered muddy field in Zurich. Particularly since it suggested he was enjoying her discomfort. What was all this? Payback for her walking away? Some kind of twisted revenge?

'You can't go about kidnapping people. It isn't civilised behaviour.'

Lord, she sounded like her mother. And, honestly, only a dimwit would put 'civilised' and 'Thane' in the same sentence. It had been his untamed earthy savagery that had attracted her in the first place. Obviously she had a screw loose.

Blasé, he gave her an insouciant shrug that said, *try and stop me*, and it made her anger boil into lava-hot fury until she felt like a mini-volcano on the verge of eruption. What *was* it about men trying to govern her life? She'd just escaped one control freak and run headlong into another.

Smouldering with resentment, she decided she wanted him to erupt too. It was as if he'd switched off his emotions. He was far too cool and collected over there. While she was sitting here losing it!

Look at him, she thought. Sitting at an angle, one leg bent and resting on the bench seat, he sprawled like a debauched lion, taking over half the enormous car—and *all* of the oxygen—in that outrageously expensive Italian suit. It *should* have oozed elegance and debonair refinement, but it made him look like pure wickedness and carnal sin.

And she detested him for making her hormones whisk themselves into a deranged frenzy over him. Wasn't she in enough of a mess?

Which reminded her… Woman on a mission, here. She wanted the playing field levelled.

'So the rumours are true, then?' she said, with as much chilly, haughty daring as she could muster.

Thane arched one arrogant brow. 'There are so many I'm at a loss as to which particular falsehood you refer to.'

'That your men steal women. That your father took your mother from her bed—stole her from her intended.' And by all accounts made her life a living hell in Galancia Castle. Rumour had it she'd thrown herself to her death to end the torment. Not that Luciana had ever believed that bit. No mother would do that to her son, surely?

Luciana waited him out. Expecting some kind of reaction. Something. *Anything.* What she got frustrated her even more. Nothing. Not even a flutter of his ridiculously gorgeous lashes.

'Ah, that one. Perfectly true. Indeed, we take what is rightfully ours.'

She was going to slap him in a second. 'And *where*, pray tell, do you get the idea that *I* am rightfully yours?'

Aha! As if she'd flipped a switch emotion stormed through his eyes. The dark variety. But right now she'd take what she could get.

'What is *rightfully* mine, Luciana, is an explanation. Answers.'

'That's all you want from me. An explanation?' It seemed a bit too easy to her, but she could answer fifty questions before they got anywhere near a plane. It was a thirty-minute drive at least. 'Fine,' she bit out. 'Ask away, Prince Thane. What do you want to know? Why I bolted in the dead of night?'

'Ah…' he said, with an affable lilt that belied the fury now emanating from him. 'So you *do* acknowledge that we have a history. Yet not thirty minutes ago you denied we'd ever met.'

Blast her runaway mouth. She should have known that would antagonise him.

'Yes, well, I don't want Augustus knowing about my personal life.'

'Worried, Luciana? That the prissy Viscount will not wish

to bed you or wed you any longer when he discovers you've been tarnished by our depraved association?'

She huffed. 'Hardly.' That would only be a *good* thing. And, absurd as it was, she suddenly had the strangest compulsion to thank her kidnapper for rescuing her from tonight's unpalatable proposal. Clearly she'd lost the plot.

As for his darkly intoned question—she'd lied through her teeth because all she cared about was making sure Augustus never put two and two together if he was ever faced with Natanael.

Natanael… *Oh, Lord.* She'd wanted to text him before he went to sleep. But it was far too risky to fish her phone from her handbag right now. The bag she clutched to her stomach like a lifeline. Thank goodness she'd carried it and not left it with her case.

More to the point, thank heavens she hadn't brought Nate to the Alps with her. The thought of Thane discovering him…carting him off to Galancia… No, that could never happen. *Never.* Thane was descended from a long line of militia. Royal males trained in guerrilla warfare. The best fighter pilots in the world. Some said all the boys were taken to the barracks to learn how to become soldiers at eight years old. The mere thought of Nate holding a weapon in four years' time made acid rise and coat her throat. Plus, she really had no idea what Thane was capable of. Considering abduction was his modus operandi for their reunion.

She shuddered where she sat, swelling until she felt she might burst with the need to protect Nate at all costs. She hadn't kept his identity a secret all this time to lose him now. Her little boy was having a long, happy and healthy life even if it killed her.

At this rate, Luce, it just might.

When she realised Thane was speaking again, she turned to face him and watched the soft skin around his eyes crinkle as he narrowed those black sapphire peepers on her.

'So you do not care? You do not care that your *fiancé* may no longer want you—?'

'He is *not* my fiancé.' Not yet anyway. And she'd rather bask in the fantasy of freedom a while longer, thank you very much.

'Now, are you *sure* about that, Luciana?' he jeered. 'Because he seemed to think you are. Or is your word now as empty as it was five years ago?'

She made a tiny choked squeak of affront. 'And what exactly do you mean by that?'

Brooding and fierce, he leaned forward, attacking her brain with another infusion of his darkly sensual scent. 'You made a promise to me. That you'd stay another week. That we would talk.'

She could virtually feel how tightly reined in he was, and Luciana delved into his turbulent stormy eyes because…was that *hurt* in his voice? Surely not. How could *she* possibly hurt this man? No. If anything she'd bruised his male ego. A man who wielded his kind of power likely wasn't accustomed to being deserted.

Though either way, to be fair, she *had* promised him she would stay. Hadn't she?

Yes. She had. They'd become hot and heavy so fast she'd wanted to tell him who she really was. Not to have lies whispering between the damp, tangled sheets. Because in her mind there'd been something so beautiful and pure about what they'd had together the dishonesty had shredded her heart.

She swallowed around the great lump in her throat. It was torture to remember. Utter torture. 'I did promise you—you're right. But that was before I found out who you were.'

With his bent elbow resting on the lip of the window, he curled his index finger over his mouth pensively and stared at her. 'So you didn't know who I was all along?'

Mouth arid, she licked over her lips. 'No, I didn't know who you were. Of course I didn't.'

'Are you telling me the truth? You swear it?'

'Yes.' Did he think she'd duped him? 'I couldn't have set up the way we met even if I tried, Thane. Don't you remem—?'

Slam! She locked the vault shut before all the memories it had taken her so long to ensnare were unleashed. Escaping to create havoc in her soul. Best to forget. For all their sakes.

'Let's just call it an ironic twist of fate,' she said, hearing the melancholy in her voice. 'We were young. Stupid. Reckless. I didn't know you at all. I'd fallen into bed with a stranger…' *And I awoke to a nightmare.* 'I found your papers, Thane.'

She'd never forget that moment as long as she lived. Standing in the dim light of their bathroom, feeling naked and exposed, his nationality papers for travel that she'd stumbled across quivering in her hand. The realisation she was sleeping with the enemy.

'And after three, almost four weeks,' he said fiercely, 'of our being inseparable, spending every waking and sleeping moment together, your first instinct was to run? With not *one* word? Do you have *any* idea…?'

Veering away from her, he clenched his jaw so tight she heard his molars groan in protest. And she swiftly reassessed the idea that she'd caused him pain by leaving the way she had.

Remorse gathered in the space behind her ribs and trickled down into her stomach to merge with the ever-present pool of guilt that swelled and churned with her secrets every minute of every day. The painful struggle between truth and darkness.

But, looking back, she remembered she'd been consumed with the need to flee.

First had come denial and bewilderment. She'd been unable to match the dark, dangerous, merciless Prince with the somewhat shy—at least around women—rock music lover who'd held her cherishingly tight through endless nights of bliss. Then terror had set in, leaving her panic-stricken, contemplating how he'd react when he discovered who she was. And heartache, knowing she had to leave before he found out. Knowing that while she toyed with the temptation of staying in touch, meeting up again, suddenly another hour was too much of a hazard, a risk, never mind some far-off midnight tryst.

So she'd run. Taken the good memories instead of tainting them with bitterness and regret. Run as fast as she could with her heart tearing apart.

Glancing out at the snow-capped peaks of the Tarentaise Valley, she took a deep breath and then exhaled, her warm breath painting a misty cloud upon the window. If he needed closure in order to forget and let her go, then so be it.

'I'm sorry I didn't let you know I was leaving. Write you a note or something. I didn't mean to hurt you that way. But it was over. We had an affair—that's all. There could never have been a future for us.'

Chills skittered over her skin and she crossed her arms over her chest, rubbing the gooseflesh from her shoulders. She was so lost in thought she didn't notice his hand reaching across the back of the bench seat until it was in her periphery and she flinched. Hard. Unsure what to expect from him.

'Are you afraid of me now?' he asked, his voice gruff as if she'd sanded the edge off his volatility.

Was she afraid of him? Genuinely?

No. Though she couldn't really understand why.

Because deep down you know he won't hurt you. Deep down you know the man who took your innocence with such gentle passionate persuasion would never physically hurt you in a million years.

But that didn't mean he couldn't emotionally destroy her. And Nate. *That* he was capable of.

So maybe she *did* fear him. Just not in the way he meant.

Luciana gave her head a little shake and he picked up a lock of her hair and rubbed the strands between his fingertips. 'I wouldn't have recognised you. How different you look this way.'

She had the ludicrous desire to ask him if he liked the way she looked. The real her. Or if he'd fallen for a black-haired hippy who didn't exist. But the reality was it was best she didn't know.

'It was a lifetime ago,' she said, immensely proud of her strong voice when she felt so weak when he was close. 'Forget the person I pretended to be in Zurich. I was just...' She had to swallow hard to push the words out. 'Acting out. Letting loose. Having a bit of fun.'

Such a lie. But maybe if he thought their wild, hedonistic fling meant nothing to her he'd hate her. Let her go...

Et voilà.

Easing back, he created a distance that felt as deep and wide as the Arunthian falls.

'Fun,' he repeated tonelessly. 'Well, that makes both of us.'

Her stomach plunged to the leather seat with a disheartened thump. Because it was just as she'd always suspected.

Stiffening her spine, she brushed her hair back from her face. 'There you go, then. There really is no point in dragging this out.'

He said nothing. Simply leaned back and glared at her with such intensity she felt transparent.

Jittery, she shifted in her seat and rammed her point home.

'Thane, you have to let me go back to Arunthia. To my family. They need me. I've got to get married soon. I—'

'No.'

'*No*? But haven't I given you an explanation? What more could you possibly want from me?'

'That is a very good question, *princesa*.'

And Luciana had the feeling she wasn't going to like the answer. Not one bit.

CHAPTER THREE

THANE IGNORED THE eyes that were boring into his skull and riffled through the mini-bar of the limousine for some hard liquor. She was turning him to drink already—he was insane even to contemplate what enticed his mind.

Snatching a miniature of bourbon, he unscrewed the lid, then tipped the contents onto his tongue and let the fiery liquid trickle down his throat in a heavenly slow burn.

From the corner of his eye he saw Luciana pick up a bottle of sparkling water and commanded himself not to look, to watch. To devour all that beautiful, riveting bone structure—her nose a delicate slope of pure femininity, pronounced razor-sharp cheekbones a supermodel would kill for—those intoxicating brandy-gold eyes and that glossy, over-full wanton mouth as she drank.

Dios, she made his flesh and blood blaze. And it had been so long since he'd felt anything that he was consumed. By want. By hate. It was a terrifically violent and lethal combination that was taking all of his will power to control.

While she speared darts of ire or disbelief in his direction, poised and elegant in her glamorous couture black and white ensemble, all *he* could think of was her pupils dilated, her hair tossed over his pillow in gloriously messy abandon, and raw, primal sheet-clawing passion.

But it was more than that, wasn't it? He'd thought his memories were long dead, murdered by the passage of time and the strife in Galancia, but since he'd touched her he'd started to remember.

Remember being held close against her bare skin, feeling truly wanted—a real man made from flesh and hot blood, willing to pay whatever price it took to sustain that feeling a while longer. And, while he wanted that back, he knew it was lost to him.

'Having a bit of fun. Letting loose.'

Any molecule of hope he'd harboured that she'd felt something for him disintegrated, and inside his chest that lump of stone where his heart should be cracked down the centre and crumbled to dust.

Good. He didn't want the weak and tender emotions involved in this. Never had to begin with. But the beguiling creature had lured him in. Lesson learned.

'Are you going to tell me what's going on in that head of yours?' she asked, before gnawing on her crimson bruised bottom lip.

'As soon as I figure it out, yes.' Because despite his misgivings, despite what she'd said, something…*something* told him she held the key to his fate. He couldn't explain it if he tried—just as he'd never been able to explain how he'd known she was in grave danger the day they'd met. How when their eyes had locked he'd known she belonged to him.

Ignorant of his internal debate, she heaved a great sigh at his cool reply. But it had taken him less than ten seconds to figure out the best way to play this game: total emotional lockdown. Which was no inconsiderable feat when that aloof haughtiness kept invading her body like some freakish poltergeist and he was overcome with the violent need to grab her and shake it loose. Then there was the way her mind clearly often wandered down a path that he suspected was paved with turmoil, because guilt would walk all over her face. It made him want to climb into her brain and seduce her secrets.

The bright lights of the Altiport runway came into view,

as did his sleek black private jet embellished with the Guerrero family crest—a large snake curling around the blade of a sword—and she clutched her bag to her chest as if it held the crown jewels. Which, he conceded, might be true. His knowledge of women's paraphernalia was zilch.

'Thane, look. Be reasonable about this. I'm your enemy—there isn't anything I could give you but trouble. For starters, the bellboy saw me drive away in your car. Does he know who you are?'

He shrugged his wide shoulders. 'I imagine so. I believe I am very difficult to miss.'

She rolled her eyes. 'Arrogance really should be your middle name. My point is: come morning, Augustus will know I'm with you. Then he'll call my father—because, let me tell you, they are as thick as thieves. Soon after my father will be on the warpath. So you *have* to let me go home. My family will worry if I just vanish into thin air.'

'Let them suffer,' he said. Just as *he'd* done. Trying to fill the empty, aching void of losing her. Had she cared for him? Obviously not.

She huffed in disgust. 'Well, how gallant of you. How would *you* feel if someone you loved disappeared off the face of the earth?'

His mouth shaped to tell her he knew exactly how it felt, but first his pride stopped him, and then her words. *Love?* This had nothing to do with love. He was a protective man by nature, and naturally that extended to her. She'd been his. Correction: she *was* his. Regardless of her true identity. Moreover, he would kiss Arunthian soil before he admitted any hint of vulnerability to *her*. To anyone. He'd been nine years old when he'd last made that mistake—telling his father that enclosed spaces made him violently sick. Twenty-four hours down an abandoned well had taught him much.

'Honestly, could you be a more heartless brute?'

It didn't escape him that he'd been called worse things in

his time—a murderer, a mercenary, a traitor—so why the devil it stung coming from her was a mystery.

'I'm sure I could if I put my mind to it,' he drawled darkly.

'But you're going to be a wanted man. Do you want to spend the rest of your days in a jail cell?'

Thane turned to face her and raised one mocking eyebrow. 'Your father would have to catch me first *princesa*—and, believe me, *that* is impossible.'

'It's not about catching *you*,' she said, pointing at his shirt before turning the same finger back on herself. 'He'll come for *me*. Do you want an Arunthian army on your doorstep?'

As if.

'They would never get through Galancian airspace. Do you forget who I am? Your security and your army are no match for mine.'

'You're probably right. But that's because we are peacekeepers. Not fighters. Our people don't live in fear of an iron-fisted rule. We are rich in life and happiness and that is more important to us.'

Thane scoffed. Did she think he didn't want those things for his own people? What did she think he fought for? The good of his health? But the topic did bring him full circle to his hellishly risky concept. She could, in effect, help him gain a better life for them. Relax that iron-fisted rule she'd just accused him of by placing his crown in his hands.

Dios, it was mad even to think any union could possibly work, but the notion spun his brain into a frenzied furore. Snagging on one name: Augustus.

He was the biggest unknown in all of this. What the hell was a woman like Luciana doing with a scumbag like him? He was missing something vital here, and he did not appreciate having only half the intel on a situation.

During the twenty minutes he'd waited for her to emerge from the lodge he'd accessed every file he could uncover.

Princess Luciana Valentia Thyssen Verbault. Born and raised in Arunthia. Schooled at Eton and Cambridge, England. No record of her time in Zurich. No surprise there, since she'd been a carousing black-haired gypsy. Five years in China. Low-key. There was only the odd photograph during that time, either with a dark-haired friend and two small boys, or back home at a royal function—as if she'd returned to Arunthia for that purpose entirely, only to travel straight back to China. So what had been there to lure her back again and again? A job? Maybe. But why did his instincts tell him it was a man?

One thing was clear: unless he got a better picture of her life his plans would be dead in the water before he'd even launched them off the jetty.

While all this circled around in his head like manic vultures, Luciana launched into another talkfest about Arunthia: how content the people were, how he could learn a thing or two. The bare-faced cheek of it! Her arms wafted in the air as she warmed to her subject. And, *Dios*, no matter what crap came out of her mouth, she was the picture of enthralling passionate beauty.

He'd adored that about her. How she could talk for hours. About nothing in particular. Silly, mundane things—music, movies and architecture. He'd revelled in that freedom from his responsibilities, the chance to forget the trouble at home for a while. Ironic that he'd chosen a Zurich festival, having been once before in his uni days, to get away from it all and met a woman from his own sphere who'd been doing exactly the same thing.

An odd memory hit and a smile curved his lips. One she caught.

'What?'

'I was just thinking of the time we went to the cinema and were thrown out because you wouldn't stop talking.'

A lie.

'Talking? We didn't get thrown out because we were *talking*. We got evicted because we were…' Heat plumed in the rapidly shrinking confines of the car, driving a flush high across her cheekbones. 'Never mind.'

He felt so smug he could hear his own grin. 'Shall I finish that for you?'

'No, thank you. It's best if we don't go there, okay?'

She was right. He should be getting a handle on her relationship with the Viscount, not testing her memory. Not watching that beautiful blush frisk down her neck and caress her collarbone. Not inhaling her subtle vanilla and jasmine scent until his body prickled with heat and unleashed a firestorm of memories that turned him hard as steel.

Like the sensation of those plump lips softening beneath his as she'd surrendered to him. The way she'd felt when he'd thrust inside her virginal tight body. The way her legs had curled around his waist as he took her over and over. Lithe, svelte legs…glossed with skin that had felt like finely powdered icing sugar beneath his palms and tasted just as sweet. The softest, most exquisite texture he'd ever touched. Legs that were taunting him now because they were fuller. Lusher. Just like her breasts…

Thane shifted in his seat, the creak of leather sharpening his arousal as his body roared to life. Feral lust pushed incessantly against his zipper. Worse still, she exacerbated his darkly erotic state by squirming and lifting her hair from her nape as if she were over-hot. Well, that made two of them.

Depressing the window button, he let the cool air slither through the gap in a wispy sheet of fog and relished the odd snowflake that settled on the back of his hand.

Luciana's answer was to snatch a bar of chocolate from the mini-bar and have ravenous sex with every bite. He could virtually hear her silent moans.

'Hungry?' he asked, his voice as thick as his throat.

She licked the sweet treat from her lips with a sensual flick of her tongue. 'Erm…yes. Dinner was awful.'

He took the opening for what it was. Perfect for getting him back on track. 'The food or the company?'

Her gaze drifted to stare unseeingly out of the tinted window. The runway floodlights flickered over her at intervals, highlighting the honeycomb strands in her lavish hair and lending her skin an incandescent glow.

Ethereal was surely the only word to describe her in that moment. Seraphic. And his ardour dulled as he was struck with the feeling that he was too dark to touch her. That he would taint her somehow.

Right at this moment she was crushed up against the door, as far away from him as she could get, and Thane hardened his body, trying to expunge the terrible self-awareness, the stomach ache that whispered of rejection. Not once had she rebuffed their volatile passion. Not once. The reason for which he wanted to know. *Now.*

'You never answered my question,' he said, his tone darkly savage. 'Was it the food or the company that was so bad you could not eat?'

Her absurdly long, decadent eyelashes were downswept. 'Does it matter?' she asked softly.

Patience dwindling, he went in for the kill. Even though he was unsure if he could go through with this if she said yes.

Astounding and unthinkable as it was, if she did he'd rather put her on an Arunthian plane without another word. The 'why' of it wouldn't be difficult to find if he cared to revisit his boyhood, watch misery trickle down his mother's face as she pined for another. But delve into the past he would not. That long-ago place was a dark punishment he would never descend to again.

'Are you in love with Augustus, Luciana?'

She massaged her temple as if he were a headache she wished to rub away.

'I wasn't born to marry for love, Thane. I have no choice over the direction my life takes.' Her voice was tinged with bitterness and he felt a flicker of suspicion spark in his gut.

Frowning, he narrowed his eyes on her face, his guts twisting into a noxious tangle. 'Have you been in his bed?'

If he'd blinked he would have missed it. Her wince of distaste.

'That is none of your business.'

'Have you been in his bed, Luciana?' he asked again—harder, darker. Almost cutthroat.

'What difference does it make?'

'For hell's sake, just answer the question!'

Up came her arms with an exasperated toss. '*No!* Okay? I haven't been anywhere near his rotten bed. Would *you* want to?' She groaned aloud as if she wished the words back, and shoved another chunk of chocolate between her pink lips.

Thane felt a smile kick the corner of his mouth as relief doused over him like a warm shower of summer rain. That temper of hers still gave her a candid, somewhat strident bent.

'And you still intend to *marry* this man?' Even though the idea appalled her?

'Yes.'

He would have to be six feet under first.

Clearly Henri was pushing her into it. *That bastard.* He should have killed the man years ago, when he'd had the chance. Fury pummelled at him to think she was being forced to the altar as his mother had been. And Thane's every protective instinct kicked in—he wanted her kept far away from Henri and Augustus. Where neither of them could reach her.

'You will not touch him, *comprende*? Nor will you allow him to touch you.'

Not that he was giving her the chance to do either.

Huffing a little, she arched one fair brow. 'That's going to prove a bit difficult when we are married, Thane.'

'Which is precisely the reason you are not marrying him.'

His mind was set. Firstly, she had the rarity of blue blood, and a union with her would give him his crown. Four years early. His struggles to build a better life for his people would end. His uncle's dictatorship would cease as Thane took total control of the throne. Finally he could make amends.

And secondly—he easily silenced the impish taunt of his earlier words—there would be no riding bareback into hell as he aligned with the enemy. Because while she might be a Verbault at this moment, Thane would soon make her a Guerrero. Tomorrow seemed as good a day as any. Saving her from a fate worse than death—namely the vapid Viscount and her father's political clutches.

Win-win. Let it not be said that he wasn't knight in shining armour material.

A faint crease lined her forehead as she fingered back the curtain of her hair to glance at him warily. 'I…I'm not?'

This could go two ways, he decided. Either he'd be flooded with a profusion of gratitude or she'd fight him under the influence of some misplaced loyalty to her father. So it was a good job there wasn't a battle he couldn't win.

'No. Instead you are marrying me.'

CHAPTER FOUR

In the distance Luciana heard the driver's door open, then close with a deft clunk. Then came a cacophony of voices that fluttered around the car—the cadence low, masculine. And all the while she stared at Thane, who wore a mask of impermeable steel. Her mouth was working but no sound was emerging as she swung like a pendulum, lurching from fighting tears of frustration to biting back a laugh that was sure to lean over to the hysterical side—because the proposal she'd expected had finally come to pass. From the wrong man entirely.

Are you sure about that, Luce?

Yes, she was sure—of course she was sure.

And the worst thing about all of this...? For a split second all she'd seen was Thane and all she'd heard was 'marry' and 'me', and the little girl inside her who'd gorged on fairytales and dreams of love—the one who *hadn't* seen the darker side of marriage and was blissfully unaware of her duties—had felt her heart leap to her throat in utter joy.

Foolish little girl. Foolish heart.

Blame it on temple-pounding awkwardness, but the silence finally pressed a sound from her throat.

'Thane? Are you crazy?'

Crazy? He was insane. Mad as a hatter. Nutty as a goddamn fruitcake.

'Quite probably.'

There, you see—he's even admitted it.

'We're enemies, or have you conveniently forgotten that?'

Oh, she could just imagine Thane having a chinwag with her father. *Hey, do you remember me? The one who tried to assassinate you? Well, I want to marry your daughter.* Yeah, that would go down well. *Not.*

If he *had* attempted the assassination. But why would her father spout such a heinous lie? Truth was, she was drowning in reasons why she couldn't marry him. And that was without broaching the topic of Natanael.

'You and I are not enemies, Luciana.'

His eyes took on the lustrous glitter of the black sapphires they reminded her of and she shivered in response.

'Any chance of that ended when I took your innocence five years ago and made you mine. If your father and my uncle wish to prolong the feud that's up to them, but it has no bearing on our future.'

She shook her head in disbelief. Bad idea. Dizziness took the car, and her, for a little spin. 'How can you say that?'

'Easily. I am my own man, and I will not be dictated to by anyone or anything.'

A scoff burst past her lips. 'Bully for you. I, however, don't have a choice.'

'Which is precisely why I am giving you an alternative.'

So it would seem. The question was: why? He wanted her away from Augustus—that much was evident. Every time the other man's name was brought up he visibly fumed, until she half expected him to snort fire like some great mystical dragon. As if the thought of the other man touching her was abhorrent to him. But not because he loved her. No, no. His biting words from earlier were enough of a clue... *'We take what is rightfully ours. I made you mine...'*

So in effect she could be a Picasso he'd spotted at Christie's and fancied would look wonderful mounted above his machete rack. A beautiful possession.

Fire-tipped arrows pierced her chest and flamed up her throat.

'Well, thank you for the offer,' she said satirically. 'But I'm not keen on your alternative, Thane. For starters, it's simply another demand. And, let me tell you, they are certainly racking up this month.' Her insides were shaking so hard it made her voice quiver. 'And another thing: unfortunately for you, as far as courting rituals and practices go, abduction does *not* score points.'

He frowned deeply and looked at the magazine pouch. As if he was spectacularly disorientated and the answer to her meltdown lay between the covers of the latest gossip rag.

Idly scratching his sexy, stubbled jaw, he glanced back up. 'Courting?'

Luciana blinked. Out of that entire speech, 'courting' was what he'd picked up on? 'Yes, Thane. Dating, courting.'

Surely he couldn't still be as mystified about women as he'd been five years ago? He must have had a truckload since then; he was sex incarnate. Not that she cared what he did. Absolutely not.

'You would prefer this?' he asked, stunned but apparently game.

Luciana squeezed her eyes shut. Lord, this was utterly surreal.

'My father would never give his blessing in a billion years.' Hypothetically speaking, of course. Frankly, she had no idea why she was engaging in this conversation. It was all impossible.

'I care not,' he drawled, his arrogance and power so potent she could taste it. 'If the man wants a fight on his hands for you he can have it. Gladly. He obviously cares little for you to subject you to such a marriage.'

Luciana eased back, pulling her spine upright. She rewound that little speech of his and replayed it in her head. Then felt butterflies take flight in her chest—winged creatures flapping furiously against her ribcage. Had he just said he would fight for her? She was pretty sure he had. As well as intimating that he cared for her happiness. Sort of.

Her thumb found its way to her mouth and she nibbled on the soft pad.

This was the behaviour of a callous mercenary? *Really?* No, of course it wasn't—she must be missing something. He had to have an agenda. Other than his ridiculous chest-thumping caveman routine, that was.

Problem was, when he fixated on the way she sucked her thumb, with wicked heat smouldering in his dark eyes, she couldn't think what day it was—never mind decipher his ulterior motives.

Maybe he wants you for you. Maybe your father was wrong about him. Maybe his reputation isn't as bad as it seems.

Luciana shook her head vehemently. No. That would mean she'd run when she shouldn't have. Made a mistake. And she refused to believe that. After all, proof of his pitiless, ruthless nature wasn't hard to descry, was it? Look where she was, for heaven's sake—atop the highest asphalted runway in Europe, about to be manhandled onto a plane!

On the verge of a panic attack, or at the very least an undignified fainting spell, she yanked at the door handle and—*yes*!—it gave way under the pressure of her grip and she flung it wide.

A second later she launched herself from the car, almost breaking her neck as her heels hit a dusty sheet of new-fallen snow and she slipped…swayed…then skidded to a stop.

Adrenaline spiked her pulse and she glanced left and right, back and forth, wildly searching for a way out. Even as her legs turned to lead at the very thought.

Stupid legs. Stupid heart.

Inhaling swift and deep, she slowly refocused her vision on the mountainous white peaks looming from all angles. Dangerous. Breathtaking. Much like the man who now strode around the back of the limousine, moving towards her with a warrior's effortless grace. And yet she felt every step like a seismic rumble.

Instinctively she staggered backwards and pushed out her hand in a stop sign. 'Don't come any closer!'

Snow drizzled from the sky in fat, puffy white flakes and swirled around his tall, commanding body in eddies and whirls as if drawn to his magnetism. The braver ones dared to touch, settle on his ebony hair, kiss his broad shoulders, tease the lapels of his jacket—only to be annihilated in an instant by his unfathomable heat.

Stupid snowflakes.

'Luciana. Don't fight me,' he cajoled, in that sinful voice that made her shudder.

Translation—*Roll over and take it. Be a good girl and do as you're told.*

Yeah, right.

His hands fisted before he stretched the kinks from his fingers and lifted them to spear into his hair; brushing the damp glossy strands back from his forehead, bringing his face into sharp relief.

Oh, Lord.

Her insides panged on a swift stab of anguish. Natanael… The resemblance was spooky. Surreal. Bittersweet and oddly wonderful at the same time.

Arms plunging to his sides, he tipped his head and gave her a crooked smile. 'We need to leave. Come with me.'

Fighting the sting at the back of her eyes, she wrapped her arms around herself, hugging her body. 'No. I can't go with you, Thane. I'm sorry. And I can't marry you. I have to take my throne in two months. I have responsibilities of my own.'

But more than that—much more—I have a son at home: one you can never find, because I'm frightened of what will become of him. I have to protect him. You keep confusing me and I can't trust my instincts with you.

Fact was, she had no idea who this man truly was.

So find out, Luce. Go with him. Find out.

It was a risk she couldn't possibly take. Something told her that if she left with him she'd never return home. Thane would never let her go. His formidable dominance would wrap her up tighter than any other person ever could. Including her father. Loath as she was to admit it, at least if she married Augustus Nate would be safe—and so would she. Her emotions would never engage with *him*.

All that swarthy, sexy maleness took on a blistering intensity as Thane dipped his chin and locked his fierce gaze on her.

'That throne will not be yours if you marry that man, Luciana. You know it. And maybe your responsibilities now lie with me.'

Temper igniting inside her, she balled her fists. 'No, they *really* don't.'

He hitched one shoulder, as if to say he wasn't going to argue about it, that she should just take his word and accept it. Talk about *déjà vu*. It was like standing in front of her father's desk, listening to the latest of his twenty commandments.

And that was it. It dawned on her that there was just no point in arguing. None.

From the corner of her eye she noticed a workman bundled in ski gear as he fought the elements, dragging safety cones across the asphalt, and knew exactly what she had to do.

Luciana took one last look at Thane's dark beauty and memorised every wicked, gorgeous inch of him. Then she hiked her chin and declared, 'I am *not* getting on that plane with you. Goodbye, Thane.'

Off she went, veering in the workman's direction, begging her feet not to slip. Cursing herself for not taking three extra minutes back at the lodge to change her clothes.

'Excuse me?' she called out. 'Hello? Helloooo…?'

His head came up, eyes latched onto her and he waved back.

Thank the heavens above.

Keep walking, Luce, just keep walking—

'Oh, no, you don't.'

An ironclad hand curled around her upper arm and next thing she knew she'd collided with Thane's hot, hard, magnificent body.

Fear and excitement shot through her in equal measure. Yet her protest went the way of her sanity when he pulled her impossibly closer, snaring her waist with one strong arm and stroking up her neck with his free hand, his fingers curling around her nape to cradle her head.

She'd have to be dead not to feel the unabashed sexual charge that sparked in the air. And, like a stick of dynamite, her insides detonated in an explosion of desire, sending an avalanche of wet heat thundering through her.

Quaking, she had to bite down hard on her lip to stifle a whimper. It didn't quite work. She let slip a hum-like cry.

Those dark, fathomless eyes locked onto her, pupils flaring as she swept her tongue across her bottom lip, and from nowhere a memory cracked through the brume of her mind…

Luciana was perched on a brick wall, waiting for him to lift her down, waiting for him to make his first move. Just…*waiting* for him. As if that was all she'd done all her life. 'Aren't you going to kiss me?' she'd asked, yearning for him to do just that.

When his expression had morphed into a giddy blend of enthusiasm and alarm she'd been flummoxed.

'Haven't you ever kissed a woman before?'

A blush so faint she'd nearly missed it had crept over the carved slash of his cheeks. A little embarrassed. A whole lot nervous.

She'd slid down the wall to puddle at his feet. 'Can I kiss you, then?' she'd asked, smoothing his frown away with her fingertips, tucking his hair behind his ears. 'Would that be okay?'

Ignoring the rhythmic tic in his jaw, she'd pushed up on her toes and pressed her lips to his. Warm. Soft. And as sensual and commanding as the man himself. Because as soon as she'd coaxed his mouth open with a flick of her tongue he'd taken over with an instinct as old as time and claimed her in a sweet, devouring…

Luciana blinked back to the here and now—to the snow whirling around them on the chorus of the breeze, the frozen wet droplets peppering her face. To Thane's dark eyes, deep and hungry and shot with shards of amber, the power of their sexual pull crippling in its intensity.

'My jet is the other way, angel,' he drawled, as if her defiance had not only been expected but he found her as cute as a button because of it.

The urge to kick him made her rapidly freezing feet twitch.

Angel… He'd never called her that before. He must have sharpened his sinful seduction skills over the past few years. It was crazy for her to wish he'd only ever been hers. Just as she'd only ever been his. Crazy. Men needed sex every day, didn't they? This man certainly had. Up close to him like this, it was easy to remember the long, sultry days and hot nights. Twisted sheets damp with sweat. Sticky skin and the musky scent of their passion lingering in the air as he was controlled by a dark atavistic need to mark her again and again. The slight soreness that only made them desperate for more. Insatiable. Never getting enough.

The base of her abdomen clenched; her core twisted with want.

Oh, this was bad. Really, *really* bad.

'Thane, let me go,' she demanded, cursing inwardly at the feathery panting that accompanied her words. 'I'm not joking. This is not funny. I'm not coming with you and you can't make me.'

His dark eyes glittered with challenge and her blood thrummed through her veins. She was scandalous—that was what she was.

'You and I both know I can and I will. So, are you going

to walk or will I have to carry you over my shoulder?' he asked, his rich velvet voice doing nothing to hide the steely threat of his words.

Problem was, her heavy breasts chose that exact moment to glory in being crushed against him, and when a fleck of snow landed on his nose she had the strangest impulse to lick it off.

'Thane…' Lord, was *that* her voice? That breathless, wanton plea?

'Luciana…' he drawled, in a tone that said *Please be reasonable about this*.

It inched her temper into the red zone.

'Don't fight this. Don't fight *me*. You don't want to go back there.'

'But I *do* want to go back, Thane.'

'No, angel. You don't.'

Argh!

'I'll scream and that man over there will come running. I guarantee it.'

His mouth tipped at the corner in a devilish smirk. 'Go ahead and I will smother that gorgeous mouth of yours.'

A gasp hit the back of her throat. 'You wouldn't dare.'

'Want to find out?' he growled.

Shameful excitement made her heart thump frenetically. 'No, I don't,' she said, though her voice sounded like a flagrant whimper to her. So she strove for forceful. 'Definitely not. Now, let go of me.'

He tutted and shook his head. 'Try again, Luciana. And if you say it like you mean it, I just might.'

Ooh, he'd asked for this.

Writhing in his hold, she pushed and shoved at his chest, drew in a lungful of air for the scream building in her throat…

And his mouth crashed over hers, taking his words from threat to carnal promise.

Oh, hell. Don't kiss him back. Don't you dare.

Within seconds he'd captured her in his invisible force field, energy swirling, flowing around them like a mini-cyclone, and her breath unwound on a blissful sigh.

He cradled her to him with one hand cupping her nape and the other splayed at the small of her back, hauling her up against his hard groin as he tilted his head and ravished her mouth as if he owned her body and soul.

Wicked was the flavour that flooded her mouth. So sinful and debauched he was. Bad to the bone. And when he stroked past her lips with a teasing flick and then a languorous lick of his tongue, that was it. She melted against him—all molten lava. Followed the sculpted line of his shoulders with her greedy hands up the column of his neck and slipped them beneath his ears, into his hair. Hair she fisted, making him growl long and low, the sound vibrating through her on a violent tremor.

The earth was moving, she was sure. Then she figured out why when he lifted her high and coaxed her legs around his waist. Luciana wrapped herself around him and hooked her ankles at the small of his back until there wasn't a sliver of air between them. He palmed the rounded swells of her bottom, squeezing her to him, and the erotic sensation of his thick hard erection nudging her lace panties made her sex throb and weep. He felt *shockingly* good and she whimpered, shivered.

Though that might also have been because she was wet, soaked to her skin. But he seemed to know what she needed, and when warmth suffused her and he sat down…*somewhere*…she straddled his muscular legs, cuddling closer to burrow into his heat.

Never leaving her mouth, he tore at her sodden coat, yanking it down her arms, and then his hot hands were back, sliding up her cool bare legs, pushing her dress up to ruck it around her thighs. And when those depraved fingers dug into the flesh of her bottom, pulling her panties indecently tight, the tug and rub of lace against her swollen folds made her cry out.

Survival instincts kicking in, she tore her lips free and dragged air into her lungs. Took a mind-numbing rush of his potent scent too. And that made her woozy. Impelled her to arch her back in a promiscuous plea for him to nuzzle her throat.

'Luciana…'

His lush, moist kisses fell on her skin like rain on drought-stricken ground and she soaked up every caress, thirsting for more. It had been so long since she'd been touched, since this man had touched her. So wonderful. Such naughty, amoral bliss.

'Thane…'

Dipping her head, she searched for his mouth and he dusted his lips over hers, teasing her cruelly. He tasted of pure virile masculinity, undiluted power. Passion and heat and lust and *Thane.*

Needing to touch, she ripped at the top buttons of his shirt, relishing his raspy curse and the sound of fabric tearing, and dived into the space she'd made, smoothing over his collarbone. Felt his heart beat a rapid staccato against her palm.

'Hot,' she whispered past his lips. 'So hot.'

His chest rumbled with a reply and yet she didn't hear a word, because a weird whooshing noise was blowing through her brain. Before she could grasp the why and the how, he scraped his stubble up the curve of her jaw in a sensual graze, making her tremble and rock her achingly heavy pelvis against him. Wanting his hardness inside her so, *so* badly.

When he let loose a feral moan from deep in his throat she did it again. And again. Her frenzied elation ratcheted up when his thumb slipped around her hip to find her sweet spot unerringly and apply just the right amount of pressure to take her to the edge of an almighty orgasm and hold her there.

'Thane, *please*.'

'*Dios*, Luciana… No bed in here, angel. But I want you to come for me. Hard. I want to hear you cry out my name like you used to.'

'Yes. *Yes…*'

Hold on.

Here? No bed *in here*?

He circled that tight knot of needy nerves and it took everything she had not to tumble into the abyss.

Her lashes were fluttering and her surroundings came to her in flashes. Cream leather seats. Small windows. Like a… like a private jet. And…were they moving?

Moving?

Luciana jerked backwards, dislodging his hand, blinking frantically, prising her eyes wide, her gaze darting here there and everywhere.

'What…? Where…? How…?'

She was the only one who was confused and disorientated, she noticed. Because the man whose lap she straddled simply sat there, his chest heaving from their passionate antics, cheeks streaked with colour, watching her with an insufferable blend of satisfaction and wariness.

Down she came, back to earth with shattering intensity. And how she didn't raise her hand and slap his face she'd never know.

'You…you *bastard*.'

Wrenching free, she tumbled backwards off his knee and landed in a messy, graceless heap. Still trembling from the erotic turbulence.

Thane lurched forward in a move to help.

'Don't you *dare* touch me.' Tears of frustration and anger pooled in her eyes.

Cautiously, he eased back into his chair, a deep V slashing the space between his brows. The look on her face must have said it all, she realised, since this was the first time he'd backed off at her word.

Somehow she clambered to her feet and stood tall before him, sweeping her palms down her black sheath, trying to cover as much of herself as she could before that horrid, vulnerable feeling of being exposed and raw threatened to strip her flesh from her bones.

Fury and self-disgust roiled inside her. Didn't diminish even when she saw a flicker of doubt and unease pass over his face. Though he soon banked it. It didn't matter. She would make him rue this day if it was the last thing she did.

'Luciana—'

'No. *Don't* speak to me.'

Spine pin-straight, she walked towards the other large leather recliner, trying to wrap her mind around her new predicament. What on earth was she going to do now? She—

A thought slammed into her, and she whirled back on a swirling spin of dizzying dread. 'My bag,' she said, unable to hide the panic in her voice. 'Where's my handbag?'

He was staring out of the small window, rubbing his mouth with the inside of his finger. 'Sit down, Luciana, we are about to take off.'

'No, dammit, I *won't*!'

Shucking off his wet jacket, he kept his eyes averted. 'Did you leave it in the car?'

Oh, God.

Her stomach pitched as the jet lifted off the runway, and she grabbed the back of the chair to keep from crumpling to the carpet.

'Go back down. Land this plane. Right now, Thane. I need my bag. My phone. I *need* my phone.'

How was she going to call Natanael? Keep in touch with home? Text Nate as she did every morning, noon and night?

Desperation made her beg the man she loathed with every ounce of her being. 'Thane, *please*, I need my phone.'

He didn't turn, still wouldn't look at her. Just inhaled deeply and closed his eyes for a beat. 'Where we are going no phone of yours will even work, Luciana. Sit down and leave it.'

She gritted her teeth, mightily glad for the return of that cool, dominant inflection because it evaporated the acidic splash behind her eyes. She would not break. Not in front of this man. Nor any other.

'I hate you right now,' she whispered vehemently. Though she suspected she hated herself even more.

One kiss. That was all it had taken to vanquish every thought from her mind.

Self-loathing slithered through her stomach to writhe like a nest of vipers and she curled into the deep bucket seat to ease the ache.

No phone. No way to call Nate. No chance of escape. And she was flying straight into enemy territory.

If she got through this in one piece and found her way home it would be a miracle.

CHAPTER FIVE

HE FELT LIKE the big bad wolf. In more ways than one. Furious self-censure and unparalleled carnal hunger took equal pleasure in tearing at his insides with razor-sharp claws until he wanted to growl.

The lust made his body thrum with pent-up energy, yet all he wanted to do was storm over there, pick her up and put her right back on his knee. Eradicate the pain in her eyes by wrapping her up in his arms and holding her tightly to him.

Dios, when tears had glistened in those big, beautiful eyes he'd felt as if a bullet had ripped clean through his chest. He'd been a little boy again, looking up at his mother, unsure what to do, how to take her heartache away. A heartache that once again he didn't truly understand. And that had made him feel lost. Racking his brains to think of some way to stem her misery. Because somehow his mother had always managed to quell his, take his pain away—back when his flesh could feel such a sensation, that was.

Rubbing over his jaw, he recalled how touching her had often worked—holding her cold, trembling hand or trying to wrap his small, thin arms around her shoulders to hug her, wishing he was bigger, stronger. Instinctively he'd reached for Luciana, but she didn't want his touch. While he'd always treasured hers. Touch was precious to him, he realised. Infinitely rare and beyond price, it was something he hadn't experienced or allowed himself to feel since he'd been seven years old. Until Luciana.

'I hate you...'

How her words tormented him. How her tears made him feel barbaric. As brutal as his father.

While he still owned what he'd had to do, he conceded his tactics might not have been the most honourable. Had he been wrong to take his chance? Hell, no. Not when the alternative was her marrying another man. A man she didn't even wish to marry! Still, luring her onto a flight using their chemistry, when she'd exploded like some hot, sensual, sultry bomb in his hands, and then almost initiating them into the ranks of the mile-high club wasn't exactly coaxing her towards a priest with a gentle hand, was it?

The memory of her furiously wild, uninhibited passion made him shift in his seat with restless virile power—as if his body had lain dormant for an age of cold bleak winters and she'd awoken the deep-seated animalistic lust inside him.

And right then the truth crashed down around him.

For the first time in years he was feeling, and he was chasing it with the urgency and fervour of a madman. He felt hungry, starved of affection, and suddenly he despised it. Didn't want her to have that kind of terrific power over him. He'd had more control when he'd been handed his first gun at twelve.

Lurching from his seat, he went to stalk to his office, where he could think straight, past the chair where she sat curled up, knees bent, hugging them to her chest, in a pose that struck him as a defensive ball—and he slammed to a stop.

Thumb-print-shaped blotches reddened her silky soft thighs, courtesy of his rough ardour, and her neck was scored pink from where he'd kissed her, dragged his unshaven jaw up her delicate throat. Ravaged. She looked ravaged.

Dios, had he hurt her?

He closed his eyes, his conscience riven by self-contempt. Maybe he didn't deserve to have her in his life again.

He could never be good inside, where it mattered. That had been twisted out of him as a boy. He was darkness and she was all golden light.

Good versus evil. Beautiful versus beastly. Flawless versus scarred.

Fatigue lent a beautiful fragility to her face. And when a shiver rustled over her honey-gold skin his guts twisted tight. She looked scared, miserable and *attacked.* So damn vulnerable.

Idiot he was—of course she'd be worried. While they'd spent one month in each other's arms there were years of animosity between their countries.

Opening one of the top cupboards, he pulled down some thick fluffy blankets and lowered into a crouch before her.

Her little bow-shaped mouth was mutinous in her heart shaped face. 'Get away from me, Thane.'

'Luciana,' he said, his voice rich and smooth, 'I am sorry I've upset you this badly.'

'*Upset* me?'

She flared up with spectacular force—his ferocious little lioness. He actually felt himself blanch when he saw her eyes, pools of brandy swimming in betrayal.

'Oh, just go away. I'm not speaking to you.'

'You just did,' he said lazily, trying to lighten the mood, get her to come round to him.

'Only because you're forcing me to. You are such a control freak. Do you get off on being Mr Big and Powerful? Taking away people's choices?'

That wasn't what he'd done. Was it…?

'No, what I was doing was preventing you from making a mistake. Giving you freedom from your father. You owe him nothing, angel. Soon you'll realise I've done you a great favour, and when you thank me I will not be so arrogant as to say *I told you so.*'

Moaning, as if his very existence was painful to her, she

squeezed her eyes shut and banged her head on the headrest. 'You're impossible. You really are.'

Gingerly, he covered her in layers of dove-grey cashmere and tucked the ends underneath her.

'What's this? A peace offering?' she jeered.

'No, a blanket,' he drawled as he slipped off her towering white glossy shoes. Unable to resist that ticklish spot, he ran his thumb over the sexy little nub of her anklebone.

She flinched and tucked her foot under the blanket, rebuffing him.

Thane sighed, stood tall, and shunted a hand through his hair. Back to that place where he was lost. Only knowing in that moment that making her smile at him was more important than anything else. And that thought was not only unnerving but also perilous and highly confusing.

His office silently chanted his name.

'I'll leave you for a while, then,' he said, stepping away.

Naturally that was when she started ranting all over him.

'How do you *do* this to me, Thane? How do you make me want you and hate you at the same time? I have no sense when it comes to you. None!'

One fat tear slipped down her cheek and his cold, stony heart cracked in two.

'Now look at the mess I'm in.'

The desolate anguish in her voice made him remember, and he couldn't just stand there paralysed. He had to do that in his own country, almost every damn day.

Ah, to hell with it.

Swooping in, he scooped her up…

'Hey!'

He turned and plonked them both back down in her seat, holding her close.

'I…I told you not to touch me again,' she choked out, trying to fight him and her tears at the same time. 'Honest to God, do you listen to one single, solitary thing I say?'

Palm to her cheek, he pushed at the side of her face to

nestle her into his neck. 'It may not seem so, but, yes. I just… Let me hold you. Warm you up. Please? Just for a moment. You're shivering.'

He tucked the blanket tightly around her, from her sexy knees to the feminine slope of her nose, until she was swaddled, unable to move an inch.

'There you go. You look like a cute furry Egyptian mummy, but that's better, *si*?'

If looks could kill, he'd be dead.

'It may be better if you remove that damp dress from your skin,' he suggested.

It was shrinking by the second, he was sure. He was also sure he wanted it off her, since he could easily conjure up far more pleasurable ways to make his thoughtless arrogance up to her.

Hiking her chin up over the cashmere, she harrumphed at him. '*As. If.* Now you're trying to get my clothes off? Forget it, Romeo. This Juliet isn't falling for that.'

Thane frowned. 'They were enemies, weren't they?'

'Yeah… Ring any bells? And there was no happy ending for them either. She killed herself, so let that be a lesson to you.'

Spine rigid, he stiffened up…then slammed down the memory before it invaded him and the blackness tainted his soul. No, that would *never* happen with Luciana. She was not his mother. He and Luciana had history. He'd made her happy once and he would again. He was a man now—stronger, more powerful—he would be enough this time. Wouldn't he?

'Thane?' she squeaked. 'Can you let me breathe? You're squashing me, here. Are you trying to suffocate me now? First you abduct me and now you're squeezing me to death. Frankly, I'm not too sure if you even *like* me, so why you'd want to marry me is beyond my comprehension.'

'Ah, sorry, angel.'

He loosened his hold a touch and nuzzled a kiss into her

hair while he could—while she was wrapped up and couldn't protest or reject him.

'Of course I like you,' he said. 'I'll have you know I don't go around kissing just anyone.' Speaking of kissing… 'Did I hurt you earlier? Was I too rough?'

The luxurious spill of her hair tumbled over one shoulder, a shimmering flow of dark bronze that Thane swept back from her face tenderly.

Those absurdly long lashes fluttered, yet she prised her eyes wide, fighting it. Fighting *him*. It just made him want her all the more.

'Yes, you hurt me. Inside you hurt me. And I'll never forgive you for that stunt you just pulled.'

'Admittedly I didn't think it would backfire in such a spectacular fashion,' he drawled, trying his utmost to ease the tension he could feel coiling in her body. Her luscious, curvy weight was glorious, he decided. 'Would you consider that I thought your tongue down my throat meant yes?'

'No, I most certainly would not.'

The haughty lash of her riposte made him retaliate with his equally devilish mouth. 'What about the way you rode my lap?'

Her lips parted on a stunned smack. 'Lord, you really *are* wicked.' Punching at the blanket for some wriggle room, she shoved at his chest. 'Go away. Go and take your guilt elsewhere. I'm not pacifying it for you. You deserve it.'

'Who says I feel guilty?'

He did. Terribly. He might have wanted to lure and beguile her, but upset her this much? No. That was the last thing he'd wanted. It made him wonder if he was missing something vital. Surely being rescued from a repulsive royal marriage was something to celebrate, not to weep over.

'I can see it all over your face. And you *should* feel guilty too. I told you I was not getting on this plane, but did you listen? Of course you didn't. Then I begged you to go back for my bag, my phone…' Sighing heavily, she thumped her head back down on his shoulder. 'I hate you.'

'So you said. But, like *I* said, your cell phone would not have worked in Galancia. At least nowhere near the castle.'

Like Fort Knox with scrambling systems, its obscene opulence was locked up tight.

And right then, for the first time, he thought of his birthright and doubt slithered its sinuous way up his spine. Not only did he loathe the place but also his uncle… He didn't want his uncle anywhere near Luciana. Because as soon as his uncle set eyes on her he'd know Thane planned to overthrow him and doubtless stir up trouble.

To hell with that. He needed Luciana to say *I do* first. And to get her there he needed time. Time only for them. When he wasn't distracted by having to peer over his shoulder.

Glaring up at him with a fierceness that verged on the adorable, she mocked, 'My phone wouldn't work in the castle? Truth or lie?'

A laugh burst past his lips—one he hadn't heard in an age. For a woman who had been in Zurich to let loose and have *fun*, she remembered quite a bit. 'Truth. Swear it. Why do you want your phone so badly?'

She flung her now unencumbered arm out in front of them, exasperated, missing his face by an inch.

'Why do you think? My family will be beside themselves with worry by morning and it's heartless of you not to care.'

He *was* heartless. Completely heartless. Yet every time he thought of that single tear he didn't want to be. Not for her. And that was akin to tying a garrotte around his own neck. By opening up he would give her the power to destroy him again, and he couldn't go through that a second time. It would kill him. No, he had to keep his head straight and focus on his end goal. The crown.

But, unlike him, Luciana had a huge heart, and he didn't want her fretting about her family so he'd have to fix that too. He didn't want her mind on anything else but him.

'Are we talking about the same family who is pushing you into an arranged marriage that you don't want?' he asked.

'First off, what *you* have offered isn't much different.'

She had a point there. What could he give her in a marriage that Augustus couldn't? Just as he despised Henri for dragging her towards matrimony, he didn't intend to do that either.

Which begged the question—how was he going to entice her there?

'Maybe it isn't. But that man will never be in your bed as long as I live and breathe.'

'Neanderthal, much?'

He gave a breezy shrug. She could call him what she liked; it changed nothing.

'And, secondly, I'm not merely talking about my father. I'm talking about my sister, Claudia. She'll be frantic by morning.' A devious light flashed in her eyes. 'Speaking of Claudia… Oh, you don't want to meet *her* husband in a dark alley. In fact when he hears about this he'll make you wish you'd never been born.'

Thane lounged back with a lazy smile on his face. 'This would be Lucas Garcia? Once head of national security for Arunthia?'

'That's exactly who it is.'

'And you think *I* fear *him*?'

She scrunched up her nose. 'Yes, well, come to think of it that *is* a flawed strategy. The devil himself wouldn't scare *you*. But one day you're going to meet your nemesis, and I'd love to be there when you do.'

He had a feeling he already had. In this woman.

'If I have my way you *will* be there.'

'On this occasion I'm afraid you'll have to accept defeat. I'm not staying with you. I'll move heaven and earth to get home, and the sooner you realise that the better. You can't always have what you want, Thane.'

'Ah, Luciana. When there is a war to be fought I will always be the victor. Especially when I want the prize so very, very badly. And I want *you*, Luciana—very, *very* badly. So I will do whatever it takes to make you mine.'

Those smooth, satiny cheeks flooded with a warm sensual blush of pleasure even as she pursed her mouth in an expression that screamed cynicism.

'Whatever it takes, huh? I don't think personality transplants are available on this continent, Thane. And, believe me, it will take more than a dishonourable kidnapping rat to woo me down the aisle.'

At the blatant challenge he felt his blood heat and he arched one brow.

'Okay. So I haven't been the most noble of men today.'

'Ha!'

'I honestly didn't think it would upset you this much. I am struggling to understand why you want to go home so desperately when there is nothing for you there but a ball and chain and a vapid viscount.'

She shifted uneasily and pulled her lip into her moist mouth with a scrape of her teeth. Before he could discern if he was seeing guilt or not, she ground that curvy, firm bottom over his rapidly hardening groin and he had to grind his jaw to stop a feral moan escaping.

Unclamping his jaw took some effort. 'All that being said, perhaps a more subtle approach *would* have been better—but I cannot turn back time.'

'You could take me home,' she suggested hopefully.

Not if the survival of mankind depended on it.

'What about if I make a deal with you instead?'

That grabbed her attention, and she focused those incredible eyes back on him. Where he wanted them to stay.

'What kind of a deal?'

'You give me two days to…what did you call it? Court you? Date you? And if after those two days you still wish to return home I will take you myself. Escort you to your father's door and never darken it again.'

Not that it would comc to that.

The knowledge that he was using military tactics to keep his princess in line did not impress his sense of fair play, but then again fair play had flown out of the window when he'd clapped eyes on her in the company of Augustus. She was his gorgeous little lioness. The answer to his royal prayers.

In his arms, he could feel the tension ooze from her body, and a corresponding flood of gratification unravelled the anxious knots in his mind.

'You mean it?'

Her brandy eyes melted to warm honey and flowed through his chest like blissful nectar, soothing his every raw nerve. He brushed the back of his index finger down her nose. Over her lips. Luscious lips that he glossed with the pad of his thumb, where they were still bruised from his kisses.

A new kind of tension sizzled in the air and a glow of unsatisfied desire filled the space between them—an invisible presence that moved over his skin, sliding over them both like a caress. A teasing, taunting, tempting caress.

And right *there* was the difference between him and Augustus. Bedevilled, off-the-charts sizzling chemistry. Black magic.

This. This was what he would play on.

Regardless of how he'd got her on this jet, he still made her weak with desire—and right now that was all he had to work with.

Rebelling against the inner voice warning him to stop, to keep his head this time and cajole her with a gentle hand, he brought his mouth to the edge of her ear and closed his teeth around her lobe.

Her breathless panting whispered over his neck and made his pulse thrash against his cuff. It was a low, husky carnal want that made him murmur, 'Absolutely I mean it. I swear it on my very life.'

Two days were all he needed to lure her over to the dark side.

'Let me show you the most beautiful place on earth.'

He knew the perfect spot for the ultimate seduction, where his Queen would surrender right into his waiting arms.

'What do say, angel?'

CHAPTER SIX

Luciana was in the throes of a wonderful dream and she never wanted to wake up. Amazingly strong, muscular arms wrapped her in the warmth of their protection and the rhythmic sound of the ocean lapping over the shore lulled her mind into a tranquil peace she hadn't felt in aeons.

A muffled lyrical trill shattered the halcyon bliss and beckoned her to rouse.

Bright was the splash of daylight behind her eyelids. Soft and sensually luxurious was the satin beneath her tummy and her cheek. Sweet was the scent of buttery pastry…or possibly French toast.

The musical chime hushed to a harmonious end.

Luciana writhed on the deeply cushioned mattress and stretched the kinks from her body, then prised her eyes open once, twice—and bolted up on all fours.

'Where the—?'

Rocking back, she sat on her ankles, her heart thrashing a symphonic staccato as her gaze bounced around the gargantuan almond-white room.

Holy-moly…

Paradise. She was in an enormous satin-drenched bed in paradise. Not only that, it felt inordinately pure. Minimalistic, all in varying shades of white, it serenaded a desperate search for solace.

In front of her and behind were the only solid walls, and when she swung to her right Luciana gasped at the fifty-foot-wide unencumbered view of a beautiful azure sky and the glistening crystalline waters of the Med as it frolicked with champagne sands. It was as if the entire wall had been rolled back and hidden to one side.

A wide wooden deck ran from the room to the shoreline and she smiled when a small lizard scurried across the sun-drenched teak.

Flipping her gaze to the left, to the opposite open expanse, she was faced with a rugged slab of rock dyed a deep charcoal-grey by the waterfall that sluiced down from some great height she couldn't see, to rush and froth and pool, then run beneath this very room…out through the other side and down toward the beach. Under the deck, she'd guess.

Gripping the edge of the bed, she tipped over to look at the floor, her hair spilling around her face. *Oh, wow.* Glass. The entire floor was glass. And she watched a vivid kaleidoscope of teeny-tiny fish dip and swerve and play beneath her.

So beautiful.

Giddiness leapt inside her at the sheer awesome natural beauty of it all—stunning architecture and a visual feast for the senses had always fascinated her. Odd that Thane was probably the only man she'd ever told that too.

Speaking of Thane… She lurched back upright to sit on the bed. Where the heck was he? And her heart-rate did *not* shoot through the roof when she thought of his name. Absolutely not. She hated the man. Yes, she did.

That would be the Thane who'd appeared so desperate to carry her into the main house, since by the time they'd arrived her insides had been battered and bruised from pummelling emotions and she'd been shivering with exhaustion. The Thane who had lain her gently in his bed…and after that everything was a bit blurry. Oh, Lord. Was it too much to ask that she'd booted him out of the room and banished him to Hades? Of course it was.

But, in her defence, her barricades had been low. And the devil was a maestro at taking advantage of that.

Lingering anger had her fisting the sheets.

She might have agreed to this bargain—*ha!* Agreed? As if she'd had *any* choice. But he was in for a nasty shock—because she was only here to prove she'd be the wife from hell. She'd evict him from her mind for ever while she focused on her end-game. Getting home to Natanael, come hell or high water.

On the plus side, seeing the real dark Prince in action, embroiled in some villainous scheme, would be just the ticket to satisfy her conscience that she'd made the right choices for them all. To ameliorate the guilt that constantly ate at her insides because she was keeping her son's existence a secret.

Though, honestly, she was mad even to trust that he'd take her home in two days. But the alternative was hauling out the big guns—her father. Who would likely kick off a military invasion. And that was the last thing she wanted. Hence she'd surrendered to the dark Prince.

Certifiable? Probably.

The opening bars of muffled Mozart trilled through the room—*again!*—and Luciana vaulted off the bed, the bare pads of her feet hitting cool glass as she searched every table-top. Because that sounded suspiciously like her phone. Which made no sense considering he'd told her it wouldn't work anywhere near the castle. But maybe he'd changed his mind about taking her there, maybe they were miles away from the horrid place—

'Oh, good Lord. My bag!' She'd never been so darn happy in her life! She could *kiss* that horrible brute right now.

Snatching the black leather heap from the side table, she shoved her hand in, rummaging to the bottom.

'Don't ring off…don't stop. *Please* don't stop ringing.'

Shaking like a windswept leaf, she barely managed to hit 'accept' and mash it to her ear.

'H…Hello?'

'Luciana?' Claudia's voice was a sound for sore ears. 'Thank God—where are you?'

'I'm...'

Common sense smacked her upside the head. Where the blazes was Thane? She didn't want him party to this conversation.

'Hold on a minute,' she whispered frantically as she ducked and dived all over the room, opening and closing doors, her heart slamming around her chest, feeling like an extra out of a badly acted eighties cop show.

Aha! There he was. The fiend. In the distance, standing on the beach, talking to a short dark-haired man. Throwing a stick into the water, of all things.

Unleashing a pent-up breath, she slumped where she stood. Looked pretty innocent to her. No dastardly guns drawn or fisticuffs. *Yet.*

'Okay, I can talk. Is Nate all right?' she whispered, stepping back out of sight, hoping the walls didn't have ears. Or maybe she was on camera. Her gaze darted around the four upper corners of the room just in case.

'Of course he's all right. He's out with Lucas and Isabelle. Now, for heaven's sake, where *are* you?'

Good question. She actually couldn't believe she was about to say this. 'I'm in...Galancia.'

'*Galancia?*'

Claudia's holler had Luciana wrenching the phone from her almost burst eardrum.

'Oh. my God. I thought Augustus had been smoking pot or something.'

'The only thing Augustus gets high on is women.'

'*Eww.* He didn't? When you were *there*?'

'Sure he did.'

'You can't marry that man, Luce.'

Oh, great—Claudia sounded like Thane. Thane who wanted her *'very, very badly'*.

Luciana rubbed the heel of her hand over her left breast.

Naïve fool that she was, she wanted to believe those three little words. Words that whispered to a secret place inside her. So it was fortunate that his mind-blowing pheromones hadn't obliterated her every brain cell. Obviously he wanted something from her—everyone always did. She just wasn't sure what.

'Did Augustus tell Father?' she asked.

'No, not yet. Lucas made him keep his mouth shut until we heard from you. Half of me wondered if you'd just ducked out on Augustus, so we were giving you today to contact us before raising the alarm. Especially with Dad the way he is. Luce, what were you *thinking*, going there with that man?'

'I didn't have much choice.'

She stormed around the room, shaking the kinky mess from her ratty locks. *Ugh*, she felt gross. And *that* was when she spied her case on a pale ecru velvet chaise longue. *Her case!*

Mid jiggy-dance, she froze as every ounce of blood drained to her toes. Had he searched it? Hauling it from the chaise, she plonked it on the end of the bed and fumbled with the lock. The still locked lock. *Phew.*

Shoulders slumping, she tuned back in to Claudia's voice.

'What do you mean, you didn't have much choice? Did he force you? Did he…*kidnap* you? *Did he*?'

Claudia's glorious indignation flew down the phone line, and it was so good having someone in her corner. She took a great gulp of air to rake him over the hot coals…

And her gaze crashed into the wide stretch of canvas over the carved bedstead, making the words jam in her throat.

'Oh.'

'What do you mean "oh"? Luce, did you hear me?'

'Yes—yes, I heard you. Sorry, Claudia.'

'Did that Galancian brute *steal* you? *Did* he? That's it. I'm sending Lucas over there right now. He'll raze that place to the ground and get you out—'

'No.' What was she doing? *What are you doing, Luce...?* 'No, he didn't take me, Claudia. I…I agreed to come.'

'Mmm-hmm. You sure about that?'

'Yes. He…he asked me to stay with him a couple of days to…talk. Yes, to talk. Then he's bringing me home.'

'Mmm-hmm.'

'Honest.'

Claudia's voice softened. 'Luciana, darling, do you really know what you're doing?'

Lifting her hand, she pressed her fingers over her mouth, felt them tremble against her lips, unable to take her eyes off the picture in front of her.

'Not really. But now I'm here I need to know. I need to…' *Prove to myself I'm over him. Make sure I've done the right thing.*

'Okay, I hear you. Even the stuff you're not saying. The feelings that put that desolate look in your eyes…they haven't gone, huh?'

'No,' she whispered. *They scare me.* 'And that's ruinous, Claudia, because he's bad for me. He's dangerous. I'm reckless with him. He makes me want to be wicked. I spiral out of control. And I can't do that because I have to protect—'

'Luce. You know who you sound like, right? If there is one thing our father is good at it's the old brainwashing technique. Stop listening to his voice. It isn't wicked to want. Maybe…' She let loose a heavy sigh. 'Maybe these two days are exactly what you need. But that's all I can give you before I have to tell Father. Though with his weak heart I'd rather send Lucas in.'

'It'll be like the clash of the titans.'

'My money is on Lucas,' Claudia said, in the confident, proud way only a wife madly in love could.

And there was Luciana with her money on Thane. What that said about her she wouldn't like to guess.

'Just…call me whenever you can, okay?'

'Okay.' Luciana sneaked another peek outside, to check

Imagine who'd been slain in his bed ever since he speared her with a warped arrow of pain and pique. 'Then clearly I created a monster.'

Laughter rumbled up from the depths of his chest. 'I think you did, angel.'

With that, he glanced up at the canvas stretched across the wall and his smile faltered.

'Right there. It's a good likeness—a stunning rendition. Don't you think?'

She had to swallow around the great lump in her throat. 'Yes, it is. It's…beautiful, Thane.'

Why? Why did he have a painting of their favourite spot in Zurich? Where they'd stayed. A dramatic panorama of the Rhine Falls. Luciana could virtually hear the roaring rush of water, feel the moist mist peppering her skin, see the craggy jutting rocks, the Prussian blue lakes.

'Do you remember the day we met?' he asked distractedly. He stared at the scene with a deep frown. As if it was the first time he'd allowed himself to really look at it.

To remember was to open a vault she'd bolted shut years ago. A perilous endeavour, just as dangerous as he was. But, as always, this man silenced the screams of her self-preservation.

'If you hadn't walked by that day…' Scary to think what might have happened.

'What were you doing there, Luciana?'

'Celebrating the end of finals.'

She'd caved in to temptation and jetted across Europe with some trusted friends from her politics class. And while her father had been under the illusion that she'd remain in London for another month, Luciana had gone incognito and ventured into her first foray into rebellion.

She'd been intoxicated by the heady taste of absolute freedom. One she'd failed to find at university, as she'd hoped. Eyes had still watched and reported back to her parents. Gossip had still fuelled the press. But in Zurich, for the first time in her life, she'd been a normal person. A woman the paparazzi wouldn't look at twice. Lost in the crowd and having the time of her life.

Until a two-hundred-pound strung-out Viking had cornered her behind a tour bus, the foul scent of beer leaching from his every pore, wanting some 'fun' of his own. And in those terrifying moments she'd cursed her naïve recklessness and prayed for someone to appear. For *this* man to appear.

It had been Thane who'd torn him off her and knocked him clean out with one punch. Thane, who'd locked onto her eyes and never let her go. Thane, who'd kept a careful distance as he'd walked her back to her apartment as if she were some fragile fawn.

The romantic little girl in her had called it serendipity. Thinking about it, dark and dangerous should have screamed at her to run, yet she'd been petrified that he'd leave. Take that awesome powerful protection with him. So she'd finagled him into having a coffee, then dinner, and drinks after that. And suddenly she'd been dependent, hooked on him like a drug, and all she'd craved was the next fix.

She'd been addicted to the intense highs. Though she'd do well to remember the aftermath. Horrendous heart-wrenching lows. Lost. Unfocused. She'd sworn she would never be dependent on another man.

Still… 'You saved me.'

'He is lucky to still walk the earth,' he said scathingly, in a fierce, low, dominant tone.

And she couldn't help it. She smiled wide—big and genuine and just for him. Because she'd been terrified and he'd been…*awesome.*

Eyes locked with his once more, she couldn't break free of his hold. They were drawn together like powerful magnets. As it had been from the start.

His initial confusion at their combustible attraction was unforgettable. As if he'd never known such passion and lust could exist. Endearing. Dazzling. He'd enslaved her in seconds.

Do you remember our first time? her heart whispered. *Yours? Mine? Teaching one another how to give pleasure and take? I remember every tender, evocative touch, every blissful second in your arms. The longing. The delirium as you drove deeper and deeper into my body until I felt indelibly marked. Branded. Claimed. Wanted. Desired.*

Yours.

Her heart ached, and Thane stared into her eyes as if the secrets of her soul were nothing more than words on a page.

Oh, Lord. She was in so much trouble here.

She was supposed to be reassuring herself that her secrets were better kept buried. Ensuring that Thane rued the day they'd ever met. Yet here she was, reminiscing about 'the good ol' times' and trying not to think of the damage they could do to the bed. They had busted a frame or two in their time…

What she *wasn't* supposed to be was more confused than ever. But within the space of ten minutes all her carefully erected defences were crumbling down around her, leaving her brain reduced to chaos and rubble.

And she hated it. Hated that the semblance of control she'd been hanging on to was as precarious as her future.

Luciana had to remember who he was and how exactly she came to be standing in his bedroom. Instead of musing that underneath, where it counted the most, he might still be the man she'd fallen for. And if that was true they were all in a bigger mess than she'd ever imagined. A wealth of pain at her hands. Because she was a mother and if her son could have a father who was a good man, hell would freeze before she kept them apart any longer.

Insides shaking, she tore her gaze from his. And as soon as that powerful connection was severed the fog began to clear.

Remember who he is, how you got here. How he once

tried to assassinate your father. Don't forget that you're enemies.

She had to stop listening to the longing of her heart. Get through the next two days unscathed, then run as fast as she could. Before she started doubting her own mind and cracked under the pressure. Told him the one secret that would change their lives for ever. The one secret she would never be able to take back.

CHAPTER SEVEN

DESPITE THE CLOAK of aloofness that suddenly settled over her, Thane had an incredibly light, airy feeling. Much like the five-foot dazzling iridescent aqua dolphin balloon he'd once bought Luciana. She'd adored the garish spectacle and, seeing that same gorgeous smile on her face moments ago—the one that made his heart kind of…*stop*—he'd known he'd played the perfect pitch by bringing her here.

She'd visibly relaxed since speaking to her sister—he'd heard her softly spoken goodbye and made a mental score to thank Seve for unearthing her case and bag pronto. By dusk today she would fall into his arms like a sweet ripe apple tumbling from a tree.

Already she was unravelling more by the second—nothing like the Princess who'd slid so gracefully into his car only yesterday. Rumpled. Tousled. Looking sublimely natural and sexed-up. No show or lipstick or pristine dress, she was sexier than anything he'd ever seen or, he suspected, would ever see in his lifetime.

He growled inwardly. Wanting her under him. Beneath him. Surrendering to him. Insane, she made him insane with want. But, as much as he knew she desired him with equal wanton abandon, something held her back, so he refused to rush this or lose his head.

Velvety rich, the scent of coffee and pastries wafted on the sultry breeze, and when Luciana's stomach grumbled

Thane satisfied himself that he could at least pacify one of her cravings this morning.

'Breakfast,' he said. 'Then you can choose where you wish to go today. *Si?*'

Her head jerked up where she stood, hastily zipping up her case, and he was smacked with the suspicion that the contents were something she'd rather he didn't see. Not that it mattered. By the time he was finished her every secret would be unearthed.

'Wow, Thane. Colour me surprised—you're giving me a *choice*?'

For now. '*Si*, of course. The first of many. Come and sit with me—let me feed you.'

As if she were an antelope and he a great ferocious lion, she approached him warily. Such an astute character, she was. Then he heard a canine sniff from behind him and accepted that he wasn't the only predator in the vicinity.

'Ah,' she said. 'Now I get why you were throwing sticks. Why are they smacking their lips as if I'm on the menu? Good Lord, they're huge. What *are* they?'

Slipping his arm around her waist, he tugged her to him and murmured in her ear. 'Rhodesian Ridgebacks. Maybe they find you as delicious as I do. Must be all those round American chocolatey…'

With a long-suffering sigh, she rolled her eyes and pushed past him. 'Yes, yes—all right, Romeo.'

All that feisty sass made him grin as he pulled out a chair and watched her sashay into the padded wicker seat.

'Thank you.'

Bending at the waist, he pressed his lips to the graceful slope of her bare shoulder and murmured, 'Welcome…' relishing both the shimmy that danced down her body *and* the way he'd already stripped her of that haughty veil.

He sank into the chair adjacent to hers and strove for nonchalance. 'I take it you spoke to your sister?' That he was ignorant of the whole conversation sat in his guts like a rock.

The sun bathed her in a warm glow, picking out the honeycomb strands in her hair, and she swept a stray tendril back from her temple in a decidedly nervous gesture. 'Yes. I told her I was staying with you for a couple of days.'

Thane didn't bother arguing that point. *Yet.*

'So, thank you for…' She shook her head, sending that wayward lock tumbling back over her face. 'Why on earth I'm *thanking* you for returning my own property to me, when it was originally your fault I lost it, is beyond me—but I do appreciate you sending for it.'

'You are most welcome. See? I am not so bad after all.'

'Oh, you are *very* bad, Thane. Of that I am in no doubt.'

A dark laugh erupted from his chest. 'Fortunately for me you like me that way. It turns you on.'

A blush that spoke more of pique than passion flurried across her cheeks, but her scathing retort perished as his man at the house—Pietro—appeared and laid a mound of homemade madeleines, croissants and cream-filled pastries on the table before her.

That serene breeding of hers came rushing to the fore. 'Everything smells delicious—thank you so much. Did you make these?'

Pietro fastened his warm hazel gaze on her. 'My wife, Your Royal Highness. But she will only cook for our Prince.'

Thane's good mood disintegrated and he clenched his teeth. It didn't matter how many times he told the man to call him Thane, he still got *our Prince*. Respectful, yes, but it shafted him with guilt—because despite his title his hands were largely tied, and if he'd played things differently he'd be in the position to do a damn sight more for them.

Luciana arched one brow in his direction. 'Why only Thane?'

'Eat, Luciana,' he ordered, knowing what was coming.

He didn't want Pietro's gratitude. It was Thane's job to procure him a better life. He was the one to blame for the mess they were in. If he'd been stronger, hidden his true ambitions better, his father would have given him the throne upon his death. Instead of passing it over to the power-hungry, greedy lech that was Franco Guerrero.

Naturally Luciana didn't take a blind bit of notice—*Dios*, she was an obstinate little thing—and she blinked up at Pietro with those gorgeous brandy eyes no man could possibly resist. Not even happily married Pietro, with his six girls and loose tongue.

'He gives us a home, our own land. No one but the crown owns land on Galancia, but Thane gives us acres of his vineyards and my family make the best wines on the island. Then he makes sure my girls can travel north, go to school. He fixes everything.'

'Pietro…don't. Please.'

Every time he heard those words it just reminded him of the thousands of others he couldn't help. Though now he had Luciana all that would change, wouldn't it? *Dios*, he couldn't wait. His patience shredded more by the day.

Luciana, whose only focus was Pietro, said, 'Oh, he does?'

As if some mental explosion had occurred in that ingenious brain of hers, so many emotions flickered across her exquisite face that he was hard-pressed to pick out one.

'Si,' Pietro said avidly. 'The best man to walk the earth. And now *you* are here, and everything will be—'

Thane glanced up to silence him. He didn't want these two days to be mired with talk of his throne. But, fisting his hand beneath the table, he warred with an internal battle to be forthright. At least with himself. Truth was, he wanted Luciana to want him. To choose *him* over Augustus. Not to feel pushed or obligated in any way. And he refused to read too deeply into that.

'Now I'm here…?' Luciana prompted.

Pietro grinned. 'He will be happy at last. All will be well.'

Guilt blanched her flawless skin and she composed a

spurious smile that made Thane uneasy. Made him doubly sure he was missing something.

'You must meet my wife. I will never have peace if she does not speak to you.'

Thane almost groaned aloud. They would be here all day and Luciana would be subjected to God knows what.

'Pietro? I don't think we have time. Luciana wishes to explore—isn't that right, angel?'

The wide-eyed gleam she launched his way was anything but angelic. It was positively devious and it made his blood hum. She wanted to hear more, he realised.

'We have plenty of time…*darling*.' She emphasised that endearment—the very one that made his heart lurch—with a swift kick to his shin as she peered up at the other man all guile and innocence. 'I think that's a wonderful idea, Pietro. I would love to meet her.'

Relishing Thane's discomfort, she flashed her teeth at him, all saccharine sweetness. The dark look he volleyed back said she would pay highly for it. Later.

Then again, Pietro had wandered off—so why wait?

Easing forward in his seat, he slid wicked fingers over the delicate curve of her knee beneath the table, then made small teasing circles as they ascended higher and higher up her inner thigh.

The light flush that coloured her cheeks made a gradual descent across her chest, down over her breasts, and the glass of freshly squeezed orange juice in her fist rippled as she clamped her thighs together, imprisoning his hand.

'See that knife?' she whispered in a rush, motioning to the lethal blade on the table-top. 'I won't hesitate to chop those fingers off.'

'Ah, you won't do that, Luciana.'

'I wouldn't be so sure, if I were you. Don't underestimate me, Romeo.'

Flipping his hand, he forcibly nudged her legs apart. 'While I have no intention of underestimating you, I believe you'll soon see sense. Because what will I pleasure you with then?'

Her breathing became short and shallow, making her deep cleavage taunt him with a subtle quivering heave, and he had the sinful urge to ramp up her erotic want higher still. So he stroked one finger over the lace of her panties and ran his tongue along his bottom lip suggestively.

'Actually…who needs fingers? I can think of various other ways to torment you.'

And he would use every one to lure her in. No matter what it took, by the weekend both Luciana and the throne would be his.

She was going to murder him. Wrap her hands around his throat and send him to meet his maker—the devil himself. That was if she didn't choke on the uncut testosterone in the air first. Arrogant and downright debauched—that was what he was.

She couldn't move or whimper a sound, since Pietro was still fiddling with a coffee pot at the far end of the deck—and of course the shameless reprobate just *loved* that…the possibility of them getting caught likely got him off. It certainly didn't excite *her* blood. A woman of her gentility and refinement should be appalled at his sybaritic behaviour. And she was. Utterly.

Squirming, she tried to dislodge his hand and alleviate the dark pulse that throbbed in her pelvis. She wanted them back on topic. Wanted to hear every word that *wasn't* being said. It was that stuff that interested her—far more than his wandering lasciviousness.

Liar.

She felt like an insect that had inadvertently strayed into a spider's web, her every move ensuring greater entrapment, but right now she didn't care. Entangled as she was, there was far more going on here than met the eye.

Pietro vanished around the corner and she smacked Thane's arm away as she spun on him, eyes narrowed.

'Your uncle runs Galancia in a dictatorship, does he not? No government, no parliament to speak for the people, all the power coming from the man at the top. The state owns every acre of land, therefore every piece of brick and mortar too.'

That did it.

He flung himself back in his seat, taking his wicked fingers with him. It was if he'd found a state of mindless pleasure and was put out at her stopping his fun. *Tough.*

'I am sure you know he does, *princesa*.'

'So by giving Pietro his own land you're breaking your own rules?'

He picked up his espresso and downed the treble shot. 'They are not mine.'

'No? Are you saying you don't agree with them?'

His nonchalant shrug belied the curious tension in his menacingly hard frame. 'I don't think it's fair that the people can't reap the benefits of their hard work, that's all.'

Fair? 'You're indirectly hinting at a democracy, Thane.'

'I might be.'

Shock made her rock back in her seat. The dark, dangerous, autocratic Prince of Galancia wanted a *democracy*? While Arunthia had been a democratic state for years, it was the last thing she'd expected here.

'Is this what you're planning to do when you rule?'

'I might be.'

Good Lord. 'And so you take from the rich to give to the poor in the meantime?'

He scratched his jaw lazily. 'On occasion. Or I may just have paid Pietro's family for building this house.'

'How much? Thirty million?'

'I'll have you know it's the going rate.'

'Is it *really*?'

This was unbelievable. Staggering. She'd been absolutely right. She had no idea who he was. And nor did anyone else.

Including her father. Which wasn't surprising. Since Thane didn't have overall control he naturally wanted to keep his true agenda firmly under wraps.

'Still being a hero, then, Thane?' she asked softly.

Just as he'd been when he'd saved her from a fate worse than death in Zurich. Just as he'd been when he'd appeared once again out of nowhere in Courchevel. As if she'd conjured him up. Like some freak happenstance or serendipity.

An assassin? A mercenary? *This* man? She doubted that very much.

But, oh, no, he really didn't like being called a hero. The angry glitter in his eyes told her that. He was a testament to leashed power, Luciana decided. No need to shout when he could incite a quake with one look or a word. So intense. And he was heart-thumpingly gorgeous with it.

'Quiet, Luciana. Or I will silence that mouth for you. *Again*. And don't think I won't.'

His dominant power pushed at her, hot and hard, and she blushed like a teenager with a crush.

'Oh. I believe you. But this time I'm not giving you the chance.' That was what had got her into this mess to start with.

She might be here against her will, or rather she'd had little choice, but the sliver of pride she had left was a precious commodity she could ill afford to lose. So there was no way she was falling for that again. She knew better. Kiss her once and he'd had her on a plane. Kiss her twice and she'd find herself bound for Outer Mongolia, or flat on her back on her way to a priest. Though why the man wanted to marry her specifically she couldn't begin to fathom.

Why can't you just accept he wants you for you, Luce?

Because that would be plain stupid.

He arched one of those devilish brows. 'You know better than to challenge me, Luciana.'

The dark promise in those words made her shiver. And if his obsidian eyes had seemed compelling before, now they were like magnets, pulling on the iron in her blood, making it race around her body.

Lifting her tall glass, she splashed some orange juice down her parched throat, relishing the tangy sweetness that burst over her tongue, determined to wrestle back her poise. *Get back on topic, for heaven's sake.*

'Anyway,' she said. 'Why build a home here? Don't get me wrong—it's absolutely stunning—but why not live at Galancia Castle?'

His gaze drifted out to sea, but not before she saw the shadow of pain wash over him. 'I live there too. But my uncle and I are not the best of housemates. Even with thousands upon thousands of square feet and over two hundred walls.'

Seemed to her they were divided in more ways than one. Even as she struggled to take it all in she dug for more. 'I've heard it's one of the most opulent, palatial castles in the world.'

'It is the devil's lair.' A deep feminine voice sounded from beside her. 'Our Prince is better here. That place makes him dark and that man drains the life from him. Welcome… *welcome*.'

Thane shoved his hands through his raven hair, discomfort and agitation leaching from him.

Luciana yearned to straddle his lap, take away his pain just as she'd once done, but instead she jiggled her chair backwards to welcome Pietro's wife.

'Buenos dias,' she said, standing to accept a warm greeting and a kiss to both cheeks. The astounding affection filled her heart with elation and almost thrust her into a stupor.

Cupping her face, the petite brunette spitfire beamed. 'Good gracious, you are a real beauty. Little wonder he will not take—'

'*Hanna*,' Thane ground out in warning.

'Ah, hush. Let an old woman be happy.' She clapped her palm over her chest. 'This will be the best Christmas we have ever seen.'

It took all of Luciana's willpower to maintain her serenity. Never mind that the woman had just told the dark Prince to hush—why the blazes was she casting her festive aspirations on Luciana? Why should she think Luciana would be here for Christmas? Was Thane so darn confident he'd been shouting it from the rooftops?

Of all the arrogant, conceited…

It was on the tip of her tongue to tell every Galancian within hearing distance that she'd be long gone by then. But as if Thane sensed her freefall he picked up her hand, lifting it to his lips. Tenderly he kissed the sensitive pulse-point that pounded at her inner wrist as he locked those mesmerising eyes on hers.

His electric energy zeroed in on her. The panicked dizziness abated. All extraneous noise drained from her perception until there was only him. Until she plunged back to her seat in a dreamlike daze.

How do you do this to me?

And then there was this couple, welcoming her with open arms despite the inbred hatred between Arunthians and Galancians, behaving as if she were their saviour. It was surreal. But it was wonderful too.

Even his beasts gazed at her with loving amber-hued puppy-dog eyes, one of them even resting its slavering chin on her knee. Lord, she couldn't resist his dogs. Had to stroke the short, furry wheat-brown coat. Brush those velvety ears between her thumb and forefinger.

Natanael would adore you, she thought with a stab of anguish.

He would adore all of this. He had pined and pleaded for a four-legged friend and he loved people, being the centre of their world. She could just hear him chattering, see him frolicking on the beach, dwarfed by these huge hounds, building sandcastles with Thane, his—

Luciana closed her eyes and swallowed thickly around the fear clotting her throat. She didn't want to make the connection—didn't want to acknowledge who this man was to her son. Had to focus on escaping, protecting Nate…

But what if in reality it wasn't Thane he needed protecting *from*? What if Thane was the only person in the entire world who could truly protect *Nate*?

He wasn't the man she'd met in Zurich. He was harder. More ruthless. More determined. And yet he wasn't the monster people claimed him to be.

Head pounding, as if it had been jammed in a nutcracker and split open, she couldn't think. Couldn't breathe.

So she smiled and nodded in all the right places while the endless waters of the Med called to her, the sound of its gentle lap, its tranquil stillness, soothing the disharmony in her heart and mind. But she didn't need to be looking at the ocean to realise she was burying her head in the sand. *Again*. That was exactly what she'd done in Hong Kong. Her utmost to pretend that her time wasn't running out. And where had it got her? Into inevitable torment when faced with reality.

If she waded through the mess of enemy nations and her throne she was a mother. First and foremost. Yes, if Natanael came to light it would ruin her in the eyes of her people and her father would likely disown her. But so be it. The only reason she'd kept him quiet was to keep him safe.

She'd pleaded to have him. The fact that he was alive right now was why she lived with the pain. The fact that his beautiful face lit up her entire world was why she lived in the dark. But if there were no danger to him there would be no reason for his true identity not to be known. His happiness was the most important thing to her. And if her little boy could have a daddy who was a good man—who would love him and protect him above all else—then Nate deserved that and so did Thane.

As for her crown… Her father would have to bend his rules and laws. Allow Claudia to take the throne despite the fact that Lucas wasn't of blue blood. Or he'd have to get over the fact he'd washed his hands of Andalina years ago and command her return from New York. Granted, the thought of Andie being Queen was hellishly scary, but her father would have no choice. If she was ruined, the damage was already done.

For the first time in years Luciana had choices. She only had to use them wisely. Be absolutely sure she was doing the right thing by telling Thane the truth.

Hanna and Pietro bade them a fond goodbye, leaving them alone once more.

'I believe I promised you a date,' he drawled. 'Lunch at the southern reef? A horse-ride along the beach or up into the vineyards? It's beautiful up there. What's your pleasure, angel?'

You. Heaven help me…you.

The man being worshipped by the sun before her. She wanted him to be real. Wanted the portentous voice inside her to be quiet, cease whispering that she was sitting in an audience watching a play—a performance being acted to perfection just for her—while she was blind to the true intent of the show.

'What do you want, Luciana?' he asked huskily.

A proper family. A wonderful daddy for Natanael. Love.

But all she said was, 'All of the above.'

CHAPTER EIGHT

In hindsight, a horse-ride probably wasn't the greatest of ideas, considering he'd almost choked on his own tongue when Luciana had poured that luscious body into some lightweight fawn jodhpurs and a figure-hugging cerise pink T-shirt—the outfit borrowed from one of Pietro's rake-thin girls. Talk about an exercise in torture.

He'd just put in the longest twenty-minute car-ride of his life. And now he cursed the *idiota* who had secreted the royal stables so far inland. He would fire the man if he didn't suspect it had been himself.

Arms folded across his wide chest, his foul temper exacerbated further still when every stable boy tripped over himself to attend her, but eventually she chose a deep chestnut thoroughbred named Galileo and Thane took his favourite black stallion, Malvado. The twinkle in Luciana's eyes told him she thought 'wicked' a very apt name for his beast of a mount. He didn't bother arguing. It was true that only Thane could dominate him.

Unsurprisingly, she rode like a pro and lured him into a race up into the vineyards, with the rich earth spraying in their wake, the fresh breeze whipping her bronze hair behind her and slapping her cheeks with colour.

Never had she looked more bewitching or more free. More real and more like his Ana.

Gradually she slowed to a trot, then an easy walk, and Thane pulled at the reins and drew up beside her.

'Good?' he asked.

'Yes. Wonderful.'

Those pink-smothered breasts rose and fell with her every soft pant and a huge smile curved her lips. Lips he wanted to make love to until her breath was ragged for *him*.

'I didn't expect it to be so gorgeous here. Warmer than home for December.'

Thane felt the muscle in his jaw spasm as he ground his teeth hard. Galancia would soon be her home, and the sooner she accepted that the better for his state of mind.

'Then again, you are closer to Africa here,' she went on. 'The air is hot and sultry. Everything just feels…'

'Relaxed? Calm?'

'Exactly. Maybe too calm—like the calm before a storm.'

A pensive crease lined her brow and she threaded the leather reins in between her long fingers, staring far into the distance as if she were a million miles away. Much as she'd done at breakfast. It vexed him because he was blind to the reason. He wanted her *here*. With him.

'Penny for them?'

She fobbed him off with a rueful smile. 'I doubt they're worth that much.'

Thane didn't believe her for a second, but let it go when she lifted in her saddle to twist and take in their surroundings. The endless rows of vines were heavy with juicy red grapes and lush dark green foliage.

'So these are your famous vineyards? Never tried the wine myself.'

'You should. In fact tonight I'll pour you a glass of one of the best wines in the world.'

She arched one brow at the vainglory lacing his words but he gave a nonchalant shrug. Why shouldn't he be proud of what they'd achieved? And moreover…

'The northern terrain is home to our much-lauded olive groves too. Far better than yours.'

'Now, now, Thane. Your head is getting a little *too* big over there.'

He grinned, amazed that they were joking about what had once been a life-threatening issue.

'Once upon a time we grew the best oranges too. Arunthian oranges are tasteless in comparison.'

She rolled her eyes. 'Of course they are.'

'I'm serious. Our crops were said to be the best in Europe. But your great-grandfather didn't like it that overseas trade demand was greater for ours, or that we made more money than he did. So he sent in men to disease our crops. Not one survived.'

Her head reared as if he'd slapped her. 'That's a lie! Nothing more than propaganda!'

'It is not. I swear it. In many ways we continue to suffer from that loss now.'

'But…but that's terrible.'

'*Si*. It is. Just one of the spats our countries—or should I say the houses of Verbault and Guerrero—have engaged in over the centuries.'

Her nose scrunched up as she grimaced. 'Hard to believe we were allies—sister islands at one time. I have heard some gruesome and horrific accounts…'

'And I bet we were always the villains.'

Thane didn't bother to wait for her to agree; they both knew he was right.

'I won't lie—I imagine we committed many an outrageous act not to be proud of, but most were in retaliation. If you care to go back far enough it all comes down to Arunthia's greed. Galancia has always been the richer in industry, and many an Arunthian leader has tried to take it by force. Almost succeeded two or three times too. But it just made us stronger. Hence we have an indomitable military presence. Now no one would dare to touch us.'

Those decadently long lashes swept downward, as if his words weighed heavily on her mind. 'I can see why you wish to be feared, in that case. To protect what you have. No matter what it takes.'

Thane narrowed his gaze on her, sure there was a deeper meaning to her hushed words—which had been spoken in a cracked parody of her usual tone. When she failed to elucidate he ploughed on, riding the imperative desire for her to know. Understand.

'We stop at nothing. Which has caused a whole new set of problems for us. Because to protect, to build an army, takes an obscene amount of money. More than you could ever imagine. So the crown hoards the land for revenue and taxes businesses until they can't breathe—until we've suffocated our own. All to make us indestructible. More powerful than any other. While our children need new schools and our hospitals are in dire need of repair.'

Sadness crept over her demeanour, making her eyes darken. 'That makes so much sense it's scary.'

'My uncle will never release those bonds on our people. Nor will he let the feud go—just like my father before him. His father before that. The hatred is inbred.'

'I know. My father is the same. But what I don't understand is why Franco Guerrero is in power and you're not. Why haven't you taken your throne?'

'Must we talk about this now, Luciana?'

'Yes, Thane, we must. You brought me here against my wishes. You talk about marrying me…which is ludicrous. We don't even know one another. And basically all you expect me to go on is rumours and secrets and lies. So here I am blindfolded, smack-bang in the midst of a labyrinth, not knowing which way to turn. Can't you see that?'

Disquiet hummed through his mind. He didn't particularly want her to know how dark he was inside, how deeply twisted by it all.

They'd reached a shaded wrought-iron arbour often used by his workers and Thane swung his right leg over the saddle and dropped onto uneven ground, determined to tread carefully over the minefield that was the past.

He was too close to success to risk everything now, by admitting he'd been a trigger away from assassinating her father. Especially when some days he regretted not doing so, since his people had ultimately paid the price. Other days he accepted it would have severed the very last thread of humanity he'd been clinging to at the time. And today, looking at the man's daughter—the woman he wanted as his wife, the woman who would give him his crown—he couldn't help but wonder if fate truly did move in mysterious ways.

Vigilance tautened his striking features, telling Luciana she was trying to open a conversational door best left shut. Then an artful devious light shone in his dark eyes and he stretched out his arms, gripped her waist and lifted her down, dragging her body against his.

The friction charged her pulse and set off a chain reaction she was powerless against. Inside her bra her breasts grew heavy, aching to be touched. Those burning butterflies went wild, flitting in and around her ribcage, and her panties suddenly felt too damp, too tight.

'Let's have lunch in the shade,' he murmured, his voice enriched with sin. 'It's stifling out here in the open.'

Translation: *I'll seduce you in the bushes until you forget your own name, never mind this discussion.*

Er…*no*. She thought not.

Though her resolve would be less painful to stick to if she stopped gawping at the man. Thane in a pair of tall sepia leather boots, black riding trousers and a skin-tight red polo shirt—collar flicked up to tease his hair and short sleeves lovingly caressing his sculpted biceps—was a head-rush all on its own.

So she made a clumsy job of sidestepping outside his magnetic force field.

Out came his arm, to snake around her waist, and she

dodged like the netball champion she'd once been and shook her head. 'Oh, no, you don't. I know full well what you're up to, Romeo, and you can forget it. *Talk.*'

Growling, he turned away. 'Fine.'

Then, just as she breathed a sigh of relief, he came at her from another angle, as if he'd played her with misdirection and now...*pounce*...stole a tummy-flipping, bone-liquefying kiss from her mouth. Only to grin with acute smugness and walk away.

Her hand shot out and she found Galileo, to steady herself, even as she bit her lip to stifle a gurgle of laughter. He was incorrigible. Couldn't stand being told no. Losing in any way. And, seriously, she shouldn't laugh—because the man was dangerous with it. Kidnapping, stealing kisses... He was off-the-charts unpredictable, and that scared her more than anything.

And it thrills you just as much.

Thane grabbed the lunch bag and Luciana rolled a blanket across the grass beneath the leafy trellised ceiling, where it was blissfully cooler. Then she sat cross-legged and unpacked a tapas feast of cold cut meats, cheeses and rosemary-scented bread.

Throat dry, she drank greedily from a bottle of sparkling water, trying not to splutter or drool as Thane dropped to the red chequered blanket and lounged back on his elbows in an insolent pose, crossing one ankle over the other. She had the shameless urge to climb over his lap, sit on those muscular thighs and feel all that latent erotic power beneath her. And—just her rotten luck—he caught her staring and fired her the most indecently hedonistic smile she'd ever seen.

Luciana deflected his corruption tactics with a haughty sniff. 'I'm waiting. So talk.'

'I have the strangest urge to take you over my knee.'

She harnessed the shiver that threatened to rattle her spine. 'And *I* have the strangest urge to get back on that horse and leave you to eat lunch by yourself.'

The brute actually grinned at that, then popped an olive in his mouth. Though when his humour faded, to be replaced by an aching torment, she almost let him off the hook, hating to see him in the throes of anguish. Oh, he banked it soon enough—but it was too late.

'When my father knew he was dying I had only just turned seventeen…' He paused, as if figuring out his next words. 'He ordered me to do a job, and at the very last moment I defied him. I thought I'd seen and felt his fury before then. I had seen nothing.' He shrugged blithely. 'I deserved every blow for going against him, and I could have lived with that, or anything else he doled out to me personally. What I hadn't expected was the depth of his wrath and the price my people would pay.'

Abruptly, he jerked upright and rested his forearm on one bended knee.

'When I failed him he decided I was too cocky, too young…too free-thinking to rule. Too liberal. I had shown my true colours. My father and my uncle are of the same ilk. Dictators. Born and bred militia. So my punishment was a stipulation that said I couldn't take power until I was thirty years old. Until I had learned my lesson.'

Outrage and the fiercest taste of bitter acrimony roiled in her stomach. To give his uncle time to work him over, no doubt. As if *anyone* could reshape Thane's mind. The very idea was ludicrous.

'I deserved every blow...'

The man didn't even flinch or care that he'd been beaten. No, all he cared about was that he'd failed his people.

'What made you break from the pack?' she asked, awed. 'Being of the same ilk and all.'

Luciana couldn't begin to comprehend the strength it would have taken to set himself apart from such men. The stories she'd heard—the ones she had nightmares about, imagining Natanael embroiled in them—brought her out in a cold sweat.

In one graceful movement he was up on his feet, leaning against an iron post, focused on the rolling hills.

'My mother, I think. It was her dream, and she used to talk about how her family would pray morning, noon and night for a better tomorrow. A tomorrow when the people could speak for themselves, have a say in how they lived. A day when they owned their own lands and could reap the benefits of what they sowed. When people's lives would be that much richer and more fulfilling if they were given the chance to aspire.'

Heaviness encroached on her chest at the grief painting his words blue. 'She sounds like she was a wonderful woman, Thane.'

Luciana knew he'd lost her young. And if the stories were true and his mother had been taken, stolen from her loved ones, his childhood must have been a war zone in more ways than one.

'A tortured soul is a more apt description.'

She could hear the dark resonance of his painful past echo through him, distorting his voice, and her eyes flared as he grabbed hold of a tangled vine from above and ripped it down, its thorns spearing into his palm. Within seconds blood dripped from his fist.

Luciana scrambled to her feet. 'Thane…?'

His eyes were the blackest she'd ever seen, and she realised he wasn't even aware he'd hurt himself. Panic punched her heart.

'Don't do that, *querido*. Look what you're doing. Thane? *Thane*!'

He blinked, over and over, refocusing on her. 'Sorry, angel, what is it?'

'G…Give me your hand.' She pulled a handkerchief from her pocket and wrapped the white cotton round his palm, biting her lip when deep red stained the cloth.

Thane searched her face with a confounded expression,

as if no one had ever cared enough before to stop him hurting. And that made her aching heart weep for him.

Pointing up to the small scar on his chin, she asked softly, 'Did that hurt when you did it?'

'I can't remember. I do not think so.'

Good Lord, his pain threshold had to be off the charts.

'When did you do it?'

'This one?'

Up came his hand and he rubbed over the thin white line with one fingertip.

A fresh stab of wretchedness almost struck her down. It was just like when Nate talked about falling out of the blossom tree at their apartment near Hong Kong. He would touch the scar on his arm when he recalled it. The likeness in mannerism was uncanny—and so bittersweet.

'I was twelve, I think. I'd dropped a thirty-five-millimetre and shattered the casing.' He smiled and shook his head ruefully. 'Let's just say I never once fumbled with the damn thing again.'

'Twelve? And he punished you? He beat you for…?' She swallowed thickly. 'How could he *do* that?'

He shrugged off her empathy. 'It's not an issue. I was born to rule, just as he was. Raised to defend, not to feel. A honed weapon. He did what he had to do. Probably what had been done to him. I accept that.'

'No. *No*, Thane. No child should have to accept that. Don't you *dare* accept that. He didn't have to be brutal or so cruel. Are you saying because you were raised like that you would do that to your children? Your son?'

Snatching his hand away, he stepped back as if she'd physically backhanded him. Anger, affront and hurt flooded the space between them. 'How could you think me capable of that, Luciana?'

Oh, God, she'd had nightmares about exactly that. As her father had filled her head with tales—and yes, okay, some facts too—she'd fought her own instincts. Scared witless, out of her mind. Missing him so badly she couldn't eat or sleep or breathe without hurting. So she'd written letters. What seemed like hundreds of letters. Only to burn them.

Tears splashed up behind her eyes. She couldn't stop them. And he didn't like it—not one bit.

Panic laced his voice. 'Luciana, what is wrong?'

'I'm sorry,' she whispered. 'I'm so sorry.'

His riveting handsome face creased with confusion. 'Why? Why are you sorry?'

Shaking her head, she forced a smile. She knew it wept with sorrow and dejection, so she made it brighter. Smoothed the damp hair from his brow.

'Do you feel *me* when I touch you?' she asked.

'You're about the only thing in the world I do feel, Luciana.'

Oh, God.

Out of control—as always with this man—she reached up in search of his mouth. Desperate to take his pain away. To take hers with it too. Because she now knew what she had to do and it would likely destroy them. Destroy this. Destroy any chance of happiness they would ever have.

As she lifted up on her tiptoes he surged downwards, closing the gap, pressing a frantic kiss to her lips.

She reached up and grabbed handfuls of his shirt, feeling the flex of his hard muscle beneath her fingertips. One kiss, she promised herself. Just one kiss so she could feel his lust and affection. Surely it would be enough to last? It would have to be enough.

Thane's fingers speared into the heavy fall of her hair, cradling her nape, his grip fierce and exquisitely firm, and with one long, languorous flick and thrust of his tongue into her mouth her knees buckled underneath her.

His cat-like reflexes kicked in and he dropped his hands to her waist to keep her upright.

'*Dios*, I crave you like a physical ache. Not here, though, angel. I can't lose it with you here,' he breathed in a rush of warm air over her cheek as he ran his nose up the side of hers and rested there for a gloriously intimate beat.

No. She couldn't possibly sleep with him. It would make everything a hundred times worse. And what was more…

'Thane, you have to stop calling me that, okay?' It tore off another piece of her heart every time he did.

'What…? Angel? Why? It's what you reminded me of last night in the limousine, with your hair this colour. Darkly spun gold. Seraphic. Beautiful. As *you* are, Luciana. Inside and out.'

'D…Don't put me on a pedestal, Thane. I'm no angel. Sooner or later I'll drop from a great height.'

And, like finely spun glass, she would shatter to the floor in a million pieces.

A rueful light flickered in his eyes as he hiked one broad shoulder. 'Then maybe we will be equal.'

Guilt. So much guilt it seemed to suffocate his soul.

'What your father did—giving control to your uncle—it's not your fault.'

Scepticism vied with his obvious desire to believe her.

'What job or mission did you refuse to do, anyway? What would anger him so much that he'd delay your taking the throne for so long?'

That had to have been ten years ago…

A shadow swarmed over his face and in that moment somehow she *knew*.

Foreboding crackled down her spine and she stumbled back a step. 'Go on. Say it.'

He shoved his hands through his wind-tousled raven-black hair and his chest swelled as he hauled in air. 'How did you know?'

'I wasn't sure until right this moment. But rumours have a way of reaching the right ears and poisoning minds.'

A muscle ticked in his jaw as he gave a short nod. 'I disobeyed a direct order and refused to kill your father.'

CHAPTER NINE

LUCIANA CURLED UP on a cushioned recliner on the beach and gazed up at the midnight sky, wishing on a billion twinkling diamond stars that Thane's business calls would take all night. But, as she already knew, burying her head in the sand would help no one—least of all herself.

The drive back down to the coast had been taut with tension, and by the time dinner had been served on the upper floor balcony Luciana had been strung so tightly she'd barely eaten one mouthful of the delicious seafood paella Hanna had slaved over. Which had only made her feel guiltier still. And she wouldn't have thought that was possible.

Closing her eyes, she recalled their brief conversation in the car.

'I didn't want to tell you,' he'd said. 'I thought you'd hold it against me.'

'I'm glad you told me. You saved his life in the end. It must have been a horrendously hard call for you. Thank you…'

Thane had saved her father's life. Paid an extortionate price for disobeying his tyrannical King. All for a man he hated. His enemy.

And how is he being repaid? His son is being kept from him. I didn't know. I didn't know any of this.

The guilt and pain tearing through her in one relentless lash after another wouldn't cease. Not for a second.

One day. She'd been here one day and the enormity of

what she'd discovered had her reeling. In truth, she wasn't sure she was taking it all in.

The rush of the ocean lapping over the shore was broken by the sound of bare feet padding down the deck, sending her heart trampolining to her throat and her stomach vaulting with a hectic tumble of dread and anticipation.

Thane straddled the recliner in front of her, one long-stemmed glass of ruby-red liquid in his large grip.

With a wriggle, she edged back to give his broad frame more room, and rested her head against the mocha cushion to drink him in.

He was breathtaking. His dark, fathomless eyes pulled at her like a hypnotic suggestion pressing against her mind. A constant murmur of want that was becoming impossible to ignore. But fight it she would.

'You are very quiet since we got back,' he said, his voice low and warm with concern.

'Just thinking.'

'No more thinking of the past tonight, hmm? Let's focus on the future. On us.'

She wasn't sanguine enough to believe there would be an 'us' come the dawn.

You don't know that for sure, Luce. He might listen to you. Try to understand.

It was a sliver of hope she clung to.

Raising her arm, she brushed his hair back from his gorgeous face and his decadent sable lashes fluttered as if weighted in bliss, as if he adored her touch. It broke her heart.

'Relax, Luciana. You seem brittle enough to shatter.'

Smooth as silk, his voice caressed her skin—a tangible touch of his magnetic heat and power that lulled her to calm.

'Here—take a taste.'

Glancing at the glass of red wine he'd promised earlier, she tried to swallow past her raw, swollen throat. Heavens, no. Thane was intoxicating enough. Half a glass and she'd be the centrefold in the tawdriest scenario her imagination could conjure up.

'I don't think that's such a good idea, Thane.'

Truly, she was way out of her depth, lying here as he towered above her, dominating her world. Thane on a sensual mission was a demonic tidal wave to be reckoned with. But she wasn't convinced sleeping with him would do either of them any favours in the long run.

Still, the yearning pushed at her soul. Stronger in force since the revelations of the afternoon. *'You're about the only thing in the world I do feel...'* That must be why he'd brought her here. Right? She made him feel and he was chasing it. Why else would he go to the lengths he had? And more than anything she wanted to bring him pleasure in any way she could.

Those devastating eyes fixed on her as he swirled the wine around the crystal, giving it air, then took a sip before dipping one of his sinfully adroit fingers into the ruby depths.

Memories of the debauched passion those hands could wreak made the briny ocean breeze stutter in her lungs and she panted out, 'Thane…I think maybe I should turn in for the night. I'm tired and I…'

I'm petrified I will give in, and it would be so reckless, so stupid, no matter how much we both want it.

She inhaled deeply, grappling for strength, only to be drugged by his dark, delicious scent. It infused her lust-addled mind and corrupted her veins. It blazed a firestorm through her midriff that eventually simmered low in her abdomen in a searing burn.

Venturing to eradicate that hot, dark pulse at her core, she squirmed to sit upright in the recliner. 'Thane…I should go to bed.'

By morning she'd have figured out what to do. What to say. How to explain.

'I—'

'Do you think I don't know what I do to you, Luciana? Do you think I can't hear and see your body crying out for mine? Stop fighting this, angel. It's inevitable.'

Claret drizzled down his finger in red droplets as he reached up and painted her lips with the lusty juice, let the rich flavour flow over her tongue, where it blossomed into an ecstasy of ripened grapes, aged wood and sunlight.

With a whimper she flicked her tongue over the very tip and sucked it into her mouth, loving the underlying saltiness and texture of his skin.

A feral groan ripped past his throat and he stared at her glistening lips, where her tongue swirled around his finger… Then he whipped it out, swooped down and captured her mouth in an erotic devouring kiss.

Push him away, Luce. Do it now...

Can't. Impossible.

Luciana laced her fingers through his hair, fisting tight so he couldn't escape, and slanted her mouth over his, licking between his lips, duelling with the sinful lash of his tongue in total surrender.

She'd missed this so much. Kissing. Being held close. The amazing feeling of intimacy with a man—*her* man. Being a sensual woman, someone who was desired. Cosseted. Craved with a burning urgency that rendered her almost weak. It was heady and powerful and she'd missed it.

The robust richness of the wine blended with the potent dominant piquancy that was uniquely Thane—something that exuded vice and sin and seduction—and annihilated her every thought until she was trapped, entangled in his wicked snare.

They tore apart to breathe and yet he never stopped the cherishing ardour, only brushed kisses along her jaw and down her neck in a slow, wet slide that made her shiver and arch in a sinuous serpentine wave beneath him. Begging for his touch. Which he gave by brushing his knuckles down over her breast, teasing her nipple into a stiff peak.

Her wanton moan rent the air, and in reward he rained kisses over her cleavage where it spilled over the top of her low-cut dress. She pressed him in close to her, never wanting to let him go.

'I want you writhing for me, Luciana.'

His hot breath gushed over her skin.

'I want to make love to you, feel you cling to me, hear you beg for release. And then I'll hold you and kiss you in the dark, watch you fall asleep. Only to wake you by sliding down your body and devouring you with my mouth.'

Her lower abdomen clenched and turned achingly heavy, dampening her panties with wet warmth. And she wrapped her legs around his waist to grind against his thick erection in a silent plea for him to do all of that and more.

Gyrating, he ground back against her with long, animalistic groans. 'Just…' He scraped his teeth over the throbbing vein in her neck. 'Just make me feel again, Luce. Please.'

Oh, God. *'You're about the only thing in the world I do feel…'*

The last wave of doubt drifted away as a tide of longing swept over her. To give him pleasure where she could. To take his pain away while he'd allow her to.

Cupping his jaw, she lifted his head to meet her gaze.

'I've missed you,' she whispered.

It was a shockingly dangerous thing to confess, because it left her so exposed and vulnerable. But in that moment the need for him to know how deeply she felt outweighed any sense of self-preservation she had left.

He eased back, his brow creased as he studied her face. 'Truth?'

'Absolute truth. I've missed you so much. So much I ached with it.'

Ah, Luce, you never had a hope of resisting him. Of keeping your heart locked away.

Farther back he moved, withdrawing from her, and her

stomach hollowed. Mind twisting, she wondered why he vibrated with rancour. And his touch…

He stroked up her thigh, burrowing beneath her floaty blush-pink sundress, his touch riding the line between pleasure and pain as if he were in the throes of anger. Suspecting she lied. His other hand roamed the curve of her waist, slid up to her midriff, where his thumb brushed the heavy underswell of her breast.

'You've missed me?' he said, flat and cool. 'Yet how many men have touched this body since I took it, Luciana? Since I made you mine?'

Staring into his turbulent eyes, she shook her head gently. 'Only you, Thane. There has only *ever* been you.'

Bizarre as it sounded, even to her own mind, she watched his barriers crumble and fall before her. Saw the floodgates to his emotions flung wide and time reversed. They stood still in the past. And there she was—his only focus, his entire world, the moon and the stars beyond. As if everything she'd convinced herself had been merely a dream was now a thrilling, breathtaking verity for her eyes only.

Her heart cracked wide open and she knew he could take it from where it lay, weak and defenceless outside her chest.

'Luciana, I…'

He cupped her face and she could feel his hands tremble as he rubbed his nose alongside hers, faltering, as if he feared what he truly wanted to say.

Instead he murmured against her lips, 'I…I need you.'

'Have me,' she choked out. 'Take me. However you want.'

One night was all they were likely to have and she would give him everything he desired. Everything in her power to give.

Tenderly he pressed his mouth to hers, then slanted his head and thrust his tongue into her mouth in a slow, languorous lick.

Luciana parried right back, glorying in his devout advance and retreat, the touch of his tongue against hers, as he took them both to passionate heights. And higher still into oblivion as he rucked her dress up and broke their lip-lock to tear it from her body. His hands were suddenly everywhere and nowhere. Big and clever, strong and capable hands. Leaving a trail of rapture in their wake.

She trembled all the while and let loose a pleading sob. 'Thane…I want you.'

'You have me, angel.'

'I want you naked. I want to feel you.'

He smiled wickedly as he stood tall, framed by the moonlit ripple of the ocean like a bronzed demigod. 'You always did,' he said, his voice raspy with lust.

The back of her head dug into the cushion as she craned her neck to stare up at him. Unable and unwilling to look anywhere else as inch by delectable inch his burnished skin was revealed.

Thane grabbed the hem of his T-shirt and with a sleek twist of his mighty fine torso, ripped it up and over his head.

Luciana had to slick her dry lips at the sight of his arms stretched high, thick with muscle and threaded with veins. The sculpted perfection of his ripped chest, the ridges of his twelve-pack and the sweat-slicked super-sexy V of muscle on his pelvis. The arrow that teased and tormented its way down to the thick ridge that burst past the waistband of his low-slung board shorts.

She wanted them off too.

His long fingers went to the fastening and he cocked one brow, faltering—*no*, teasing, tormenting until her heart beat in her throat, thump-thump-thumping in excitement and exhilaration. Waiting. Wanting.

He unpopped the button. Excruciatingly slow.

Her impatience spiked. Two could play at that game.

She unclipped the front of her bra, but held it closed.

He growled.

She smiled.

And then he shoved the material down his densely corded legs.

Oh, wow.

Lord, she'd forgotten how big the man was. Thane—naked in all his rock-hard, battle-honed glory, frosted by moonlight—was a mind-bending orgasmic pleasure all on its own.

'You like, angel?'

'I absolutely *love*,' she breathed. 'Far more than any angel ever should.'

His dark eyes zeroed in on the lacy confection veiling her breasts, which were rising and falling under her laboured breathing, and he dropped back to the chair and unwrapped her as if she were a precious, delectable gift, slowly tugging the lace free. Then with splayed hands he smoothed down her midriff, watching, enraptured, as her flesh shimmied and pimpled in delight.

He'd always used to look at her that way. Fascinated. Glorying in what he could do to her. Just as his restraint had always evaporated when he reached the satin that shrouded the tight curve of her femininity, sending her torn panties somewhere over his left shoulder.

'This is better,' he rasped thickly, leaning down, closing in, teasing his tongue along her bottom lip. 'Much better.'

Possessive and heated and bruising in his intensity, he ravished her mouth, her throat, winding his way down to where he moulded her breast and thumbed her tight nipple. And when his tongue glossed over the plum-coloured peak her sex clenched around thin air, desperate for him to fill the aching void she'd languished in for years.

Arousal at fever-pitch, she hooked her legs around his back and ground against the erection that lay snug over her folds, the sinuous movement pulling a deep groan from his chest and making him suck harder, drawing the tight bud into his mouth. The responding tug in her core ripped an inarticulate cry from her throat.

'Thane...'

Feverish, she felt her pulse rocketing into the stratosphere and...*heck*, she was seconds away from hyperventilating. Had to remind herself to breathe.

'Patience, Luciana,' he growled, coercing her legs wide, lifting one up and over the chair-arm, then the other, until she was splayed for his depraved enjoyment.

'I'm going to kiss you until you can't breathe,' he said as he nuzzled down her stomach, grazing her skin with a day's growth of stubble and glancing up to meet her eyes through the sable fringe of his lashes. 'Lick you everywhere. Touch you everywhere. And you, Luciana, are going to lie there and *take it*.'

Oh, *yes*.

He crawled backwards, like the sleek, rapacious predator he was, dipping his head to drop a hot, open-mouthed kiss to each of her inner thighs. Luciana moaned and lifted her arms above her head to grip the top rail of the chair. Knowing he was about to blow her sky-high. Just the sight of his dark head bent, the feel of his hot breath teasing her throbbing sex, already pushed her to the brink.

'Oh, God, Thane. Come on—do it, *please*.'

She was sure he laughed. The callous brute. Though he did make up for it by parting her and raking over her folds, lavishing her with the velvet stroke of his hot tongue. He blew against her, then lashed his tongue once more.

'You're so aroused, angel. I forgot how sweet you taste—like honey. I could eat you alive, Luciana.'

She whimpered in shameless pleasure and thrust her hips in a rhythm that matched his tongue. He found her nub unerringly, sucking it into his mouth, and the cords of erotic tension inside her pulled tighter and tighter, until she was a boneless, quivering mass of desire.

'Thane. I can't...hold...on...'

She gasped for air. Then cried out when he pushed two thick fingers deep inside her saturated channel and stroked her to a splintering crescendo so magnificent her mind blanked with sensory overload.

Every muscle in her body stiffened and seized for one, two, three beats of her heart—then she exploded. Screamed as hot, hard sexual pleasure short-circuited her every nerve, shocking her into ecstasy so powerful she levitated off the lounger…suspended on an erotic plane, eyes locked on the midnight sky, the stars glittering above her…then literally slammed back to earth.

When she roused herself from delirium he was leaning above her and her heart fisted. She adored the way his damp hair hung around his face, making him look wicked. A perfect picture of debauchery.

He licked his lips and let rip a feral growl that seemed to come from the depths of his chest. 'I'm going to take you, Luciana. Fill you up. Pour myself into you. But I'll be damned if I'll do it on a beach. I want you in my bed.'

He lifted her up effortlessly and she wrapped her legs around his waist as he strode up the deck into his bedroom, kissing her all the while, never leaving her mouth even when they tumbled onto the bed, hands everywhere as they desperately tried to touch as much of each other as they could reach.

She tore her lips from his. 'Thane, please. Don't make me wait.'

Pushing his arms beneath her shoulders, he cupped her head in his hands, pinning her completely as he trapped her in his dark hypnotic gaze. 'You're mine, Luciana. You've always been mine.'

And then he pushed inside her in one long, deliciously hard thrust.

The stupendous clash of their cries filled the air, caromed off the walls.

Lord, the relief. The screaming, delirious relief and joy and rightness. The inordinate power they created was so all-consuming she slipped into that boneless delirious state once more.

Every one of her senses was as sharp as a pin and yet the moment was dreamlike. Even the erratic rhythm of his breathing seemed in perfect tandem to the thrash of her own heart.

Thane crushed her to him, cradling her, still embedded deep, his strong, muscular body shaking, his face buried in her neck. '*Dios*, Luciana. You feel so snug. So incredible…'

As if being inside her, reuniting their exquisite connection, had doused some of the urgency, deeper emotion now flooded the space between them, and Thane lifted his head and tenderly brushed her damp hair from her face, kissed her cheeks, her nose, her brow. So lovingly, so affectionately, that her heart splintered.

Too much, Luce, this is all too much. Back off or you won't survive this. Him.

No. She couldn't let go. Not yet.

His touch sculpted her behind, hooked around her thigh and urged it to curl over his hip as his pelvis locked with hers.

'That's it, angel, now let me watch you.'

He ground against her, watching, as if taking in every nuance of her feverish response, and when he hit her sweet spot she shivered and cried out, gripping his hair. He exploited it, rolling his hips, pushing his iron-hard length deep inside her, thrusting over and over until she was mindless, begging, delirious beneath him.

'*Thane…*'

Bliss opened up before her, fathoms deep, a chasm that would take her—body and soul. For one shimmering, breathless moment she teetered on the brink…and then she was falling, falling, tumbling, crashing as she hurtled towards ecstasy.

Thane picked up the pace, slamming into her, chasing his own nirvana, until he stiffened with a guttural cry of release, pouring himself inside her, racked with convulsions that left him weak and heavy in her arms. Trembling with the aftershocks like tiny flashes of lightning as the storm dissipated. And she loved it. Revelled in his weight, in his ragged breath whispering over the sensitive skin beneath her ear, his pounding heart against hers.

When lucidity fully returned she realised silent tears were tracking down the sides of her face. She saw again the Rhine Falls of Zurich—a stoic, bittersweet witness to her fragile joy. Because it didn't matter how tightly Thane wrapped her in his arms, as if she was all he'd ever wanted. As if she truly were his angel and they basked in the heavens. Because come the dawn all hell would break loose.

Luciana wrapped herself in a robe—the black silk her only armour and sat at the base of the bed, leaning against the carved footboard, watching the morning sun dapple over the hard contours of the man who lay sleeping, naked, on his stomach.

He was a study in masculine perfection. So beautiful. His face reminded her with exquisite poignancy of Natanael. And for the first time she didn't look at him and feel fear or trepidation or anger or dismay. She looked at him with one crystal-clear thought. Or rather she allowed herself to.

This was the man who had given her the son she loved so much. This was the man who'd helped to create a miracle of joy and wonder and beauty.

This man was the father of her child. The very man she'd fallen in love with so long ago. And she could not, *would* not keep their son from that man a moment longer. No more than she could keep Thane from Natanael.

And that man would not cast her out or take Nate from her. He would protect them both always. Even through his anger and rage. And, darn it, she would be strong through this. As lion-hearted and courageous as he was.

Satin shifted across the sumptuous mattress as he stretched and smouldered in all his abeyant heat. Her gaze locked on the muscles in his back, on the flex and bunch of his ruthless power.

Luciana fisted the folds of the robe at her neck, ordering herself not to reach out. To touch. Become lost in him all over again.

He prised his eyes open and smiled sleepily at her. Lord, it *hurt.*

'Come back up here, Luce. Let me hold you.'

She inhaled a lungful of fortifying air.

Come on, you can do this.

'I…I can't, Thane. I have to go home today. I have to go back to Arunthia and I need you to take me—like you promised.'

He sat up in one lithe rippling movement, like a panther uncurling, and pushed his tousled air back from his forehead. 'No, Luciana, don't say that.' His husky, lethargic voice grew stronger, firmer. 'You belong here with me. There's no reason for you to go back.'

Luciana swallowed around the searing burn in her throat. 'But there is, Thane. Someone is there that I can't leave. *Ever.*'

His expression darkened and she felt a frisson of fear. Flinched when he suddenly ripped the sheet from his body, vaulted from the bed and shoved his legs into a pair of black silk lounge trousers.

Hands on his hips, he spun on her. 'You love this person?'

'Yes,' she said, her voice cracking under pressure. 'I love him more than life itself.'

His eyes grew furious, dark as rain-laden thunderclouds. And she knew it was only going to get worse. This, she realised, was merely the beginning. God help her.

'Who do you love?' he demanded.

You can do this, Luciana. For him—for Natanael. Thane will rip your heart from your chest but this is not about you. It is about the little boy you love and his father. You are doing it for them. They deserve this from you. Do it. Do it.

'Please don't hate me, Thane,' she whispered, begging him. 'I was only trying to do the right thing. I was scared. I only wanted him to be safe—'

His beauty took on a terrifying, dangerous edge. 'Who, Luciana?' He flung his arms wide. 'Who do you love?'

'Your son. *Our* son.'

CHAPTER TEN

THANE'S PULSE ROCKETED and the room took an untimely spin, making his breath whoosh past his lips in a sickening rush.

'You…you had my child? I have a son?'

He couldn't have heard her correctly, he assured himself. But her beautiful brandy eyes filled to the brim and one drop escaped, glistened as it fell. Shimmered over her pink-washed cheeks, along the side of her nose and down to the corner of her full mouth.

A mouth that whispered, 'Yes…'

Thane shook his head jerkily. No. He could *not* be hearing her right. He would know. If he had a son he would know. Yet her words wouldn't stop ricocheting around his mind.

'You were pregnant?'

'Yes.'

'How?' he asked stupidly, feeling adrift and as vulnerable as the boy he'd once been. Trembling inside, feeling weak. He loathed it.

Luciana blinked, her brow pinching, her voice so small she appeared just as lost as he. 'Do you mean which time? I was on contraceptives, so I don't know. There were…'

So many times? Yes, there had been.

And they had made a baby. Together. His child. His *son.*

Then—*then* it hit. Like a bullet ripping through his chest. And it tore his world apart.

He jabbed his fingers through his hair and fisted the silky

strands. 'How does no one know my son exists, Luciana? How do *I* not know my son exists?'

'I fought to have him. I went away to have him. I—'

Acid flushed through his stomach and surged up to his throat. 'Ah, so he is your dirty little secret? My son. With Galancian blue blood. The man who will take my throne. He is *your dirty little secret*?'

Affront clawed inside his chest with merciless razor-sharp talons and he slammed his hand over his bare ribs to rub, to try and ease the gashes of pain tearing through him.

With an unsteady hand she reached out imploringly. 'I made a pact to have him. To keep him. I went to Hong Kong, where we were safe…'

'Safe? You kept his identity secret to keep him safe? Safe from *who*?' he hollered.

He didn't understand this. Any of it.

A sob racked her frame and she covered her mouth with one hand, fingers quivering over her lips. Lips bruised red and swollen from his kisses.

Dios, he had just made love to a deceitful, dishonourable bitch. He had just been embedded inside a liar and a thief. The woman who had stolen his son. Who *did* such a thing?

She's an Arunthian, Thane, what did you expect?

His brain was working so fast his thoughts tripped over themselves before he could even process the last.

'No one ever asked? *Suspected*?' he asked, dark incredulity pouring from his tone.

Sitting at the base of the bed, she bent her knees and wrapped her arms around them, curling that incredible hateful body into a defensive ball.

'No. We had a nanny—Crista—who has a son of her own. Very few other staff. I wanted him to have a normal childhood. A free life without the constraints of the crown. Without being suffocated by duty—'

Thane flung his arms wide. 'Yet you take away his rights

as a born royal! Why didn't you tell me? Were you *ever* going to tell me I had a son?'

Dios, he had a son. Maybe if he kept repeating the words it would sink in.

'I tried. So many times. I wrote letters—so many. I burned them. We didn't really know each other, Thane—you didn't even know my true identity.'

With the tips of her fingers she rubbed the moisture from the tender skin beneath her eyes and took a deep breath.

'Our countries are enemies—you know this. Only yesterday you admitted you almost assassinated my father. He knew, Thane. He *knew* it was you. I was so scared. And the rumours, the horrors I'd heard of this place—they chilled me. Your childhood…' She rocked a little, as if the mere thought of his youth pained her. 'The fact that you're staunch militia…raised for war, for fighting. I couldn't bear the thought of him being raised like that. Getting hurt. I still can't.'

She looked up at him through the veil of her lashes, those huge eyes pleading. Thane had to stiffen himself against their power.

'Please try to understand. I didn't even know you and your uncle were divided. I just—'

'Stop. Just *stop*.'

He couldn't abide her voice any more. Because it was becoming increasingly clear that the person she'd been trying to protect their son from was *him*. The only woman he'd ever let past his shields, the only woman he'd wanted to live his life with, thought him so monstrous that she'd feared for their son's life. And that almost killed him right where he stood.

'I cannot bear to hear your excuses any longer. Where is he? *Where* is my son?'

'At…at home—'

He sliced her off with a razored slash of his hand through the air. 'No, Luciana. He is not at home. His home is here—with *me*.'

Unable even to look at her, he pulled on his T-shirt and

bounded out onto the deck. Oblivious to where he was going. Blind to what he was doing.

He felt vile. That ever-present blackness was rising like a demonic tide inside him, swirling like a toxic storm. He despised it. Despised *her* for causing it. Would do anything to stop feeling—*anything.* And she'd done that too. Torn down the walls that had barricaded his emotions, leaving him defenceless, only to stab him in the back.

He brought his hand up in front of his face, watched his flesh tremble and gritted his teeth as he balled it savagely until his knuckles and wrist cracked and his strength began to return. Until his heart was black and his blood ran cold. Then he spun on his heels to stride across the patio.

'Thane, *wait.* Where are you going?'

That was one thing he *did* know.

'To get my son.'

A flash of memory arrowed through his mind and he crashed to a halt. Turned with lethal calm to see her climb from the bed and stand tall on those amazing legs—such works of art. He'd had them wrapped around his waist as he'd taken her against the shower wall, not two hours ago, and it sickened him.

'The photograph I saw. Of you pushing a young boy on a swing. In a park. When you were in China. He had ebony hair just like mine…'

Dios, he'd been staring at a picture of *his own son.*

She frowned and her flawless skin went impossibly paler. 'Photograph?'

'*Si.* I pulled files on you back in Courchevel. I saw him and I didn't even think he could be mine. Didn't even *think* you would be capable of such a heinous crime.'

His tone was getting louder and louder and he couldn't seem to stop it.

'I brought you here from the Alps—where you were… what? Vacationing? Having *fun*, were you, Luciana?' He felt as if the blood rushed downwards from his head and there was a roaring in his ears. '*Dios*, no! You were with that sleazy bastard Augustus. Does *he* know about my son?'

'No—no, Thane. He doesn't know. No one does.'

'*Si*. Well, this is fortunate for you both. Still, you didn't even tell me you'd left *my son* behind in Arunthia. I brought you here and you left him there in that…that *place*.'

He was drowning in an ocean of pain. Betrayal.

'I'm sorry but, Thane, I didn't know what to expect from you. You practically abducted me in broad daylight, for heaven's sake!'

What did *that* have to do with anything? Anyway… 'It's a damn good job I did. Otherwise my child would've been lost to me for eternity. Two days you've been here. Not once did you say a word.'

'I…I'm telling you now—'

'Ah, yes. So you are. Did I pass your rigorous testing, Luciana? Am I good enough to be in my son's life now? My son… *My son!* My own flesh and blood and he doesn't even know me.' Something was tearing apart in his chest. 'Well, he will soon enough.'

'You can't go and get him. How will you get past my father? I don't want any fighting or trouble, Thane.'

He jabbed a menacing finger in her direction. 'On *your* head be it.'

With that, he surged across the limestone patio, rubbing his face with his hands.

Within seconds Luciana had gripped his arm, was pulling him round to face her.

'No, Thane. Where my son is concerned you *will* listen to me.'

There was a fierce light in her eyes. As if she had some voracious maternal instinct.

Cynicism curled his lip. This woman? Who'd denied her son his father for more than four years? Thane's father had been a brutally fierce man, but when Thane had asked for him he'd come. Just as Thane should have been given the chance to be there for his son. But, no, he'd had that opportunity *stolen* from him.

'Do you honestly want your introduction to Natanael to be throwing punches or behind prison bars? He isn't like you, Thane. He's not big and tough, resilient and strong. He's small and kind and loving and beautiful, and he's only four years old. Please. Let me go and get him. Bring him here.'

Thane wrenched his arm out of her grasp. 'Let you go and not return? Disappear off the face of the earth? With my son? *Again?* I think not, Luciana. To suggest it just shows how much of a fool you think I am.'

'Then let me ask Lucas to bring him.'

'Lucas Garcia?' he said disgustedly. 'Are you mad?'

'Natanael loves him and Claudia—they're his family. He's with them right now.'

The sharp teeth of anger bit into his heart. '*I* am his family.'

Her eyes closed momentarily. Those long lashes were coated with crystals and it vexed him that he was still noticing such things about her. Vexed him beyond belief.

'Just...please let us make this as easy on Natanael as possible. I don't want him scared. Let him come here on your turf and meet you properly. Peacefully. *Please*, Thane.'

He hauled in air, trying to think through the clattering maelstrom. The last thing he wanted to do was frighten his son; the boy didn't even know him. But he didn't trust Luciana to come back. He didn't trust her at all. Never would again.

Furious that she'd pushed him into a corner, he bit out, 'I will give Lucas Garcia three hours. Then I will go for my son myself and to hell with your father. I will get past him if I have to crush Arunthe Palace into the ground.'

She curled her quivering hand around the base of her throat. 'They'll be here.'

When she glanced up at him, with those brandy tarns full of anguish, for a moment he felt himself falling under her spell. So bewitching. Making him blind to anything but her…

Not any longer.

Thane forced himself to deflect her considerable charms. She'd lured him in for the last time.

'They'd better be here,' he incised. 'I'll never forgive you for this, Luciana. Four years I have missed of him. And if you think I am missing one more day you are grossly mistaken. When he steps foot on Galancia he is here to stay—and so are you. You will not leave here. Neither of you will. We will marry without delay and he will be acknowledged if it is the last thing I do on this earth. And *that* I promise you.'

CHAPTER ELEVEN

LUCIANA STOOD IN front of the double porcelain basin in the sumptuous marble bathroom suite and flipped on the faucet. Cupping her hands beneath the flow, she watched the icy clear liquid pool and then splashed it over her face, dabbing the tender puffy skin beneath her eyes.

Keep it together, Luce. You'll get through this.

She plucked an oyster hand-towel from the rail and patted her face dry, daring to peek at her reflection in the mirror. Lord, she still looked ghastly. And the black jeggings and white shirt she'd chosen to wear didn't help a jot. Not that she cared for her appearance—she just didn't want Lucas to latch on to her wretched state or he wouldn't leave. Didn't want Natanael to pick up on her mood either. This would be hard enough on him as it was.

Insides shaking, she gingerly walked back through to the bedroom…and, darn it, just the sight of those rumpled sheets and the lingering scent of their passion brought the wave of misery rushing back—so tall and wide it flooded over her in a great gush and she couldn't stand up in it. Couldn't even seem to breathe through it.

Crumpling to the bed, she tried her damnedest not to break. Not to splinter apart. She had to stay strong, because the next few days would be hard enough. *Days?* Try weeks. Try a lifetime.

Her conversation with Lucas played back in her mind.

'Please, Lucas, you're the only person I trust to get past

my father and do as I ask. Thane knows. If you don't bring him I don't know what he'll do.'

Already he paced like a caged animal, face dark, implacable. Cold. And if his brutal, austere demeanour wasn't enough for her to know she'd destroyed any chance of happiness between them, his words tormented her heart and soul.

'I will never forgive you for this... We will marry without delay...'

Luciana was unsure what was worse. An emotion-free marriage in which her heart was safe. Or being married to the man who'd always owned her heart and yet hated her in return. And loathe her he did. She'd never forget the look on his face. Such disappointment. Such hatred.

But Nate will have his daddy and you won't have to leave him any time, any place, anywhere. You'll spend every day with him and see him grow into a great man and that will be enough.

Of course it would be enough. It was all she'd ever wanted since the day that little stick had turned blue.

Lucas had promised to be here on the hour—though he wasn't happy about it. His tone had suggested she'd gone stark raving mad. But luckily Claudia had smoothed the way. Thanks heavens for Claudia and her huge heart and quick mind.

Breathe, she told herself. In and out, slow and even as she made her way up four flights of stairs to the vestibule.

The future was staggeringly vague—and wasn't that the story of her life? No idea what tomorrow would bring, how they'd live in this strange place where they didn't know a soul. She was asking herself how they would fit in, how she'd explain to her father that she wasn't taking her crown, how her own people would react on discovering they'd no longer have a new queen in the spring.

Thane had said she'd never leave, but that had to be his anger talking—he couldn't possibly be serious. She'd have to go home before they wed…give a speech renouncing her birthright. Then enter a marriage she couldn't bear to contemplate. And, *wow*, that seemed to be happening a lot lately.

All of it was churning in a relentless, nauseating roll. Until she felt insecure. Vulnerable. Defenceless. And by the time she stepped beneath the overhang of the palatial entryway, restless angst clutched her midsection, making her bow forward so hard she faked tying the satin bows on her pumps to cover it up.

Come on, Luce, you can do this. It's just like being at home, right? Serene smiles. Cool façade. Think...poise and grace. By Christmas you'll be a carbon copy of the ice queen that is your mother and in a barren, loveless marriage.

Oh, God.

Luciana pinned her spine straight and stood on the top step, squinting at the black dot swelling beneath the sun. Plagued by the need for someone to take her hand, tell her everything would be okay.

No, not someone. Not just anyone.

Chancing a look at Thane, she sneaked a peek towards the base of the stairs where he stood—separated from her by metres that felt more like a vast yawning chasm she had no clue how to fill.

As if he could feel her eyes on him Thane turned his head to catch her stare. His dark eyes were stormy and full of condemnation as they snared hers in an unbreakable glare.

She wanted to battle it out with him, make him see her side of things, but this wasn't the time or place. And deep down she knew he'd never look at her in any other way. Certainly not the way he had last night. With need and adoration and respect. Something close to joy.

Luciana sank her teeth into her bottom lip, unable to sever the dark, hypnotic pull, and for a second—when the faintest crease lined his brow—she imagined those beautiful obsidian eyes shimmered with striations of golden warmth.

Hope spun its crazy web inside her…

Then, with a curl of distaste at his mouth, he tore his

gaze from hers. And that web disintegrated into the pit of her stomach.

Deafening, the whoop-whoop of the helicopter grew louder and louder. Her hair whipped around her face and she focused on the only thing that truly mattered.

The colossal machine lowered into a lethal squat on the landing pad in the centre of Thane's huge circular driveway. And the need to run to Natanael—see him, hold him, touch him—had her bolting forward and hurtling down the steps.

At the bottom, Thane snagged her arm to pull her back.

'Wait,' he ordered fiercely.

'Let go of me, Thane.' She felt as if she was hanging by the slenderest of threads over a vast, dark churning abyss and at any moment now the line would snap.

'It is too dangerous—wait a moment.'

He stood with rigid tense-jawed focus, but when the black door swung wide, and Natanael emerged, for a split second he looked as if he'd seen a ghost.

Nathanael careened towards her at a speed of knots. And though he swam in her vision she could still see those gorgeous dimples in his smooth caramel cheeks, those deep expressive eyes so much like his father's.

His father—whose entire body had gone rigid, as though he was desperately fighting to maintain control.

Luciana threw hers to the winds and ran.

Thane had a curious feeling in his chest—as if someone had reached in and taken hold of his heart.

It was like looking at himself. Turning back the clock and gazing in the mirror to see himself as a small boy. And at that moment Thane vowed to do everything in his power to ensure his son would not suffer hurt or cry in pain. He swore it. Swore to move heaven and earth to prevent any of it.

He'd always been adroit at killing his emotions—with the exception of those evoked by Luciana—but he'd never felt anything close to this. Emotions…so many emotions flooding over him. All-powerful. All-consuming.

Natanael—meaning 'God has given'. He tried it out on his tongue for the first time, because maybe he hadn't truly believed it until now, and acknowledged how good it felt—how right.

Thane's fingers burned with the need to touch all that smooth skin, his silky hair—ebony, like Thane's own. But he didn't want to frighten him. The scars on his face were enough to scare anyone, let alone a child.

So instead he ground his feet into the gravel and soaked up every nuance as his son shouted in utter joy, with the biggest smile Thane had ever seen, when he spotted Luciana.

'Mamá!'

Luciana lowered herself into an elegant crouch to catch him and ended up on her bottom in the dirt, not caring about it one iota, hugging him with a glorious smile of her own, smoothing the thick glossy waves of his hair, kissing his brow, his soft cheek.

Never had he seen anything like it. Or maybe he had. Maybe the sight before him resurrected memories he'd rather keep buried six feet under.

Dios, his chest was imploding.

A sweet strum of a giggle flew past Natanael's perfect lips and Thane wondered what she was doing to make him laugh. Saw her fingers tickling his sides, realised he must like that, even though he was yelling, 'Stop! Stop!' And then she was wrapping him in her arms again, kissing him and touching him. All over.

And in that moment there was something so profoundly, exquisitely beautiful about her he felt the strangest sensation in his throat, behind his eyes. Like tiny hot needles pricking.

'Did you see? I was in the big black 'copter, Mamá!'

'I know, darling, and I'm so glad because it brought you to me.'

Darling. The endearment fisted Thane's heart.

'I've missed you so much. My goodness—I swear you've grown an inch.'

Natanael gazed up at her with a fierce male pride that punched Thane in the gut. He was a Guerrero through and through.

When his little mouth geared up for the next zealous outpouring, he stalled—his attention seemingly snagged on Thane.

His insides turned over and he wondered if this was what it felt like to be nervous.

Natanael gaped at him with steady unblinking eyes, scrutinising the scar on his chin as if he couldn't quite believe what he was seeing. Then he looked up at Luciana, and then back to Thane, his tiny mind processing.

It was utterly fascinating, Thane decided. And—for want of a better word—nerve-racking. *Dios*, he felt ill.

Then, as if Natanael had finally accepted Thane was real, he exclaimed, 'Wow! He looks like me. But a whole lot bigger. Do you fly?'

Huh?

'*Si*...actually, I do. I am a pilot and I have my own fighter jet.'

'I knew it,' said Natanael, unequivocally awed. 'You're one of the New Warriors. Did you just come down from InterGalactica?'

Thane blinked. 'Is this in Europe?'

'No, silly. It's in outer space.' With a smile and a nod he gave Thane a knowing look. Then he tried for a wink that scrunched up his entire face as he whispered, conspirator-like, 'You *know* it is.'

Luciana lightly cleared her throat. 'He's into...er...superheroes. Like Batman and Ironman...that kind of thing. And one of them looks uncannily like you. And him too.'

Thane supposed he could live with that. Although what would happen when Natanael asked him to actually fly? He was far too small to go in his military jet.

He hunkered down until they were at eye level and commanded himself to relax, to think of something to say.

'Actually, I *am* a warrior of a kind. I'm the Prince of Galancia and I live here, and I was hoping you would come and live with me too.'

It occurred to him that they'd have to have the 'I'm your daddy' conversation—but, frankly, that petrified him. Plus, he wasn't keen on Garcia being within hearing distance for that. Right now all he wanted was for his son to agree to stay.

Natanael huddled into Luciana, a spark of panic blanching his beautiful face, and Thane realised a second too late his mistake.

'Mamá too?'

He cursed inwardly. Of course he would panic. The love he could feel between them was palpable. 'Yes. Of course. Absolutely. Mamá too.'

Luciana nodded and achieved the perfect smile—though to Thane it verged on brittle, and made him ache even more.

Natanael peered around him, unconvinced. His nose was scrunched, as if he wasn't overly impressed with the tree-lined driveway or the kaleidoscope of manicured blooms flourishing in the borders. Granted, the mansion looked like a one-storey cottage from the top of the cliff. The towering five-floor vista from the beach was far more dramatic and arresting. Though perhaps not for a child.

Thane scratched his jaw. Stumped. Then intuitively he glanced at Luciana. Who, in turn, mouthed a word at him.

He frowned, striving to catch her meaning. What the hell was she saying? 'Dog?' he asked.

'Dog?' Natanael said, perking up. 'You have a dog? *Really*?'

Ah. This, Thane realised, was of great importance. '*Si*. Lots of dogs. And horses too.'

'You have horses?' Dark eyes, the precise shade of Thane's own, grew huge and glittery with excitement.

He didn't seem afraid, so hesitantly Thane reached out

and touched the soft caramel skin of his cheek. The astonishing surge of connection rocked him to the core. Phenomenal. His little boy was the most miraculous thing he'd ever touched. Just like his mother, Thane thought, with a wrenching tug on his guts.

'Many, many horses. You can have your very own. But they don't live here… Yet,' he added hastily, thinking he could easily build a stable for a few. Dozen.

Natanael jumped up and down on the spot. 'I can have my own *horse*, Mamá! Can we go and see the dogs? Right now? Can we? *Can we?*'

Relief poured down Thane's spine. Victory. This was good. He could kiss Luciana for that dog hint. Though he quickly squashed the impulse.

'I think so. Thane, are they downstairs?'

As if she'd experienced the same kind of bone-melting sense of appeasement he just had, she made a clumsy effort at rising to her feet and Thane bolted forward, curled his fingers around her tight waist and lifted her upright.

Surprise widened her eyes. 'Oh. Thank you,' she whispered.

And when he saw her perfect white teeth bite into her bruised red bottom lip a surge of heat spiked his pulse. One he couldn't understand. Didn't want to feel.

Jerking his hands away, he stepped backwards and cleared his throat. 'Pietro will let them out. When I've had a word with Garcia I'll join you.'

With a strained smile she nodded, and glanced at Lucas Garcia herself.

Thane wasn't sure what he'd expected, but it was certainly not her embracing him like some long lost lover. He had to clench his fists to stop from tearing her off him.

'Thank you so much, Lucas,' she said softly, shakily. 'For everything.'

Garcia pulled back and shot her a meaningful look that

pricked Thane's nerves. 'Remember what I said, Luciana. Any time, night or day.'

Another of those frangible smiles, but she brightened it for Natanael and took his small hand in hers—as if she was physically unable to stop touching him. Thane felt an absurd pang of envy that filled him with self-disgust. Surely it wasn't healthy or natural to feel envious of his son? *Dios*, he truly was black inside.

Those clasped hands swayed back and forth as they waltzed into the house, then he turned back to Garcia.

Voice stony, he bit out, 'She will not be contacting you. Everything she needs is right here.'

As if in a standoff, they weighed one another up. One soldier to another.

Garcia's midnight-blue gaze hardened. 'You hurt either of them and I will come for you.'

Thane almost laughed. Almost. Instead he sneered at the other man. 'If you had any sense, Garcia, you'd never set foot on my island again. I've allowed you into restricted airspace to bring my son to me. Next time it will be denied.'

'Do you think that will stop me? I'll be honest, here—I'm not getting a very good vibe between you and Luciana, so I'm not entirely convinced that leaving them here is the right choice.'

'I care very little for what you think. My relationship with Luciana is none of your business.'

'*That* is where you are wrong. She is family, and I will not have her here against her wishes. Are you understanding me?'

Thane's mouth shaped to tell him she was emphatically *not* here against her wishes, but then he realised he'd given her little choice. *Dios*, he'd been so angry. Still was. Couldn't remember half of what he'd said to her.

Whether or not Garcia picked up on his inner turmoil Thane wasn't sure, but he abruptly let loose a sigh that marginally shrank his impressive shoulders.

'Look, I understand this must be a shock—difficult for you.'

Thane wanted to ask him how the hell *he* would know how it felt, but then he remembered the man had just had a child of his own.

'But know this: she has not had one moment of peace in the last five years. Knowing you were out there has tormented her. There is a reason they say ignorance is bliss. She's had to live with her decision for years. Do not forget we have been enemies for a long time, Guerrero. She begged. She bartered. She made a pact. Just to bring Natanael into the world. I know she wanted your son more than anything in this life.'

Begged? Bartered? Meaning Henri had wanted her to destroy their son? For the umpteenth time in history Thane wished he'd pulled that trigger. Vibrated with the urge to rain a hellish firestorm on the man's head. Crush him beneath his almighty foot.

Of one thing he was certain. He would do everything in his vast power to ensure Henri Verbault was erased permanently from his wife's life. And his son's too. Their relationship was officially at an end.

Dios, he was so vexed his insides shook. In fact blistering fury was all he could feel in every molecule of his body as it ran like red-hot lava through his veins. Anger towards every person who'd kept him from his son. He wanted to punish them all.

And that still included Luciana. Because she should have come to him five years ago. He would have protected her from the start.

Thane crossed his lethal arms over his wide chest. 'You love your daughter, don't you? How would you feel if she'd been kept from you for the first four years of her life?'

His voice was iron-hard but he was genuinely interested to hear this answer. What would a normal person feel right now? Should his insides be so black with hatred? Or was he truly twisted with darkness inside?

But then Garcia had to shock him by being brutally frank.

'Not just angry. Furious. Cheated. Betrayed. All of the things you are doubtless feeling. But if I looked at the bigger picture I would see that above all else Luciana put her son—*your* son—first, believing he was unsafe. I have no idea how much of your reputation is true, but one fifth of it would be enough to persuade me. She protected him as any mother would. And I could not hate her or blame her for that.'

On that note, he spun on his heels and strode back to the helicopter.

Thane watched the blades whip into a frenzy, slicing through the air. The vociferous clamour lent him a moment of mental peace. A chance to breathe without it physically hurting.

'I only wanted to keep him safe... We're enemies... I was scared...'

Then the sonorous roar receded and it all came rushing back in one titanic tsunami of agony—and he turned and ploughed his fist into the stone wall.

Dressed in Hawaiian-style shorts and a funky matching T-shirt, Natanael was a red blur, sprinting along the shoreline, dragging a long stick that drew a wavy line in the damp sand, while those great lumbering dogs pranced around him. Her little boy in seventh heaven was a glorious sight to see.

Slanting another glance over her right shoulder, she kept watch for Thane. The helicopter had soared into the sky over an hour ago and she felt flimsy and tenuous—like a kite that would blow away with one gust of wind.

Sloshing through the shallow waters, she slowed her step, 'Hey, Nate? Shall we build a sandcastle and wait for Thane?'

'Sure, Mamá.'

Together they scooped sand into a mound, and Luciana watched those sweet little hands pat-pat-pat their creation into shape. This was good. She had to keep busy. Too much time to think and regret and fret would drive her loopy.

'May I join in?'

She flinched at Thane's low, masculine tone and rocked back on her knees to peek up at him.

'Of course,' she said, her stomach hollowing at the pain that darkened his eyes. At the way he shunted frustrated fingers through the swarthy mess of his hair.

When his hands plunged to his sides her gaze snagged on his raw swollen knuckles and air hit the back of her throat.

'Thane?'

Lord, had he hit Lucas? Reaching up, she dusted over his torn skin.

'Did you fight?' she whispered.

'No.'

He snatched his hand away and she curled her fingers in her lap. He'd closed himself off to her. Emotionally. Physically.

Natanael—oblivious to it all—said, 'Sure, you can help. You can build the moat of the castle if you want. That's a *biiig* job.'

'I think you're right,' Thane said easily, sinking to his knees. 'Where do you think I should put it?'

'Right there.'

Nate pointed to a slope that was close to him, Luciana noticed. As if he wanted Thane closer, in his space.

That was a big enough clue for her and she shuffled backwards, giving them some room, some time together, while her heart lodged itself in her throat. It was like watching a fantasy she'd replayed in her mind, but reality was even more incredibly beautiful.

'Is your name really Thane? Like the warrior?'

Those broad shoulders seized up. 'Yes. But…'

Dark turbulent eyes darted her way in a silent plea that said he didn't want Natanael to call him Thane. Of course he didn't.

'Do you want to tell him now?' she whispered.

Incredible as it was, he blanched—as if drowning in pure fear. Almost as if he expected a rejection.

She couldn't abide it. This was her doing and she didn't want him hurting any more than he already was.

'Nate…' she began. 'You know how Auntie Claudia is Isabelle's *mamá* and Uncle Lucas is his *papá*?'

'Mmm-hmm.'

'Well…' She licked lips salty from the sea breeze. 'Thane is…your daddy. He's your papá.'

His dark head jerked up. *'Really?'*

'Yes.'

A huge smile stretched his face as he looked at Thane, then back to her. 'Oh, *wow*—my daddy is a New Warrior.'

'He is,' Luciana agreed, fighting tears. 'He saved me once. Many years ago.' Her throat felt thick, and it burned as if aflame. Stung so badly her words came out on a choked whisper. 'He's a real superhero.'

She could feel Thane's eyes searing into her cheek, but before either of them could exchange a glance or say a word Nate launched himself at Thane like a cannonball, almost knocking him over.

Luciana watched those big, strong, protective arms curl around their son, wrapping him in instantaneous instinctual love. And knew, no matter what the future held, she'd done the right thing.

So while she kissed goodbye to any chance of a loving marriage those glorious sounds of male bonding were sure to keep her warm at night. And as Nate tugged on Thane's hand, to coerce him down to the water's edge, half of her felt as if she'd lost her little boy. The other half reasoned that there had merely been a part of her son that was never hers to begin with. That part was solely for his daddy.

As for her and Thane… Some things were meant to be. And some things were not.

CHAPTER TWELVE

HIS SON NEVER stopped talking, Thane realised, not even to take a breath. And within three days he had the entire household wrapped around his tiny butterscotch pinkie finger.

He said, 'Christmas tree!' and Pietro was lugging ten-feet-tall firs into the main lounge, trailing dirt across the antique Persian rugs. The biggest monstrosity Thane had clapped eyes on was deftly smothered with garish ornaments and enough twinkling lights to illuminate the Taj Mahal.

To say Thane didn't 'do' Christmas was the understatement of the millennia, since it ordinarily tainted his mind with an abundance of achingly dark memories. But he couldn't seem to say no to Nate any more than anyone else could.

Luciana included.

Which was how now, fresh from his shower and dressed to kill in sharp business attire at the ridiculous hour of seven in the evening, he'd known where to find them. Known she'd be clearing the debris in the kitchen after baking Nate his favourite white chocolate cookies for supper while he happily munched and drank his milky way into bed.

Pandering to his every whim. As if she yearned to be needed. As if she had to keep busy or she'd shatter to smithereens. Not that her outward regal poise had faltered, but he didn't trust that cool façade of hers. It wasn't the real Luciana and it set his teeth on edge. Though he only had himself to blame. By creating this ever-widening gulf between them.

But, *Dios*, he'd felt so volatile after her revelation. Drowning in emotions he was ill-equipped to handle. So angry. Betrayed and devastated. So black inside he'd been petrified to go anywhere near her. Unsure whether he wanted to yell and vent or bury his pain inside her. Beg her to touch him, make him forget—which felt tantamount to an insult to his pride. So conflicted. Torn. His usual ruthless decisiveness obliterated until he felt weak. Less of a man. At the whim of dangerous emotions that no hardened commanding warrior should feel.

Every day he waged an internal war. Knowing that in many ways her arguments held weight. They'd been enemies for centuries. He *had* almost assassinated her father. And for the last three nights he'd been engaged in political warfare with his uncle, who was going to extreme lengths to keep Thane from his throne. Instigating trouble left and right. Leaving Thane uneasy, in no doubt that he needed to get Luciana down the aisle—preferably yesterday. Needed to claim his heir before Christmas. Ensure his absolute safety.

And if this was the way she'd felt years ago—afraid, panicked, verging on desperate to shield their son—Thane would have to be made out of stone not to understand her predicament. His uncle's reputation wasn't founded on fresh air, and nor was Thane's. He was lethal even in his sleep. So, prevaricating aside, could he honestly blame her or hate her for doing what any mother would? *No.*

But all the reasoning in the world wasn't eradicating the ache. Or helping him forget that he'd missed four years of his son. Lost the sound of his cry when he came into the world. Had Nate's first word robbed from his ears. Missed the amazing sight of his first step. And the thought that he couldn't get any of that back drenched his heart in sorrow. Coated his mind with resentment and fury.

It was taking everything he had to switch off, just so he could function like a rational member of society, wrestle for control where he could and pave the way for their future.

Leaning against the kitchen doorframe, he crossed his arms over his chest and did a swift recon of his flour-bombed kitchen. Only to be hit with bone-deep longing, wishing he was a part of the warmth that pervaded the room. But, no matter how much time he spent with Nate, at times like this he felt like an outsider looking in. Unable to breach the dense walls of their love. As if they were the family and he the dark intruder who didn't belong. Unworthy as he was. And envy was so thick and poignant it pervaded his chest, making it hard to breathe.

Then one look at Luciana and he was back to battling in the internal war. Distrusting her. Still wanting her.

Wrapped in a long, thick wheat-coloured cardigan, chocolate-brown leggings and socks that scrunched around her ankles, she looked so young, so adorable. So hatefully sexy. All that lavish honeycomb hair was pinned in a messy knot atop her head, the odd stray tendril curling, caressing her cheek, and when she lifted one hand to brush it away with her wrist she left a smear of creamy buttery sugar streaking her flawless skin.

He wanted to lick it off. Taste the honeyed sweetness of her skin. Let it saturate his tongue.

Damn him to Hades for allowing her to beguile him.

Nate's voice yanked Thane from his turmoil and he watched him swipe at his milk moustache with his Batman pyjama sleeve.

'Eight sleeps until Christmas, Mamá. What would you like from Santa?'

Luciana plopped down into the seat beside him and dabbed his mouth with a tissue. 'I want you to be happy. Are you happy here?'

So loving she was with him. Selfless. Protective. So much like his mother. And Thane realised then that never had he thought so much of his childhood since Luciana had stormed back into his life. Something else to mess with his head, shove him to the edge of sanity.

'Yep. I like living on the beach, and my new dogs, and my new daddy, and my room isn't great…it's *awesome*.'

That would be the room that now resembled outer space, with a galaxy of stars painted across the ceiling that shone in the dark.

'You won't fit into my new spaceship bed tonight, Mamá, so will you sleep with Daddy, like Auntie Claudia with Uncle Lucas?'

Luciana closed her eyes for a beat. 'Er…no, I don't think so, darling. Maybe I'll sleep in the suite next to yours, in case you need me.'

Aversion constricted his throat. Was that how it would be between them? Separate suites? Strangers who shared a house? A son? The thought made him cold to his bones.

'I'm a big boy now,' said Nate, all Guerrero fierce pride. 'You can go further down the hall with Daddy.'

Thane couldn't think of anything worse. Luciana lying beside him in that slippery, silky, lacy black camisole and shorts, that vanilla and jasmine scent taunting his senses. So close yet unable to touch. Bad, *bad* idea. He didn't trust himself not to reach for her when his defences were low. When his anger was asleep. When he craved oblivion from the pain.

Frankly, she didn't deserve to be used in such a way. Since he doubted she still shared their fatal attraction. Since she'd moved in with Nate and shrank from him the odd time he accidentally touched her. As if he were some dangerous predator who would maul her at any moment. And he could hardly blame her for that since it was exactly how he felt. Toxic. Lethal.

Luciana, who was clearly reading from the same map, said vaguely, 'We'll see.'

Nate gave an immense cat-like yawn, hair flopping over his brow, and Luciana stroked the ebony tufts back and smiled indulgently. 'Come on, sleepy-head. Time for bed.'

Heavy eyes blinked up at her. 'Can I have a carry?'

Thane pushed himself off the doorframe. 'I believe that is my job.'

Luciana glanced up and for a split second he was sure he saw pleasure light a fire in her brandy eyes, but then she trailed that gaze down over his attire and the flames flickered and died. He took a scissor-kick in his stomach and when he drew up close suffered another swift jab. She looked like an exhausted Botticelli angel—the violet smudges beneath her eyes a vivid contrast against her unusually pale skin.

And right then he realised they couldn't go on like this much longer. While he'd never wholly trust her again, completely forgive and forget, he had to try and move on—for all their sakes. He just wasn't sure where to start.

Nate found a burst of energy to bounce in his chair and raise his arms. 'Daddy! Will you give me a carry downstairs?'

'I certainly will.'

Down they went, Thane stealing a hug on the way, inhaling that glorious warm bathtime scent, loving those fragile arms wrapped around his shoulders trustingly, giving him a 'squeezy cuddle' right back. He'd been initiated into the realms of squeezy cuddles yesterday, and found they were strangely addictive displays of affection.

Luciana pulled back the star-encrusted navy bedcovers and Thane eased him down and kissed his brow, stroked the back of his finger down that cherubic cheek. 'Sleep well.'

'You too, Daddy.'

He walked to the door as Luciana fussed.

'Love you, tiger,' she said.

Nate mumbled sleepily, 'Love you too, Mamá.'

Thane leaned against the hallway wall outside his room, telling himself to leave now. Avoid confrontation. Any kind of temptation.

His traitorous feet didn't like that idea—suddenly had

a mind of their own, wanted to be with the woman that haunted his body and his mind.

Luciana pulled thc door closed and warily met his gaze. *Dios*, she was so beautiful. Made his heart ache. And he couldn't fathom that any more than he could understand anything else he was feeling.

Nate's words from earlier penetrated his brain, and before he knew it he said, 'He expects to see a marriage like your sister's.'

Her eyes drifted downwards to where she scuffed the parquet with the toe of her fluffy sock.

'He does. But all marriages and families are different. He'll learn that too.' Her husky voice teemed with yearning. 'Claudia's marriage is…unique, I suppose. They love each other intensely. Talk constantly. Wouldn't dream of being in separate beds. They married for love, not because of duty or a child. Ours won't be that kind of marriage.'

He knew that, so why a dagger lanced through his heart was a mystery.

'I suppose ours will be more like my parents'. They always had separate beds. It didn't affect me…'

A small furrow lined her brow as she nibbled on the pad of her thumb.

He didn't believe her. Not one iota. Began to wonder if the revered Verbault union was more myth than fact and had affected her in ways he couldn't see. Throw in the longing in her voice and he was more certain than ever that their marriage would be a far cry from what she truly coveted. Which was why he didn't trust her not to run again.

'Where did you sleep last night, Thane?'

Wrapping her arms around her gorgeous curves, she frisked her gaze down his midnight Italian suit, his ice-blue shirt, and he'd swear a shiver rustled over her skin.

'Are you going there again?'

'*Si*. Galancia Castle,' he said easily, unsure why that

would sadden her, or wreak the anxiety he could see clouding her brandy gaze.

He had to grind his jaw to stifle the explanation hovering on his tongue. He didn't want her knowing there was trouble afoot. Didn't want her worrying for their safety. He'd prove to her he could protect them if it was the last thing he did. She hadn't believed in him five years ago, so this time he'd move the planets out of alignment to ensure she did. And if that meant he was running on two hours of sleep, constantly looking over his shoulder in the hellhole that was his birthplace, so be it.

'Guards will be posted here, upstairs and down.'

'All right,' she said, her body deflating as she gazed down the hallway and out of the west-facing double doors, towards Arunthia, in a way that dropped an armoured tank on his chest.

Heart-wrenchingly familiar, it said she wanted to be a million miles away from here. From *him*. It said she wanted to be with her family, with people who truly loved her. Not a black hearted prince. It was a look he remembered well. The look of a woman imprisoned.

Dios, he couldn't bear it. Didn't know how to get rid of it. He'd never been able to with his mother, had he?

He pushed off the wall. Hardened his body into the emotionless indestructible weapon it had been honed to be. Focused on what he could control with some semblance of rationality.

'Nate has asked to see Santa Claus and the Christmas fête is in Hourana this weekend. I was thinking we could all go as a family. For Nate.'

He knew that would sway her so he used it abominably. But they had to go out and paint a united front. Play happy families. Deflect his uncle's attempts at undermining him. Word of his impending marriage had spread like wildfire and his people were in a celebratory mood. It was the perfect time to introduce them.

'For Nate. Right.'

She gave him a short nod and forced one of those serene smiles that sparked his temper. Made him want to shake it out of her.

'I'm sure he'd enjoy that.'

Another victory. But no relief in sight. 'Good. I'll see you in the morning.'

He stepped towards the staircase, stopping when her fingers tentatively touched his sleeve, sending a fresh arrow of heat through his veins.

'Thane? Please wait. Don't go yet. We need to talk. About when I can go back to Arunthia.'

Never.

'I need to leave now. Maybe we'll talk tomorrow.'

A soft sigh slipped past her lips. 'I can't marry you without tying up my life at home. I have my own responsibilities. And you said we'd talk about it yesterday, when you dropped the "we're getting married on Christmas Eve" bomb on me. As you were walking out of the door, I hasten to add.'

That spark of temper ignited in the pit of his stomach and raged through his body, firing his voice to a blazing pitch. '*Si*, well, you owe me four years, so I'm damn sure you can wait another day.'

Guilt thrashed him and he instantly wanted the words back. He was unsure why he'd said them with such a vicious lash of his tongue. Maybe because she'd called Arunthia home. Maybe because he knew she didn't want to marry him, only wanted to leave, no matter what excuse she gave herself. Henri was quite capable of tying up her life. She wanted her freedom. Something he could not, *would* not give her. His son was here to stay.

Moreover, the date was set, their marriage arranged. She would become his wife in less than a week. And if the thought that they had to perform for the crowds tomorrow wasn't enough to convince him to tame his tongue and start building bridges, the way she flinched as hurt darkened her beautiful eyes certainly was.

Luciana knew regret when she saw it. Though it still failed to lessen the strike of his words—each one like a knife-blow to her chest.

At the searing impact, his deep pained frown vanished behind her eyelids and the sound of his retreating footsteps gave way to the forlorn thunder of her heart.

Three days of this and she was ready to crack. Living on a knife-edge while a red river screamed through her blood, chanting for her to escape. Sleep was a fool's dream. One day blurred into the next. And stone-cold silences caromed off the oppressive walls until she felt a relentless ache of loneliness that refused to abate.

The only thing keeping her standing—Nate.

Luckily enough she knew the drill. Had seen it all before. And so, with the asset of royal breeding, she kept her head high and smiled on demand. Her mother would be so proud.

Why was he avoiding the subject of her going home? There was no way she could marry him without renouncing her throne. How would *that* look to her people? What was more, she at least wanted her sister at her wedding—but had he asked her who she would like there? No. She'd just been told when and where. Truth was, she couldn't understand the hurry. Why not springtime?

Ah, come off it, Luce, you're petrified. Scared stiff of committing to a loveless marriage. Where you'll be eternally powerless. Trapped by invisible shackles. His mistresses secreted behind closed doors...

Slumping against the wall, she slid to her bottom, bending her knees to hug them to her chest.

Stop. Just stop jumping to conclusions. Stop with the portentous predictions.

Problem was, three days of silence had slowly turned her mind inside out—and with it came unadulterated panic exacerbated by Thane's sporadic vanishing acts. Every day he spent with Natanael, every evening he disappeared until dawn, leaving her with enough bodyguards to secure Fort Knox. His cousin Seve being one of them.

Could the man scream, *I don't trust you not to steal my son* any louder?

She felt like a captive, with no way to escape. And, since he couldn't seem to tolerate the sight of her, was he getting comfort from elsewhere now? Was that where he was? Did she have the right to know who he was sleeping with?

Her mother would say not.

She'd always divined that her mother truly loved her father but it was disastrously one-sided. Luciana could have only been twelve or thirteen when she'd spied one of her father's mistresses slipping down the hall, seen her mother's tear-tracks when Luciana had sneaked in her bedroom to ask about her.

'We don't talk about such things. Go back to bed, Luciana.'

Considering how cold Luciana had felt in the last few days, Marysse Verbault deserved a gold medal for that cool façade she'd perfected. Imprisoned by duty. Funny thing was, Luciana could have put up with all of that from Augustus. But the thought of Thane being in another woman's bed…

Squeezing her eyes shut, she dropped her head to her knees and forced air into her lungs, past the heavy, tumultuous maelstrom that swirled like a thick brume. Tried to cling on to the rapidly fraying threads of hope that he'd come round. That they could somehow find each other again.

She shoved desperate thoughts into her brain to keep faith afloat. Telling herself he'd brought her here for a reason. That she was the only person he could feel. That the fact he wanted them to go out tomorrow as a family meant there was light at the end of the tunnel.

If only she could believe it.

CHAPTER THIRTEEN

WHETHER IT HAD been her midnight sniffle-fest to Claudia—who'd told her to stop being such a darn pessimist, painting her future blue when it was only early days, which Luciana conceded was a fair point—or whether it was Nate's hyper-chatty mood as they clambered out of the luxurious bulletproof Range Rover to behold an authentic winter wonderland, she wasn't sure. But for the first time in days her spirits had lifted and she was determined to make the most of their first family affair. To think positive *unpessimistic* thoughts and refrain from pondering on why Thane looked exhausted. What *exactly* he'd been doing all night.

No, she wasn't torturing herself with any of that. Nor was she allowing his invisible power storm to buffet her like a ship in a restless sea. And that ominous slinky dread coiling in the pit of her stomach, warning her that trouble was coming…? Not listening. Not today. Today she was channelling her inner cheeriness—Nate deserved nothing less.

The rich nutmeg and cinnamon scent of gingerbread wafted over her, courtesy of the warm breeze, and she inhaled deeply. 'Wow, that smell is amazing. It's the strangest thing—to be looking at Santa's grotto, surrounded by reindeer and heaps of snow, in twenty degrees—but I've got to admit what they've achieved is fantastic. It's Lapland!'

Slamming car doors, Thane murmured, 'It is…' in that distracted manner he'd worn for days, as if his mind was in constant turmoil.

Guilt and unease weaved in and around her ribcage, and for the thousandth time she wished he would speak to her. Let her past those impermeable steel barricades he'd erected so they could work through this.

'Would you like your bag?' he asked, his voice making a sudden shift to that deep drawl she loved so much, as if he'd just found something amusing. 'You have a tendency to leave them in vehicles and make me fetch them.'

The return of his humour—however slight—was so shocking, so wonderful, she smiled up at him, squinting against the burnt orange and red haze of the lowering sun. 'Yes, please. I would. And, just think…you don't have to send someone to France this time.'

'What a relief,' he said sardonically, even as he frowned. As if he was just as surprised at his quip as she was.

Her heart was buoyed up a little more and she wondered if their moods rubbed off on each other. Vowed to be extra chipper, just in case.

'Oh, actually,' she said, 'I think I'll leave my coat in there. I can't believe how warm it is.'

With a roll of her shoulders she shrugged off her long cream jacket and pushed it into Thane's waiting hand. When that hand didn't move a muscle she glanced up and caught his heated stare—which doused her in his particular brand of fire.

Another return. The first time in days that he'd paid her the slightest attention. And as that searing gaze trailed down her body, from the V-neck of her coffee and cream polka dot dress to her cinched waist, all the way down to the flared kick of the skirt, where the fabric kissed her skin just a peep above her knees, her heart floated higher still and beat an excitable thrum in her throat.

He lingered on her bare calves until she felt positively dizzy.

'You look…stunning, Luciana. Truly beautiful.'

That voice was husky. Intimate. All *Thane.* And wanton

heat surged upwards into her cheeks as her stomach imploded with shameful want.

She dug her cream kitten heels into the asphalt to curb her squirm. 'Thank you. You don't look too bad yourself.'

Understatement. Right there.

Suave and sinfully hot, that commanding body was sheathed in one of his *de rigueur* custom-made Italian suits. The biscuit hue was striking against his olive skin as was the torso-hugging crisp, white open-collared shirt he wore beneath. In short, he oozed gravitas from his every debauched pore, and the brooding expression on his face made him look as dangerous and piratical as ever.

Those dark eyes fixed on her mouth as she slicked her glossy lips with a flick of her tongue. 'Luciana…' he murmured. 'I…'

And when they flicked back up to meet hers a meteor shower of dazzling sensation exploded inside her pelvis.

Oh, Lord, he still wanted her. She knew it. Also knew he was fighting it. Fighting it with all his might. As if his anger lingered and he wanted to hate her but couldn't persuade his body to obey.

'You were going to say…?' she prompted.

His throat undulated on a hard swallow. 'Only that I'd like us to try and be a family today.'

She wanted to ask why. For whose benefit. But caught herself in the nick of time, annoyed at her suspicious mind. Who cared why? He wanted to try and that was okay with her. An enormous step in the right direction.

'I would too,' she said softly. 'And maybe later we could talk?'

The sooner they discussed her going home and their marriage the better for all of them. They couldn't go on like this.

Thane gave her an enigmatic smile that failed miserably to instil her with any kind of confidence. But before she could pin him down Nate burst between them, bouncing on his loafered feet like a coiled spring.

'There's Santa's house! And look over there! A big sleigh! Can we ride in it? *Can we?* Oh… Is that the Three Kings? They look *scary*.' Of course he looked up to his big warrior. 'I don't want to see them, Daddy.'

Luciana watched those wide shoulders relax, watched bad-boy, dominant Thane disintegrate like milk-sodden cereal in the face of all that cherubic idolisation.

'I'll take you to meet them and show you there is nothing to be afraid of—okay?'

Nate didn't look convinced, but climbed up Thane like a monkey all the same. 'Okay. I'm ready.'

'Are *you* ready, Luciana?' Thane asked.

To spend an evening being a family? Something she'd always dreamed of?

'I'm definitely ready.'

Ten minutes. That was all it took to sense that Nate's insuperable case of hero-worship for his father was nothing in comparison to that of Thane's people.

The intense magnetism he exuded grew in strength the further they walked, until he was an imposing impression of vibrant and unrelenting power. But those waves of energy flowed with a palpable warmth that was positively endearing. And for the first time she didn't see a ruthless soldier, born to fight, she saw a prince of the realm born to be King.

It was such a thrilling sight she couldn't calm the flurry of burning butterflies inside her, their tiny gossamer wings stroking her heart with pride and her stomach with want.

The town was utterly delightful. Stone façades with deep wooden lintels and picturesque fairytale windows lined the intricate alleyways, and there was a lovely blend of quaint bespoke shops and chocolate box family homes. A few were a little shabby, and there was a subtle cloud of poverty in the air, but it wasn't so obvious as it had been in the outskirts they'd driven through to get here.

As Thane had told her, his uncle's tyrannical rein choked his people. The fact that they were still so pleasant and joyful was humbling. In truth, she still found it amazing they were so accepting of *her*. The enemy in their midst.

By the time they reached the main square night had fallen, and the colossal fir tree taking centre-stage near the clock tower burst into a dazzling display of a million twinkling stars of light.

Nate gasped in delight, cheering along with the flock of festive gatherers, and Thane laced his warm fingers through hers with a gorgeous half-smile that sent a shower of unadulterated happiness raining over her. It was one of those moments in time she wished she could freeze-frame, because it held the promise of unaccountable tomorrows. Of what might be.

He was trying so hard tonight. And she was determined not to suspect that his efforts were merely for the cameras. The cameras that now flashed around them in a dazzling firework display.

Squeezing his hand, she relished the spark of their fiery magical connection and tugged him towards a carpet of colour: rows of stalls that were a complete festive indulgence. Jingle-bell-shaped cookies. Apples dunked in glossy red candy and Swiss white chocolate. Unique crafts and *objets d'art*. Handmade jewellery and amazing tree decorations—intricate blown glass figurines, hand-carved wooden rocking horses and baubles etched with snowflakes.

Thane bought half of that stall, since Luciana and Nate oohed and ahhed over it all.

The yummy, nutty smell of roast chestnuts and frangipane Stollen floated in the air and lured them to the food tent, where Thane and Nate indulged in pancakes drizzled with chocolate sauce. Luciana chose the Galancian version of mulled wine, its scent heady and seductive, and by the time she cradled her third cup she felt half sloshed.

'Thane, is this stuff strong?'

'A little.' He narrowed those black sapphire eyes on her. 'Do you drink often?'

'Nope.'

'Okay, no more for you.'

His hand a claw on the rim of her cup, he tried to wrangle it from her death grip. Then he pursed his lips to stem the laughter that glittered in his gaze.

'Let go, Luce.'

Luciana peeked up at him through the veil of her lashes, feeling naughty and reckless and so happy that he was smiling again. 'Make me.'

He growled—the sound dangerously feral. 'Are you drunk?'

'Don't be daft. Of course not.'

The tent made her a liar by taking her for a spin.

'Good, because we are going ice skating.'

Oh, heck.

'Fancy a coffee?'

For four minutes Nate was like Bambi on ice—all legs and flailing arms. Not that he was discouraged by smacking off the hard surface every five seconds. Guerreros were made of stronger stuff than that. He just picked himself up, wobbled a little, and off he went again.

As for Luciana, she was all style and grace—but the Galancian mulled wine had put her in a fun-loving, giggly mood that was so infectious it obliterated the darkness that had been festering inside him.

'Daddy, watch *me*.'

Nate perfected a double twirl and Luciana clapped, sending a battalion of bystanders cheering along with her.

Daddy. Why he'd chosen that over Papá was a mystery, but Thane liked it. Every time he heard it his heart did a funny little clench.

Nate suddenly faltered and Thane skated over, scooped him up by the waist and lifted him high into the air like an aeroplane. His huge grin as he squealed in delight etched itself into Thane's memory, his heart.

Time slowed.

Snow drifted lazily from the canopy ceiling as they spun round and round.

Nate screeched his name and whooped with joy. And realisation hit him with the ferocity of a thunderbolt.

He wouldn't even be a daddy at all if it weren't for Luciana, would he? She'd gambled with her reputation, risked bringing disgrace upon her house, her country, overturned the colossal expectations of a royal firstborn heir and fought to have his son out of wedlock. Without her courage Thane wouldn't have this moment. This perfectly wonderful moment in time.

No matter where he'd been for the last four years, no matter what he'd missed, without Luciana he wouldn't be gazing into eyes so like his own. Wouldn't have this precious fragile body to hold, to cuddle or to spin in the air. Wouldn't be able to incite the adorable innocent smile that never failed to lift his soul. Without Luciana he wouldn't have this moment or one hundred more just like it. The opportunity to have a million more after it.

And then came a crack of lightning, incinerating the remnants of his anger, leaving him awash with need. The need to wrap Luciana in his arms and thank her from the bottom of his black heart. Come to think of it, the fact she'd wanted Thane's son so badly at *all* astounded him.

When Nate was safely perched on his blades and had tootled off, Thane instinctively swivelled to find her—and somehow, like a whirl of fate, she crashed into his arms, her gorgeous curvy body plastered flush against his.

'Oops,' she said breathlessly. 'I nearly went over. Are you okay?'

Why? he wanted to ask. *Why did you want my son so badly?* The son of her enemy. That had to mean something. Right?

'Thane?' Affectionate concern etched her brow as she stroked his jaw, rubbed her thumb over his cheek. 'What's wrong? Why are you looking at me like that?'

He speared his fingers into the fall of her hair and dived into her eyes. 'Thank you.'

'For what?' she whispered.

'For fighting for him. Making sure he took his first breath. For telling me now, for trusting me now, so I can have him in my life.'

Tears brimmed in her eyes. 'Oh, Thane, I'm so sorry you've missed so much. If I could turn back the clock I would do it in a heartbeat.'

He believed her. He did.

'I can tell you everything,' she promised in a frantic whisper.

'I'd like that.'

'Every last detail. Show you a million photographs so you can see it all…'

'Shh.' He pressed his index finger to her mouth, then dragged it downwards, curling her plump lower lip, coaxing her to open for him as that ever-present magnetic pull—the one he'd been battling for days, the one he was powerless against—drew them together. And when their lips touched that blistering crackle of electricity jolted through his body, sizzled over his skin, fired heat through his veins. Stronger than ever before.

Luciana made a sound that came perilously close to a whimper and Thane let loose a soft growl as they shared one pent-up breath. Then he slanted his head to find the perfect slick fit, desperate to taste, luxuriating in heady relief, because she still wanted him after he'd put her through hell.

Her hands clutched at his broad shoulders, followed the column of his neck, and slid under his ears into his hair as her tongue skated against his. Thane's danced right back, and the slip and slide of their lips took them higher and higher.

The seductive pull of her mouth was a pure exhilaration he never wanted to end.

Dios, he'd missed her. Missed this.

The rapid flash of cameras lit the air around the vast indoor rink, but it was the joyful chorus of spectators chanting their names that brought him back to earth with a thud.

Ending their kiss, he pulled back a touch and pressed his lips to the corner of her lush mouth, the high curve of her cheekbone, inhaling the rich jasmine and vanilla scent from the decadent tumble of her hair.

'Oh, Lord. We're making out in public,' she said, a smile in her husky voice as she buried her hot face in his neck.

'Want to make out at home instead?' he rasped, curving his hands around her sculpted waist to steady her and pull her tightly against him. *Bad* idea, when the crush of her heavy breasts took his arousal up another notch.

Her wanton sigh of 'Yes…' was a stream of warm air over the skin beneath his ear, coercing a shudder to rip up his spine, and when she lifted her face he grinned at her bright pink cheeks.

If the crowds hadn't adored her before they were soon smitten when she spun to face them and dipped into a beautiful little curtsey, stealing the heart of every Galancian in the room. She was going to be a fabulous queen—he knew it.

As if the crowd had picked up his thoughts they began repeating a mantra: 'Queen Luciana of Galancia!'

Her dark blonde brows nigh on hit her hairline. 'They're a bit premature, aren't they? How bizarre. I'm years away from *that*. And you know what's stranger still? I know you'd gladly take your throne now, but I don't feel anywhere near ready.'

The ice shifted beneath his feet, tilting his world on its axis. 'Of course you are ready—you were born ready.'

'You sound like my father,' she grumbled. 'I may have been raised to be Queen, but I would never have chosen it for myself.'

Dios, he hadn't thought for one minute she would be averse. 'But you were about to take power…'

'Not through choice. I was being pushed early because my father is— Thane?' Her palms splayed down his chest, settled over his pecs. 'Why have you tensed up?'

Rolling his neck to slacken his body, he cursed inwardly at the idea that he was about to give her yet another reason to leave. Not to desire their marriage.

She narrowed her eyes in suspicion. 'Why do I get the feeling I've just stumbled on a landmine that's about to blow up in my face? What's going on, Thane?'

'We'll talk later.'

'Ah, no. You're not fobbing me off this time. I'm missing something here, and you're going to tell me *right now.*'

'Luce, I…' He cleared his throat. 'I will take my crown after we marry next weekend.'

She jerked backwards, her footing skewed, and a sense of *déjà vu* rocked him—the jet back in Courchevel—as he instinctively reached out and snatched at thin air as she dodged him. The loss of her warmth froze the blood in his veins.

Skidding a little, she found her balance. 'Wh…What did you say?'

Something told him he was about to have another battle on his hands. He had to remind himself that he hadn't lost one yet.

'By marrying you, a blue blood heir. I can take my crown four years early.'

CHAPTER FOURTEEN

THE SMILE SHE'D been taught in the cradle carried her through fond farewells and the car-ride back to Thane's beachside mansion to tuck a happy, sleepy Nate into bed, even while her heart was tearing itself apart and her mind was working her into a pained frenzy, connecting the dots.

By the time she walked into the suite that had been her palatial prison for days the riotous flow of turbulent emotions was a swirling, churning, flaming volcano at critical mass. And she fanned the flames of that anger—because the alternative was crumbling, breaking, shattering and she steadfastly refused to be that woman. The very woman she'd found curled up against the wall last night in the hallway. Loneliness burrowing into her stomach. Fighting defeat. Almost broken. Allowing *him* to control her. All for what? Because she was desperate for the love of the dark Prince?

Clearly it wasn't him who was crazy. It was her. She should know better. Since when had love or romantic happiness ever entered the equation of her life? *Never.* From the day she'd been born she'd been a means to a crown.

Her hands shook as she gripped the bed-rail and lifted one foot like a flamingo to tug off one kitten heel, then switched legs to yank off the other. And when she spied Thane walking through her door, his dangerous stride a purposeful prowl, only to close it behind him and lean against it, crossing his arms over his shirt-clad chest, ready for battle, she *blew.*

She launched her shoe across the room to clatter off the

wall—and, *God*, that felt great!—then spun on him like a furious firestorm.

'You seduced me for your crown, didn't you? You played me from the start—abducted me from Courchevel, brought me here against my wishes—to get you your throne. *Didn't you*?'

'You could say that,' he hedged, his easy stance belying the tension emanating from his honed, dominant frame.

How she didn't go over there and slap his hideously handsome face, she'd never know.

'Makes perfect sense, really. Why else would you want me "very, *very* badly"?' she bit out, throwing his perfect passionate prose back in his face. 'Your scruples really are abhorrent—do you know that?'

Fool, she was. Total, utter fool. She'd known he had an agenda but, as always, self-preservation had taken a darn hike and cowered in the woods with this man.

There she'd been, protecting Nate from a power-play, and she'd walked headlong into the lion's den. Blind to the warning signs flashing in glaring pink neon, brighter than a Vegas strip. Hanna and Pietro going on as if she was their saviour, for starters…

He'd played her like a puppet on a string. And she'd followed his every beat.

She didn't miss the way he shifted slightly on his feet, thrust his despicable hands through his hateful hair.

'Luciana…angel…'

'Ah, no, Romeo. You can forget the charm. No longer required. You've got me right where you wanted me. *Bravo*, Thane. Really, you should be proud.'

Was that her voice? That fractured aria of sarcasm and bitterness—that portrayal of a heart betrayed?

He rubbed at his temple as if she was one of those Sudoku puzzles that twisted her brain into knots.

'I cannot see the problem, Luciana. You didn't wish to marry Augustus and so we would both benefit.'

Of *course* he couldn't see the problem. While he'd been polishing his crown she'd secretly been building castles in the sky. But that was *her* problem. Not his. One she'd simply have to accept. Because she'd given him the one guarantee that would get her down the aisle: Natanael. Not that she'd ever feel regret over that. Seeing them together made remorse utterly impossible.

Now all she had to do was face those portentous predictions she'd been battling for days. A loveless prison of an autocratic marriage would be her future if she wasn't careful.

With a shrug she tore off her coat and slung it to the bed. 'See, Thane? Right there. *You* decided we would both benefit. *You* made that choice for me. Much like the wedding you arranged yesterday, behind my back. Has it never occurred to you that I would like to be asked?'

Hopeless, pathetic romantic, she was.

'I told you the other day we were getting married.'

'Precisely. You *told* me.' But she hadn't argued the toss, had she? No,' she'd allowed him to control her. For the last time.

He hiked one devilish brow. 'So what is the problem?'

She shot him a glare which he impudently ignored.

Lord, he just didn't get it, did he? While she could feel the ropes of a noose tightening around her neck.

From the start it had been the same. No choices. No requests. Only kidnappings and kisses and demands. Either it was ingrained in him to dominate, literally stamped into his DNA, or he respected her so little he didn't value her opinion or her own wishes. Whichever the case might be, what kind of marriage would they have? A hell of a lot worse than her parents'—she knew that much.

Her lungs drew up tight, crowding her chest until she could barely breathe. She'd been under the command of a control freak all her life and suddenly she couldn't commit to a moment longer. Heaven help her, she would *not* live under another man's rule for eternity.

'The problem is,' she said, pleading with her strength not to fail her now, 'I would like some control over my life. To at least be involved in decisions. I would like a partnership, Thane. *Not* a dictatorship. You talk about giving your people a voice. Yet you silence mine. Don't you think that's hypocritical?'

'That is absurd, Luciana,' he said fiercely. 'You speak when you wish to and I listen.'

She groaned aloud. The man was delusional.

'Did you listen in Courchevel, when I told you I wasn't getting onto that plane? *No.* Did you listen when I told you I had to go home before we could get married? *No.*'

A frigid draught swept over her, pebbling her skin with goosebumps.

'*Home*?' he incised. 'Galancia is your home.'

It wasn't his words that bothered her—it was his granite-like tone. The one that said Arunthia was to be forgotten and she should accept that.

He'd have to bury her six feet under first.

She wrenched open the antique armoire and hauled out her suitcase.

'Luciana? What the hell are you doing?'

'What does it look like I'm doing, Thane?'

She was leaving this place. This island. As soon as the dawn broke. And *nothing* would stop her.

'I don't think—'

'Oh, Thane, right now I don't care what you think. And if I were you I would start listening to me. Because your days of controlling my life are *over.*'

Frustration mounting, his pulse spiked, making him feel light-headed as Luciana whirled around the room like a tornado, shoving clothes into the sinister suitcase that sprawled over her bed like a black stain on pure white satin.

'Would you like to tell me why you are packing?'

He had no idea why—she wasn't going anywhere.

Seeing her beautiful clothes and those delicate bottles of cream that made her radiant skin smell sweet being haphazardly tossed into that vile contraption made his fists clench into thwarted balls of menace.

'I would've thought that was obvious. I'm leaving. I need to go home for a few days. I need time. I need to sort out my responsibilities there. If you had stood still long enough this week we would've already had this discussion—but, no, you dictate and you command. And I've *had* it.'

Darkness fell over his eyes until he was blind to everything around him. She was not leaving him again. Nor was she stealing his son a second time.

'No, I am sorry, Luciana, but you are not going anywhere. And *that* is final.'

His conscience was screaming at him to stop. To think about what he was doing. Saying. But if he let her go she wouldn't come back. He knew it. Just as she hadn't five years ago.

Her heavy sigh infected the air. 'You need to trust me, Thane.'

'*Trust*?' The vicious swirling cyclone in his chest picked up pace and he whirled on her in a gust of fury. 'Trust the woman who disappeared in the night and never told me I had a son? Are you *serious*, Luciana?'

Those thick decadent eyelashes descended and her voice turned heartbreakingly weary. 'I know it's early days, but are you *never* going to forgive me? Are we ever going to get past this?'

The memory of earlier tonight, when he'd peered through a different lens…her frantic whisper that she would show him what he'd missed…doused the furious fire in his blood.

He thrust his fingers through his hair and exhaled heavily. 'I'm trying, here, Luce.'

Truth was, even before this evening he'd started to appreciate the turbulence she must have gone through. Which was why he didn't want her or Nate anywhere near Henri

Verbault—the man who'd almost cost him his son. Thane would never forgive him or trust him, and he was amazed Luciana could contemplate either. Obviously she was blind to the man's influence over her, so Thane would protect her from that too. By keeping her here with him.

'Just let your father deal with the Arunthian crown. He places it above your importance anyway. You don't need to go back and see your family ever again. You have Nate and I.'

Her hand plunged from where she'd pinched the bridge of her nose and her jaw dropped agape as she spluttered, 'Of *course* I need to see them. You can't expect me to give up my family. That's just *insane…* Whoa—hold on a minute. Did you expect me to get married next Saturday without my family there?'

'Basically? Yes. I do not want your father anywhere near my wedding.'

'And what about my sisters? My *sisters*, Thane! And, no matter what grudges you have against my King, he's still my father and he's sick. I don't know how long he has left and—'

That stopped him in his tracks. 'He is sick? I didn't know this.'

She flung her arms wide in an exasperated flourish. 'Why *would* you? Since you've never asked or cared to know about that part of my life. If you had you'd know why I was being pushed into taking *my* crown early.' Her smooth brow pleated and she shook her head. 'It's almost as if you haven't accepted who I really am. Do you still wish I was the nobody you met in Zurich, Thane? Have you even acknowledged that I'm a Verbault?'

He flinched. Actually flinched. And he wasn't sure who was more surprised.

'Oh, my God.' A humourless laugh burst from her mouth. 'Did you honestly believe giving me your name would erase my heritage? Stop me from being my father's daughter?

Even if I become Queen of Galancia I will still be a Verbault in *here*.'

With her fist she thumped her chest, and when her voice fractured he felt the fissure in his own heart.

'I'll still be the enemy. You are kidding yourself to think otherwise.'

Pivoting, she spun back to the dark wood armoire, yanked open another drawer and scooped up a mound of pretty, frilly, lacy garments to dump in her case.

Thane slumped against the wall, rubbing over his jaw, his mind going a mile a minute.

In a way she was right. He'd never truly acknowledged who she was: a sister, a daughter, a friend, even the heir to the Arunthian throne. Simply hadn't wanted to admit it to himself. Not because she was his enemy, but because he would have been slammed up against the naked truth—she had responsibilities of her own. To her family, her people. Responsibilities that could take her away from *him*.

So not once had he considered or asked if she wished to take her rightful place. Because he feared her answer. Was scared she'd choose her crown over his. Her family over him.

Self-loathing crawled through his veins. He was so selfish with her. Was it any wonder desperate panic loitered in her brandy-gold eyes—a silent scream that confessed she wanted to be away from here? From him. It cut his black twisted heart in two.

And the way she eluded his own gaze struck him. The night his mother had died Juana Guerrero hadn't been able to look at him either. Her every move premeditated, she'd known what she'd devised. Just as Luciana did. She'd move heaven and earth to leave him. Permanently.

Luciana was kidding herself if she believed otherwise. Why else pack her every solitary possession into that case? A case he hadn't failed to notice had been already half full of Nate's clothes when she'd opened it.

The walls began to loom from all sides and suddenly everything appeared malefic and pernicious. Even the black rails of the ironwork bedframe seemed to uncoil and distort and writhe in front of him. Every drawer she flung open clattered and squealed and rattled, as if it bore the menacing teeth of a monster.

'You are wasting your time, Luciana. There is no way for you to leave here.'

'I'll ring Lucas to come for me.'

His heartbeat raced, threatened to explode. 'I will deny him access to Galancian airspace.'

She froze in her frenetic rush, head jerking upright, eyes slamming into his. Even from the other side of the bed he could see her glorious, voluptuous frame vibrate with pique and pain.

'Are you serious?'

'Deadly.'

Up came her trembling hand, her fingers curling around the base of her throat. 'You can't do this, Thane. I am *not* your property. I am my own person. And you can't keep me here against my wishes. It isn't right. I've felt like a prisoner in this house for days.'

Her pitch escalated as her breathing turned choppy, raspy, and she clutched her chest as if struggling for air.

Every ounce of his blood drained to his toes and a cold sweat chased it. Bolting forward, he thrust out a pleading hand. 'Luciana, calm down.'

'No, you need to *hear* me this time. What I said before—it's right and you don't see it. You don't listen to me.' Her eyes pooled with moisture, making them overly bright. 'By controlling me you take away my choice. You silence my voice. My whole life I've had this gag around my mouth, and I can't *breathe* when I think I'll have a lifetime of that with you.'

Thane raked his hand around the back of his neck, tearing at the clammy skin. He did *not* silence her; he only wanted what was best for her. She hadn't wanted to marry

Augustus. He only wanted them here so he could keep them safe. Protect what was his. And yet his conscience argued vehemently. Because he *had* told her she was marrying him. And he knew precisely why—even if he wasn't eager to admit it.

She collapsed against the hardwood drawers as if she no longer had the energy to stand upright. 'For once, just *once*, I would love someone to ask me what I truly want. Everyone who is free in the world is asked that very question every day, I imagine, and I often wonder if they realise how precious it is. If they take it for granted. I want to yell and scream at them that they shouldn't. They should cherish it. I *envy* them, Thane. I envy their freedom of choice.'

It was like being tossed into the past, hearing his mother's wistful voice—the hopes of a woman trapped like a bird in a gilded cage. And suddenly he felt like the damnable hypocrite Luciana had claimed him to be. He refused to ignore the truth one second longer. The reason he had never given her a choice.

'What are you saying, Luce? You don't want to marry me?'

'No, Thane,' she said, shaking her head, her brow pinched. 'I don't.'

And when one single diamond teardrop slipped down her exquisite face he felt as if noxious venom infected his veins, surged through his body, making him destructive, malevolent, black. As if he contaminated her with his darkness.

What more proof did he need than the evil voice whispering in his mind to *make* her marry him? Force her by threats to take away her son. And that disgusted him. It made him sick to his stomach even to think of it. The idea he was turning into his father.

She smoothed her hand over her midriff, as if he made her ache inside, but her tone strengthened as if she was resolved. Her stance one of weary resignation. 'But I will marry you. For my son. He needs you and he loves you.'

Thane closed his eyes. Why didn't that make him happy? Why couldn't he be satisfied with that?

Verity hailed down on him in an icy blizzard, pummelling his flesh through to his bones. He longed for her to want only him. For Thane to be enough.

Idiot, he was. He'd done the one thing he'd sworn he'd never do. He'd let her creep past his defences. *Again*. And that petrified him—because he'd never be enough to make her happy. Just as he hadn't been enough for his mother. To make her want to stay. He was too much like the man he'd sworn he'd never be. Twisted, selfish, possessive, dark inside.

Look at her, his inner voice whispered.

She was so beautiful she made his breath catch, his heart stall in his chest. But that solitary tear-track that shimmied a pearlescent dew down her cheek said it all. It said that one day she would hate him for imprisoning her here. Despise him. It said that one day she might fly to her death with a euphoric look of peace on her face as she finally found freedom. From him. From her life here.

And he couldn't do that to his son. Take away the woman who loved him beyond Thane's wildest imagination.

He wanted Nate to be happy. Have the kind of childhood Thane had never had. Peaceful and joyous. Learn how to be a good man with a pure soul and to be able to love another with his whole heart. Surely that was the greatest gift he could give him? More than horses and dogs and spaceships and candy canes. And to be that person Nate needed Luciana. Not Thane.

Unchaining the doors to the cage, he threw them wide open, his throat so swollen and raw every syllable hurt. 'You are right, Luciana. Of course you are right. You need to go back.'

That glorious body slumped as she gave him a tight, grateful smile. 'We'll just be gone a couple of days. Back for this…this wedding on Christmas Eve—'

'No.' He cut her off with a shake of his head, commanding his tone not to falter, to stay strong. 'There is no need. No hurry. Spend Christmas with your family if you like.'

That had been his mother's worst time for missing her loved ones. Had once made blood trickle from her wrists as the depths of her depression found no bounds.

Unwanted, harrowing, his dark, tormented mind made one of those incongruous leaps, placing Luciana in that bloodbath…

Dios, maybe her leaving long-term was for the best after all. It would only be a matter of time before he destroyed her. He'd rather have her alive somewhere else in the world than dead by his side. And, while he truly believed Luciana had more strength than his mother had, Thane could easily kill her spirit—was already doing so—and that would be a great tragedy in itself.

He lavished himself with one last long look. At that incredible dark bronze tousled tumble of hair. The perfect feminine curves of her body. Those big, beautiful brandy-gold eyes now swimming in confusion.

'Well…if you're sure,' she said, relief blending seamlessly with her bewilderment. 'We could think about getting married in the New Year. But don't you want to spend Christmas with Nate? He'll miss you.'

'No,' he said, turning his back on her, unable to lie to her face as he strode to the door.

If he thought for one second that she might come back he would hold out hope. And it had almost killed him waiting night after night in Zurich, praying she'd walk through the door. A second serving of that persecution would ruin him.

Fingers curled around the door handle, he pushed his final retort past his lips. 'I won't force you into a marriage you don't want, Luciana. In the long run that will only harm Nate. I'll explain to everyone that things haven't worked out between us.'

'Wha…What do you mean? What about Nate? Your crown?'

'I'll find another way.'

There *was* no other way. But in that moment he realised he'd crawl through the dust of his heart to give her what she wanted, needed. He'd make up for the delay to his people somehow.

'As for Nate—we will arrange visits.' Though how he'd manage to say goodbye every time, he wasn't sure.

'Thane? Turn around—look at me, please.'

He couldn't. He'd change his mind.

'I'll arrange a jet for early morning. But I can't be here when you leave. I'll be at the castle. Business.'

The barracks was his destination, and he knew it. He needed to be out cold when she left. He didn't trust himself otherwise. And there was no better way to vanquish his emotions than via his father's legacy.

'Be careful, Luciana. Love my son for me.'

'Thane, *please* wait. Talk to me.'

The soft pad of her footsteps sounded behind him and he momentarily stalled as her sensual jasmine and vanilla scent curled around him in an evocative embrace, luring him back.

No. No more talking. He didn't want her to see what lay beneath. Something too dark to describe.

Thane hauled open the door before she could touch him and vaulted up the staircase to the foyer, where he snatched his keys from the side table and stormed into the night.

CHAPTER FIFTEEN

TWELVE HOURS LATER thousands of miles separated them, and not only was Luciana still reeling from their final showdown but the man refused to leave her be.

Blind to the lush Arunthian vista as the car snaked up the steep incline towards the palace, she saw only those intense obsidian eyes searching her face before he'd sped from her suite, as if he were committing her to memory, as if she were the brightest star in his universe—it was a devastating impression she couldn't erase.

Nor could she erase the questions trying to wade through her woollen, sleep-deprived brain—why was he suddenly willing to give up twenty-four-seven access to his son, delay taking his throne?

Because despite his inglorious method of coercing you into Galancia, his intentions were pure. His only thought was for his people, and he wouldn't force you down the aisle for anything.

And she couldn't have made her desires clearer, could she? *No.*

A fiery arrow of self-censure tore through her chest and she squeezed her eyes shut. *'No, Thane, I don't want to marry you.'* But in that moment—that gasping, suffocating moment—she truly hadn't. Had only envisaged a life of dictatorship, one-sided love and the misery of duty. Where she became a dark blonde replica of her mother.

And that had petrified her. Thrown her into a panic that

had whirled out of control. Muscles burning, aching to run and never, *ever* return. And the idea that she could consider, even for a millisecond, parting him from Nate again made shame crawl over every inch of her skin.

With a restless shake of her head she cuddled Nate to her side, forcing herself back to the present, and glanced up at the fairytale façade of Arunthe Palace—all cream stone walls and fanciful turrets with conical slate roofs—as the car rocked to a stop outside the grandiose scrolled iron gates.

And when the habitual dread *didn't* pervade her body, *didn't* line her soles with lead, suddenly, astoundingly, she watched a smile play at her mouth in the reflection of the window. Apparently battling with the dark Prince had given her the courage to face anything. Even her mother's disapproving glare and her father's steely, vexed countenance as he rehashed her latest escapades in reckless rebellion.

But, unlike five years ago, he would not make her feel guilty, dirty, shameful or unworthy—he no longer held that power over her. She *refused* to grant it to him. It was not wrong to want her son or to wish for the hedonistic passions of love. To reach beyond her expectations. Thane might fight dirty at times, but at least he fought. *Hard.* For what he believed in, what he desired above all else. Taking a leaf out of his book wouldn't hurt.

Thinking about it, right at this moment she'd never felt so strong in her life.

Claudia—tall and dark, striking and radiant—appeared at the arched entryway, shielding her eyes from the sun, and leather creaked as Nate bounced at the sight of her.

'Go inside with Auntie Claudia, darling. I'll just be a few minutes.'

'Okay, Mamá,' he said, darting from the car and bolting up the stone steps.

Luciana raised splayed fingers—*five minutes?*—and on her sister's nod, the door slammed shut.

The locks clicked into place and she depressed the internal speaker for the driver.

'Another limousine, another town. How are you, Seve?' She'd swear she'd seen more of this man in the last few days than Thane.

Down came the privacy screen on a soft whirr, until she stared into deep-set titanium eyes sparkling with amusement in the rearview mirror.

'You beat me to it. I'm impressed. What gave me away?'

'Let's just say I can feel his protection.'

All around her. Wrapping her in warmth when she was so cold inside, missing him already. Wondering what he was doing in that darkly disturbing castle, who he was with. Why her inner voice shrilled that he was with no one, had only his dark pain for company.

'How does it feel, driving a car embellished with the Arunthian royal crest?'

Seve grimaced, and she couldn't help but laugh a little.

'So...are you my new shadow?' she asked.

'I sure am. Until he's satisfied you're safe and that your father won't push you into anything you don't want.'

Wry was the smile that curved her lips. Leopards and their infallible spots. He couldn't quite let go. And the hell of it was she adored him for it. They might not share love, but he cared.

'What is he doing in that castle, Seve? Who is he with?'

Unease permeated the air-con cooled air and he rolled his brick-like shoulders.

'Please, Seve, he won't talk to me.'

Exhaling heavily, he met her gaze in the rearview mirror. 'If I know Thane he's into his third bottle of Scotch after a bout in the barracks while my dear old dad cracks open the champers, celebrating his continued reign.' Anger rode his tone hard. 'I don't know what infuriates me more.'

Luciana frowned deeply. 'Barracks? What would he be doing there? And, hold on a sec—your dear old dad?'

He arched one dark brow. 'Much like Thane, I lucked out in the father stakes. My dad is Franco Guerrero.'

'Oh, Lord.' It struck her then, with everything that had gone on last night, that she'd never given Thane's uncle a thought. 'By marrying me Thane would have overthrown him. I imagine he isn't best pleased about that.'

'Understatement of the millennia, Princess. He's been causing Thane trouble for days—ever since you dropped the Nate bomb on him.'

She groaned aloud. 'Dammit. *That's* why he's been going to the castle. Practically pushing me down the aisle. Why didn't he tell me? The insufferable man doesn't *talk*.'

But she knew the answer before Seve muttered it. He wouldn't have wanted her worrying. Had to be the hero, didn't he? While she was doing her usual—painting a prophesy of desolation in a gilded cage.

Why did she *do* that? Claudia was right—she was a darn pessimist. An optimist would believe fate had brought them together again, regardless of Thane's agenda, say they had a son and that in time love could grow. An idealist would reason that duty didn't necessarily bode a farewell to happiness. They were not her parents—they could strive to have both.

And the duty that put the fear of God up her didn't have to be a noose around her neck—it could be an adventure with Thane. The greatest adventure of all. She just had to fight for it. Make it happen. Be her own hero. And maybe Thane's too, for once. Give him the crown he so desperately wanted. Help him free his people from tyranny. Make his mother's dreams come true. The woman he couldn't even speak of without pain engulfing him with a tenebrous shroud.

'His mother…' she began warily. 'Does he ever talk about her?'

'Never. The world could end tomorrow and he'd die with those memories locked in his soul. She was a manic depressive, you know? She self-harmed and…' Seve blew out an anxiety-laden breath. 'That's why I hate him being in that mausoleum. Makes him blacker than night.'

Panic gripped her stomach at the thought of him hurting somewhere she couldn't reach. 'Listen, I need a couple of days here. So right now you're going to go back there, tell him I'm fine—perfectly safe—and get him out of that castle for me. Aren't you, Seve? Tell me. Give me the words.'

He gave her an incredulous look that said *hell, yeah*, which did a somewhat splendid job of easing the crush in her lungs.

'Good. Okay. And after that I need a favour. Or three…'

A few days later. Christmas Eve.

He had the hangover from hell. Why Seve had ordered him to haul his 'sorry ass' out of bed and get in the shower he'd never know. That Thane had actually obeyed the man was even more incongruous. All he'd wanted was to sleep through Christmas. After that he knew he'd be fine. Great. Wonderful.

His groan ricocheted off the onyx marble as he braced his hands, palms flat, against the shower wall and dipped his head beneath the deluge. The cold water was like shards of glass, biting into his scalp and skin. And this was *post* eight shots of espresso. Some big tough warrior he was. He was just glad Nate wasn't here to see his hero slide down the drain, and Luciana—

Ah, great. He'd just blown his 'I won't think of them for ten minutes' pact.

The floor did a funny tilt—his cue to jump ship—and he stepped onto the rug, wrapping a towel around his waist.

Spying a bottle of headache relief on the countertop, he

reached for it, his hand freezing in mid-air as a shard of light sliced through the dim haze.

'Turn the damn light off, Seve!' he hollered. Was he trying to split his head open?

'Not Seve,' said a delectable honey-drenched tone. 'And, no, I don't think I will.'

His heart stopped. His jaw dropped. And he stared at the door that was cracked ajar. Was he hearing her voice now? His mental state was seriously disturbing these days.

With a shake of his head that made him curse blue when his brains rattled, he turned back to the basin and picked up his razor.

'Are you going to be in there all day? I'm gathering dust, aging by the second, out here.'

Clatter went the blade into the porcelain sink.

He watched his hand move at a snail's pace towards the handle…fingers curling, gripping. Heart leaping, hoping, as he eased the door fully open.

Two steps forward and—*Dios…*

'Luciana?'

Hallucinating or not?

Perched on the vanilla-hued velvet chaise longue, one leg crossed over the other, she rested her elbow on her bent knee and propped her chin on her fist. But it wasn't the sight of that exquisite serene face that jolted his heart back to life, it was the seraphic vision she made dressed from head to foot in ivory-white.

The gown was pure Luciana. No fuss or bustles or froth. Simply elegance that sang a symphony of class. Straight, yet layered and sheer, with a sensual V neck and a pearl-encrusted band tucked beneath her breasts. Lace was an overlay that capped the graceful slope of her shoulders and scalloped around her upper arms in a short sleeve. And atop her head was a diamond halo from which a gossamer veil flowed and pooled all around her.

He rubbed his bare left pec with the ball of his hand

where he ached—God, did she make him ache—and those hot needles pricked the backs of his eyes.

'Luciana…' Her name was an incoherent prayer, falling from his lips. 'You look so beautiful. Like an angel.'

She gave him a rueful smile and spoke softly, 'I've told you before, Thane, I'm no angel.'

Whether it was because he felt utterly broken inside, or because the sight of her had turned the gloomy morning into pure sunshine he couldn't be sure, but his mouth opened and for the first time in his life he was powerless to stop what poured free.

'But you were *my* angel. And you never stopped being mine—not for one minute. Even when I was furious with you, you were still my only light in the dark. And no matter where you are in the world that will never change.'

Down came long lashes to fan over her flawless cheeks as she bit down on her lips. Lips she now covered with trembling fingers.

Panic punched him in the gut. 'Luce?' He took a tentative step closer, relieved when she breathed deeply, pulling herself up to sit tall and straight, with a gorgeous watery smile just for him.

'My sister,' she said, with an airy wave that belied that quivering hand, 'who is somewhere around here, tells me it's bad luck to see the groom before the wedding—but you know what I think?'

While Thane knew nothing about these things, the fact that she resembled a bride and spoke of weddings and grooms wasn't lost on him—but hope was a fragile beast he tethered. Because despite the agony of losing her he would not take her down the aisle without happiness in her heart.

Brushing his wet hair back from his face, he eased down onto the edge of the bed, never taking his eyes off her in case she disappeared. 'What do you think, Luce?'

'I think we make our own luck. I think fate offers us opportunity but *we* are the masters of our own destiny. I think

I've allowed people to control me for too long, and now I'm going to take my life and my happiness into my own hands. Are you ready, Thane?'

Happiness.

He was ready for anything as long as she didn't leave.

CHAPTER SIXTEEN

SHE WAS GOING to propose. Any minute now.

It wasn't every little girl's dream. But, when you'd been governed since the day you were born, being the commander of tomorrow was a unique dream all its own.

So here she was. Sitting opposite a handsome man—*the* most beautiful she'd ever seen. The dark, dangerous divinity that was Prince Thane of Galancia. And maybe she hadn't set the stage so superbly—no dimly lit chandeliers or intimate tables for two, but it was *their* scene, their intimate paradise—the place where she'd been reunited with the other half of her soul—and to her it was perfection. Beyond price.

So all that was left were the words.

And Princess Luciana Valentia Thyssen Verbault had to press her palm to her stomach, desperately trying to calm the swoop and swirl of anxious butterflies, their dance wild with exhilaration and anticipation, before she stood tall. Because she had the horrible feeling she might pass out. She'd felt less nervous renouncing her throne yesterday, before hordes of press. The news would be broadcast at twelve noon and by then—hopefully—she'd be this man's wife.

Sucking in a shaky breath, she rose to her feet and walked over to where he perched on the edge of the bed, his honed body glistening, those black sapphire eyes holding hers captive. And, despite the fact he looked like hell, the mere sight of him, in all his myriad beauties and unguarded mercies, still made her weak at the knees.

Down she went onto the floor before him. Never leaving his gaze, loving the way he opened his legs to let her in. The way he reached up hesitantly, fingers trembling, as he brushed a wayward curl from her temple.

'Luciana…' he murmured. 'I…' A faint crease lined his brow. 'What are you doing down there?'

'I'm doing this right. On one knee.'

'Doing what right?'

When light dawned, he shook his head vehemently.

'Like hell you are.'

He grasped her waist and lifted her up, plonking her astride his knee with a rustle of her skirts.

'You will not kneel before me. And isn't that *my* job?'

'Not when we're living in this splendid era called the twenty-first century, Thane.'

Not when she heard that hint of panic in his voice—the one that reminded her of the day on the beach with Nate. That fear of rejection. She could kick herself for not considering it before. That by taking away her choice he gave her no option to say no. To reject him. Lord, it was amazing what a mess two people could make in a few days.

Wriggling back, she tried to clamber off his lap. Thanks to Thane, she somehow ended up on the bed, where she hoisted up her skirts—slipping and sliding as tulle and chiffon met satin sheets. By the time she was on her knees again she felt like a triathlete after a three-day event. Likely resembled one too, with her tiara askew. But one look at the man of her dreams, wearing a towel that left *nothing* to the imagination, getting on his knees too, as if he needed them equal, and her every thought zeroed in on him. Only him.

'And why shouldn't I kneel before you?' she said. 'I respect you. I'm proud of you. For breaking free of your father's hold, for fighting for your people.'

She trailed her fingertips down the scimitar line of his jaw and stared into those beautiful dark fathomless eyes.

'You're going to be a powerful and noble King and I'll

be honoured to stand by your side. Our son needs a wonderful daddy too, and that man can only ever be you. And *I* need the man I love with my whole heart to be with me always. So…Thane Guerrero of Galancia…will you do me the great honour of becoming my husband?'

His throat was convulsing, and his magnificent chest shook as if he fought his emotions. Until one rogue teardrop finally spilled on his first spoken word.

'L…Love? You *love* me, Luciana?'

Holding his jaw in her hands, she leaned forward and kissed his tear away, breathing him in. 'Oh, I love you. I always have. Since the moment you knocked out a Viking in my honour.'

'Really?'

'*Really*, really. I just didn't believe in fairytales and happy-ever-afters. Didn't believe in happiness for myself at all. The right to dream beyond duty was drummed out of me when I was three feet tall. Duty was why I would marry—not for love. So, like a self-fulfilling prophecy, I ran years ago, when my heart screamed at me to stay and tell you who I was. I listened to my father and an age-old feud, ignoring my every instinct to come to you with our son. Duty would never bring happiness—my parents are proof of that—so when I discovered I was the key to your crown I ran scared again.'

She brushed his damp hair back from his temple, tucked one side behind his ear.

'But I think if we try we could have both. I promise I'm not running any longer. I'm here to stay—more than ready to be your Queen. Your wife and your lover too, if you want me. So what do you say?'

'Yes.'

Swooping in he came, and back down she went to the mattress, the heat of his body spilling over her.

'Yes. Yes, I'll marry you.' He wrapped her in his arms in a cherishing crush and breathed against her neck. 'I want it all too, Luciana. You'll always come first to me. *Always.* I love you so much. You've always owned my heart. Only you.'

A sigh feathered the aching wall of her throat and she closed her eyes as the last stain of doubt was erased. Replaced by the sweet sherbet-bright happiness that fizzled inside of her. If she'd heard him right, that was.

'I have?'

'Always,' he said, his lips moving over her skin.

For long moments they held on tight. Breathing. Loving. Calming. Trying to accept a dream beyond dreaming, a thing too precious ever to risk again. Then he was kissing her with exquisite annihilating tenderness and she was melting beneath his fervid ardour.

'Why else would I search for you for weeks, turn over every stone in Zurich looking for you, while my heart wouldn't beat and my lungs could barely breathe?'

She felt one fat tear trickle down the side of her face. 'Ah, Thane, why didn't you tell me?'

'I didn't want to give you that power over me again. Stupid to think I had any control over it at all. I even kidded myself I was only after my crown. That worked for…'

He hiked his shoulders and she felt the play of muscle against her palms.

'I don't know—maybe a day? I wish I'd told you that at the ice rink, instead of making it all about the throne. I was a coward.' Red scored his cheekbones. 'And now I'm rambling.'

She laughed at his newfound candour. 'No, you're not—you're talking, and I love it. It's wonderful. That's what I need.'

'To share. You told me. See? I do listen to you, Luciana, I just… At first I thought I was doing the right thing. And, *Dios*, I should have asked you to marry me, but I didn't want to hear your voice say no. I *was* silencing you, and that made me as bad as my father. Black. Twisted up inside. I kept having these visions of you hurting yourself, like my mother used to, and—'

'Hey, look at me. *Never* going to happen. She wasn't well, Thane. And that was your father's doing—it had nothing to do with you. You're nothing like him. You're a heroic man in *here*.' She placed her palm over his heart…a heart that thumped in tandem with hers. 'Will you tell me about her one day?'

Closing his eyes, he rested his brow against hers. 'One day soon. Just not today. Let me enjoy having you back in my arms.'

'Okay.' That was plenty good enough for her. 'Just promise me you'll keep talking. If you're hurting I need to know, so I can be there for you. In the silence I'd convinced myself we were doomed. When you don't share with me my mind runs wild. You were at the castle, trying to keep us safe, and I was picturing you with mistresses, you know?'

His eyes sprang open and his head reared back. '*Que*? You are *crazy*, Luce.'

'Yeah, well, one day I'll tell you about my childhood. Or, better yet, I'll sleep out one night and not bother telling you what I'm doing and who—'

'Like hell you will.'

'Need I say more?'

He growled. 'I didn't think of that. But I swear you'll see a snowball in hell before I ever take a mistress.' He brushed his lips over hers, back and forth. Teasing. Tormenting. 'Only you.'

Then he began to rain lush, moist kisses down her throat in a golden trail.

'I've been the only lover in your life, yes?'

Blood thrumming, she writhed against the satin sheets. 'Y…Yes, you know that.'

Nudging at the lace covering her breast, he swirled his hot breath over her skin as he murmured, 'And you are the only lover in mine. There has only been you and there will only ever be you.'

Blame it on the havoc being unleashed on her body, but it took her a second to catch on—and then she pushed at his shoulders to gauge his expression. 'You mean you haven't slept with anyone since *me*?'

Nonchalance made his shrug loose, as if he didn't see the big deal. 'No. It felt wrong. Like I was betraying my heart.'

'But…but you're a *man*.'

A laugh rumbled from the depths of his chest. 'I am *so* glad you've noticed that, angel.'

'And you're…*hot*.'

His eyes smouldered along with his smile as he towered above her, dominating her world, as always.

'I am *hot* for you right now,' he growled, with such sexual gravitas she shivered. 'Hot enough to show you exactly how much of a man I am.'

His sinful tongue licked across the seam of her lips in silent entreaty and she fisted his hair and surrendered, holding him to her as that black magic enthralled her.

It was the distant tinkle of glasses and music that pierced her lust fog.

'Oh, Lord, Thane, our guests! You have to get dressed. We're getting married on the beach in…' Lifting her head, she peeked at the bedside clock. 'Crikey—seven minutes.'

And she wouldn't like to guess what she looked like. Their wide eyes met and they both burst out laughing like lovestruck teenagers.

'Seriously, though, I was thinking this private ceremony could be for us. We'll have a big splash at the cathedral, before your coronation. It will give my father time to come round too. We need peace between our houses, Thane. I want us to end this feud. You and I. Together.'

'Whatever you want—whatever makes you happy. I can be nice to your father. For thirty seconds at least.'

'Make it sixty-nine and I'll pay you in kind.'

He growled like a virile feral wolf. 'I'm having you back in this bed within two hours.'

'Then move it.'

Tornado-style, they whirled around the room, yanking suit hangers and buttoning shirts and shoving feet into shoes. Before she knew it they were at the door.

'You look indecently gorgeous, Prince Thane. I adore you in this black Armani. All dissolute and wicked. How do *I* look?'

He pointed his index finger north. 'Your halo is wonky.'

Her smile exploded into laughter. 'You mean my tiara?'

'*Si*. Not that I care. To me you look perfect. A debauched angel.'

'And I bet you like that, huh?'

'Of course,' he drawled.

She was beaming—she knew it. 'Okay, Romeo, are you ready to marry your Juliet?'

'I am ready to marry *you*, Luciana. To finally make you mine.'

She laced her hand through his and he gripped it with warm fingers and devout love and the promise of unaccountable tomorrows.

'Then let's do it. Let's make our destiny our own.'

* * * * *

CHRISTMAS BRIDE FOR THE SHEIKH

CAROL MARINELLI

CHAPTER ONE

I PROMISE I'LL be good.

Florence Andrews lay on her side beneath the sheets, with a heavy male arm pinning her, and promised that if the powers that be could possibly reverse the mistakes made last night then she would be good for the rest of her life.

'Morning,' he said sleepily, and she felt the morning swell of him on the back of her thigh. It was so insistent he might just as well have been prodding her to get up.

She said nothing, deciding it was far safer to feign sleep.

Flo was all too used to getting it wrong with men.

Petite, with blonde hair and china-blue eyes, Flo had found that she attracted a rather specific type of male—ones whose names began with a B and ended with a D.

Bad.

Bastard.

Either would fool her.

The last man she had dated had practically had to come with written references before she'd even agreed to go out with him, yet he had turned out to be just like the rest.

A louse.

In fact, even thinking of him had Flo screwing her eyes more tightly closed in shame.

She'd sworn off men, so it had been an awfully long time since she'd gone out with anyone.

Not that she and Hazin had ever *been out*. It hadn't even been a date.

She opened her eyes and the view of a cold, grey London in autumn was as stunning as it had been last night. Big Ben let her know it was just after eight and from the dizzy height of the presidential suite it looked like a black and white photo, except for the rain hitting the vast windows.

Flo knew she had outdone herself in the rake stakes this time.

Sheikh Prince Hazin al-Razim of Zayrinia came with warnings attached rather than references.

She knew his title, not because he had told her but because of her friend.

Well, she had actually known of him before Maggie had got mixed up with his brother. Scandalous photos of Hazin were plastered over the Internet. His handsome face and naked body—with a generous black rectangle covering the necessary—appeared from time to time in the trashy magazines that the mothers read on the maternity ward where she was a midwife.

They would sometimes even giggle with Flo about him.

His reputation was appalling. Hazin was completely irredeemable; in fact, he was bad to the bone.

Yet he was adored by all.

And last night he had been, without a shadow of doubt, the best lover of her life.

Hazin had either fainted from a lack of blood to the head or he was asleep again, because the arm that had been pulling her back was loose now on her stomach and his breathing was even.

It gave her a pause.

How long the peace would last, she could not be sure.

Did she tell him she knew who he was and explain how their seemingly chance meeting had come about?

Would there even be conversation, given all they had between them was sex?

How the hell had she got into this mess? Flo wondered as she lay there. She was supposed to have been helping out her friend!

Flo had no intention of going out this evening. Maggie had texted and asked if Flo could stop by at the café where Maggie worked. Her friend had brought a souvenir home from her backpacking trip around the world—she was six months pregnant.

By Crown Prince Sheikh Ilyas of Zayrinia!

'I have to tell him.' Maggie said as they lunched. 'But I don't know how to.'

Privately, Flo wasn't too sure that Maggie did *have* to tell the father.

Oh, she was all for parental responsibility, but her friend was her main concern and she was pregnant by a future King, no less!

The baby was due just after Christmas. But as well as that, Maggie had recently found out she was having a little boy, and Flo was concerned how that might impact the situation.

Still, it wasn't for Flo to decide and so she told Maggie what she knew.

'His brother will be at Dion's tonight.'

'How do you know?'

'Because he gets kicked out of there every Friday. Hazin is the reason they're so popular now!'

Flo knew all about where the rich and beautiful gathered.

Dion's was a bar set within a very plush hotel. It had once been a sedate place to gather for pre-theatre drinks and dinner.

It was old-fashioned and had become oddly trendy, a sort of retro fifties-style bar that people now lined up to get into.

'You could go there tonight and tell Hazin that you need to speak with his brother.'

'Just walk in and tap him on the shoulder?' Maggie rolled her eyes.

'Get talking.' Flo shrugged. 'Flirt a little…'

'I'm nearly six months pregnant by his brother!'

'Oh, yes, I see your point.'

'And I doubt Hazin would be particularly pleased to see me. I caused an awful lot of trouble for him. No doubt he thinks I was involved in the plan to set him up.'

Maggie had been unwittingly used in a plan to stitch up Hazin and bribe the Palace. She had ended up in Hazin's cabin aboard his Royal yacht where a camera had been hidden overhead.

But whoever had assumed that Maggie would drop her bikini bottom for Hazin had not known her.

Maggie and Hazin had done nothing but have a conversation.

Not that the Palace had known that at the time. Ilyas had kidnapped Maggie to find out what had happened aboard the yacht.

Yes, *kidnapped*, Flo reminded her friend. 'Which, in my opinion, means you're under no obligation to tell him.'

'I want to, though.' Maggie said. 'Flo, I know I've given you an awful impression of Ilyas but he really was wonderful to me.'

He must have been, Flo conceded, because Maggie trusted so few people.

Flo thought for a moment. She didn't want to go to Dion's, it was where she had met her ex and he still drank there on occasion.

Maggie didn't know about that; she'd had enough troubles of her own since she'd returned from Zayrinia, without Flo piling on hers.

That wasn't the full reason, though. Maggie and Flo were close and usually she would have told her, but the break-up that had happened last Christmas, when Maggie had been away, had hurt Flo deeply.

And Flo was still terribly ashamed.

No, she did not want to go to Dion's tonight.

In fact, Flo hadn't really had a night out since last Christmas.

Maggie's baby was due a week after this one.

She looked at her friend, who had no family and was pregnant and scared, and Flo put on her smile.

She was very good at doing that and keeping her thoughts to herself. 'I could always come with you to Dion's after my shift,' Flo offered.

And so it had been arranged.

'I have to go.' Flo glanced at the time. 'I'm going to be late.'

She was often late, though not usually for work. It tended to be the other way round—she would stay on at work and arrive late for her life.

Men didn't seem to like that, Flo had worked out.

At least, not the ones she was used to.

Flo's shift had been a good one.

She was a midwife on the maternity unit at the Primary Hospital in London. It was a busy, modern hospital but, as much as Flo loved it, sometimes she yearned for more one-on-one time.

She had been rostered to work in Delivery but had instead been moved to the ward. There she had caught up with a mother she had cared for in the delivery unit the previous day. It had been a difficult birth and had ended in an emergency Caesarean.

Tonight, at the end of her shift, Flo had held the outcome in her arms.

Rose.

'She looks like one.' Flo had smiled, for Rose was delicate and pink and utterly oblivious to the terrible scare she had given everyone.

'Thanks for all you did, Flo,' Claire, the mother, had said.

Flo had smiled as she'd looked down at the tiny baby. Very rapid decisions had needed to be made and the petite, fun-loving Flo had snapped into action and become extremely vocal.

In her private life she did not stand up enough for herself, but at work, when looking out for the mothers and babies, she was very different indeed.

Her job was exhausting.

Quite simply, it was always so busy and it was a constant juggling act to give enough attention to the mothers.

Tonight, though, she had a moment.

Several of them.

At twenty-nine, and with her ovaries loudly ticking, Flo would have loved a baby of her own. Still, she got more than a regular fix of that delicious newborn scent each working day. 'Your beautiful daughter has reminded me exactly why I love my job,' Flo said.

She popped the sleeping baby back into her Perspex crib and then reset Claire's IV.

'Are you on tomorrow?' Claire asked.

'No, but I'm back on Monday. You should be about ready for discharge then but I shall do my best to come in and see you both.'

She looked again at little Rose, so peaceful and safe, and then Flo turned at a knock on the door and saw it was her senior.

'Flo, it's time to give your handover.'

It was just after nine, and for the first time in a very long time it seemed that Flo might just get away on time.

She did.

Flo raced back to her flat and had a very quick shower. She was used to getting ready quickly to go out.

Or she had been.

Not all men were bad, Flo knew that.

She saw evidence every day that good guys existed. Her parents had just celebrated their thirtieth wedding anniversary and her brothers and sisters were all happily married. At work, she regularly saw fathers support their partners and she worked with an amazing team.

Yes, she knew there were good guys, but she had met the other kind too.

Flo grabbed a sheer, grey dress and high-heeled shoes and then quickly set to work on her hair and make-up.

She put her hair up and quickly did her eyes, followed by a slick of neutral colour on her lips. She was about to add earrings when her hands paused over her jewellery tray.

It was a testimony to her disastrous love life. Flo knew she had been too easily appeased by bling.

She had thought the more expensive the gift, the deeper the commitment.

Flo knew now she could not have been more wrong.

And so she left the earrings off and raced for the underground, firing Maggie a quick text on the way.

Ten minutes

It would be more like twenty, Flo knew, but she also knew Maggie would be terribly nervous and looking for an excuse to walk away.

Flo was more than a little concerned at the predicament her friend was in. Maggie had been raised in foster and care homes and had no family to advise her. As a midwife, Flo was well versed on single mothers who were facing difficulties alone. She wasn't exactly trained, though, in advising women who were pregnant by a future King.

Goodness!

She hurried up the escalator, came out of the underground and arrived out on the street a little breathless.

Even from that distance she could see the queue and wondered if there was even a hope of them getting in. She knew just how exclusive it was.

'Flo!'

Marcus, the doorman, called her name and Flo flashed her winning smile as she walked over, thrilled to be remembered. 'I'm just waiting for my friend to arrive.'

'Well, you could both be waiting for a very long time if you don't come in now,' Marcus told her. 'I'm being moved to security inside in a moment so there will be someone else on the door.'

Flo wavered and looked down the street, but there was no sign of Maggie.

'You can leave your friend's name at the front desk,' he suggested.

To the moans of the queue, the velvet rope was lifted and Flo was allowed in.

'You have to hand in your phone,' Marcus warned. 'So maybe text her now.'

'Why do I have to hand in my phone?'

'Orders from the top.'

Ah, so Hazin *must* be here.

His bad-boy ways had been captured on camera one too many times, Flo guessed, and the management would not want to upset him. She fired Maggie a quick text to meet inside, left her name at the desk and then made her way in.

Dion's was very beautiful. There were intimate velvet booths for diners, a gleaming walnut bar, and occasional tables where patrons could sip their cocktails and beverages of choice.

The place was packed with endless, rich beauty, and though it had once excited her, now it left Flo rather cold.

She had been caught up a little in this world once and, having been a lot more innocent back then, she'd believed that men had actually wanted to get to know her!

Instead, they had wanted her to hang quietly on their arm and not ask too many questions.

Yes, she'd been hurt.

Badly so.

But she pushed it to the back of her mind and squeezed her way over to the bar.

A couple looked as if they were about to vacate a table and Flo debated whether to grab it or to go and order first.

But then she saw him.

Sheikh Prince Hazin al-Razim.

He wore a suit that was as black and superbly cut as his hair. His tie was loosened and he was so stunning that he actually stopped Flo in her tracks.

How the hell did a person even begin to approach that? she pondered, thinking of her suggestion to Maggie to approach casually. And then she thought of Maggie alone in a cabin with him for two hours!

Had she been the one alone with him on a yacht, they would not have been talking!

Hazin was as utterly gorgeous as that.

He wasn't banned from bringing in his phone, of course.

In fact, he was checking it and Flo could tell he was getting ready to leave.

Indeed, Hazin was about to go.

He was supposed to have met his older brother an hour ago and hadn't been looking forward to it in the least. He did not need another lecture on taming his ways, but Ilyas had been insistent that they meet.

And then hadn't bothered to show.

They were not close. In fact, thanks to their upbringings, Hazin and Ilyas were practically strangers. They had been segregated as children and when Hazin had proven rather a handful he had been sent to be schooled in London.

Ilyas wore the robe in the relationship and Hazin the suit.

Ilyas would be King.

Hazin simply did not care for any of that and did all he could not to return home, for there was no welcome waiting, just lectures on his behaviour that had been on repeat from as far back as Hazin could remember. As well as that, he loathed how his father ran the country, for it was in the same way in which King Ahmed parented—no empathy and with disdain for those he was charged to care for.

To Hazin's eyes, Ilyas was as staid and cold as his father.

There was no message on his phone to explain his brother's lateness, and looking up Hazin glanced around the place.

He was sick of Dion's and the empty, painted people.

But then he saw her.

Or rather he heard the barman laugh at something and looked to its source.

She was ordering a glass of wine and a sparkling water and as she waited for her drinks she turned to look around. Her china-blue eyes met his.

'Hi,' she said.

He gave a very slight nod, but he didn't find her forwardness particularly fetching. She was gorgeous, that was a given, but Hazin was more than used to women making a move on him and the gloss had long since worn off.

Flo could sense his disinterest and that he was about to leave; she wondered what she should say and how best to introduce herself. She glanced towards the main door and wished Maggie would arrive, but there was no sign of her. 'I'm waiting for a friend.'

Hazin said nothing, for it had nothing to do with him.

'She's late,' Flo pushed.

Hazin accompanied his tight smile with a put-down. 'And I'm leaving.'

He had no interest in offering to keep her company. He was tired of being chatted up just for his Royal title and the empty sex that followed.

These days, he practically had to pat them down first to check for cameras anyway.

Then he watched as she stifled a yawn.

It was not the response Hazin was used to. Usually they hung on his every word.

Yes, he was jaded.

'Excuse me,' Flo said. 'I just came from work…'

She was tired and yet also energised in the magnetic presence of Hazin, and unsure whether to tell him who her friend was and that Maggie would soon be arriving, but then he asked a question.

'What do you do for work?'

'I'm a midwife.'

He pulled such a horrified face that it made her laugh.

And then Hazin became curious.

'I haven't seen you here before…' Hazin said, because he would have remembered if he had.

She wasn't just pretty, she was animated and a shade different from the rest, he thought.

'No, I used to come here quite a lot but I've banned myself,' Flo said, and took a sip of her wine.

'Why?'

'I'm not telling you.' She smiled.

Oh, hurry up, Maggie, she thought, because he was utterly, recklessly stunning and now that he was talking to her she could peek shamelessly without looking odd.

He had smoky grey eyes and his skin was a burnt caramel. As for his mouth, she couldn't not watch it when he spoke, and those plump lips needed to be kissed.

She should have gone out more, Flo thought, for she felt like a convent schoolgirl set free.

'Do you want to get a table?' Hazin offered, because all of a sudden he wasn't that jaded and was very much up for being used.

Well, a table would be perfect actually, Flo thought. It meant he wouldn't be leaving and Maggie would get here to find them both sitting and talking, like sensible adults.

Only right now Flo didn't want to be sensible, and she was suddenly nervous about going and sitting down.

There was a crackle of awareness between them, stronger than she had ever known.

'I doubt we'd get a table…' she said, terrified of her own lack of resistance to him, and then pulled a little face behind his back as he had a word with the bar.

'Done.'

But they didn't get a table.

Hazin and his glass of water were worthy of a booth.

He was so broad shouldered that the people parted like the Red Sea for him and she should have walked a smooth path behind, except her thighs felt like they were made of rubber.

'After you,' he said, and she slid into a velvet-lined seat and let out a tense breath of relief when he took the seat opposite, instead of sliding in beside her.

'I'm Hazin.'

She noticed he did not offer his title.

This man did not need a title to have her feeling weak from the waist down.

He thought that perhaps, if she hadn't been coming to Dion's for a while, she might not know who he was. It was a refreshing thought—to losc the burden of it for a night.

'You?' he asked.

'Flo,' she said. 'Florence.'

'Like that old nurse?'

'Florence Nightingale?' she checked, and he nodded. 'Well, she wasn't old in her day,' Flo corrected him. 'Do you perhaps mean that nurse from olden times?'

'I do.'

She smiled.

Hazin was well schooled but English was his second language and occasionally he slipped. Anyway, language and its intricacies could hardly be expected to be at the forefront of his mind when in the presence of such loveliness.

He liked her matter-of-fact correction that had come with a smile. Hazin had been raised to know any deviation from perfection would not be tolerated.

Yes he was wild, but whether it was a misspelt birthday card to his father, a torrid fling, or being born second in line, the verdict was always the same.

Not good enough.

So he no longer tried and instead happily disappointed everyone.

His sins would never be forgiven so Hazin had long since stopped apologising for them.

It made no difference when he did.

'So,' he asked, wanting to know more of her, 'why have you banned yourself?'

'Because the people here are terribly shallow.'

'Yes.'

'And my ex comes here...' Flo explained just a little.

'Were you hoping to see him?'

'God, no.' Flo grimaced at the very thought. 'I'm not just avoiding Dion's, I've been staying home a lot of late.'

'For how long?'

'All this year.'

'Why?'

'I'm off men.'

He looked at Flo and he wondered, in a way that was unusual for him, what on earth had happened that she would hide her light away.

'Why?'

'I don't want to talk about it.'

Flo hadn't told anyone.

Not a single soul.

Yet his eyes looked right into hers and his smile was non-judgmental and kind.

But, no, she would not be telling him.

'So are you off *all* men?'

She swallowed because just a short while ago her response would have been an unequivocal yes.

Except he was ravishing.

And funny.

But mainly he was ravishing.

His eyes weren't a uniform grey—this close she could see there were little flecks of green and amber.

'I think so.'

'Isn't it a bit extreme?' he asked. 'To hide yourself away…?'

'Perhaps,' Flo said. 'Yes.'

'Would you like another drink?' he offered.

'No, thank you.' She glanced at his empty glass. 'Can I get you one?'

She was frantic to get some control here—to go and

stand at the bar again so she could remind herself how to breathe, but Hazin would not let her get away that easily.

'I don't drink,' he said. 'I can have your friend's soda water. It doesn't look as if she's going to show.'

'No.'

She looked around the bar and wondered what to do. Perhaps Maggie had changed her mind about letting Ilyas know about the baby.

Flo felt a little lost without her phone.

And then she saw him.

Her ex.

The reason why she had been hiding for so long.

Bastard.

She flicked her eyes away from her past and back at Hazin.

At least this man didn't pretend he wasn't one.

'Are you okay?' Hazin asked, because he didn't usually lose his audience.

'My ex is here,' Flo said, and she held her breath as out of the corner of her eye she saw him make his way over.

Hazin watched her very pretty face pale rather than flush and he knew she'd been badly hurt.

And then he knew why.

Hazin was a regular here and had watched this creep pick up someone on one night and bring his wife for a meal the next.

Hazin might be wild now, but he had been married once and he'd taken his vows seriously, so, when it was clear from her panicked silence that she could not deal with her ex, Hazin was more than happy to.

'Flo's busy,' Hazin said in a surly tone. 'Please leave.'

'Now look here—' the man started, but then Hazin stood up.

'I did ask politely,' Hazin said and Flo could not believe there was about to be a fight.

What the hell?

He was more than up for a fight, but instead he gestured with his head for Marcus.

'I just want to speak to Flo,' the man insisted.

'Well, you can't,' Hazin said, 'because, as of now, you are barred from this establishment.'

It was Marcus's problem now because, as Flo's ex loudly protested as he was steered away, Hazin took his seat again. 'He shan't trouble you again,' Hazin said. 'At least, not when you're here.'

The shadow in the room was gone and she experienced the giddy feeling of some measure of retribution at last.

Now Flo examined him and no longer did she hide that fact.

And Hazin did the same.

She was used to the roaming of male eyes over her body but his eyes did not leave her face.

And yet his gaze was indecent.

He traced the curves of her lips with his eyes so thoroughly that Flo fought not to run her tongue over them.

It felt as if he studied each eyelash in turn until she silently pleaded for him to fully meet her gaze.

Then when he did it was fire versus fire.

Beneath the table, she could envision his spread knees for they seemed to encircle hers, which were pressed tightly together. She could feel their surrounding warmth and almost craved the tight pressure of his grip.

'I think I should go,' Flo said, because it was clear Maggie wasn't going to show.

'I can't hear you.'

Liar, liar, Flo thought as she gazed deep into his eyes, for here in the booth they were sequestered from the thrumming noise of the bar.

She could say it a little louder, reach for her purse and leave, or she could lean in a little closer to that delicious mouth and repeat what she had just said.

Or she could simply make the complicated so terribly easy.

Flo chose the latter—'Come and sit by me, then.'

No, she didn't want another drink, or conversation; she wanted this…

His kiss.

CHAPTER TWO

It felt as if the oxygen masks had tumbled out on the plane, for even before he was seated she reached up for his tie and pulled him in.

The attraction had been instant, the effect close up magnetic, for they were so strongly drawn to each other that first contact offered Flo a heady feeling of relief. Hazin lowered his head and their mouths met before he was even fully seated. His lips were warm and Flo's pouted to his.

Soft and sensual, his mouth claimed hers as he slid into the booth beside her.

She had never known a kiss like it, for it sent a river of shivers through her and the brief bliss of relief faded for she *had* to taste his tongue, yet Hazin made her wait. His hands came to her upper arms and he held her steady when she ached to lean into him.

Still no tongue, just the bruising of his mouth and a breathless rush of desire in an outwardly chaste kiss. Then his mouth left hers and she felt its warm drag against her cheek and the scratch of his jaw as his lips found her ear. His breath was warm and he told her his truth. 'I want you so badly.'

His voice was so loaded with lust that it sounded as if he were already inside her.

Her sex clenched to his words.

She had no resolve.

None.

For a second she sat, his cheek pressed to hers, his ragged sexy breathing in her ear and his hands firm on her arms, and Flo closed her eyes in a vague prayer for common sense to prevail.

It didn't.

Fired on by one kiss, her body crackled like a chip in hot oil and she offered her response to his indecent request. 'Take me to bed.'

As soon as the night air hit her, sense would appear, Flo reassured herself as they stood. He took her by the hand and she was rather glad for the support as he led her through the bar.

But not to the street.

No cool air to hit her.

No car or taxi to calm her mind.

They were in an elevator. He hit the button and even that jab of his finger had her almost fold. And then that same finger stroked her nipple and she simply watched, entranced.

Was it her self-imposed ban on men that had her so frantic? Flo wondered. But, no, that wasn't right, for she had never felt like this in her life.

She was turned on to her very core. When he removed his hand she took it and pressed his palm to her face then deep-kissed his hand.

He moaned and said something in Arabic and then, when the elevator doors opened, Flo dropped his hand and they stood for a second facing each other.

She had to have his mouth.

Yet he just gave a slow smile and with an utter lack of haste he turned and walked down the long corridor.

For a hotel, there was a distinct lack of doors, Flo thought vaguely, for her mind was muddled by him.

They came to one, though, and he opened it. They stepped in and she realised the lack of doors was because his suite took up the entire floor.

A rainy London night glittered before them. Flo could see the Houses of Parliament, and Big Ben told her it was after midnight, yet the landmarks, so loved and familiar to her, were now altered in her mind. How could she ever gaze upon the time again and not remember the feel of him coming up behind her?

His hands dealt with her zipper and she just stood there as her dress fell to the floor.

She turned her head, needing his touch, for little slivers of doubt were raining in.

'Kiss me…' she said.

'Of course.'

But still he denied her the taste of his mouth for his lips went to her shoulder and he tasted her there as he slowly removed her bra.

'Hazin…'

'Do you mean, kiss you here?' he asked, and turned her around so he could kiss her breast.

Softly, slowly and indecently.

The doubt he'd sparked was intentional, Flo realised, and it now felt delicious. The hovering of uncertainty was dizzying as he kissed down her stomach.

Hazin removed her knickers and then he kissed her calves as he carefully slipped off her shoes.

'Sit down,' he told her.

'Where?'

'You choose.'

She couldn't.

Flo looked around at the stunning surroundings and

blinked in confusion. She was naked while he was fully dressed and she was actually trembling with desire.

'How about here?' Hazin suggested as he indicated one of the high-backed wooden chairs from a large polished dining table.

'It doesn't look very comfortable.'

'Poor Flo,' he said as he brought the chair over.

The wood was cold and hard on her bottom and she wasn't certain she liked this game, yet she complied willingly.

He was still completely dressed—he hadn't even removed his jacket—and the only concession to her nakedness was that he further loosened his tie.

'Are you going to spank me?' Flo asked, curious because she had never been spanked before. In fact, she would absolutely refuse it.

Not with him…

'Why would I spank you?' he asked. 'When you've been so good?'

'Oh.'

'I'm going to reward you.'

He knelt down and his hands parted her thighs. 'Hazin…' Flo objected. It was all too clinical. She didn't want flowers but, hell, a kiss would be nice.

And then he did kiss her.

But…*there*.

He just scooted her bottom out before lowering his head and thoroughly kissing her. He could be as clinical as he liked if it meant this! He moved her calves to rest on his broad shoulders as she hung onto the edge of the chair.

His tongue was insistent and he moaned with intent. It was so focused and thorough and Flo found that tears threatened. Her thighs were trembling but his arms clamped them down. She let go of the chair and buried her hands into his hair. His tongue grew more rapid in its intimate perusal and her bottom tried to lift as she began to climax, but he pinned her down and she tugged at his thick black hair as she met utter bliss.

Then he stood and simply picked her up and did as she had asked.

He took her to bed.

It was already turned down, but he pushed the sheets further back and deposited her there.

And she lay on her side, trying to recover and somewhat bemused as she watched him undress, for she had wanted to do that part.

Hazin was like no other lover.

He kicked off his shoes and peeled off his socks.

She wanted to feel the muscled arms beneath the white shirt.

Yet he denied her that pleasure.

She wanted to tug at his belt and to feel him, yet she breathlessly watched instead.

God, he was exquisite.

Lean and strong and completely unabashed. He smiled over to her, an arrogant smile, and she returned it, for they were feasting on each other with their eyes.

He went into the bedside drawer and took out a condom. She reached out to touch him but he slapped her hand back. Again she had to settle for watching and she bit on her lip as he stood and gave his long thick length a couple of deft strokes before sliding on the condom.

It shouldn't have been sexy, yet it absolutely was. She was burning from her roots to her toes, on fire as he climbed into bed beside her.

And then finally, *finally* he kissed her.

He rolled her onto her back and he gave her all that

had been denied until now. His tongue was probing and his mouth was urgent and rough. Finally, she felt those muscled arms and the satin of his skin. He drove into her and she cried out because he was not a gentle lover, but his controlled power was the just the right kind roughness, for he stroked her deep inside and seemed to read her wants instinctively.

Hazin spoke in Arabic, yet she somehow understood every word, for they *were* so hot together and so damned good.

Worries fell like dominos.

That row at work? Gone.

The bastard earlier? Forgotten.

Obsolete.

Hazin felt the same.

For the first time utterly attuned to another person.

He had tasted her first peak of pleasure, but the second gripped him and the shudder and pulsing grip of her just about finished him.

'Hazin,' Flo begged, because she was utterly spent, and then, when it should have been over, he kissed her back.

A kiss so soft and slow it tasted of the romance both had denied.

It was like finding herself in the wrong dream.

Scary almost to know him tender as well as urgent and passionate.

And even scarier for Flo to reveal her other side.

Flo opened her eyes and met his and there was a moment of utter connection. Her legs loosened their grip on him and he thrust slowly. So intimate and slow were they that she deep-kissed his neck, tasting the salt of his skin, as they locked into each other; tasting each other, and raining kisses as he took her to a place she had never been.

It felt like the edge of something, like she had finally stumbled into the right dream as he called her name and reached his own moment of release. And when there was nothing left to give, her body found an untapped resource, for she beat to his tune, this utter giddying orgasm, that only he could evoke.

His weight on her felt necessary and, oh, so right.

She could lie there and not think for a moment, just enjoy the bliss of them both sated.

He really was bliss, for there was no dark silence afterwards, just a light kiss and the warmth of his embrace.

'I'm glad you were there tonight,' Hazin said.

So was she.

Flo awoke, of course, with regret.

Please, she bargained with the powers that be, reverse this mistake and I will give up men for life.

Then she felt the wetof his tongue and the warmth of his breath on her neck and the light dusting of his fingers on her stomach.

And then the tearing of the condom foil lit her like a match as he pulled her against him.

Tomorrow, she vowed as he slipped inside her.

She would start being good tomorrow.

CHAPTER THREE

HAZIN SHOWERED AND thought of the woman who now lay in his bed.

He liked her being there.

Flo made him laugh and that in itself was unusual for there had been little laughter of late.

As a rule, Hazin offered no breakfast with bed that might encourage an overnight guest to stay longer, but he came out and dried himself with a towel and found he had not changed his mind—he wanted her here.

'Do you want breakfast?'

'That would be lovely,' Flo said, and sat up as he picked up the bedside phone and ordered breakfast for two.

She did not know how to tell Hazin that she knew who he was and wished that she had got it out of the way last night.

Now she stood watching him dry off. There was a bruise on his chest that her mouth had made and another on his neck. He was muscled and toned and his length was rising from his thigh. He watched her watching it.

'Did I miss a bit?' he said, holding the towel out to her. She wanted to take it, to dry his glistening skin and then wet him again with her mouth. Their want and desire was so matched, and her body so willing, but she had to clear things up first.

'Hazin,' Flo said, declining the towel, and she swallowed nervously as he resumed his leisurely drying off. 'Last night, I came—'

'I know.'

'I mean I came to Dion's in the hope…' Her words were coming out wrong, Flo knew that, but she just didn't know how best to tell him. So she simply did. 'I knew that you'd be here.'

The towel stopped in mid-stroke of his thigh.

'Meaning?' he said, and then gave a derisive laugh. 'You know who I am.'

'Yes, but—'

'Did you get your photo of me?'

'Hazin!'

'Or are you off to sell your story now?'

'Please listen—'

'No, you listen.' He pulled on his clothes with some difficulty for the angry words had fired him, and as he attempted to tuck himself in, words hissed out through his teeth. 'Do what you want. I don't care…'

'I'm a friend of Maggie's.'

'Who?'

'The woman you met on the yacht…'

'You mean the one who bribed me?'

'No.' Flo knelt up on the bed, shaking her head, and then she pulled the sheet up to cover her for everything had vanished in a heartbeat—the intimacy, the carefree nakedness, the laughter, all that they had so recently found swept away by her careless words.

'Hazin…' She took a breath, and though her mouth was open she did not know what to say.

Clearly Maggie had stayed away last night for a reason. Perhaps she had changed her mind about telling Ilyas that she was carrying his child?

And now certainly wasn't the time or place to tell Hazin!

'Get out,' he said, and his voice whipped the tense air.

'Hazin, what happened last night had nothing to do with Maggie. I didn't come to the bar intending to sleep with you.'

He was too used to this, Hazin thought as he marched through to the lounge and retrieved her underwear and dress that they had so happily disposed of last night. He walked back to the bedroom and tossed them to her on the bed.

'Get out!' he said again.

But then he changed his mind, for he could not wait however long it would take her to dress for Flo to be gone. 'Actually, I'm going to go,' he told her. 'I want you out of here by the time I get back. If you're not, I'll ask Security to have you removed.'

She knew how effective his security was.

He grabbed his wallet and phone and pocketed his keys.

'Stay for breakfast at least,' he sneered. 'You certainly earned it.'

Hazin kicked at the kerb as he walked down the street.

It was grey, raining and cold.

His phone kept ringing and he was in no mood to talk to anyone. It couldn't be Flo because they hadn't exchanged numbers yet pulled it out to check.

It was Ilyas.

Ilyas was persistent and Hazin was in just the mood for a row.

'What the hell happened to you last night?' Hazin shouted by way of greeting when he took the call.

'We need to speak.'

'Well, had you turned up as arranged we would have.'

'Hazin, this is important.'

They met at a café and drank strong coffee.

Hazin could feel his brother's eyes sweep over his neck and the bite mark Flo had left. 'I don't need another lecture.'

'I'm not here to lecture you,' Ilyas said.

'And I don't need to be reminded that the yachts and jets will be pulled. I can afford to pay for my own.'

Hazin was not idle.

After Petra's death he had returned to England with the intention to further his education and attend university, as had always been his aim. He hadn't been able to focus, though, so had started to dabble in property.

Whatever Hazin dabbled in did well.

He did not need Royal privilege to survive; in fact, without it Hazin thrived. Yes, he had been given an amazing start but he had a good eye and even if he had been born to a beggar he still would have done well.

His parents knew it and loathed that fact.

'Hazin,' Ilyas said, 'I have already told you that I am not here to lecture you. I have something important to tell you—yesterday I spoke with our father in front of the Palace elders and I told him that things are changing—'

'They will never change.' Hazin dismissed the notion. 'Not while he is King.'

'I have told him that there are to be no decisions made without my approval and that there is to be a transition of power to me.'

Now Hazin looked up. 'He would never agree to that.'

'I gave him no choice but to agree. I made it clear that if he refused then I am prepared to take it to the people,' Ilyas said. 'Would I have your support?'

'You don't need it.'

'I want it, though.'

Hazin looked at his brother.

A stranger.

He wanted to believe change could happen, yet could not really see it taking place. Yet there was a stir of relief within Hazin that his brother would be stepping up, an intrinsic trust that Ilyas would get things right, yet he did not know where that feeling came from for they had been raised apart. 'You have my support.'

'I want you beside me.'

'Oh, no.' Hazin shook his head. He would support his brother in his ventures but he would not be returning home.

'Hazin, there has been a lot of damage done by him. If things are to be put right it's going to take a lot of work to win back people's trust. You returning to Zayrinia would speak volumes.'

'You expect me to upend my life on the premise that things *may* change?'

'They shall change. And there is something else I am here to tell you,' Ilyas said. 'I am going to marry in two weeks' time.'

'So much for change.' Hazin shrugged and took a drink of his coffee. Ilyas had always refused to marry, insisting the harem more than sufficed. 'You simply gave in to him.'

It had infuriated their father that Ilyas had refused to marry. He had long wanted to select a bride for his son and for there to be a Royal wedding.

At the age of eighteen Hazin had received his exam results. He had worked incredibly hard and the results had been outstanding.

His father hadn't even commented.

Instead of attending university in England, as had been Hazin's dream, finally he'd found something he could do that might please his father the King.

There was going to be a Royal wedding—Hazin's.

Petra had been chosen as his bride and they had first met at the wedding itself.

Both had been eighteen and Hazin could well remember looking out from the balcony at the cheering crowds and wondering what the hell he had done, while trying to hide it from his bride.

Ilyas dragged him from his introspection. 'You remember Maggie?'

Hazin frowned at the sound of that name again.

He hadn't seen her in six months. Even then, all they had shared was a conversation and that alone had caused so much trouble.

Yet in the space of an hour he had heard her name twice.

Once from Flo, now from his brother.

'What about her?'

'Last night I asked Maggie to marry me.'

Hazin suddenly felt caught.

Nothing at all had happened between Maggie and himself. It had been a set-up and the cameras watching had hoped something would.

It hadn't.

But Hazin had asked the Palace to pay the ransom demand because of the conversation that had taken place between them. Thankfully, though, their voices had not been recorded and so no one other than Maggie knew what had been said.

He had spoken openly, perhaps far too openly, but he had felt safe in the knowledge he would never see Maggie again.

Yet now he was being told she was to marry his brother!

Had she told Ilyas what he had said?

'Maggie is pregnant,' Ilyas told him. 'The baby is due in three months.'

'So while you were nailing me to the wall for something Maggie and I didn't do, all the time you were—'

'Hazin,' Ilyas interrupted, 'I had Maggie brought to the desert to find out what was going on, because I assumed she was blackmailing you. She wasn't. We fell in love.'

And that silenced Hazin, for it was something he'd never thought he would hear from Ilyas's mouth.

His brother had always seemed cold and aloof and yet he was sitting in a café, telling him there would be changes in the Palace and that he had fallen in love.

And, yes, Maggie had spoken.

The content of the conversation had been private. Words had been said to a stranger with confidence they would never meet again.

Instead, Ilyas relayed what he had said that day.

'Maggie told me you said on the yacht that you hoped to be disinherited.'

'Well, she shouldn't have repeated what was clearly a private conversation,'

'It remains just between us. I shall not be taking what was said to the elders.'

Oh, Ilyas was so controlled and formal, Hazin thought, and shot him a look as he spoke on.

'I understand too that you don't want to speak at Petra's anniversary…'

'Maggie's been busy!' Hazin sneered.

'I had to drag the conversation from her.'

Hazin felt as if his most private thoughts were being raked over by a stranger.

'I know this must be difficult for you,' Ilyas attempted. 'You must miss Petra—'

He knew *nothing.*

Ilyas, who had always been so distant, suddenly reaching out did not sit right with Hazin.

'We don't talk, Ilyas. We never have, unless it was you telling me to raise my game. You know nothing of my life yet ten years after Petra's death you sit here and tell me you know how I feel?' Hazin shook his head. 'Too late.'

'No.' Ilyas said. 'I want—'

'You can keep wanting, then,' Hazin said. 'But I have no desire to come back home, and certainly not for a wedding.'

The last one he had been to had been his own.

They had all assumed he had been blinded with grief since Petra's death and that was why he had gone off the rails.

They didn't know him at all and it was too late now to try.

'Why didn't you show up last night?' Hazin asked.

He saw Ilyas's slight eyebrow rise at the odd question, given the rather vital news, but Hazin was starting to realise what might have occurred.

'I went to see Maggie,' he said. 'She was actually on her way to try and meet you, so you could have me contact her.'

Hazin pressed his fingers into his forehead and closed his eyes. He could see now what had happened. Worse, he could see himself tossing Flo her clothes and shouting at her to get out.

He had to get back and try to explain somehow, and now had no desire to play catch-up with his brother.

'Good luck with the wedding,' Hazin said, and stood.

Ilyas did not try to dissuade him from leaving. They may not have been close, but he knew his younger brother would take time later to think it through.

And Hazin would.

Right now there was somewhere else he needed to be.

He walked briskly back to the hotel and took the elevator up to his floor. He pulled out his card and swiped the door open.

Too late.

Flo was gone.

He had known that she would be.

Hazin really hadn't imagined he'd find her sitting there, tucking into breakfast. Instead it had been set up on the table and remained untouched.

He walked through to the bedroom and the unmade bed.

There was the towel he had dropped on the floor and there was another so he guessed she must have showered and left.

Hazin walked back to the untouched breakfast and

felt a curl of guilt when he saw a box of tissues by the window and a little pile of knotted ones.

She'd been crying.

Hazin was very used to being a deliberate bastard.

This morning he'd been an inadvertent one.

CHAPTER FOUR

IF EVER THERE was a walk of shame, this was one. Not only was Flo clearly wearing last night's clothes, she'd also had to go down to the bar to retrieve her phone.

When she stepped out onto the street it was raining.

Of course it was, Flo thought as she trudged in high heels towards the underground.

What on earth had she been thinking last night?

Only she hadn't been thinking—one look into those smoky eyes and she'd forgotten why she was even at Dion's. How the hell was she going to tell Maggie the mess she had made of things?

And where the hell was Maggie?

Flo turned on her phone and on a cold, miserable wet morning there was suddenly a reason to smile.

Ilyas had proposed.

Oh, she was going to start crying again and hadn't thought to stuff her purse with tissues from the hotel.

So she used the back of her hand and read on and saw that Maggie wanted her to come straight over.

Er, that would be a no.

Flo first went back to her tiny flat and pulled on something a bit less *last night*!

Then she did what she could with foundation because

her chin was a little red and her mouth was all swollen from his delicious kisses and soft nips with his teeth.

She was going to start crying again, but that would not do.

So, instead of weeping, Flo headed over to her friend's and bought a bunch of flowers on the way.

'What happened?' Flo smiled, putting her own woes aside to celebrate the wonderful news with her friend, though there were rather too many stars in Maggie's eyes to see the threat of tears in Flo's.

'A lot,' Maggie said. 'I was just on my way to meet you when Ilyas came to the door. I'm so sorry I left you waiting…'

'Of course you did!' Flo said, for she totally understood the wonderful surprise that it must have been. 'What did he say about the baby?'

'He's thrilled,' Maggie said, but then her face became worried. 'I don't know how the people will react, though, or his family. Flo, there is so much going on back in Zayrinia—Ilyas has challenged his father, the King.'

'What does that even mean?'

'That Ilyas is to be the silent leader. From now on nothing is to get passed without his approval. He has told his father that if he doesn't comply then he will take it to the people.'

'What does that mean for you?'

'I'm not sure. I know that there's unrest amongst the people and that there has been a lot of unhappiness at the Palace. Ilyas wants change. He's gone to speak with his brother to see if he has his backing.'

Flo held her breath. She doubted she'd be at the forefront of Hazin's thoughts when he found out his brother was challenging the King, yet there was a tiny dart of hope that Hazin would maybe understand that she hadn't been at Dion's last night to seduce him.

Maggie had more news as well. 'After Ilyas has spoken with Hazin he's heading back to Zayrinia. Now that I've accepted his proposal I'm not allowed to see him until we marry.'

'At all?' Flo checked, and Maggie nodded. 'So when will you marry?'

'Two weeks' time!'

'Oh, my!' Flo looked at her friend and asked, perhaps, a stupid question, but it was all too much to take in. 'You'll live in Zayrinia?'

Maggie nodded. 'I'll still see you, though.'

Yes, Flo thought, but it won't be the same. She looked around Maggie's room within a flat, which she had helped her move into not long ago. She was thrilled for her friend but at the same time Flo was daunted by the distance. Maggie felt more like a sister than a friend. Flo stopped by the café where Maggie worked most days for a catch-up. She had a drawer full of clothes and necessities that she'd been buying for the baby.

And now both Maggie and the baby were moving away—in two weeks' time!

'I'm going to miss you,' Flo admitted.

'I won't give you a chance to. But, Flo, I'm so scared it will all go wrong. What if his father doesn't accept his choice of bride? This challenge to the King is so new and it was made before he knew about the baby. Ilyas knows that nothing happened between Hazin and me on the yacht but what if his parents don't believe us?'

'Maggie…' Flo attempted to calm her friend but Maggie was a touch frantic.

'I just don't want anything to go wrong.'

'It won't,' Flo said assuredly, deciding that now possibly wasn't the best time to tell Maggie she had just come from Hazin's bed! Maybe once the wedding was over and done with she would tell her friend what had happened last night.

But maybe not!

'You will come to the wedding?' Maggie checked.

'Of course I'll be there,' Flo said as she mentally stared down the eye of the off-duty roster. She had fought hard to have three weeks off at Christmas. It would be her first Christmas off since she had started nursing, but she would forfeit it if meant she could be there for her friend. 'I'll call work now.' Flo said. 'I'll see if I can swap some annual leave.'

Yet she didn't have to!

She and Maggie would arrive two days before the wedding and, Flo was delighted to find out, they would be flying in on Ilyas's plane.

And, given Maggie and Ilyas would be off to the desert straight afterwards, she didn't need much time off work.

It just meant a jiggle of the roster and Flo got to keep her Christmas leave.

Of course, while organising her leave there was a coil of hope rising that she would get to see Hazin!

It was the busiest run-up to a wedding and was beyond exciting.

Maggie sorted out her life and planned her big move, and Flo worked right up to the last minute.

'I am so tired,' she admitted, as she and Maggie, along with a couple of other good friends—Paul the café manager and his wife Kelly—all collapsed on the sumptuous leather seats on Ilyas's private jet. 'But not too tired for champagne!'

It was brilliant.

A whirlwind.

The take-off was abrupt and then they were served a sumptuous lunch of dips and then a delectable *kuku sabzi*—a Persian herb frittata with walnuts, decorated with crushed rose petals and berberis leaves, all washed down with a sweet hibiscus tea.

Paul and Kelly went for a rest in one of the guest cabins but Flo refused hers; instead, she and Maggie went into the Royal suite.

'Oh, my gosh!' Flo said. 'You and Ilyas get to have sex here!'

There was a huge bed draped in furs, and the lighting was demure. It was just a sexy man cave miles in the sky. 'Is this just for Ilyas?' Flo asked, fishing a little.

'It is.' Maggie nodded.

'What about his parents?'

'They have their own plane.'

'And the brother?' Flo, oh, so casually asked.

'Hazin has his own, I believe,' Maggie said. 'They do their own thing.'

They lay on the bed together and marvelled at the journey ahead, as well as the one that had brought them here.

It was so nice to take some time out, for they simply had not had a chance to just relax and talk.

'What will happen about your antenatal care?' Flo asked.

'I'll have the Palace doctor apparently.'

'What about scans and things?'

'Anything I need shall be brought to the Palace but if there's a problem in labour and I need to go to the hospital there'll be a helicopter on standby.' She must have seen the dart of concern in Flo's eyes for Maggie spoke on. 'It's a ten-minute flight away. I don't think they'll be taking any chances with the future King.'

'Of course not.' Flo agreed, and then sighed. 'I'd have loved to deliver you.'

'Well, I know it's your job and everything but I'd find that strange.' Maggie smiled. 'A doctor that I rarely have to see suits me just fine.'

They decided to get some sleep so they put on the eye masks provided and lay there, drifting off. Flo wasn't offended in the least at Maggie's dismissal of her suggestion to deliver her. It was a moot point now anyway, given that she would be living so far away. Flo just knew how things changed when you were actually in labour. Maggie had no family. Well, of course she now had Ilyas, but when Flo had first offered, it had been because Maggie really had no one else.

She had Ilyas now, Flo consoled herself. And as Maggie herself had said, they were hardly going to take any risks with the future King.

It was her friend who concerned her, though.

'Hey, Flo…' Maggie said, as they lay in the dark, and the question that Flo had been anxiously avoiding, while simultaneously waiting for Maggie to ask, arose.

'Did you ever catch up with Hazin?'

'Sorry?' Flo pretended that she'd misheard.

'At Dion's, when you went there that night, did you speak to Hazin?'

'Is he going to be the best man?' Flo asked, terribly glad of the eye masks to cover her obvious change of subject.

'I don't think they have best men,' Maggie said. 'Anyway, he's not coming to the wedding apparently.'

'Not coming?' Flo frowned, whipping off her mask and sitting up. 'But he's Ilyas's brother.'

'I know that.' Maggie yawned. 'I hope he changes his mind.'

'Are they arguing?' Flo asked. 'Is that why he's not coming?'

'They don't talk enough to argue,' Maggie said. 'But I don't think it's that that's keeping Hazin away, I think it's more…'

'What?' Flo prompted, tempted to whisk off Maggie's eye mask and shake her for more information. But she held back from doing that and just hovered over her unseen.

'Hazin's wife died,' Maggie said. 'It's coming up for the tenth anniversary of her death and Hazin's dreading it apparently. They're opening a new oncology wing in her name. I think he still misses his wife and that's why he hates going back so much.'

Oh.

'How long were they married?'

'A year, I think,' Maggie said. 'They were very young.'

Flo sank back on the bed and lay there, listening to the hum of the engines, and she thought of Hazin and his lovely eyes and smile and the pain that must be behind them.

She could not get him out of her mind.

Despite working right up to the last minute, despite helping Maggie with all the wedding plans, she had not forgotten, even for a moment, the bliss of that night.

There should have been a stab of relief that there was now little chance of Maggie finding out before the wedding that she had slept with Hazin.

There wasn't, though.

Flo had been desperately hoping to see him, knowing that surely by now he would have worked out that she had been there about Maggie and not simply for a hook-up with a royal prince.

Perhaps he didn't care enough to work it out, Flo thought as she lay there.

She did, though.

She cared, not just what he thought of her but Flo had found that she cared for him.

The Rebel Prince.

A widower.

And also a man who would decide not to attend his own brother's wedding.

There was so much she wanted to find out and also to explain.

But if Hazin wouldn't be attending the wedding, there would be no chance to. None at all.

CHAPTER FIVE

THE PALACE WAS INCREDIBLE.

Maggie had told her just how amazing it was but nothing could have properly prepared Flo for its splendour. The plane came in over the sea and Flo got her first glimpse of the stunning white building, a stark contrast to the burnt orange canyon it sat atop.

And, because they were aboard the Royal jet, they would land at the Palace. It was both terrifying and exhilarating as the plane aligned with the canyon. 'How big is this place?' Flo asked, still unable to fathom that it had its own landing strip.

'Huge,' Maggie said. 'And magnificent.'

They landed and were met by a woman named Kumu, who greeted them warmly, and they were then driven to a side entrance.

'The grand entrance,' Kumu explained, 'is used only by the Royals and for official occasions.'

And Maggie wasn't quite that yet, though the side entrance wasn't exactly shabby! They were led into a huge marble foyer and introduced to the wedding coordinator, who told them where they would be sleeping.

'Maggie, you asked to stay in the westerly wing in your previous suite and that has been accommodated.

The Palace is very full, though, with wedding guests arriving so your friends are in another section.'

It would seem that the westerly wing was rather *the* place to be, but Flo was just so thrilled to be here she really didn't care where she had been put.

Paul and Kelly were led off. 'Miss Andrews, I shall take you to your suite now and—'

'I'll go with Flo,' Maggie said. 'I want to know where she is.'

They were led through long corridors and up ancient steps and finally they arrived at what would be her home for the next few nights.

It was stunning.

The beautiful suite was bigger than her entire flat and the centrepiece was a high four-poster bed that was draped with heavy gold silk.

'There is no direct *hammam* access from here,' the co-ordinator regretfully explained.

'That's fine,' Maggie said. 'There's access from my suite so we can go from there.'

'Of course,' the co-ordinator agreed, 'but you cannot wander, Maggie. It is imperative that you do not see the groom, so when you are out of your suite, Kumu or I shall escort you.' Maggie was handed a schedule and when the co-ordinator had gone she and Flo went through it.

Basically, it was two days of utter bliss.

There was to be a lot of *hammam* time and a cleansing diet of fruit, then an hour from now the dressmaker would come to Maggie's suite to make adjustments.

'Dressmakers,' Flo corrected as she read through it. 'Oh, it's like a luxury retreat.'

'With a wedding at the end of it,' Maggie said, and Flo could hear the nervousness in her voice.

'It's going to be wonderful.'

'I know it is.' Maggie nodded. 'I just hate it that I can't see Ilyas until then. It feels like him coming to the flat was all a bit of a dream.'

'Well, it clearly wasn't,' Flo said, and she opened the huge French window. They stepped out onto the balcony to breathe the fragrant evening air.

'You have to come to my suite and see the sunset,' Maggie said. 'You've got planes for a view.'

'I like planes,' Flo said.

She actually did.

As Maggie went off for her fitting it was incredible to watch the private jets come in over the desert and see the helicopters land.

Dignitaries descended the steps of private jets in richly coloured robes. Some were taken by car while others walked across a small ornate bridge. It took an evening of sipping fragrant tea and eating slivers of fruit for Flo to work out that the more esteemed guests crossed the bridge rather than being met by a car.

Maggie clearly wasn't royal yet!

In the two days prior to the wedding, the bride-to-be and her guests were pampered and spoiled. There was a huge *hammam* beneath the Palace and because Paul and Kelly were married they were taken to the couples' area. Due to her impending status, Maggie had her own private section and Flo was allowed along for company.

'Think of it as one of our spa days,' Maggie had said the first time they had gone down there.

More often than not they gave each other a spa day for birthday presents. This meant that twice a year they got a wonderful girly day.

They weren't like this, though.

Their spa days had been taken in a swish hotel and

had always felt decadent as they lay wrapped in fluffy towels with face packs on, followed by a dip in a gorgeous pool.

Here, though, they were underground and they walked through tunnels decorated in mosaics. It really was another world. There were natural steam rooms and waterfalls and maids who took care of everything.

Maggie's long red curls were oiled in preparation for the big day and Flo's blonde hair received several treatments. Her skin was pummelled with salt, and by the time it came to Maggie's wedding day, all that was left to do was relax and prepare for the service, which was just a few hours away.

Maggie was nervous and Flo didn't blame her a bit. She hadn't seen Ilyas since he had proposed to her! Apparently his family was being difficult as Ilyas enforced the new order. Hazin was still a no-show, though his jet was apparently in Dubai. Yes, there was a lot for Maggie to be tense about. Not just the service—afterwards she would go out onto the balcony and the people would get their first glimpse of the obviously pregnant bride.

'It's going to be wonderful, Maggie,' Flo said as they lay being massaged, but despite her brave words even Flo could not let go of her tension.

Not just about the no-show of Hazin.

Today her best friend would be married and become a princess and the future Queen.

Flo looked over and, given she was so pregnant, Maggie lay on her back. Her eyes were closed as one maid massaged her scalp. Two others worked quietly on her feet.

No, it was not a regular spa day.

Flo was scared of change and did not want this valued friendship to slip away, yet she did not see how it could possibly stay the same.

She said nothing, though, for today was about the wedding, and Maggie was already nervous enough.

'What happens now?' Flo asked as they were led, wrapped in *hammam* towels, back through the tunnels to Maggie's suite.

'I guess hair and make-up,' Maggie said. 'I'll ask Kumu to have your clothes and things brought over to my suite.'

But it was not to be, for they found out that Flo could not be with Maggie in the final preparations.

'Only family can be present,' Kumu, who took care of details, explained.

'But Maggie doesn't have any family,' Flo said. 'I'm her closest friend. We're like sisters.'

'There can be no exceptions,' Kumu responded, and then turned to the bride-to-be. 'I am sorry, Maggie.'

'Surely…' Flo started, and was about to put on her assertive midwife voice, but she knew it might be best not to use it today so she changed her tone and turned to her friend. 'Maggie?' she checked. 'What do you want me to do?'

'I'll be fine,' Maggie said, but Flo could see that her teeth were chattering. 'You go and get ready.'

'In a bit,' Flo started, but it was clear she was no longer welcome.

'I'll see you at the service.' Maggie tried to be brave. 'Wish me luck.'

'You don't need luck,' Flo said. 'You're going to do beautifully. I just know it.'

Flo was not best pleased as she made her way to her suite, but there was nothing she could do.

The next time she saw Maggie it would be at the ceremony.

After that, Maggie and Ilyas and other Royals would appear on the Palace balcony and then there was to be a formal meal before the couple went to the desert.

She doubted there would be even a moment to speak properly with her friend.

And tomorrow Flo flew home to London.

Things were changing and there was nothing she could do, except get herself ready for the wedding.

Her hair had never been silkier and Flo decided she would leave it down, so she took out her tongs and added a few curls.

Then a few more.

Whatever oil they had used was amazing.

The treatments had done wonders for her skin and all she needed was a little blush and eyeliner and then mascara and she was done.

Flo put on a silk robe that had been left out for her and headed out onto the balcony, willing herself to be calm. Yet the sight of all the planes and helicopters was daunting. This was a huge Royal wedding and Maggie was facing it alone.

And as for Hazin…

She scanned the tails of the jets but she didn't know what she was looking for.

Flo just wanted to see him.

Not for the sake of his brother.

It was selfish of her perhaps, but she had an aching need to see Hazin again.

She and Maggie had been shopping before they'd left for Zayrinia and Flo had found the perfect dress.

It was full length and worked with all the guidelines, but it was bright red and as sexy as hell.

And had been bought with Hazin in mind.

She put on her very red lipstick, which had been bought with *both* the dress and Hazin in mind!

It killed her that he wouldn't be there to see it.

Surely he might still come, Flo thought as she headed to take her place in the gardens.

There was still no sign of Hazin, so the dress and lipstick were rather in vain.

But then she forgot about him when Maggie arrived.

She was smiling so widely and seemed utterly relaxed, so unlike the tense woman Flo had left.

It was the most beautiful ceremony, and it was clear they were deeply in love.

And there *was* time to speak after.

Maggie made the time for them.

'Did they drug you?' Flo beamed. 'You looked so calm…'

'Stop it.' Maggie laughed. 'Ilyas and I spoke before the ceremony.'

'You saw him?'

'No.' Maggie shook her head. 'We just spoke and it calmed me down a lot. I have to go out to the balcony now. Will you come up and wait for me there?'

'Of course.'

Ilyas and Maggie led the way back to the Palace and the Royals and Flo walked behind.

She wouldn't be going onto the balcony, of course, it was just nice to be a part of things. But then, just as they turned on the grand stairs, the entrance doors to the Palace opened and a sight for sore eyes staggered in.

Hazin.

His hair was dishevelled, and he was dressed in a crumpled suit and carrying a bottle of cognac. He clearly hadn't shaved in days.

'Keep walking,' someone advised, but of course the procession halted while Ilyas took charge and went to deal with his errant younger brother.

'Ilyas!' The Queen called him back but he ignored her summons. 'You…' the Queen said, and Flo was startled as she met the Royal glare. 'You're a nurse—deal with Hazin.'

'I'm a midwife, actually.'

'It's the same thing.' The Queen dismissed Flo with a wave of her hand.

Flo would have loved to tap her on the shoulder and correct her, but she had actually done her general nursing too.

It had been a very long time since she had been in the emergency department and dealing with drunks, though.

It was like riding a bike once you got down to it.

Hazin was led off by the guards and on the Queen's instructions Flo followed.

Down corridor after corridor they went and she found herself in an apartment within the Palace.

There the guards placed him on the bed.

'Thank you.' Flo smiled at them and when they were gone she stood there and looked at Hazin.

He really was terribly gorgeous with his tie undone and his shirt untucked. His eyelashes were flickering and she knew he was only pretending to be asleep. She looked at the bottle of cognac in his hand.

'I'm surprised you didn't drop it,' Flo said, and took it from his grip.

Yes, it *was* like riding a bike, for her training was ingrained and she knew he wasn't drunk!

Drunks weren't so pretty!

And Hazin had told her himself that he didn't drink.

'I know you,' he said as he opened one eye slightly.

'Indeed you do.'

She bent over and he frowned as her lips hovered over his.

'Is that within your nursy duties, Florence?'

'You're stone cold sober, Hazin. Couldn't you at least have taken a swig from the bottle?'

He smiled.

Busted.

'I can't stand the stuff.'

'Why didn't you just stay away if you didn't want to come?

Hazin didn't answer that.

It was a good question indeed.

'Why didn't you want to be at your brother's wedding?'

'It isn't the wedding so much…' He closed his eyes and it was all too hard to explain. 'Maybe it is,' Hazin said. 'The last wedding I was at…'

'Was yours.' Flo said. 'Maggie told me.'

'What else did she tell you?'

It was time to be honest, Flo decided, for pretending she had no idea who he was hadn't served them well. 'That you hope to be disinherited.'

'I never meant that to get out,' Hazin said, and he told her first-hand what had happened in his cabin that day. 'I was fed up,' he said. 'I had tried coming home for a visit but ended up taking out the yacht. I invited a few friends and…' He shrugged. It had been the usual debauched party. 'I was just tired of it and I went into my cabin and Maggie was there. She'd gone to lie down. I could tell she was upset and she mentioned it was the anniversary of her mother's death. She said how she missed having a family. I told her she was lucky, how

I was sick of mine, and that I wouldn't mind being disinherited. It was how I felt on the day. I might have no choice in the matter now.'

He was making the choice for them, Flo was sure, and she was rather sure she knew why. 'Maggie also said that you have to give a speech for the anniversary of your wife's death.'

'Ah, yes.'

He sank back on the pillows.

'When is that?'

'December.'

'It would be hard to do…'

'You have no idea,' he said, though not unkindly, more wearily. 'Go,' Hazin said after a little while. 'I don't need a nurse.'

'Could you use a friend?'

'I don't need one of those either.'

'Are you sure you want me to go?' Flo checked, and he nodded.

Hazin liked it that she didn't push and he watched her depart and close the door.

It felt odd, having her here.

Hazin behaved badly, but never when he was at home.

Not in this bedroom.

There had been no one since Petra in this bed.

The Palace and furnishings were intricate and ancient. Hazin could hardly have a clear-out and pop out to the furniture store, so he had asked for a new suite in the Palace.

His father had told him to toughen up.

Hazin could tell no one his feelings.

He looked out at the glorious sky and wished the drapes were closed.

Everyone assumed they knew why he had gone off the rails—Hazin's grieving, they'd said.

Of course he had been grieving, for Petra had been nineteen when she'd died and he had done everything he could to save her. Flying in different doctors for opinion after opinion. An operation had left her unable to have children and he would never forgive his parents for their reaction to that news.

They felt they had chosen unwisely.

Hazin could not forgive them for that.

He had been by Petra's side every step of the way and had held her hand through the hell of surgery and chemotherapy. And, when there had been nothing more that could be done, Petra had asked to come home.

Here.

Her parents and brother had moved into the vast apartment and they had done all they could to love and support Petra.

Sometimes when tears had refused to remain hidden, Kumu, Petra's assistant, had stepped in and read to her or sat a while.

Hazin and his in-laws would step out onto the balcony and comfort and draw strength from each other before heading back to her side.

Now and then, Hazin would carry her from the bed to glimpse the desert and enjoy the warm breeze on her skin. Hazin had made her smile as often as he could. In fact, making Petra smile had been his daily mission.

But for all Hazin had cared, he hadn't loved Petra.

On his wedding day, staring out at the cheering masses, he'd known he had married in an attempt to please his father, rather than follow his dream and study classical archaeology and ancient history at university.

He had told Petra how much he loved her, though,

and had done everything he could not to let her know his truth.

Yet she had.

Right near the end of her far too short life, he had lain with her on this very bed, holding her to him, refusing to believe it was close to goodbye.

And then she'd said it. 'I want you to find true love, Hazin.'

'I have already found it.'

'No, Hazin. You have been a wonderful husband. I have been so happy in my time with you but I know you don't love me.'

'Petra—'

'Stop.' She had told him and he'd been able to see her struggle to open her eyes and that every breath had been an effort. 'I want you to find the one who makes your heart beat too fast.'

And then hers had stopped.

He loathed it that she had felt unloved.

To Hazin's eyes he had even messed up on Petra's deathbed.

CHAPTER SIX

FLO HEADED BACK down to the wedding celebrations, which were in full swing.

The feast was incredible and Maggie and Ilyas looked so happy. It was a wonderful occasion and full of food and much dancing.

And then came the gorgeous candle dance. Flo had no idea what it was but smiled as Maggie stood with two lit candles, just enjoying the goings-on, when unexpectedly she was handed one herself.

All the woman were, and with candles lit they stood behind the bride and followed her to the sounds of a soulful song. And then Flo was moved along the entourage so she stood by her friend and Flo realised then that this should have been Maggie's mum.

It was a special moment and Flo danced alone with her friend, who had been through so much.

And then it was the men's turn to dance and Maggie must have been thinking the same thing—that Hazin should be here.

Yet Flo understood why he could not be.

'How's Hazin?' Maggie asked.

'He'll be fine,' Flo said, but she didn't divulge to Maggie that he hadn't been drunk at all. 'I'll check on him later.'

As the celebrations eased down, and the bride and groom were about to leave for the desert, she said goodbye to her friend.

'Thank you for coming all this way.'

'It was hardly a burden. I've had the most wonderful time.'

And now it was goodbye.

Flo held back from crying until she could be alone in her suite. But she would miss Maggie terribly. They had been friends for years. When Flo had first started at the Primary she had found the chocolate café and their friendship had soon formed.

And she didn't know how this marriage and Maggie's new title might change that, only that she knew it would.

She was so ready for a good old howl that she actually forgot about Hazin, right up until she got to her suite.

His apartment was quite a walk from hers but she trudged down there.

Yes, she wanted to check on him, but not because he was drunk.

She wanted to check on him, *on them*, while she had the chance, for she loathed the way they'd parted.

There was a guard outside, one of the guards who had deposited him on the bed, and he gave Flo a nod and let her in. She walked down a long corridor and when she got to his bedroom she knocked softly and opened the door quietly.

Moonlight lit the room.

Hazin was asleep on top of the bed. In fact, he was just as he had been when she'd left. Flo slipped off his shoes and covered him with a large throw and he stirred.

'I told you,' he said, 'I don't need a nurse.'

'I know you don't,' Flo said. 'And whether or not you

need a friend, tonight I do.' She slipped off her shoes and climbed onto the bed beside him. Without a word, he pulled her in and covered her with the throw.

It wasn't sexy or anything, it was just nice, to lie there in the quiet.

'I'm sorry I didn't tell you I knew who you were.' Flo said.

'It doesn't matter.' He gave her arm a squeeze. 'It was a good night until then.'

'It was.'

'So you were there for Maggie?'

'She wanted to tell Ilyas about the baby.' Flo nodded slowly as she looked back at that night and then sighed. 'I'm going to miss her an awful lot.'

'You'll still see her. She's hardly going to have to save up her frequent flyer miles to come and see you.'

'Perhaps, but it won't be the same. I was so happy when she came back from her year away. I was looking forward to being like an aunty to the baby…'

'You still can be,' he said, and then asked a question. 'Did you used to go out on the town together?'

Flo smiled to herself. 'We met for coffee most days. Maggie's not into clubs.'

'And you are?'

Not any more, Flo thought, but she did not say it.

'So when does your self-imposed exile end?'

Flo lay there and still said nothing.

It had ended with him, but she could not see herself heading back out there.

Something had shifted within her on the very night she had met Hazin, though she hadn't explored it properly and could not do so now, for she doubted that Hazin wanted to hear on this night that she was completely crazy about him.

He misread her silence.

Or not.

For there was sadness in the air; he just didn't put it down to being about him.

'What happened, Flo?' Hazin already knew that her ex had been married but he wanted to hear it from her. 'Why have you been hiding yourself away?'

She hadn't just been hiding, it had been a punishment, one she had inflicted on herself.

'He was married,' Flo said. 'I honestly didn't know, though looking back I should have. I knew he went away on business a lot. At the time, I was fine with it because it was coming up for Christmas…' She thought about it some more. It had actually been a bit of a relief when he'd gone away for he'd liked to see her at short notice and would be put out if she had other plans. On-call sex, really, now she looked back. 'We didn't actually go out that much,' Flo admitted. 'I met him at Dion's and after that it was always bloody hotels.'

'What's wrong with hotels?' Hazin asked.

'Nothing at all, if sex is all you're after. He would sometimes come to my place but it was mainly hotels—he told me his apartment was being renovated. We were always staying in when I wanted to go out.'

'Where?'

'Anywhere, just on a date.'

But the concept of a date was clearly as unfamiliar to him as her aversion to hotels so he asked for more clarification. 'But where would you go?'

'Anywhere. Movies, theatre, meals…'

He yawned and Flo lay there. 'I haven't been on enough dates,' she told him. 'I can see it now.'

Her year off men had served her well.

'How did you find out he was married?' Hazin asked.

She was silent.

'Tell me.'

'I'm too embarrassed to.'

He could feel the tension lock her arms tight against her body. 'Flo,' he said, 'do you know my reputation?'

'I do.'

'Then you must know that not much shocks me.'

Flo had held it in for so long. She remembered the night she and Hazin had met and his kind, non-judgmental smile. She had come close to telling him then and so she told him now.

Hazin was the first person—the only person—she had ever shared this with.

'He came into my department with his wife. She was booked in at a private hospital but it was all happening too fast…' Even with months having gone by, even with the shield of his arms, she could not complete it, but Hazin knew her job and soon worked it out.

'I stand corrected,' he admitted, for he was shocked. 'Bastard.'

They lay there together and he thought about it.

'You didn't have to deliver her?' Hazin checked.

'Oh, God, no, never!' Flo said. 'I hid in the IV cupboard and I never wanted to come out.'

It had been rock bottom for her.

'Then I told my colleague I had a bad period and I needed to go home. I called in sick for two days…'

She looked up and he pulled a face at her ailment choice.

'Well, I guess I could have just pretended to be drunk, as a certain person does when he wants to get out of something.'

They both smiled just a little, but hers wavered when

she recalled that time and the explosion of feelings it had produced.

'It was Christmas Eve and the next day I had to go to my parents' home and pretend to be all happy...'

Hazin frowned. 'I never feign happiness, I'm just a miserable bastard whenever I feel like it.'

'You don't feel like one now.'

He felt lovely, all big and strong and so very kind, and then he said something she did not understand.

'I used to, though.'

'When?'

He thought back to the early months of his marriage, before Petra had taken ill. He had been the dutiful Prince then, attending endless functions with his gorgeous bride. Petra had been very hands on and had liked to get close to the people. At night they would get into this very bed and make love—yet it had not really been love, for he would lie there afterwards in the dark of the night with a hollow longing in his soul for the life he had once led in London.

Yet he could never tell anyone that.

And so he asked Flo a question instead of answering hers. 'Why did you have to pretend to be happy?'

'Because that's what I do,' Flo said.

'Would your parents have been cross with you?'

'No, no, they'd have felt awful for me. It was Christmas,' she said, as if that explained it.

It didn't.

So she tried.

'You do what you can to make it happy for the people you love, especially at Christmas, and me sobbing into the turkey wasn't going to help anyone.'

He lay there, waiting for her to explain further. It took a moment to realise she had fallen asleep. Confession really was good for the soul.

CHAPTER SEVEN

IT WAS THE best sleep.

For both of them.

Hazin woke first and he lay there, both liking the feel of her in his arms and dreading the day ahead.

He would be hauled over the coals by his father and asked to explain his behaviour yesterday.

Yet he could not.

His jet had sat at Dubai Airport for hours as he'd toyed with whether or not to attend the wedding.

He had been cross with Maggie for spilling his secrets to Ilyas, yet he understood why she had.

And though a part of him had wanted to be at the wedding, it had been the balcony appearance that Hazin had not been able to face.

The last time he had stood there had been with his young bride, on the day they'd met.

And sitting in Dubai, the thought of the speech on the anniversary of her death had loomed and on a foolish impulse he had decided to do the unthinkable and ensure once and for all that he was removed from the lineage.

Except Ilyas was now in control.

And he wanted Hazin to stand beside him.

Yet Hazin did not know how.

Growing up, he had loathed being the dutiful Prince.

Hazin had felt like a charlatan, for he had known that thc poverty in which so many of the people lived was unnecessary. And he had also known of the unrest with the Bedouins under his father's ruthless rule.

Yet the people had loved him.

They always had.

As a young teenager, his father had been giving a speech and the cameras had caught Hazin rolling his eyes.

He had been severely disciplined, but with each lashing, he had—to his father's fury—smiled contentedly.

And, newly married, he and Petra would go into town and dine at the restaurants and actually speak with the locals, who had in turn adored the young couple.

Now his father apologised to the people for his son's sins.

It should be the other way around.

Without words, perhaps, but there was so much good he could do.

Hazin felt Flo stir in his arms.

She would be the best part of this day, Hazin knew.

And he was the best part of hers, for to lie there all warm and rested and to open her eyes to his welcoming smile was such a lovely awakening.

Flo stretched her neck like a swan and reached for his kiss. He met her midway and their lips mingled in an intimate morning caress.

He pulled her up his body and, like Scotch mist rolling in, he slowly engulfed her. Their tongues teased in tender exploration as beneath the rug his hands moved to her breast.

She longed to be naked as they kissed. Flo craved

those fingers stroking her hardened nipple and the palm with which be caressed her bare skin.

And yet it remained at a kiss, for he halted the mingling of their mouths and she could almost taste the regret he left on her lips.

'I have to go,' he told her.

'Do you?' Flo didn't quite believe him.

'I have to go and speak with my father,' Hazin said.

But while his actions yesterday needed to be faced, the truth was that it was all too new and surreal to have someone else in this bed. It took things to a far higher level, though he could not explain that to her, so he applied logic instead. 'And you have your flight to get ready for.'

However gently he did it, Flo knew she was being dismissed.

'What will your father say?' Flo asked as she climbed out of bed.

'Plenty.' Hazin rolled his eyes.

'Did you ever get on?'

'Never,' Hazin said, but then amended, 'For the two weeks while my wedding was being arranged he was more amenable. But that was only because I was dancing to his tune.'

He stood from the bed and gave her a smile—though it was not a smile she liked. It was a smile of farewell. 'Thanks for everything, Flo.'

'I didn't do anything.'

'Well, thanks for looking out for me yesterday when you thought I was drunk.'

'I never did think that, Hazin.'

She had known right away he'd been staging things, and it hadn't all been down to her training. Flo felt a connection with him, though it was clear it was something Hazin didn't want. There was no suggestion that he would see her before she left and no offer to catch up when they were both in London.

'I'll say goodbye, then,' Flo said.

'Goodbye, Flo.'

He might just as well have shaken her hand, Flo thought as she left.

He saw the slight slump of her shoulders and he fought not to call her back as she walked out the door.

It would be the easiest thing to do.

To call her back and blot out the morning and the weeks and months ahead. To fly her back to London on his jet and sex the miles away up in the air.

Yet Hazin knew the easy solution was not the correct one here.

And so he bathed and changed into a robe and put on his *keffiyeh*, and when Mahmoud, the King's vizier, called and said that King Ahmed wished to speak to him, Hazin was ready.

It was not a welcoming committee that waited.

His father sat at his huge desk, with Mahmoud standing beside him. The surprise was that his mother was standing there too.

'Mumia!' Hazin greeted her with the Arabic word for 'Mummy', but it dripped sarcasm for he had not used that word even as a child.

He hadn't been taught to and he'd certainly never had the chance to.

Being back made his skin crawl, for he could remember long nights in the nursery, crying out, only to be ignored or met by a stern nanny.

'Discipline him,' his mother would hiss on her rare visits, and well he remembered her tone now.

She stared coolly at the son she had reluctantly borne

and then addressed him. 'Your behaviour yesterday was despicable. Many esteemed guests witnessed your display.'

'You're not upset that I might have upset your son and his new wife?' Hazin checked. 'Just that I embarrassed you in front of guests.'

'You always embarrass me, Hazin. You do nothing right.'

'For such a rebel, I excelled at school.'

'You hardly needed qualifications to support yourself,' the Queen sniffed. 'Perhaps you might wish you had gone to university now, when you hear what the King has to say.'

Hazin looked at his father as the King spoke. 'My strong recommendation is that you will be disinherited. I want the people to see the consequences of your despicable behaviour. However…' King Ahmed's face twisted as the new order in the Palace choked him. 'Ilyas is determined that your title will remain. Your brother has more faith in you than I do. Though that is hardly a compliment for I have none. I would wash my hands of you with satisfaction.'

'You washed your hands of me before I was even born,' Hazin responded, then looked at the Queen—she did not deserve the title of Mother. 'And you washed your hands of me on the day that I was,' he finished, looking at the King.

He had been fed by wet nurses and visited by his mother on rare occasions. And when at six years of age he had kicked up, he'd been offed to a country where he didn't even know the language.

Hazin was angry now.

Furious, in fact, not just about his childhood but for the utter lack of support shown to his late wife. Once she had become ill they had treated Petra as if she had been a poor choice of bride—even though they had been the ones who had chosen her.

Yes, his hate ran deep and it built the more she spoke.

'It does not have to be Ilyas's choice,' the Queen pointed out. 'You can always step down.'

They wanted him to, Hazin realised. They wanted him gone before Ilyas returned from the desert.

It was their only chance at wresting back control, for there was safety in numbers. He thought of Ilyas standing alone against these two.

He had no doubt now in Ilyas, and he was a formidable force indeed. But these two were pure poison, and not afraid to use it.

His brother had said he wanted him there by his side.

But Hazin didn't know Ilyas.

Simply, he did not know him.

Yet there was intrinsic trust between them. He thought back to the coffee bar and that stir of relief when Ilyas had told him that things would change.

So he spoke in a steady voice to the Queen, for his decision was made. 'I shall not be stepping down,' Hazin said, and he watched her blink rapidly. 'And, given that you no longer have the power to disinherit me, there's really no point to this conversation.'

'Oh, but there is,' Ahmed said, and he played his final card. 'If you refuse to step down, Hazin, then it is time to step up. The formal invitations for the anniversary of Petra's death are about to be sent. The date is the twenty third of December and the ceremony shall commence at two p.m.'

And Hazin stood there as his father outlined Hazin's own personal hell.

'We thought it fitting that Petra's family be there as

you open the new oncology wing. They shall be on the stage beside you. Naturally, it shall be televised, for it has been a long time since our people have heard from their missing, errant Prince. I am sure they will listen closely to what you have to say for yourself.' The King watched the sweat bead on his son's brow and with a black smile he looked over at his vizier. 'Not to worry, though, Mahmoud is working on your speech.'

Hazin turned and walked away.

Through the guarded doors and into the grand entrance, where there hung the portrait of him and Petra, taunting him. How the hell could he face her parents after all he had done in the years since he had last seen them? How could he sit on a stage, with the world watching, and deliver a speech about how much he'd loved and missed his wife. He looked into her chocolate eyes and did not know how to face the day. He just did not know, but as he stared at Petra he remembered her kindness.

Such kindness, and it had been so alien to Hazin that he had not known how to accept it at first.

And, no, his heart had not raced in her presence or at the thought of her, but he had done all he could to return the gentleness of her nature.

I want to do the right thing by you but I don't know how.

He said it in his head, but Petra only smiled back for her smile was fixed on the wall.

The easiest thing to do would be to head back to bed and bury himself in Flo, but that would not honour either of these women. He turned to leave.

It was a familiar sight at the Palace—Hazin flying out the day after he had flown in.

But it was not familiar to Flo.

She was on the balcony, drinking in the view and watching the constant activity as various dignitaries left, when she saw him stridc across the bridge and board his jet without a backward glance.

No goodbye, no kiss.

Nothing.

She watched the plane with its black and silver tail hurtle down the runway and lift into the clear blue sky.

And she watched until the speck in the distance had gone, scanning the sky in the ridiculous hope that the plane might return. He might realise that he had left something important behind—her heart. He might change his mind and come back to the Palace…

Of course not.

And so to life without him.

CHAPTER EIGHT

DECEMBER.

It had always been Flo's favourite month.

Not any more.

She had worked a lot of late shifts in the first two weeks, but more so that she would have a genuine excuse not to attend the many functions and get-togethers that came with this time of year.

The unbelievable had happened and Christmas had lost its gloss.

She had finished up work yesterday to commence her long-awaited leave and was determined to inject some enthusiasm into the season. Yet she decorated the tree and her tiny flat with something more akin to grim determination than enthusiasm.

Then Flo headed out to make a start on her Christmas shopping.

The bus stopped right beside the chocolate café. If Maggie had still been working there, Flo would have dropped in for a hot chocolate and a gossip.

Then, after her shopping, she might well have ended up back there again.

They spoke online often enough, but it was in the day-to-day things that Flo missed her an awful lot.

The shops were all decked out for Christmas yet Flo's

shopping wasn't done. She traipsed around the various stores, but the music was too loud and the crowds overwhelming. As well as that, she had seen what was surely the perfect necklace for Maggie.

Yet, just as she had been admiring it, Flo had thought of the stunning jewels that Maggie now had access to and had put it back.

Somehow she could not get in the mood.

Last Christmas had been awful.

This one was faring no better.

Well, that wasn't strictly true.

Last year at this time she had been happy, decorating her tiny flat and dashing to the shops to get the perfect presents for family and friends and her now ex-boyfriend.

Yes, this time last year she had been busy and happy.

It was Christmas Eve that had been hell.

She had felt so ashamed yet, looking back, she hadn't cried tears over the loss of him.

Yet, after one night with Hazin, Flo had cried.

And she had cried over him several times since.

Today, as she took the bus back to her flat, it felt as if it could be one of those times.

The bus made its way along the busy London street and Flo looked down and saw Dion's.

She hadn't been back since that night when he had first turned her life around.

According to the gossip columns, neither had Hazin.

That morning, after the wedding, when she had woken in his bed and they had shared that lovely kiss, had been the last time she had seen or heard from him.

Flo had found out from Maggie that he hadn't been back to Zayrinia either.

It would seem he really did not want to deliver that speech or stand with is brother.

He was off in the Caribbean, according to the last gossip rag Flo had read.

Flo let herself into her flat. She pulled off her boots and scarf and refused to cry over a man who clearly had no real interest in her.

Another one.

Only with Hazin it didn't feel the same as it had with other boyfriends, for when she had been with him, his interest in her had felt real.

Get real! Flo told herself.

It had been three months.

She pulled out her laptop, trying not to think about Hazin, and to decide what to get Maggie for Christmas. Flo had left it rather too late to post something, so she'd have to spend a small fortune for a necklace Maggie might not even want.

Suddenly Maggie messaged her. Great minds think alike, Flo thought.

Free to chat?

A few seconds later there was Maggie, smiling from the screen. Her red hair was thick and glossy and she was clearly rocking those pregnancy hormones.

'You look amazing,' Flo said. 'Three weeks to go!'

'It feels like for ever,' Maggie sighed.

'How's it all going?'

'Very well,' Maggie said. 'Well, at least I think so…'

'What's wrong?'

'Nothing. I just…' Maggie closed her eyes. 'Flo, do you remember when you asked if you could deliver me?'

'Yes, and you said that you could think of nothing worse than that.'

'I could think of nothing better now,' Maggie told her.

'Are you okay?'

'Honestly, yes. I'm getting the best care and I really am fine. I'm getting all worked up, though. I have to deliver at the Palace, unless something goes wrong, of course. But as well as the Palace doctor there has to be a Palace elder present at the birth.'

Flo held in her own thoughts about that.

Maggie didn't need them.

At the end of the day, she was giving birth to the future King. Of course there would be certain customs that had to be adhered to.

Yet Maggie was a very private person.

Late pregnancy was often a difficult time, especially given that Maggie was in a new country and didn't speak the language, and it made sense that she would want someone from home with her.

But Flo wasn't sure if she wanted to go.

Not that she said it out loud; instead she pointed out a fact. 'Maggie, what happens if the baby's late? First babies often are and I'm due back at work on the fifth of January.'

'I know. It would just be so nice to have you here for a while.'

Flo thought about it.

She wanted to be there for her friend but she loved Christmas, and the thought of not spending it with her family was daunting.

'Flo, it honestly would be a holiday,' Maggie said. 'We can go out and you can go off exploring. I'll take you out to the desert where Ilyas and I met.'

'You're thirty-seven weeks pregnant.'

'And there are helicopters lined up outside like a taxi rank. Though I do have a couple of functions to attend, so long as the baby's not here. I just…' Maggie hesitated. 'I'm asking too much. I know how much you love Christmas and being with your family.'

Flo had always loved Christmas—the tree, the scents, the gorgeous dinner—but she had been feeling so low of late.

Flo needed to think about it, yet she could see the pleading in Maggie's eyes and she was absolutely useless at saying no, or even asking for some time.

'Of course you're not asking too much,' Flo said. 'I'd love to come.'

Maggie gave a squeal of delight. 'When?'

'How soon do you want me?'

'Now!' Maggie said, and started to speak of arrangements. 'Don't bring a thing. I've got a wardrobe of robes and I'll get Kumu to—' but Flo cut in.

'You'll have to message me the details. If I'm going to be flying to Zayrinia at short notice then I need to hit the shops now.'

'I just said you don't have to bring anything.'

'I've got my family's presents to get,' Flo pointed out.

This was more like it, Flo thought as she entered the huge store that she'd so listlessly walked around just a couple of hours before.

On the bus ride over, she had thought about it and a working holiday in Zayrinia, and delivering a future King, wouldn't look too bad on her résumé.

Hazin might be there; after all, he had that dreaded speech to give.

He wasn't the sole reason for her cheery mood. She

and Maggie were very close, but the chance to see Hazin again was certainly a factor.

She simply couldn't get him out of her mind, though she had to now because Flo had so much to do.

So much!

Yet this time around it all happened with ease.

Her brothers, sisters, parents, nieces and nephews were soon off her list and Flo left the bags at a counter to collect later.

Ilyas?

Impossible.

So he got a box of dark-chocolate-covered ginger.

A big one, though.

Maggie had become newly impossible to buy for, but she utterly refused to think like that, so Flo went back to the necklace and bought it, along with a book that she knew Maggie would enjoy.

And then Flo went to the place she longed to be most—the baby floor.

Despite seeing, holding and smelling newborns each and every day, it was never too much for Flo.

Shopping for her friend's baby was an utter delight, though she would love to be shopping for her own.

Flo had wanted a baby as far back as she could remember.

Every doll she had begged for at Christmas and birthdays had proven a secret disappointment when she'd finally held them, for she had longed for them to be real.

It wasn't like she was peering into prams and longing to scoop the babies out, it was just that she hoped to be a mother one day.

Flo knew Maggie was having a little boy but, rather than blue, she loved the more neutral mint greens and pale lemons and she searched for just that.

And then she found it—a little playsuit in the palest green with the face of a rabbit, or dog, or something of that nature on the front.

It wasn't very regal, but it was gorgeous.

And he got a teddy, because from the little she knew of the al-Razim brothers, they hadn't exactly been plied with toys as children and a palace could be a cold and lonely place.

So she splurged and got him a little play mat and a rattle too in the shape of a ladybird.

Done.

Not quite.

Hazin!

Her mother had trained her well, and of course there must be spare presents for the unexpected and, in this case, much-hoped-for, guest.

For that was what he was, Flo thought, more a guest in the Palace than a much-loved son.

Hazin had been born a spare.

So an extra box of chocolate ginger would not cut it, Flo thought, even as she bought some for him anyway.

She stood in the middle of the store as that Hazin-shaped wave hit her again.

It had swamped her on too many occasions of late.

What were you supposed to get for someone you desperately fancied but who might not even be there. What present were you supposed to get a man who could afford absolutely anything?

Flo couldn't fight it any more.

While it might have been sex in a hotel to him, it had been far more than that to her.

She was crazy about him.

That night in his arms in the Palace where nothing had happened had been the most amazing of her life.

She loved sex, but Flo had found out that night just how nice it was to hold someone and be held for no other reason than to hold and be held.

It had never happened to her before.

She'd been held before, of course, but there had never been one without the other.

Until Hazin.

She *had* to get a present for him, just in case he was there, but what?

It had to be light, Flo thought.

But she wanted more of Hazin, not less…

And suddenly Flo knew what to buy.

It could prove an expensive mistake, Flo thought as she grabbed her many bags and headed off to make her purchase.

And it could prove a rather lonely exercise.

But then at least she'd know.

CHAPTER NINE

ZAYRINIA WAS BEAUTIFUL, Flo thought as the plane came in to land and she got a glimpse of the Palace sitting atop the canyon on the very edge of the desert. She could absolutely see why Maggie had been drawn to the place.

Flo was nervous, though.

Last time she had flown here it had been on a private jet and they had landed in the grounds of the Palace. She had been with Maggie, revelling in the bliss of Ilyas's jet and so excited about the wedding. This time, an itinerary had been sent to her by Kumu. She was being flown first class, which was terribly exciting, although a part of Flo would have preferred to be back in economy and the flight paid for by herself.

Just a friend visiting a friend.

Flo's itinerary stated she would be met at Zayrinia airport and then be taken straight to the Palace.

It was as impersonal as that.

But as she stepped into a small lounge area, the first person shc saw was Maggie.

Hugely pregnant and waving to her friend.

Although it was the VIP lounge rather than the chocolate café of old, immediately they clickcd back into familiar ways.

'I didn't think you were coming to meet me,' Flo admitted.

'Didn't Kumu tell you that you would be met? She told me she'd sent you all the details.'

'The itinerary just said I'd be taken to the palace,' Flo said. 'It didn't mention you.'

'Well, Kumu's super-organised and was no doubt making provisions in case I was in labour. Otherwise, of course I'd be here.'

The Palace was as beautiful as when Flo had left it and she was shown to her former, now-familiar suite.

'I told you not to worry about clothes,' Maggie said when she saw Flo's cases waiting in her suite. 'It's all robes here and I have loads.'

They had always borrowed and swapped clothes. As Maggie had pointed out, it was a bit pointless to fork out for a new wardrobe when she had so many.

'I just didn't know what to pack.'

That wasn't true.

Flo had packed plenty and had warned the maids that she wanted to unpack the cases herself, because they didn't contain many clothes—her luggage was mostly filled with presents.

They went for a walk in the gardens and though cool it was nice to breathe in fresh air and to walk for a while after being on a plane.

'I can't believe you're here,' Maggie said.

'Nor can I.' Flo smiled.

It had all been a huge rush to get here—dropping Christmas presents off to her family as she'd told them of her sudden change of plans.

Her mother, Flo could tell, while excited for her, had been disappointed that she wouldn't be there for

Christmas, but they had promised they would have a big dinner as soon as Flo got back.

'How's work?' Maggie asked.

'It's great but always too busy,' Flo said. 'I seem to spend more time writing up notes than anything.'

'Well, you don't have to write any notes up on me. I'm just so glad there's a chance you'll be here when he's born.'

'I'll be here whenever he arrives,' Flo said.

She had made up her mind.

Just as she wouldn't leave a woman in the second stage of labour, neither would she walk away from her friend so close to the end. 'I told the unit manager that I'm staying until the baby's here. I'm not officially due back until the fifth but we can work something out if your little man isn't here by then.'

'Oh, I hope he is,' Maggie sighed, and finally explained some of what was on her mind. 'I told you that an elder has to be present at the birth?'

Flo nodded.

Since Maggie had asked her to be there, Flo had looked into things and had thought through her approach. Instead of fighting the system and getting Maggie all worked up in the process, she was practical instead.

'Maggie, you are giving birth to the future King. If there wasn't someone official present, I could well be smuggling him in under my robe.'

Maggie smiled but Flo could tell she was still concerned.

'I'll talk to the Palace doctor and find out what *has* to happen and how we can all work around it.'

'Will you?'

'Of course I will,' Flo said. 'You're going to have a fantastic birth, I just know it.'

'Thanks.' Maggie's smile was more relaxed now. 'And we're going to have an amazing time. Ilyas has to go to the desert next week and, as long as the baby is behaving, we can spend the day at the tent!'

'Where you two met,' Flo said.

'Well, not met exactly,' Maggie said. 'Where he had me brought to him!'

They both laughed at all that had happened.

'So what's been happening with you?'

'Oh, you know,' Flo said. 'More of the same.'

'Meaning?'

'I've just been really busy with work.'

'You're always busy with work,' Maggie said. 'But you still manage to squeeze in fun. Are you seeing anyone?'

'Not really.'

Flo knew she was being evasive, yet she was also telling the truth. It had been almost a year since she'd gone out with anyone. Hazin had been her only slip-up.

And they had never really gone out.

It had been just a one-night stand really, except to Flo it felt so much more than that.

But instead of talking about her lack of a love life, Flo asked about Christmas plans.

'There aren't any,' Maggie said. 'It's just another day here. Ilyas and I have to go to Idihr a few days before…'

'That's fine,' Flo said. 'I don't need a babysitter.'

'And then there's Hazin's speech on the twenty-third.' Flo felt her stomach clench as Maggie mentioned his name. 'If he gets here.'

She looked at Maggie as they walked.

They chatted about a lot.

A lot.

Yet Flo simply did not know how to chat about this.

'*If* he gets here?' Flo checked.

'It would seem that he's still doing his best to get disinherited. He was in the Caribbean the last Ilyas heard. No doubt partying hard.'

Maggie knew no more than her, Flo realised.

No one really knew Hazin.

Not his parents.

Or his brother.

And clearly not the King's vizier, Mahmoud, who, a few days later emailed the first draft of Hazin's speech, to be delivered on the tenth anniversary of Petra's death.

Hazin lay on top of a bed, drinking iced sparkling water, but it did not cool his building temper as he read through the words.

The proposed speech belittled the brief joy Petra had brought to the people of Zayrinia and it cited her death as the cause for Hazin's reckless years.

It made *her* into an excuse for *him*.

Hazin flung the glass of water across the room and it smashed against the wall. But it brought Hazin no relief.

He then walked out onto the beach. The water was azure and crystal clear and the beach so white, unlike at home, where the sands were a rusty, beautiful orange.

Home.

It had never really felt like Zayrinia was home, but there was no denying that it called to him now, for the commemoration of Petra's life was just a few days away.

And he had decided to attend.

Hazin intended to fly in on the morning of the ceremony and back out that same night, though he had not told Ilyas that, for he knew he would try to coax him into staying longer.

There was little chance of that.

As for the speech, Hazin would not be reading from Mahmoud's draft. He wanted to honour Petra, but to stand there and say such empty words would dishonour her memory.

Hazin called his brother.

'I write my own speeches, Ilyas.'

'Since when?' Ilyas clipped. 'You're never here to make one.'

Hazin had no smart reply to that.

'You had better be here,' Ilyas warned. 'And sober this time, unlike at my wedding.'

His brother had no idea that Hazin didn't drink.

But Flo did.

After one night together she had worked it out. But he could not think of that now and so instead he tore the current version of his speech apart. 'What is this about the black sheep, and grief making a foolish guide?'

'Hazin,' Ilyas sighed. 'We've thought long and hard and decided that your reckless ways cannot be ignored.'

'So you make Petra's death into an excuse for me? How dare you use her in that way?'

'No one is using Petra but, for whatever reason, since Petra died you *have* gone off the rails.'

'Rubbish.'

'Hazin, your brother is the person who is honest with you, not the one who believes you.'

He did not need some old saying stuffed down his throat and Hazin told his brother that. 'You have the gall to criticise me when you had your harem?' Hazin pointed out. 'All you had to do was pull a bell—at least I indulge in a bit flirting and conversation.'

'Don't try and condone your behaviour,' Ilyas said. 'From all I have read there is little conversation and no flirting where your lovers are concerned.'

Hazin closed his eyes for there had been plenty to read and most of the kiss-and-tell stories were true. He was on the cover of trashy magazines, and there were articles and photos all over the Internet.

Not recently, though, and Ilyas admitted that at least. 'But there have been no scandals of late.'

'No.'

'Can you keep it that way until the ceremony at least?'

'I don't need you to tell me how to act,' Hazin said as he looked out at the lonely island where he had holed himself away from the world.

An idyllic romantic retreat—without the romance.

What Ilyas had said was true, there had been no scandals recently. But that was not because he was attempting to redeem his name, neither was it because all temptations had been removed.

They simply no longer held any appeal for him.

'I need to go.' Ilyas cut into his thoughts. 'Not only am I sick of discussing your sex life, Hazin, but I am taking Maggie and her friend out to the desert abode today.'

'Playing tourist guide,' Hazin sneered.

'Not playing,' Ilyas responded. 'I am meeting with the Bedouin leaders to solidify our political ties and to invite them to join a roundtable so they can play a bigger role in shaping the country's future.'

Hazin frowned, because this had been something

the Bedouins had long been pushing for yet his father had always dismissed the notion.

But Ilyas had more to say.

'I also happen to enjoy my wife's company and I am more than pleased to show Flo where we first met.'

'Flo?'

'Maggie's friend. You would have met her at the wedding…' Ilyas paused. 'Oh, that's right, you were too drunk to attend.' Ilyas stopped the lectures then. 'Flo's also a midwife and has been staying with us. I think Maggie is nervous about giving birth with an elder present and—'

'Ilyas,' Hazin interrupted. 'Just as you don't want to discuss my sex life, neither do I need to hear about Maggie's plans for her labour.'

'Fine.'

Hazin was curt, but there was no emotional bond between them and not a single memory Hazin could call on that softened his brother. He had always been forbidding and distant. Certainly it was too late to be friends and have cosy chats but, more importantly, Hazin did not want to hear about Flo.

Not now.

'Enjoy your time in the desert,' Hazin said, and rang off.

He stripped and placed his phone on his clothes, then headed into the surf and swam for the best part of an hour. But no matter how far or how hard he swam, he could not outswim his own thoughts.

Flo was in Zayrinia.

How was he supposed to feel at hearing that news?

There would be warmth and laughter for once at the Palace, and if he did not care about her so much she might even have served as a pleasant distraction.

Yet he did care.

Hazin wanted to address how he felt about Flo, *after* the anniversary.

Not before.

First up, he *had* to finally do the right thing by Petra.

CHAPTER TEN

ILYAS CERTAINLY WASN'T playing tour guide.

When they arrived at the desert abode he disappeared to prepare for his meeting and Maggie showed Flo around while the maids set up for lunch. 'This is where I slept on the first night I was here.'

'And by the second you were in Ilyas's bed,' Flo reminded her.

It was gorgeous, with a huge satin-draped bed and a luxurious bathing area. It was mysterious and beautiful and Flo could absolutely now see why Maggie loved to come here. 'When you've told me that you and Ilyas were heading off to the desert, I've always felt a bit sorry for you, but I won't now.'

They stepped back into the main living area and Flo was entranced. 'I don't think I've ever seen anywhere more beautiful.' And that was saying something, having come from the Palace. But it was just so lavishly furnished. A huge fire was in the centre of the tent and the flue ran up to the ceiling. On the walls hung tapestries and the rugs on the floor were so plump and inviting that you could easily sleep on them. Ilyas joined them and they sat on cushions around a low table and ate from an array of tajines.

The food was smoky and delicious. Flo's favourite was a mild chicken and date curry, which she tucked into as Ilyas told her why he would be leaving them for the rest of the day.

'I am to speak with the Bedouins and invite their representatives to join us at some Palace meetings.'

'Do you think they'll come?' Flo asked, surprised that Ilyas had even said this much. He was very formal, or at least he had been when they had met at the wedding, but recently he had opened up a little.

Perhaps he had realised just what good friends she and Maggie were, Flo thought as he answered her question.

'I expect so. Being consulted and given a voice is something they have wanted for a long time,' Ilyas said. 'I have forged a good relationship with them over the years but there is a lot of history. It is not only the Bedouins whose trust I hope to win, though. That is why Maggie and I are heading to Idihr tomorrow. There has been a lot of damage done to our standing with neighbouring countries. I hope Hazin changes his mind about returning on a more permanent basis; there is a lot of work that needs to be done.'

At the mention of his name, Flo had to fight to keep her features impassive as she asked, 'Do you think he will?'

'I doubt it,' Ilyas admitted. 'I spoke to him this morning and I can't even pin him down to an arrival time for the memorial event for his late wife.'

'He'll be here for that,' Maggie said assuredly.

'I am not so sure.' Ilyas shook his head. 'He has few fond memories of Zayrinia and little desire to come back. Whenever he does return…' he gave a slight smile in Flo's direction '... I am sure my wife will have told you he tends to take out the yacht.'

It was a little tease about how he and Maggie had first met.

'Ah, yes,' Flo said. 'Well, perhaps the yacht will need to go in for a long service after three months in the Caribbean.'

There was, though she fought it, a slight edge to her voice and she watched as Ilyas's perceptive eyes narrowed a touch.

'Is it really three months?' he asked. 'I admit, I haven't been counting.'

'Well, Maggie was six months pregnant at the wedding and she's due any day now. I have a midwife's mind rather than a mathematical one.'

She'd got out of that one.

Just!

But it was becoming harder and harder not to reveal just how much she liked Hazin.

'Your desert abode is beautiful,' Flo said, quickly changing the subject.

'You should see it at night.' Maggie gave a wistful sigh. 'When it's dark and the fire is burning and all the lanterns are lit and the music...' She stopped and looked at Ilyas. 'Why don't we stay tonight?'

'I can't.' Ilyas shook his head. 'I have to be at the Palace for an engagement tonight and I am in back-to-back meetings all day tomorrow. Still, there's no reason you two can't stay.' He must have seen Flo's flicker of concern at the thought of being deep in the desert with a heavily pregnant woman for he immediately addressed it. 'Once I get to the Palace I will send the helicopter straight back. If there is a need to return sooner you would only be an hour away.'

A taxi ride to the hospital really, by the time they turned up! 'Sounds wonderful.'

And it truly was.

The afternoon was spent in the kitchen.

With much laughter, Flo learnt from one of the maids how to prepare the date and chicken curry and then she and Maggie went for a gentle walk around the tent.

It was a feast for the eyes outside too.

There were beautiful Arabian horses and even a little white foal. His tail was high and his long legs so slender that he looked as if he should be on a carrousel.

'Oh, I want him,' Flo breathed.

'Be careful speaking like that in front of Ilyas,' Maggie teased. 'Or that cute little creature might be a surprise gift waiting on your doorstep when you return home.'

It was such a glorious afternoon. Ilyas returned from his meeting with the Bedouin elders and then headed back to the Palace, and soon it was just the two of them.

There was a deep sense of peace here that Flo had never known. It was such bliss to lie on the cushions and chat with her friend as the fire bathed them in a warm glow and they spoke about life in Zayrinia.

'Do you miss home at all?' Flo asked.

'I miss you and my friends but…' Maggie thought for a moment. 'I haven't really had a home as such since I was seven.'

Flo nodded.

She understood completely what Maggie was saying. Maggie didn't have any family, whereas Flo was very close to hers.

'It's going to be so odd, not seeing them at Christmas,' Flo admitted.

'I don't miss Christmas either,' Maggie sighed. 'It's the time of year I always miss my mum the most. It's kind of nice to bypass it.'

'You can't bypass it, though, Maggie,' Flo said. 'You're always going to miss her.'

'I know I am. I guess Christmas just isn't the big deal to me that it is to you. I could have the staff try and make a dinner for us…'

Flo laughed. 'Please don't. I'm very specific with my trimmings. Mum's freezing me a huge dinner and I'm going to have it when I get back.' She smiled at the thought and then frowned. 'Have there been any deliveries for me?'

'No.' Maggie shook her head. 'Are you expecting one?'

'Not really.' Flo shrugged. 'Mum said that we'd do presents and things when I get back, I just thought she might have sent something for me to open on the day.'

Flo resisted an unhappy sigh and reminded herself that she was twenty-nine! But it was still quite a daunting prospect to have nothing to open for Christmas. Clearly Maggie had given it little thought but she had hoped her mum would have sent something. Still, there was one thing that would certainly cheer Christmas up.

'You might have a Christmas baby!' Flo said.

'Perhaps, but I really want to have the baby tomorrow,'

'Why?'

'Because I'd like to have you here for some time after he comes,' Maggie said, and then she gave a cheeky smile as she admitted another truth. 'And I want to get out of the trip to Idihr as well as the hospital opening.'

'I can write you a note from your midwife to say you

can't possibly attend,' Flo joked, but then, more seriously, she asked a question. 'Why don't you want to go?'

'Well, Idihr will be lovely but it's going to be a very long day. Then it's the hospital opening the next day and it will take for ever. Still, it's so important to the people…' Maggie admitted to a further truth. 'I'm terrified my waters will break.'

'Well, labour usually starts with contractions and they don't generally break with a sudden gush…'

'It *could* happen, though.' Maggie sighed. 'I'm going to sit at the back for the hospital opening and the trip to Idihr is an informal one. Ilyas says that Queen Atisha has had five children…'

'You'll be fine,' Flo said. 'But if it's really working you up, perhaps it might be time to stay home.'

'I'll think about it,' Maggie agreed.

'Do you really think Hazin will come for the opening?' Flo asked, because Maggie had sounded so sure that he would when she'd spoken about it with Ilyas.

'I don't know,' Maggie now admitted. 'No one knows. Ilyas has tried to talk to him but never gets anywhere. Hazin doesn't get close to anyone.'

'He spoke to you on the yacht that day,' Flo pointed out.

'Ah, but only when he thought he'd never have to see me again.'

'How is he with you now?'

'Flo, I haven't seen him since the wedding, and that was just for a moment when he arrived half-drunk. Hazin will do what Hazin does.' Maggie looked at her. 'Please don't like him.'

'But I do.'

'Then please don't act on it, Flo—he's a rake. Well,

he's been lovely to me and everything but that was only because he didn't fancy me.'

'Maybc I should tcll Ilyas I like him so Hazin can be waiting with a bow on my doorstep when I get home,' Flo said, making light of her feelings.

It was odd.

Flo had squeezed out all the details from Maggie when she had come back pregnant from her round-the-world trip.

Maggie, certain that she and Ilyas were over and scared to be having a Royal's baby, had told Flo everything.

Yet Flo could not tell her this.

It wasn't because she was ashamed of it, as had been her reason for not telling a soul about the married man.

It was more that she felt she had to protect whatever fragile flame she and Hazin had.

And exposing them could not help, Flo knew. Even if she ached to confide in her friend. Even if she yearned to eke out whatever information she could about him, Flo felt it better to keep what had happened between her and Hazin private for now.

It was a gorgeous night and a really wonderful retreat, just what they had both needed, but all too soon the chopper was landing them back at the Palace.

It really was stunning and so vast.

A plane was landing and there was another waiting to take off.

'The Flying Royals,' Maggie called them as they disembarked, and then she held her stomach.

'I'm having one.'

Flo felt her stomach and all Maggie was having was wishful thinking along with a mild Braxton Hicks contraction, and she gave a slight cackle. 'No, Maggie, you're not.'

There was no sign of the baby making a move anytime soon.

'I'm going to have to go to Idihr, aren't I?' Maggie sighed as they walked across a pretty bridge from the helipad that would take them back to the palace.

Yes, Maggie was Royal now.

'Maybe not. It's your antenatal check tomorrow. If things are starting to move along you'll have a good reason not to go.'

As they walked into the Palace, Ilyas came down the main staircase to the grand entrance to welcome back his wife, which he did with a kiss, and then Maggie asked what he was doing there. 'I thought you had meetings all day.'

'I do.' Ilyas nodded. 'But Hazin's plane just came in. I want to see how he is and if there are any last-minute things he wants added in for the opening.'

Flo didn't know what to do. A part of her wanted to go and hide in her room and have him find out she was here when she wasn't around to see his reaction.

Another part, though, wanted to see his face when he found out.

In the end there was no reaction at all.

He walked in scowling, when the Hazin she knew was always pleasant.

Hazin felt he had actually walked into hell, for Flo, Maggie and Ilyas were standing beneath a huge portrait of himself and his late wife. Everything he was trying to separate was there together in his line of vision.

'Hi,' he said to the gathered trio. His tone was dry

as he kept on walking. 'I really don't need a welcoming committee.'

'You don't have one,' Ilyas said. 'Flo and Maggie have just got back from their trip. I came out to meet them.'

That wasn't true, Flo thought. Ilyas had just told Maggie he had come out to greet his brother.

There was no warmth between the brothers, she thought.

None.

But at least Ilyas tried. 'Would you like to join us for dinner, Hazin?' he offered.

Flo found that she was holding her breath.

'No,' Hazin said. 'Thanks.'

The simple words came in two separate sentences. Even an attempt at politeness had to be forced.

'Please join us, Hazin,' Maggie pushed. 'It would be nice for us all...' She didn't get to finish as Hazin gave a terse shake of his head.

'I already have plans for tonight.'

Hazin did indeed have plans.

As he stalked off to his apartment, Hazin nodded his thanks to the maids who were sorting out his luggage but then asked if they could please leave.

He waited until the doors closed on them and then let out a tense breath.

That had been hell.

This was hell.

He walked through to the bedroom to get to the balcony but, of course, he had to pass the bed.

Flo was the only other woman to have slept with him there—not that she could have known that.

Guilt clawed at his throat like fingers and he loosened his tie.

Hazin hadn't been lying about having plans for tonight when he had declined Ilyas's offer to join them for dinner.

He was dining with Petra's parents.

Hazin did not want to have to meet them for the first time in many years on a stage in front of a gathered crowd.

Instead, he had called them and Petra's father had invited him to come to dinner.

It was going to be a long and difficult night.

CHAPTER ELEVEN

IT WAS CERTAINLY a long and difficult night for Flo.

Knowing that Hazin was here in the Palace had her on high alert and caught in the vague hope that he might make contact.

Yet why would he?

Hazin had left Zayrinia last time without so much as a goodbye, and on his return had barely graced her with a glance.

Flo had fallen asleep, trying to work him out, and had awoken none the wiser.

Breakfast was delivered by a smiling maid. Flo sat up and a bed tray consisting of fragrant tea, tiny pastries and a lovely fruit platter was placed over her lap.

Flo could only pick at it.

This morning it was Maggie's antenatal check. Her due date was days away, though first babies were often late.

Maggie, who had first thought it would be awkward having a friend as a midwife, was now a lot more relaxed about it. Flo had spoken with the Palace doctor and also the elder who had to be present for the birth. They were both charming. The doctor did indeed have to, if at all possible, deliver the future King. If there were complications and a Caesarean was required, he would be present in the hospital theatre. 'However…' he had smiled at Flo '…if things are going well, you don't have to rush to call me.'

He really had been kind and understanding and he wanted the same for Maggie as Flo did—a wonderful, uncomplicated birth.

Flo had given in on the few clothes she had brought and was now more at ease about borrowing Maggie's robes. They were so comfortable and light and today she selected one in a deep jade green and tied her hair up high.

There was a flutter of nerves in her stomach as she made her way through the Palace, in case she saw Hazin. Flo had decided that if she did then it was time for her pride to kick in and to coldly ignore him.

Of course, now she had decided that, Hazin was nowhere to be seen. She smiled at the guard and knocked on the door to the suite where Maggie lived and was let in by one of the maids, who explained in broken English that Maggie was bathing.

'That's fine.'

Flo took a seat in the lounge and looked around the exquisite furnishings but all she could see was the complete lack of Christmas.

She wasn't homesick as such for she had spoken with her family regularly while she'd been away and she was loving being here….

Flo was just homesick for Christmas.

As glum as she had been back in London, with Christmas just a few days away, excitement would surely by now have been kicking in as she rushed to the shops to get last-minute things for her mum.

'Hi, there.' Maggie came in wearing a bathing robe with her hair wrapped in a towel. 'I have to get my hair and make-up done later so there didn't seem much point in getting dressed.'

'None at all!' Flo beamed.

'I have to say,' Maggie admitted as they headed through to the bedroom, 'it is so less awkward seeing you for my antenatal checks than I thought it would be.'

'Good,' Flo said, 'but I have to say, the Palace doctor is very nice. He delivered Ilyas and Hazin.'

'Really?'

'And I can see now why you need an elder present,' Flo said cheekily as she checked the specimen Maggie had provided and was relieved to see it was all clear. 'It's hard to believe their parents ever had sex!'

Maggie laughed as Flo spoke on.

'Are they not the coldest people you have ever met?' Flo said as she took out her blood-pressure machine. 'I saw her the other day and she stared right through me.'

At least Hazin had scowled when he'd seen her, Flo thought. The Queen had ignored her so completely that Flo had felt like a ghost, utterly invisible to those noble eyes.

'She's actually better than she was,' Maggie said as she sat on the bed while Flo checked her blood pressure. 'She speaks to me occasionally now and King Ahmed seems to be accepting the transition a little better. He's not in the best of health,' Maggie added.

'They might even be relieved to hand over the reins a bit.'

'Not that they would ever admit it,' Maggie said as Flo took off the cuff.

'Your blood pressure is perfect. You do look tired, though.'

'I didn't sleep much last night.'

'You have a perfect excuse not to go today. No one

would blame you a bit for staying home and putting your feet up rather than being out on official business.'

'I know.' Maggie nodded. 'But I doubt I'll want to leave the baby for a while after he's born. Ilyas is trying to repair a lot of damage and apparently bringing me on this visit will show that he's sincere in his efforts to get along better.'

She lay on the bed and Flo checked her impressive bump. 'You really are all baby.' The size was spot on, plus there was lots of movement. 'He's wide awake!' Flo laughed as the baby gave her hand a little kick.

He was head down and engaged, Flo told her, and then examined Maggie further.

'All seems quiet,' Flo said, and explained that there was no sign of the cervix thinning. 'For some women it happens over days and weeks, with some it happens in hours.'

Maggie gave an impatient sigh.

'You can still stay home. Just because there's no sign that you're in pre-labour it doesn't mean it won't happen and you're certainly entitled to rest up and enjoy these last days or weeks at home.'

'I know. It's not that I don't want to go to Idihr today and to the hospital opening tomorrow, it's just…' Her voice trailed off but Flo could guess what was wrong.

'You just want to meet your baby.'

Maggie nodded. 'I think this trip today might take my mind off it.'

'Well, I think it's good that you're keeping busy, and also, if you can get as much work out of the way now, you won't be putting so much pressure on yourself after the baby comes.'

'I also feel terrible asking you to come here and then practically leaving you alone for the next two days.'

'I'm hardly slumming it,' Flo said.

It was true. There was a driver at her disposal if she wanted to go in to the city, and if she wanted some time in the *hammam* all she had to do was let Kumu know.

They chatted for a while but soon it was time for Maggie to get dressed and be made up for the trip to Idihr. Again Maggie, checked that Flo would be okay on her own. 'What will you do with yourself?'

'I might go for a wander,' Flo said. 'Or I might do something about the lack of Christmas in this place!'

Maggie laughed. 'Well, good luck finding decorations.'

Flo didn't need luck.

She had come with tinsel!

Back in her suite she set to work.

There was no hope of a tree so she wrapped it around a stunning vase that was in the corner of the lounge area and then set about wrapping the presents she had bought.

There was a knock at the door. She guessed it might be Kumu and gave a cheery, 'Come in!'

It was Hazin.

Hazin looked exquisite. He was wearing a pale gold robe with buttons that ran the length of the front and he wore a *keffiyeh*.

Flo had only ever seen Hazin in a suit. She was so surprised to see him—and so taken aback by this exotic side to his beauty—that she didn't even say hi, just sat there, with her lost voice, holding the little outfit she had bought for the baby.

'How are you?' he asked.

'I thought you were Kumu.'

'She needs to shave, then.'

She laughed, but midway it faltered as she remembered how he had blanked her yesterday and how she had been determined to ignore him. Yet now, on closer inspection, she could see the tension in his features and guessed that he hadn't dropped by idly.

Hazin could see her sudden wariness. 'May I still come in?' he asked.

'Of course you may,' Flo said, and sighed at her complete inability to sulk around Hazin or play hard to get.

But games were not needed here, for he had come to apologise.

'I just wanted to say that I'm sorry I was rude to you yesterday,' Hazin said, and closed the door behind him.

Flo was rather unused to such a direct apology—in fact, she couldn't remember receiving such a sincere one before. 'It's okay. I guess it must have been a bit of a shock, seeing me here.'

'No, Ilyas had already told me that you were here when you were leaving to go into the desert.'

That surprised her.

Hazin came and sat down on the floor where she was wrapping up her presents.

'You're wearing a robe,' he said, and smiled. 'It suits you.'

'It's Maggie's,' Flo admitted. 'I might go to the souks and get some of my own as it feels a bit odd wearing her clothes. It didn't used to. We used to borrow each other's clothes all the time.'

'So why is it awkward now?'

'I keep waiting for her to change.' Flo sighed. 'It's nothing to do with her and all to do with me. I'm just worried that we're going to grow apart.'

'Have you spoken to her about it?' Hazin asked.

'I'm not very good at that sort of thing. I don't like making waves.'

'Flo tends to go with the flow.'

'I do.' She sighed. 'Wherever it leads.'

And in the casc of Hazin it had led straight to bed.

She met his eycs and they just looked at each other for a long time.

'I'm sorry I was rude,' he said again.

'Apology accepted,' Flo said, and did not look away.

His scent was intoxicating and she liked him unshavcd, as he was now. She could not help but wonder how rough his kiss would be, and she tried to haul herself back from such thoughts.

But she didn't try very hard.

There was an elemental want that danced between them and there was desire that ran like a cord, one that should have tightened and drawn them together, except he remained upright and out of reach.

She did not move closer, yet she begged for a kiss with her eyes and it seemed to her that he was feeling the same inexorable pull, yet it was he who broke eye contact. He looked down at the little rattle and all the presents she had shoved in her case.

'What's this?' he asked, and picked up the ladybird.

Flo battled with disappointment for she had been certain a kiss was just a breath away, but she tried to keep it from her voice as she answered his question. 'A rattle.'

He gave it a little shake. 'Won't he be too young to be into music?'

'It's not a maraca.' Flo laughed but then it faded. She couldn't really believe that he didn't know what toys were for. 'Well, I guess it could be for music, but really it's just a plaything.'

He was looking past her shoulder and Flo turned and followed his gaze to the vase she had decorated. 'It's tinsel.'

'That I had worked out.'

'I'm having Christmas withdrawal. I miss all the build-up…' Flo admitted. 'I'll ring my family on the day and we're going to have another Christmas when I get back home, but it's not the same. Mind you, last year was awful,' Flo said. 'I couldn't stand to admit to my family that I'd found out he was married. I was ashamed enough without all of them knowing.'

'So you pretended you were fine.'

Flo nodded. 'I didn't do a very good job of it, though. I forgot to put my stocking out…'

'Stocking?'

'You know!' Flo couldn't believe he hadn't heard of it. 'You practically grew up in England.'

'Ah, but I came back here on the Christmas breaks.'

'Well, on Christmas Eve you hang up a stocking at the end of the bed, and then when you wake up it's filled with presents and nuts and fruit.'

'Who fills it?'

'Father Christmas.'

Hazin frowned and she guessed that if he hadn't heard of Christmas stockings and thought a baby's rattle was a musical instrument then some further explaining might be required.

'Some people call him Santa.'

But she had misread his confusion for it was entirely aimed at her.

'Flo, I have heard of Santa. Please tell me you don't believe in him.'

'Of course not,' Flo said, 'but there is a certain magic to Christmas.'

'So who fills it up?' he persisted.

'Stop it,' she said.

'Oh, so it's a magical stocking that you put at the end of your bed?' he teased.

'Of course not. It's my mum who fills it.'

He blinked.

'While I'm sleeping, though I don't tell her that I know it's her…'

'You live with your parents?'

'No, but I go home for Christmas.'

'And you're telling me that at the age of…' He waited and she reluctantly gave her age.

'Twenty-nine.'

'At the age of twenty-nine your mother creeps into your bedroom and pretends to be Santa while you pretend that you don't know it's her…'

'Pretty much.' Flo nodded.

'How bizarre.'

'It's actually very lovely,' Flo said, and then she sighed. 'I was so excited to come here, and I still am, but I really am missing Christmas.'

'It hasn't happened yet.' Hazin pointed out.

'And it won't—Maggie's never really been into it. I think because it stirs up memories of her mum. I just love it, though.'

She told him about the other traditions her family kept up, which right now she missed, like presents under the tree and the decorations. 'On Christmas Eve Mum lights these redcurrant candles and she makes this gorgeous mulled wine with a little sachet of spices. It's my favourite scent in the whole world,' Flo said, but then she flicked her eyes away at the sound of her own lie, for she had a new favourite scent.

Hazin.

Raw and masculine with crisp fresh notes. If she could bottle him she would and dab it on each day.

Yet it did not come just from a bottle, for she had tasted his skin and even now she could recall that taste. She moved her gaze back to his and the note of lust in the air was back and she swore he could sense it too.

He looked down at her mouth and then back to her eyes. A kiss was as inevitable as the night they'd first met—though perhaps she was imagining it, for Hazin spoke on as if the air did not thrum with lust and as if they were not alone in her bedroom.

'What else will you miss?' Hazin asked.

Flo had to peel sex from her mind like a reluctant stamp and attempt to remember what they were discussing.

'I'll miss Christmas dinner.'

'I remember at boarding school they would serve it to us on the last day of term. I tried it once…' He pulled a face. 'I cannot see how you could miss that.'

'My mum makes an amazing one. I was just telling Maggie that she's going to freeze it for me.' Flo gave a small shrug. She was tired of talking about a Christmas that wasn't and so she asked about him. 'What's it like for you, being home?'

'I had dinner with Petra's parents last night.'

'How was it?'

'It went better than expected,'

Hazin had been so filled with dread yet their warm welcome had touched him.

His brother and the elders had thought that some sort of public acknowledgement of his rather reckless behaviour was required.

Hazin thought not.

He had privately apologised to her family for any pain his indiscretions had caused them, and he felt this was a far more appropriate gesture.

'They were as lovely as she was. I care for them very much.'

He looked so intently at Flo that she felt as if she was missing something, but then the moment was gone.

'What else have you done?' she asked.

'My parents have lectured me at length. Prior to that it was Mahmoud, the King's vizier, and no doubt later I'll be talked down to by my brother.'

'Talked down to?'

'No one thinks I am capable of writing a speech. They all want to check it first and are annoyed that I won't let them.'

'Have you written it yet?' Flo asked, and she was surprised that he laughed.

'No.'

His laughter had been at her perception but then it faded because writing this speech had been hanging over his head for weeks.

'Why don't you just speak from your heart on the day?' Flo suggested.

'The day is tomorrow,' Hazin said.

Flo could see he was almost grey, just at the thought of it. 'So, just say what feels right at the time.'

'We don't speak off the cuff here in Zayrinia.'

'I thought things were changing.'

Oh, they were, they were, Hazin thought, for he ached to take her to bed. He ached for the feeling her mouth gave on his and the company and comfort she brought him. Yet he knew he must wait and so he rolled his eyes and spoke of his brother instead.

'I'm glad that Ilyas is away today. He's so staid…'

'Ilyas is gorgeous,' Flo refuted. 'He's not staid at all.' Then she smiled. 'Maybe a tiny bit.'

It was like sharing a little secret.

'All my family do when I am here is complain to me about me. Then they wonder why I don't like coming back.' He looked at her. 'This time, though, there was a rather compelling reason.'

'The speech?' Flo said.

'No, the midwife.'

His flirtation was very direct and it swept through her like relief, even if she didn't believe him. 'You didn't come back here for me.'

'But I did.'

He should not be here, Hazin knew, for he couldn't help himself when he was around her, and he had to fight to resist reaching out for Flo with each and every breath he took.

No, he should not be here, yet here was exactly where he wanted to be. Hazin looked down at the presents she was wrapping and the little mint-green suit with an odd face embroidered on the front.

'Is that a dog?' Hazin asked.

'It's a dog with rabbit tendencies, I think. I just thought it was so cute that I had to buy it.'

'You like babies a lot.'

'Far, far too much.' Flo sighed. 'You'd think I'd get my fill at work…' She shook her head. Really! She was hardly going to tell Hazin just how much she would love her own baby—Flo had learned many times over that it wasn't the best flirting technique!

Yet Hazin seemed unfazed.

'The carpenter's door is broken,' he concluded, and when she gaped at his odd choice of words Hazin better explained. 'It is an Arabic saying. It means that you rush around taking care of others while neglecting your own needs.'

'I don't neglect them,' Flo said. 'I just…well, you don't just go out to the shops to get one.'

'No.'

'But, yes, the carpenter's door, while not broken, is very squeaky.' She started to laugh as she decided she liked his saying better than thinking of her ovaries as some ticking clock.

'I thought you would be with Maggie today,' Hazin said, but Flo shook her head.

'No.'

'Aren't you supposed to be watching her?'

'She's not going to suddenly pop!' Flo laughed, although Maggie's water could break at any minute! She very much hoped not, though she chose not to air *that* concern with Hazin. 'I'm sure if anything *starts* to happen then Ilyas will get her back home. First babies usually take ages.'

'Oh.'

'And she's not ready yet.'

'How do you know?' Hazin asked.

'You don't want to know.'

He pulled a face. 'I like how babies get in there, not how they come out.'

'I had rather worked that out, Hazin.'

She just had not worked *him* out for, despite the thrumming between them, he made not a single move and Flo was too wary to make one of her own.

'So, what are you going to do with your day?' he asked.

'I thought I might wander,' Flo said. 'I have to speak to Kumu and work out where I can go, but I wouldn't mind a day exploring. What about you?'

'I have to work on my speech.'

'Can I help?'

He gave a wry laugh that Flo could not interpret. She could not possibly know that she was, in fact, the problem, and yet, *here*, with her, was where he wanted to be.

A day with just them was completely irresistible. Like wagging school instead of buckling down to work on his speech.

And as he sat there, he remembered something, a long-ago day when no one had shown up in the nursery and his brother had come to the door.

He had been so surprised to see him. Hazin could absolutely recall the feel of the smile that had split his face at the unexpected sight of Ilyas unaccompanied by an elder.

But then the memory faded and he shook his head, trying to recapture it. They had gone exploring together.

'Come on,' Hazin said suddenly.

'Where?'

He didn't tell her.

Hazin didn't have to.

Like an eager Labrador, when he stood up so too did she.

Had there been a lead she'd have rushed off to grab it! She reminded herself she had to be more aloof, more restrained, less available.

Except her heart was already utterly available to him.

CHAPTER TWELVE

THEY WALKED ALONG a corridor she had not been down before. It was dark and, unlike most of the palace, dimly lit. In fact, the only light came from a small arched window at the end of it.

'This was the nursery,' Hazin explained, and pushed open a huge unguarded door. 'Of course, it is not used now.'

Flo rather hoped it wouldn't be used anytime soon! Unlike the rest of the palace, which was lush and oozed luxury, this room was incredibly dour.

'Is this where you and Ilyas were…?' She didn't know what word to use. Housed? Kept? It was just so drab and gloomy.

'No, Ilyas was raised in the leaders' wing, but one day the elder did not come to school him…' He could remember it just a little clearer now. 'Ilyas came and fetched me.'

He pushed open a heavy wooden door and, having experienced the trip from Maggie's suite before, when she saw the steps leading downwards Flo knew that it led to the *hammam* beneath the palace.

'Are we going swimming?' Flo asked.

'No, we're going exploring,' Hazin said as he led the way, determined that they would not be getting naked.

They passed under a low archway and through decorated tunnels but he took her beyond anywhere that Flo had been with Maggie.

'Down there is Ilyas's private area…' Hazin pointed, but as Flo went to head down he called her back. 'We can't go there.'

'Why? He'll never know, he's not here today.'

'We just can't.' Hazin said and then smiled at her ease at breaking the rules.

'Do you have your own area?'

'Not really.' He shook his head. 'I declined.'

Flo frowned, unsure what he meant, but Hazin was already heading in a different direction.

'We came down here.'

'Who?'

'Ilyas and I.'

He was starting to remember a time so long ago and so buried that Hazin had until now completely forgotten its existence.

'Come on,' he said as they walked further down natural stairways until they came to a low tunnel that they had to stoop to go through.

It was worth it, though.

They came out to a huge cave pool surrounded by the soft sounds of fountains. They were no longer plunged in darkness for it was dimly lit by a natural window in the cave that looked to the desert sky.

'I can remember coming here…' Hazin said, looking up. 'Ilyas and I, we were children…'

There hadn't been a single good memory of his childhood, not one.

Yet as he looked at the huge cave he remembered them as children. 'We came exploring.'

'Here?'

'I'm sure it was here.' Hazin nodded. 'But it was far lighter. It seemed to glow. We swam and then we sat over there.' Hazin pointed. It was all coming back to him. 'And I told Ilyas that I wished he was King.'

Hazin could remember that feeling exactly—the absolute assuredness and trust that he'd had in his older brother then.

'He was always sensible. That day, even before we headed off, he stopped and got food and drinks. I was annoyed at the time because I wanted to head straight off…'

'Then you were hungry after your swim.' Flo laughed.

'Yes.' Hazin nodded. 'It was such a good day.'

'How old were you?'

'I don't know. Little. We had an amazing day but when we got back to the Palace it went back to being the same. I hardly saw him.'

'How come?'

'He lived in a different part of the Palace. I have my own area. I was a lot of work for the nannies and it was soon decided I should be schooled overseas.'

'Why not here?'

'I was too rebellious,' Hazin said. 'They didn't want the people to know that.'

'So they sent you away?'

'Yes, and now they complain that I stay away. I cannot stand the way my father rules. He has no compassion for his people.'

'Ilyas is changing that,' Flo said. 'He's the real leader now.'

She knew everything, Hazin realised.

He was not used to outsiders knowing Palace business, but he found that Flo knowing it did not unsettle him.

The world felt more open than the closed one he had grown up in.

'Could you give Ilyas a chance?' Flo asked. 'You trusted him once.'

'I trust him still,' Hazin said. 'I know he will do the right thing by the people. He wants me to have a more prominent role.'

'Do you want one?'

It was refreshing to be asked, but he could not answer yet.

'I'll tell you what I want, Flo. I want to get past tomorrow. I want the speech made and to get it right for Petra's family.'

'It will be,' Flo said. She looked at his taut features and wished she could melt the strain away. She wished, how she wished, that he would reach for her, that he would suggest they swim, so she might wrap herself naked around him.

Yet he made no move.

Hazin, the Playboy Prince, had, since their one torrid night, been a complete gentleman.

Flo just wished it wasn't so.

And then something lovely happened. Fingers of light that had been streaming into the cave spread as the sun became aligned with the window and they were bathed in light.

It was how he had experienced it all those years ago, when he'd come here with Ilyas.

'Shall we swim?' Flo said, oh-so-casually.

Hazin stared out at the pool and his memory recalled the perfect temperature of the water. He longed to shed his robe and take her in; for their legs to tangle beneath the water; to kiss her wet as he took her deep; to lose themselves in each other for a while.

'No,' Hazin said and stood. 'We ought to get back.'

He knew he had confused her, for he could feel the signals his body gave out. He was as turned on as she, yet he had sworn he would wait.

That he would do this right.

She walked ahead of him this time and he tried not to notice the single blonde curl that coiled on the nape of her neck.

And when she stooped to make her way back through the tunnel, he did all he could to ignore a bottom dressed in velvet waving inches from his face.

What the hell had he been thinking, bringing Flo down here?

And they were not out of the caves yet.

Flo did not wait for Hazin to follow her out. Instead, she walked ahead and tried to sort her head out, which was rather an impossible ask with his footsteps behind her in this intimate, magical space.

'Not that way…' he called out to her when she turned to the right, but Flo ignored him, for she was intrigued.

There were huge white pillar candles lighting a passage and she saw that the tunnel was lined with red mosaic tiles.

'We're not allowed here,' Hazin told her.

'Since when did you care for the rules?' Flo said, and she looked at the softly lit tunnel. 'Who lights the candles?'

'The *hammam* maids do. Each candle burns for seven days and seven nights.'

'Is this Ilyas's area?'

'No,' Hazin said. 'Well, sort of. This leads to where his harem used to be housed.'

She was right, he did not care for the rules, so he took Flo by the hand and they walked down a long red tunnel until they reached a boudoir.

'This was his harem.' Hazin explained. 'That tunnel over there leads to Ilyas's area of the *hammam*.'

'We came in through the back door?'

'So to speak.' Hazin nodded. 'Only those summoned by Ilyas can go through there.'

Flo felt her cheeks go pink.

There wasn't much that made her blush, but for some reason that this had once been a harem did.

She looked around at the plump velvet cushions where they must have lain, awaiting his summons. There were many mirrors and glass bottles. Flo took the stopper off one and inhaled.

It was the most sensual space she had ever been in.

'Would Ilyas come in here and choose?'

'No,' Hazin said. 'This space was for them.'

Hazin watched as Flo pulled out silk scarves and tassels from the chests that lined the walls. Her curiosity had been aroused and he ached in his groin.

'The harem was disbanded when Ilyas announced he was to marry…'

'I would hope so!' Flo said, and she draped a scarf over her shoulders as if playing dress-up. 'Was yours disbanded too?'

'I never had one.'

'Oh, I guess you were too young,' Flo said as she draped herself over some cushions.

He frowned. 'I told you, I declined.'

She looked at him. Hazin fascinated her, he truly did. 'Why?'

He gave her a smile as he answered, a smile that simultaneously warmed her as it sent a little shiver of energy through her. 'I like the thrill of the chase, Flo—or at least I used to.'

'Used to?'

'People know who I am now so they tend to chase me.'

No wonder he had been so upset when he had thought she had been targeting him simply because she'd known his title. 'Hazin, I came over and spoke to you so that you'd stay long enough for Maggie to arrive. I didn't really think it was my place to break the news of her pregnancy to you.'

'I know that now.'

He stood looking around the luxurious space where Ilyas's harem had awaited his summons, then smiled at Flo, who was draping the scarf over her face.

'It's sexy isn't it?' she said.

'I guess, but there would certainly be no chasing required here. The only thing you need to pull is this.' He reached up and pulled a thick velvet rope and the bells in the centre rang out.

'Ooh,' Flo said, and got up and danced towards him. 'How do you want me, master?'

He laughed, but then the mood changed all of a sudden. He wanted her so much, and as she shimmied over to him he felt the pull of his eyes but then, when she neared him, he gave her a slight push of his hands instead of an embrace.

'Let's go back,' Hazin said, wishing she would leave it there.

Flo could not, though.

'I couldn't make more of a fool of myself if I tried,' she said, stinging at his rejection of her all over again.

'It's not that, Flo. I didn't bring anything.'

But she just stared back at him through narrowed,

hurt eyes. 'Excuses, excuses,' she said. 'A simple no will suffice.' She turned to walk off, embarrassed and cross with herself, for she had sworn that he would make the first move. And confused too, so confused, for she had been so certain of their mutual want.

'Flo.' He caught her wrist and turned her around. He loathed the look of shame he had caused on her face. 'It is not that I don't want you…' He could not explain, because Hazin had promised himself that he would not speak of his feelings for her until Petra's memory had been laid to rest. His rejection of her had been unintentionally cruel, and he didn't know how to make it right without breaking his promise.

How did he explain that if he touched her he might crack and reveal all that was on his mind? 'I do want you but…' He could not reveal himself fully, but he tried to a little. 'I would not be a considerate lover. I have a lot on my mind…'

'I don't need cartwheels!' Flo cried. As her anger dimmed she could see the utter wretchedness in his eyes and the desire between them was almost palpable. She guessed he must feel guilt, yet she could not really fathom why. 'I know tomorrow is huge but it's not as if you've been celibate these past ten years.'

'No,' Hazin said. 'But I can't have sex with feeling today.'

For if he did, he might break apart.

'Then don't,' Flo said. She looked at his mouth and the set of his jaw and she felt his hand hot on her wrist. For him she would risk rejection again.

'As I said…' Flo smiled seductively. 'How do you want me, master?'

She saw the stretch of his lips and watched his Adam's apple dip and then rise. She dragged her eyes down to the buttons on his robe. Flo removed her hand from his grip and he did not reclaim it, as one by one she undid the buttons.

There was no question he wanted her, as she could see how hard he was through his sunnah trousers, and she felt a little dizzy with lust herself.

So she tasted his neck again—just the light brush of her lips and the tip of her tongue this time. It shot her back to the night when they *had* made love. Not at first, but later, when their eyes had locked and her soul had leapt and met his.

But this was just sex, she reminded herself. Yet as she moved her mouth lower and tongued his flat nipple, she heard his ragged breathing and knew she was just kidding herself, for this was more than pure need because there might never be a *them* again.

She kissed and licked across his flat, taut stomach and she nipped the dark snake of hair with her teeth before slipping him out to her full view.

On that morning when they had woken up together, just before it had all gone wrong, she remembered how it had been between them as she slid her tongue around his head and wetted him as she had wanted to then. Her hands slid up his thighs and she cupped his balls. She felt her knees press into the velvet cushion on which she knelt, and he moaned with craving as with her other hand she circled the base of his shaft and applied light pressure, her lips dusting the delicate skin in pure torture. Then she licked his long delicious length over and over as he fought not to guide her head, but then came the bliss of her lips closing over his heated tip.

Hazin sucked in his breath as she took him all the way in and his mind went blank.

He moaned with relief for she was not gentle or tender, her mouth was as hot and hungry as he needed it to be.

Flo had never been more into anyone. She tasted every delicious inch of him, and she could feel the fight in him not to thrust so she worked him faster with her hand.

She could feel her own sex heavy and wet as Hazin lost his desperate fight and put his hands on either side of her head to control the movement. He cursed in Arabic and then he warned her.

Flo knew it was coming.

She had felt the tight swell of him, and the salty rush came with a shout and it was so primal that even as she slid him from her mouth she felt herself coming.

She knelt back on her heels as the waves of her climax rocked her body. He looked down at her flushed face and right into her china-blue eyes as she swallowed.

'Come here,' Hazin groaned, and he hauled her up and held her against his body. Flo leant her head on his chest and breathed in the sexy scent of them, and for a moment his arms wrapped around her.

He was breathless, but for the first time in months it felt as if he could breathe. 'When I can,' he said, 'I will make things right by you.'

'I enjoyed it too, Hazin. It wasn't a favour.'

That hadn't been what he'd meant, but now was not the time to explain.

He and Flo had to be on hold for now.

Yet on the slow walk back through the caves to the palace they were holding hands. They came back through the wooden door to the stark old nursery.

'You go out first,' Hazin said, but not unkindly.

They were both dishevelled and it would be awkward indeed if anyone saw them like this. It was not said dismissively either, for he smoothed her hair and straightened her robe and did what he could to make her not look as if she'd just had sex.

'Good luck tomorrow,' Flo said. 'I mean that.'

'Thank you.'

He made her feel brave, because normally she put on a smile or made a little joke, but now she said what she felt she must. 'Promise me one thing?' she said, and he nodded. 'Don't leave this time without saying goodbye.'

It had hurt.

And he knew that.

'I won't.'

That promise, at least, he could give.

CHAPTER THIRTEEN

HAZIN FACED THE MORNING.

He had slept, and he awoke in that damned bed to the sound of his breakfast being brought into the lounge.

Usually he called down for it at his chosen time, but no doubt it had been sent to serve as a check that he was awake.

Well, he was.

He took his breakfast out on the balcony that looked out to the stunning city and, beyond, the ocean.

Ilyas's balcony faced the desert, but Hazin preferred this view. And on a day he had been dreading for such a long time, he actually smiled as he remembered how Petra had loved to sit out here.

It was nice to remember her with a smile. He hadn't been able to do that in all these years, but then the moment was broken when he heard a knock on his door. No doubt it was Ilyas to check he was on track for today.

Or Mahmoud to cast his beady eyes over his speech.

He could try, but Hazin had taken Flo's advice and decided that he would speak from thc heart. He knew all the formal parts that he had to say, and as for the rest he still did not know.

But it was neither Mahmoud nor Ilyas, but Kumu.

'I have that number for you.'

Hazin blinked, He had not expected Kumu to be able to get the information he had asked for so soon.

And certainly, if she had, he had not expected her to give it to him today.

'Thank you,' Hazin said. 'And, Kumu—'

'You don't have to say,' she interrupted with a smile. 'I won't say anything, I never would.'

'Thank you.'

'If I can be any further help, please just ask.' She gave a small bow but as she turned to go she remembered a request from the Crown Prince. 'Ilyas has asked for a copy of the speech so it can be translated for his wife.'

'Ilyas will not be getting a copy of my speech,' Hazin said. 'He is quite capable of telling his wife what is said.' He watched a tiny smile play on Kumu's mouth but he did not want her to get into trouble on his behalf. 'If he gets annoyed, tell him to speak with me.'

'Ilyas always speaks kindly to me,' Kumu said.

He didn't know his brother. This was something Hazin knew, but he was constantly being surprised by the way Ilyas was changing things around the palace. And through those changes he was getting to know his brother.

It was clear that Ilyas loved his wife, and the atmosphere in the palace was so much lighter than it used to be.

Back when they had been boys, Hazin had said that he wished Ilyas was King.

He had trusted him then and he still did.

He always had.

As Kumu turned to go, he called her back. 'Kumu, wait there, please.' He went through to the study and opened up a drawer, taking out two slim packages.

'Please,' he said when he returned, 'take a seat.'

It was most irregular for a prince to invite one of the staff to take a seat in their apartment and he could see her confusion but she did as she was told.

'How old is Rami now?' He asked after her daughter.

'She is eleven.'

'Petra was so excited when you brought her in to visit her. You made her days so much brighter with the pregnancy and the baby…'

'I miss her so much,' Kumu admitted.

'I know, and so I have something for you.' He handed her a package. When she opened it, she saw it was a beautifully bound book that Petra had loved to read and sometimes Kumu had read to her.

Inside was a jewelled bookmark and he saw her fingers trace it.

'This is too much.'

Hazin had considered that, for he knew they must struggle to send their child to Zayrinia's best school. As he had wrapped the gift he had thought about Petra, for she had tried to give Kumu a necklace once and she had declined. 'She could never sell it,' Petra had later explained to Hazin, 'so that would make it a burden.'

He hadn't understood then, but he tried to now.

'I want you to have something that Petra loved and that is the bookmark. I would also like you to have this.'

She opened the envelope he gave her and tears fell from her eyes as she read that Rami had been offered a full scholarship at the prestigious Zayrinia school.

'How did you know?'

'Because I thought of Petra and this is what she would want for you.'

It was a nice start to the day he had dreaded. When

Kumu had left he looked down at the number she had brought him.

He was about to put it off when he thought of his own words…

I thought of Petra and this is what she would want for you.

Hazin made the call.

Flo made her way to the grand entrance hall to say goodbye to Maggie as they left for the ceremony.

Well, mainly to say goodbye to Maggie, but also in the hope of a glimpse of Hazin.

He wasn't there.

In fact, few of the staff were, for Ilyas had insisted that all who wanted to could attend the ceremony, and so most were there.

Yes, times were changing indeed.

'Hopefully, if Hazin does make it, he'll appear sober this time,' Ilyas said to Maggie, and headed off to find out what the hell was keeping his brother.

Maggie rolled her eyes. 'I don't know what Hazin is playing at. He won't let anyone see his speech and he's been holed up in his apartment all morning, receiving guests.'

'Who?'

'I don't know. I just know that I'll be really glad when today's over.'

'Are you sure you don't want me to come with you?'

'You keep telling me I'm not made of glass.' Maggie laughed and then she realised what was going on. 'You weren't asking to come to the ceremony for *me*, were you?'

'No,' Flo admitted.

'Flo…' Maggie's face worried. 'I love Hazin, I really do. He has always been an utter gentleman to me but—'

'I already know his reputation,' Flo cut in. 'Maggie, don't worry. I went into this with my eyes wide open. Or at least I thought I did.' Flo hadn't expected to find love.

'When you say you "went into this"…' Maggie closed her eyes. 'I'm too late with my warning, aren't I?'

'You were too late three months ago.'

'Oh, my God,' Maggie said, and she sort of laughed and groaned at the same time, but she was clearly concerned for her friend. 'I don't want you to get hurt.'

'I've a feeling it's a bit late for that, too.' Flo said. 'And the only person I'll have to blame is myself.'

She didn't even pretend that she wouldn't hurt when they ended. And end they surely must. Flo just hoped this time he would keep his word and say goodbye.

But it was Hazin who was hurting today, Flo was certain.

'I just wanted to be a friendly face in the crowd.'

'Liar,' Maggie said. 'You just want to hear it for yourself.'

'True, though I'll have no idea what's being said.'

'Well, given my due date is so close, I think I might need my midwife to accompany me after all…' And then she stopped speaking and looked up. Flo followed her gaze.

Hazin looked regal. Together and composed.

He wore a silver robe and over that a black *bisht* that was trimmed in silver. His *keffiyeh* was elaborately wrapped and tied with a thick silver cord.

The King came out then and barked something at him but Hazin did not answer, just made his way slowly down the steps.

He did not look at the portrait and he did not look

at Flo, he just made his way through the open doors to the first of the waiting cars.

'Can Flo travel with me?' Maggie asked Kumu.

'Flo will come with me,' Kumu said. 'I shall take care of her and should you need her, just give me a discreet wave.'

Maggie looked at Flo. 'I'm sorry, I tried…'

'I was hardly going to come in the car with you.' Flo smiled. 'And Kumu's right, if you need anything just let me know. I'm glad I'm here for you today.'

The official cars were waiting to move off, and Kumu took her to another that was, of course, not part of the procession. In fact, she and Kumu left first so they could be there before the Royals arrived.

They drove through streets lined with people all waiting to glimpse not just Hazin but the Crown Prince they held out so much hope for and also his very pregnant bride, who they were desperate for news of.

As they headed towards the hospital, a huge crowd of people began cheering and Flo could not quite believe the turnout.

'Princess Petra was very popular,' Kumu explained. 'When she and Hazin married she came down and met with the people. It was as if a breath of fresh air had breezed into the palace, for the Royals had always kept themselves separate until then. Unfortunately, that breath of fresh air did not last.'

Flo was surprised at how much Kumu was telling her, but guessed she must be feeling sad today and perhaps needed to share.

Kumu turned then and smiled. 'Now that Maggie is here, things are different again,' she said. 'Now the people see Ilyas smiling. Do you remember the cheers on their wedding day?'

'I do.' Flo laughed. 'I was standing right at the back of the ballroom and I still had to put my hands up to my ears.'

It was so sad that Petra had died, and maybe Flo was torturing herself by going today, but it would be torture too, to stay away.

Once they had arrived, Kumu went to greet the Royal cars and Flo stood with the caterers and maids and security and the many people who were there to ensure that things went seamlessly.

The Royals would be seated on a covered platform. There was a lectern and beside that a beautiful image of Petra, and the platform was dressed in gorgeous desert blooms. There were rugs on their seats for the air was cool. That had actually been Flo's suggestion to Kumu and it had nothing to do with the weather, more the very pregnant princess and those waters breaking on a very public stage!

She watched as Maggie took her place on the platform and she smiled as she saw that Maggie was the first to cover herself with a rug. And Ilyas, because he loved her and did not want her to stand out, did the same.

But not the Queen.

There wasn't an empathetic bone in her body, Flo thought, but then ate her own words because the Queen did the same then too.

Hazin did not.

He sat absolutely still, like a statue.

There were moments, though, when she felt closer to him than she ever had to anyone. She could tell him things, reveal things and be entirely herself.

They had moments of absolute connection.

Now was not one of those moments, for he looked so

alone up there on the platform. Not sad, or lonely, just separate from the people who surrounded him.

He did stand and smile as three more people came to the stage, presumably Petra's parents and brother. They all sat beside him and then the crowd hushed as the ceremony began.

It was all very formal. There was a band that played for *ever*, and a whole lot of speeches, and then the band played *again*.

And then Petra's brother made a speech and Flo watched as his mother dabbed at her eyes.

Not the Queen. She remained remote and untouched.

And then Flo held her breath as Hazin came to the lectern and the crowd hushed immediately. You could have heard a pin drop as everyone listened intently as their long-absent Prince, for the first time in a decade, made a speech.

He spoke in Arabic, so of course Flo had no idea what was said, but his voice was clear and only a couple of times did it become husky with emotion.

Flo stood, her teeth working her bottom lip, watching his pale features, the only real sign of how difficult this was for him. And then she straightened her features to appear more impassive as Kumu came and stood by her side.

'He just thanked all the medical staff and he said that this new facility is much deserved and needed.'

'I see.'

'And now he says that Petra's family draws a lot of comfort from this new facility.'

Flo nodded.

'Hazin says now how kind Petra was. He says he would like to reiterate that, for…' Kumu hesitated. 'She truly was.'

Kumu was crying, Flo realised.

'Now Hazin says that it has taken him a long time, but he understands that seeds of kindness were planted in him and that this is how she remains with him. For now, when he is angry, he tries to think of Petra, and what she would do. Hazin says that it is never too late to change…'

Flo watched as he turned briefly and looked back at the people behind him, and she wondered if he had looked directly at his parents as he spoke on.

'He says,' Kumu continued, 'that we can all learn from her. And even today he tries to follow her wise words. He hopes that today she smiles on all of us.' Kumu choked and then added, 'And him.'

The crowd applauded and then it built and built to a cheer. Flo could see how much the people loved him.

And so did she.

He had made the dreaded speech without notes and she knew that every word had come from his heart. Flo felt her heart twist with misplaced jealousy, for her rival was a ghost.

As the crowd's applause faded, he turned and guided Petra's mother to cut the ribbon and officially declare the facility open.

He was very patient with her, Flo thought, and watched as he steadied the emotional woman's arm with his hand as she cut the ribbon.

Hazin might have a scandalous reputation but, Flo knew, he really was a very nice man.

And she was more than a little in love with him.

Flo felt nothing like she had this time last year.

Then it had been about dressing up and going out and all the stupid superficial things.

With Hazin it was all the little things that mattered.

Finally it was over, yet perhaps not for Hazin. Flo watched as he mingled with the guests and duly made small talk as waiters milled around.

A sad garden party really, Flo thought.

Even Flo was not ignored. In fact, just before it was time to leave, Hazin made his way over to her. She decided to take a lesson from Perfect Petra and be…

Kind.

'Well done,' she said.

'Thanks.'

'It seemed to go very well.'

'I think so.'

She didn't know what to say, for there was a stretch of awkward silence so Flo filled it.

'I know that you must miss her so much.'

'Please…' He took a breath for he could not deal with it today. It *had* to be later. Hazin's eyes shuttered as he braced himself to get through the rest of this most difficult day. 'Not now, Flo!'

His words came out too harshly, Hazin knew, and yet there was no chance to rectify things with the world watching.

And so he walked away.

CHAPTER FOURTEEN

It was Kumu who brought Flo's breakfast in the next morning and it took more than a moment for Flo to register that it was Christmas Eve.

Not that it felt like it here in the desert kingdom.

'How did you sleep?' Kumu enquired as she placed the breakfast tray on Flo's lap.

'Very well,' Flo lied, and then asked a question. 'Kumu, have there been any deliveries for me?'

'If there were they would have been sent straight to your room. Is there anything you need that I can get for you?'

'No, I have everything.' Flo smiled. 'I just…' She held in her disappointed sigh. 'I thought my family might have sent something for Christmas.'

'I shall look into it myself,' Kumu said. 'If anything comes, it shall be delivered straight to your suite.'

'Thank you.'

'Flo, I know that we don't do Christmas here, but I wondered if, as a treat, you might like to sleep in the western wing tonight. The view of thc desert at sunset is spectacular.'

'It's lovely of you to offer…' Flo smiled '…but, no, thank you. I really like it where I am.'

'You're sure?' Kumu checked.

'Absolutely.'

It was madness, Flo knew, yet the first thing she had done when Kumu had opened the drapes had been to check for Hazin's plane.

She could read the insignia on the tails a lot better now and it soothed her to know that he was still here. Yes, he had promised not to leave without saying goodbye, but men would promise anything after a good blowjob.

And if that was crass, she was only being crass with herself, because distance from him made Flo bully herself. And that bully rearranged her thoughts until she had decided that she had thrown herself at him in the *hammam*.

And though they had both enjoyed it, there had been nothing since then bar that brief exchange after his speech. Flo picked at her breakfast and then cast her mind back to yesterday and the moment they had shared.

Not now, Flo!

She could still hear his words and feel the tension with which they had been delivered. Flo could kick herself for being insensitive and for saying what ten thousand people yesterday had surely already said to him.

From all Flo could gather, Hazin had not returned to the Palace last night.

Where had he spent the night?

Give it up, Flo told herself, and hauled herself from the bed.

Yet she could not let it go.

She had known from the start that he came with a warning attached.

Yet it wasn't his reputation or other women that concerned her.

It was Petra.

Flo, dressed in a soft, indigo velvet robe, stepped out onto the balcony and tried to shift her low mood. It was cold, though not, Flo thought, cold enough for it to be Christmas, not while the sky was so high and blue.

And his plane was still here.

Of course there were no decorations in the palace. Flo noted their absence as she made her way to Maggie's wing.

'Morning.' Maggie smiled and greeted her friend. 'Have you had breakfast?'

'I have.' Flo nodded as she wandered in and took a seat on one of the couches. Maggie came and sat with her and they gazed out at the stunning desert view. 'It feels odd not to be hitting the shops today,' Flo admitted. Usually she was the last of the last-minute Christmas shoppers but had made sure that she'd got it all done before she'd left. 'It doesn't feel like Christmas at all.'

'I feel bad that I've let it slide.'

'Well, you've been pretty busy.' Flo shrugged. 'I'm just a Christmas tragic.'

'And this is going to be your worst.'

'No.' Flo shook her head. She didn't want Maggie feeling guilty. 'I'm having the most amazing time and I am so glad that I came. It was *last* Christmas that was the worst ever.'

'Oh, that's right, while I was away you broke up with…?' Maggie frowned. 'I can't remember his name.'

Flo smiled at her friend's irritation with her own brain.

'What was his name?' Maggie said, clicking her fingers in exasperation, as if that might make his name suddenly appear.

Flo decided it was time to share with Maggie his rightful description—and it was far worse than one that began in B and ended in D. 'His name was Married Man.'

'Oh, Flo.' Maggie put her arms around her friend. 'Why didn't you say?'

'Because I was just so ashamed. His wife came in to have her baby…'

'You poor, poor thing.' Maggie was completely lovely. 'You could have told me.'

'I know, I just didn't know how.'

It was since she'd told Hazin that she'd felt if not better then a little less brushed by the shame. 'I do know how to pick them, don't I?'

'You really, really do.' Maggie sighed and then told Flo what little she knew about Hazin. 'Apparently he came back very late last night and left early this morning.'

'Do you know where to?'

'I don't,' Maggie said, and then her voice was serious. 'Though he's asked to speak formally with Ilyas tonight. Ilyas seems to think that now Hazin has got the speech out of the way he's going to formally request to step down.'

'And how does Ilyas feel about that?'

'He wants Hazin beside him.'

'Don't we all,' Flo said, and then buried her face in her hands. 'I'm sorry, Maggie, my disaster of a love life is the last thing you need to hear about right now.'

'It's exactly what I need,' Maggie said. 'I've missed you so much, you know.'

Maybe she could address it? Flo thought of Hazin's

suggestion to talk about what was on her mind. But Flo did not want to heap pressure on Maggie now and tell her her insecurities about the future of their friendship. So instead she did what she did best—shook off her mood and pushed out a smile.

'I'll be fine.'

'Better than fine,' Maggie said. 'I've told the *hammam* to expect us this afternoon! I think we could both use a spa day.'

It was a very different Christmas Eve indeed.

Flo left Maggie and met with two nursery nurses who would be helping once the baby was here. She also spoke with the palace elder who went through a few details about what was required after the birth had taken place.

'There are already people gathering and watching activity at the palace. It is one of the reasons that we prefer the birth to take place here. It allows the family some time before it is announced to the world.'

'How long before it is?'

'That is a choice for the parents. For Ilyas it was two weeks after his birth and for Hazin I believe it was a couple of months.'

'A couple of months?'

'The baby is brought onto the balcony, or that is what used to happen. Ilyas says that the announcement shall be made on the day the baby is born but the balcony presentation can come afterwards, whenever Maggie is ready.'

Flo could more than see the merit of giving birth here without the world waiting impatiently to hear the news. Maggie was shielded from a lot of what was happening, for certainly Flo would not be telling her about the crowd already gathered. It really sounded as if Ilyas had done all he could to ensure his wife was well looked after.

And that included having Flo here.

After lunch, she and Maggie made their way down to the *hammam*, but Maggie could not relax at the foot massage. She was just as tense through all the gorgeous treatments so Flo suggested they go into one of the pools.

The water was bliss and just the right temperature. Maggie lay on her back as Flo leant over the edge and stared out at the desert.

It was late afternoon and in a couple of hours the sun would be setting. Flo could have accepted Kumu's kind offer and had that view all to herself.

Yet she had placed herself on Hazin-watch, furtively checking for his plane and all too aware that at any moment he could leave. It sounded as if he would tonight.

He was surely stepping down.

Why else would he want to see Ilyas?

And it made her sad.

There was a guilty shard in her soul that relished the thought of him living in London and the chance it might give them, but mostly she was sad.

She didn't blame him for turning his back on his parents, who had treated him so abysmally, but the people all loved him so much, that was clear to Flo. And, despite his rather staid exterior, Ilyas wanted to right the wrongs that had been done to them and to have a relationship with his brother. Yet Hazin pushed away anyone who attempted to get close to him, that was abundantly clear.

And so she would close her drapes on the view tonight and stop watching for planes leaving and searching for signs.

She had a job to do.

Maggie was in pre-labour, Flo was quite certain, for she was irritable and unable to relax, though the water seemed to be doing the trick now for there was a lovely feeling of calm.

Flo was on Maggie-watch now.

CHAPTER FIFTEEN

IT WAS A very quiet Christmas Eve indeed.

Tired from the massages and time in the pool, Maggie was early to bed and Flo lay in hers with the drapes firmly closed. If she was right and Maggie was in early labour, at any time her phone could go off so Flo was more than happy to have an early night. But first she called home.

'Flo, I can't talk for long,' her mother warned, which wasn't exactly a great conversation starter. 'I have so much to do.'

'Tell me,' Flo said, desperate to be a part of the celebrations, but her mother didn't have time to indulge her suddenly homesick daughter. And so Flo lay on her bed watching a Christmas movie on her computer and eating chocolate.

It would be perfect, really, if it wasn't Christmas Eve.

And if she wasn't bracing herself for a broken heart.

She was all floppy and tired from her spa and she frowned when there was a knock at her door. But as she pulled on a wrap Flo was sure it was Kumu to tell her to come and see Maggie.

It was Hazin.

'What do you want?' she asked, and her voice was all surly, for she refused, yes, *refused* to jump to his tune.

'I want you to come to bed,' he said.

'Excuse me?' Flo checked, not sure if she was hearing things right. It would seem that she was! 'Hazin, what happened to the thrill of the chase?'

'You're easy, though,' he teased, and then saw her murderous expression and quickly amended with a slight triumphant smile, 'Flo, I prefer the thrill of you.'

He melted her.

Her resolve popped in the same way she'd feared Maggie's waters would until it lay in a puddle on the floor. Still, she did *try* to resist him, even if he had just made her smile.

'I'm not your sex toy, Hazin. Anyway, I need to sleep.' She went to close the door but his shoulder got in the way.

'Sleep in my bed, Goldilocks.'

'Ha-ha.'

'We've managed to just sleep before,' Hazin pointed out. In fact, it rather suited him *not* to have sex tonight, for he desperately wanted the air cleared between them before they did. He was holding onto a secret indeed. 'You have to come to my apartment, I've got a surprise there for you.'

Flo was intrigued.

And she wanted to know what had been said between him and Ilyas, not that she could admit she knew he had just been in a meeting.

'Bring your phone,' he said. 'You may be gone some time.'

She really was a pushover where Hazin was concerned, Flo thought as she quickly pulled on her robe and happily collected her phone.

Down long corridors they went and then they entered his apartment.

He led her towards his bedroom and as she opened the door to darkness, there was a familiar scent in the air. It wasn't pitch dark, for there was a candlc burning and he handed her a glass of warm mulled wine.

'It's a redcurrant candle,' Flo said shaking her head in wonder, because it most certainly was.

'Happy Christmas Eve,' Hazin said.

'This is the nicest thing you could have done.' Flo beamed. She was very close to tears, for she could not quite believe what he had done! There was one problem, though. 'I can't have a drink tonight,' Flo said, and told him the real reason she had to sneak in some sleep. 'I've a feeling I'm going to be needed by Maggie.'

'Really?' He thought for a moment. 'Well, you can have some tomorrow then.'

He took the glass from her and put it down and then turned on the side lights as she breathed in the lovely scent of a Christmas at home. Well, minus the pine and the mince pies and things, but quite simply he had taken her breath away.

'Thank you for this, Hazin!'

'You are so welcome.'

'I was starting to feel a bit homesick.'

'Then come here,' he said, and lay on the bed. A moment later she had joined him. It was bliss to be in his arms and just to lie and chat and be held. 'Do you really think Maggie will have the baby tonight?' he asked.

'Well, it's not an exact science, but I think things are starting to move along.'

'How come?'

'She's distracted, a bit irritable…' Flo couldn't really explain it. 'I haven't said anything to Maggie, of course. You just get a feeling about it, I guess, though I may well be wrong and I shall have foregone my mulled wine for no reason.'

'There's plenty whenever you're ready.'

'So you're going to stick around?' Flo asked, not so subtly fishing for information.

'I think so,' Hazin said. 'I just spoke with Ilyas.'

'And?' Flo asked.

'I don't want to talk about it now,' Hazin said.

In many ways she was happy not to hear his decision just yet.

Whatever he had chosen, it would hurt.

Still, there was a part of her that simply wanted more information.

'If you're ever back in London…'

'Flo…' He warned that the subject was closed.

'I'm just saying we might bump into each other.'

'Like we did the first night, when you just *happened* to be at Dion's?'

Flo smiled. 'No, maybe on the tube…'

'I think we did cross paths once.'

'Really?'

'I'm sure it was you. It was winter and I specifically remember you were wearing jeans and boots…'

It took a second to realise she was being teased because half the women in London would have been wearing jeans and boots in winter.

Still, Flo smiled at the thought that their paths might have crossed one day and accepted that the subject of his chosen future was closed. And so she asked him another question instead. 'Are you looking forward to being an uncle?'

'I don't know. I've never had anything to do with babies.' He thought for a moment. 'Ilyas seems happy, though.'

'He does.'

'And the mood at the palace has certainly improved since the last time I was here. It's nothing like it used to be.'

'What was it like when you came home at Christmas from school?' Flo asked.

'Well, it wasn't Christmas, for one thing.'

'But what was it like?'

She wanted to know.

'I had nannies when I was younger and then from the age of about eleven I took care of myself. Really, I didn't see anyone when I was here in the holidays, unless there was an official function. Ilyas was housed in the leaders' wing or taken out to the desert and immersed in the teachings.'

'Did you eat together?'

'No,' he said. 'Well, we did on formal occasions.'

'So where did you eat?'

'I was served my meals in the dining room here.'

'In the apartment?' Flo said, and she swallowed and thought of a child virtually alone in this huge space.

You really can have everything and nothing, Flo thought.

'I loathed coming home,' Hazin admitted, and he gave her arm a squeeze. 'But not this time.'

'I'm glad I've entertained—'

'You're not the entertainment, Flo,' Hazin said, and he meant it. So much so that it was then that he remembered she might soon have to work. 'Let's get some sleep.'

They undressed and slipped into bed. He turned off the lights so that all that lit the room was the scented candle.

He lay on his back with Flo curled up into him, her

head on his chest. He smelt heavenly and the feel of his naked stomach beneath her fingers had her wonder if she might just have to change her mind about sex.

He was so unexpectedly romantic this evening.

But she must not get ahead of herself.

As nice as tonight had been, it was a glass of mulled wine and a candle.

Yet it was the little things he did that made her heart glow, and she could not help but hope that there was more to come, for he had made this night away from home so special.

She had assumed, right up to now, that the gesture had been a bit of a ruse to get her into bed.

Not that he had needed a ruse.

Yet Hazin didn't seem to mind a bit that she needed to sleep.

But now she wanted a kiss.

Except Hazin really was asleep!

Not just asleep—his breathing had gone from deep to a gentle snore.

Flo lay there smiling as the noise from her less-than-perfect Prince grew louder.

'Hazin,' she said, and gave him a little prod.

It didn't do the trick.

'Hazin!' she said louder, and this time he got a kick.

He awoke a little and disengaged her from his arms, then rolled onto his side so they faced each other. They shared a smile. 'I don't usually snore,' Hazin said.

'Liar.'

'I don't, I'm just wrecked.'

These last few days had been busy. Racing around to get things done and seeing Petra's family, followed by the drain of relief at having given the speech.

And the guilt.

For Hazin had been busy making plans.

But he did not want to examine guilt now, for rather than speak their mouths met in a sleepy kiss.

There was just a whisper of resistance in him, for he wanted a clean slate, a clear head before he lost himself, but that whisper faded in the melding of their mouths.

Softly and slowly Hazin kissed her, his large hand lightly stroking her bare arm.

His calf came over her and she felt its heavy weight hook her in as they drank the intoxicating lust from each other's mouths.

Hazin's hand moved from her arm and stroked her waist, shooting arrows of desire to her centre. It was such an unhurried kiss yet it was the most sensual of her life.

Hazin had not brought her to his bed for this, yet there was no thought process now, just the sensation of being lost in a kiss.

Sometimes it had felt as if they'd been playing a game of cat and mouse, but not now.

Desire wrapped them closer. She opened her eyes to his and his gaze awaited her, and suddenly Flo remembered the first night they had met.

That moment when their souls had locked had felt the same as this, only this was deeper and this time they did not hide from it, or look away.

She was burning at his kiss and his touch, wrapped so tightly in his embrace. Flo freed her leg so that she could move it over his thigh, thus opening herself to him, for she had to have him inside, right now.

Her hand stretched down and felt him, hard and strong and ready. Hazin's hand encircled hers, and together they stroked him until they could bear it no longer. She guided him there but one of them at least was sensible, and his hand released hers as he went to reach for a condom.

'I'm on the Pill, Hazin.'

Those were words Flo had never said before, but to break contact now would feel criminal.

They were words that Hazin had always ignored.

Until now.

Hazin entered her slowly, relishing the feel of her tight, warm grip and he swallowed her sigh of pleasure.

Utter pleasure as he stretched her completely and their mouths met again. There was a delicious daze at his tenderness as they moved together, slow and unhurried.

Those strong arms were Flo's to explore tonight and she felt the silky skin that sheathed his muscles, while his tongue stroked hers in enticing circles. The heat they made could surely light the dark desert sky.

He rolled her onto her back and kissed her in a way Flo had not known existed until now. She found out first-hand how that rough, unshaven face felt when it rubbed against her soft skin.

He took her hands and held them over her head, their fingers laced.

Her legs wrapped around him and Flo arched into him. She knew, beyond a shadow of a doubt, that he was making love to her.

Hazin was drowning in the intimate embrace of her and he swallowed down the soft moans that came from her throat.

He freed her hands so she could explore his facc, and he drew up on his hands so he could watch her and kiss her. He took her in rapid, measured thrusts that had her grit her jaw together at times and had her stretch up for a kiss at others.

Hazin took her harder, holding nothing back. He watched as she helplessly grasped at pillows to anchor herself, then give in to the absolute force of his thrust. He felt her climax gather and the zip of tension in her made his stomach lift.

The room felt like a vacuum that sucked the air from him as he shot into her. He released with a breathless shout, and *this* was how it should be, Hazin knew.

This, he thought as he felt her release beneath him and revelled in the softness of the air in the aftermath of lovemaking.

His eyes opened to darkness and there was a shiver of guilt that ran through Hazin for the love Petra had never known. The defences inside with which he had walled that regret were temporarily down and Hazin wished, how he wished, that she had known love. In the still of the night, his soul spoke and he voiced that regret out loud. 'Oh, Petra.'

Flo froze beneath him.

Lost to her orgasm, utterly gone, she was hauled back as her lover said his late wife's name while still inside her.

It was like being sluiced with filthy water.

Lost in bliss, about to float gently back to earth, she was instead hurtled into high alert and her eyes snapped open. There was no denying what she had heard and Flo shoved him off her.

'Flo…' he attempted, but she was already half way out of the bed. His hand reached for her and came down on her shoulder but she shrugged it off.

'Don't touch me!' she told him through tense white lips.

She could not believe what had just happened and

what she had just heard, but knew there could be no coming back from this.

She flicked on the light and then scrabbled on the floor, trying to find her robe, desperate to get out and feeling as if she might well throw up, when her phone rang.

Not now! Flo thought.

Please, please, not now.

But she looked at her phone and, yes, it clearly wasn't Flo's night for it was Maggie.

Flo couldn't even bear to sit on the bed as she took the call, she just turned her back on Hazin.

'Hey,' Flo said, and tried to keep her voice as upbeat as possible.

'Flo, I've been having contractions. I think the baby's close.'

Flo asked a few questions and told Maggie she would be along very soon. First, though, she had to have a shower.

'Is she having it?' Hazin asked. He was sitting on the edge of the bed with his head in his hands.

'What do you think?' Flo sneered.

'Can we speak for two minutes?'

'You don't get another moment of my time,' Flo said, and grabbing her clothes she headed into his bathroom and slammed the door behind her.

Flo was very used to quick showers but this was the quickest of her life.

She felt as if she had been beaten all over and she was desperate to cry but there was no time to.

Hazin tried to speak to her, though.

He went into the bathroom just as she was turning off the taps and stepping out.

'Please, Flo. Let me explain—'

'Don't even try,' she said as she dried off and dressed with lightning speed. 'I've been made to feel bad in my time, but what you just did to me…' She picked up his comb and quickly ran it through her hair. In the mirror she could see the redness of her face as she practically glowed with humiliation and pain. 'Why don't you go back to bed, Hazin, and get off to your late wife.'

It was nasty but, hell, it was merited and Hazin closed his eyes as she brushed past and walked out.

They were done.

CHAPTER SIXTEEN

FLO WALKED SWIFTLY through the Palace.

There was no IV cupboard to hide away in this time.

No other staff she could call on to cover for her.

There was the Palace doctor, of course, but she would never let down her friend.

She had to push aside what had happened.

It was hard to, though.

Flo wanted to pause and have a cry, or to catch her breath.

A few moments ago she had been in his arms, locked in bliss…

As Flo walked through the grand entrance towards the leaders' wing she ignored the portraits, yet it felt as if Petra's eyes were following her.

'Have him!' Flo said out loud, to the bemusement of two guards who stood at the foot of the stairs.

And with that small outburst she did what she could to let it go.

She would examine her pain later but right now she had Maggie to focus on.

Flo loved her job. As she climbed the staircase and entered the Royal wing that housed Maggie and Ilyas, she drew on that fact. This was about Maggie and being with her as she brought life into the world.

Flo put on a smile and walked into the Royal suite. Maggie was leaning against Ilyas and deep in the midst of a contraction.

Flo went over and felt the strength of the contraction. 'How long have you been having them?' Flo asked.

'Since Ilyas got back from seeing Hazin.'

'Maggie!' Ilyas said in slight reprimand and then addressed Flo. 'I think she started to have them when I was about to go and speak with my brother. I told her I could speak to Hazin at another time, but Maggie insisted she was fine.'

'So since around seven,' Flo checked, and Maggie nodded.

It was now just coming up for midnight.

Flo got Maggie up onto the bed and gave her a gentle exam to see how far along things were.

'Should we call the Palace doctor to come?' Ilyas asked.

'You can call if you would prefer to,' Flo said, 'but he'll be around for quite some time.' She smiled at Maggie. 'You're three centimetres dilated.'

'Three?' Maggie's voice was a touch incensed. 'That's it?'

'That's excellent,' Flo said, in positive midwife-speak, but Maggie didn't want to hear it!

'How can I only be three centimetres dilated?' As another contraction hit she started to moan. 'How bad is it going to be?'

'It's going to be absolutely fine,' Flo assured her.

Flo let the Palace doctor know what was happening and he came and checked on Maggie, but was very affable and understood her desire for as much privacy as possible during the first stage. Flo assured him she would call when things had moved along, or if she had any concerns in the interim.

Ilyas suggested that Maggie lie down for a while and try to relax, and when Maggie agreed Flo thought it best to leave them to it for now. There was an area outside the main bedroom, once used for maids and such, but tonight it served as Flo's staffroom.

She made a huge mug of tea and curled up in a chair, keeping her thoughts on Maggie, rather than dwelling on Hazin.

It was too hard to do both.

Her broken heart would be there waiting at the other end of the birth, so for now she pushed it aside and focused on Maggie and the baby soon to be born.

Maggie dozed between contractions and then had a bath, and as she climbed out her waters broke.

'I was so worried it would happen on the stage…'

'I know you were.' Flo smiled as she listened to the baby's heart rate. 'Your baby is behaving beautifully for you.'

The contractions strengthened and started coming closer together and when even the huge bedroom felt confined, they moved out onto the balcony as the dawn broke.

'What a beautiful day to have a baby,' Flo said.

A Christmas baby.

It *was* magic.

Somehow Christmas always was.

Even last year when she'd been so low, it had been a wonderful family day.

And on this one she would deliver her best friend's child.

Or the Palace doctor would.

But Flo got to do this part.

This lovely part where the world was all hushed as Maggie leant on the stone wall and tried to breathe through the pain. The contractions were coming close together now and Maggie was finding them overwhelming.

'You are doing so well,' Ilyas said in his deep voice.

He wasn't staid, Flo decided. In fact, he was incredibly stoic and calm and exactly what Maggie needed.

As Maggie groaned, Ilyas put his hand on the small of his wife's back and massaged her there as Flo had shown him, but now it did not appease her and she pushed his hand off.

'Go and get Flo her present,' Maggie said, and Ilyas frowned.

'Now?'

'Yes, now,' Maggie said, and her voice was urgent.

Flo knew things were moving along, just by her friend's need to set the world to rights.

'I thought you'd forgone Christmas,' Flo said.

'Not for you.'

And that touched her heart, because they were such good friends and while it wasn't a big deal to Maggie, it was to Flo. She smiled as Ilyas returned to the balcony with a beautifully wrapped gift.

'Open it,' Maggie ordered.

It was a *hammam* towel and a gorgeous glass bottle of oil that smelled the same as the one the maids had applied to her hair.

'They're gorgeous,' Flo said. 'Thank you so much.' But Maggie still wasn't appeased.

'Read the card!' Maggie shouted.

Flo loved a woman in transition!

The dominatrix effect, she jokingly called it, and gave Ilyas a smile.

But then, when she did as she was told and read her card, Flo felt tears well in her eyes.

Dear Flo,
Any time you need a spa day, know that I do too and that the hammam *awaits. I still can't get used to being rich, but you can come here whenever you want, even for a weekend.*
We are best friends and we need our spa days,
Maggie xxx

Flo had wondered if things might change between them, and if Maggie being a princess might somehow be the end of their friendship. Over and over she had told herself it would not and had reminded herself that this was Maggie. Yet at times she had doubted and worried, and Maggie had clearly understood that she might.

It meant so much.

'Thank you,' Flo said. 'I shall be sure and use my gift often.'

'Well, make sure you do!' Maggie snarled, but then she wavered as her body took over. 'I want to push.'

'Then do.'

For an hour or so more it was still just the three of them. Maggie moved onto the bed and asked for darkness so Flo closed the drapes on the gorgeous day, and with just the sidelights they got down to the gritty end of birth.

Pushing was hard and exhausting work, but Maggie got the hang of it and real progress was being made.

'I'm going to call for the doctor,' Flo said, and as Ilyas encouraged his wife, Flo made the call and opened up the delivery pack.

'Another push,' Flo said. 'You are so close to meeting your baby, Maggie…' She looked up and smiled as the doctor and elder came in.

The elder was lovely and he went and sat where Flo had throughout the night drunk an awful lot of tea. The doctor too was charming and did not rush to take over.

It was just a gorgeous, natural birth and as Ilyas held Maggie's leg, Flo held the other and then hugged her friend through the very end of it as Ilyas watched his son being born.

He really was a beautiful baby.

Long-limbed and with a lusty cry, he was delivered onto Maggie's stomach and Ilyas cut the cord.

'I've got a son,' Maggie said, and though they had all already known that the baby would be a boy, it was wonderful to watch her friend's pure joy that her son was here.

Flo covered them in a blanket so the baby lay on his mother's chest, and his cries soon faded. He had a little feed, which helped with the delivery of the placenta.

And there was still no rush, there was plenty of skin-to-skin time before the doctor asked for him to be brought over so he could be checked.

He really was perfect. With huge dark blue eyes and thick black hair, he was the image of his father.

'Your son is very healthy,' the doctor said, and Flo wrapped the little man up and handed him to Ilyas.

Often, first-time fathers were awkward, but Ilyas was confident and held him close as he carried him over to Maggie.

It was a lovely family moment, so as the elder and doctor went to inform the King and Queen of the birth of their first grandchild, Flo stepped out onto the balcony to give them some time alone.

And for some time alone for herself too.

Now that the baby was safely here and the intensity of the past hours was fading, Flo could feel anew the hurt that had propelled her from Hazin's bed.

She closed her eyes on the bright mid-morning sun because tears were dangerously close.

She was thrilled for Maggie, absolutely so, yet Flo ached, she just ached because it felt like a knife was twisting in her gut at another appalling mistake made in the romance department.

Maybe she should be more like Maggie and be mistrusting of people. Instead, she was like that bloody eager Labrador, jumping whenever the master called.

No more.

She was through.

Of course, she would stay for the rest of her leave and she would return often, because there was no way she would let Hazin affect her friendship with Maggie. But as for Hazin she was done.

Flo was angry and hurt and felt cold to the bone.

But there was still work to be done so she pressed her fingers to her temples and took in a deep breath before heading back inside.

'Where's Ilyas?' Flo asked when she saw Maggie alone, holding the baby.

'He wanted to speak with his parents and not just leave it to the elder.'

'Do you think they'll come and see him?'

'I don't know,' Maggie admitted. 'I don't think they took any interest at all in their children, but things do seem better sincc we married.'

'Well, let me get you tidied up just in case,' Flo suggested.

It was all very seamless.

With no expense spared, the room had been very

well prepared for the Royal birth. Flo soon had all the equipment moved out, and the new mother sitting up in a fresh bed and gown, holding her baby.

'How are you feeling?' Flo asked.

'So happy,' Maggie said, and looked down at her sleeping son. 'He looks so like Ilyas.'

'He does. I certainly didn't smuggle him in under my robe.' Flo smiled. 'He's definitely his father's son. Do you have a name?'

'We like Bassam,' Maggie said, and then looked up at her friend. 'Thanks for being here, Flo.'

'I wouldn't have missed it for the world.'

'After Mum died I never thought I'd love Christmas again,' Maggie admitted. 'But now I want him to know the same magic that I had growing up. I haven't even got him a present…'

'I have,' Flo said. 'I got a few extra bits too and they're all wrapped and waiting.'

Christmas was back.

At least, it was for Maggie.

Flo was beyond tired and looking forward to crawling into bed and pulling the sheets over her head until the day was done.

But that wasn't an option yet.

She didn't want to leave Maggie until she was ready for a long sleep, but that wasn't about to happen as Ilyas returned and informed her that his parents did indeed want to visit.

It was both surprising and nice to see them make an effort. They didn't stay for long, but the Queen even had a small hold of the little baby.

'Congratulations,' King Ahmed said. 'Have you chosen a name?'

Flo watched as Maggie went to respond but Ilyas cut

in. 'We are still deciding.' For whatever reason, Ilyas didn't want to share that particular piece of news just yet, Flo guessed. When the Queen looked over at her, Flo went over and took the baby as Ilyas spoke on. 'I have asked the palace elder, later today, to announce the birth of a healthy son. That is news enough for now.'

The King and Queen left, and with that visit over Maggie sank back on the pillows in relief.

'I think he's starting to get hungry,' Flo said, and handed her back her son. But feeding time wasn't going to happen just yet for there was another visitor.

'Hi, Hazin,' Maggie said, and Flo felt the colour drain from her cheeks.

She simply wasn't ready to face him now, not that she could show it. The last thing Maggie needed was to pick up on even a hint of the tension between them.

It was hard not to show it, though.

Terribly hard, to stand with a fixed smile and pretend that this man had not hurt her deeply.

Hazin came over and gave Maggie a kiss on the cheek and then peered down at the baby.

'He's very cute,' Hazin said, and Flo could hear his attempt to sound bright. He was as pale as he had been on the day he had given the speech. Beneath his eyes there were dark smudges and he looked as if he'd had just about as much sleep as she had.

'Do you want to hold him?' Maggie asked, but Hazin shook his head and politely declined.

'No, thank you. I'm sure he needs his mother right now.'

'Well, I think he'd like to meet his uncle,' Maggie refuted, and held the little baby out.

Hazin rather awkwardly took the baby.

Flo didn't want to look; she didn't want Maggie to get even a hint of the hurt she carried today.

Yet she couldn't not look.

Hazin gazed down at his nephew and watched as he struggled to focus in this very new world, but then Hazin lowered his head and their eyes met. 'Hi, there,' he said to the infant and did not take his eyes from him as he spoke to the proud parents. 'Does he have a name?'

There was no evasion as there had been with the parents. 'Bassam,' Maggie answered, then Ilyas explained why they had chosen that name.

'It means the one that smiles. It is what we both want for him.'

Hazin's face crumpled a touch as he looked at the newborn and heard his new name.

Hazin didn't cry as such, but it was this moment where all could see the pain that he'd kept hidden for so long. Here, today, for a brief moment, it was on show for all to see. Yet for all the pain of the past, there was so much hope for his nephew, who lay so tiny and yet so content in his arms, as if he already knew he was wanted and loved.

Flo went over, only because she was the midwife and could sense he was ready to hand the baby back. The less professional side of Flo could tell he was struggling to keep it together.

'I'll take him,' she said, and as Hazin looked up she saw his eyes were glassy.

'Thanks.'

It was an awkward transition—Flo, who could easily juggle twins on her lap while speaking on the phone, was suddenly all fingers and thumbs as he handed her the little bundle, but of course she clicked into working mode and seamlessly handed him back to his mother.

She could still feel the touch of Hazin's hands on her skin and she had seen the despair in his eyes.

'I'm going to go,' Hazin said. He was a bit embarrassed by the brief slip of his mask so he again offered his congratulations and then left.

As the door closed, Maggie spoke to Ilyas about Hazin and his reaction to the baby. 'He must have been thinking about Petra.'

Flo knew she was brilliant at her job then, because somehow she bit down on a very smart retort about Hazin thinking of Petra at inappropriate times!

And then her anger towards him simply faded.

There was just a hollow ache of sadness.

It wasn't a vague ache, for it gnawed inside her and it felt like hunger.

But hunger she could rectify.

What had happened earlier she could not.

The baby was fed and settled and Maggie too, after a light meal, was ready to sleep. Flo was more exhausted than she had ever been.

Not just physically, she was utterly drained.

'Why don't you go and get some sleep, Flo?' Ilyas suggested.

'I'm going to.' Flo nodded. 'Wake me up when Maggie wakes and if the baby—'

'Rest now, Flo,' Ilyas said. 'We have the palace doctor and there are two nursery nurses. You have been up all night and you need to sleep too.'

Flo nodded, because she knew he was right.

Over the next few days she would be hands on, helping Maggie with little Bassam, but right now she wanted to curl up in bed and just cry.

'Thank you for everything,' Ilyas said, and saw her outside.

She ached, and the walk through the Palace felt like a long one. The high of a successful delivery had faded and the rest of the world, her world, awaited—she just could not bear to face what had happened last night with Hazin.

She would deal with her thoughts later, Flo decided, for right now she was too depleted to think straight.

As she passed the portraits, very deliberately Flo kept her eyes fixed ahead and thought only of bed and sleep. Yet before that she had to ring her family and pretend, for the second year in a row, that everything was okay just so that she didn't ruin their Christmas.

This time, though, she hurt way more than last year.

A married man had been awful.

A grieving widower hurt like hell.

And the sight of Hazin waiting for her as she turned the corner was not a sight she needed right now.

'Not now.' Flo was the one who said it this time and she put up her hands and attempted to just walk past.

'Yes, now.'

'No, because I'm too tired to be polite,' Flo said. 'And I don't want to be mean…'

'I don't blame you if you are,' Hazin said, 'but, please, just hear me out.'

CHAPTER SEVENTEEN

He guided her into a room, a library, and she sat there, shivering with cold and tiredness and the hurt of it all.

'I didn't feel for Petra the way I feel about you,' he said, and Flo let out a hollow laugh.

'You've had all night to come up with something and that's the best you can do?'

Flo stood and went to brush past him but he halted her.

'I knew that I was…' He stopped. Hazin was certain he had messed up too much for the plans he had made. 'Flo, I wasn't thinking about Petra.'

'You said her name when you came.'

'*After* I came,' Hazin said, and those seconds mattered. 'Afterwards,' he reiterated, 'I just felt this terrible guilt because I've never felt like that before. I didn't love Petra the way I love you.'

But Flo was so wary and way too used to lies to simply believe him.

She did sit down, though, while Hazin did his best to explain.

'Just before she died, Petra told me that she knew I didn't love her and I can't stand it that she died never knowing love. Because I didn't. Ilyas had again refused to marry and my father had asked me if I was prepared to step up. I said yes. For the first time I didn't feel like a substitute. I did the right thing by my father and I married the bride they chose for me. I did my best and I treated her like the princess she was but—'

'Hazin,' Flo interrupted, 'love doesn't just happen, well, not most of the time…' She had to qualify what she had just said because love *had* just happened to her on the night they had met. 'You married a stranger…' Flo was not a mean person by nature, so she was kind. 'I've seen the way you treat others, I don't doubt you were wonderful to your wife. Perhaps she was just trying to set you free…'

Hazin was quiet as he thought back to those times because that was the type of thing Petra might have done, and then he swallowed as Flo spoke on.

'Maybe love would have grown.'

He nodded.

For in many ways it had.

'You were eighteen when you married, Hazin, and did your best at the time…' Flo shook her head. 'I can't do this now. I need to sleep.'

'Of course.'

She walked away from him, and as she did so his words were playing in her head.

Though the words that were playing on repeat in her head weren't—Petra, Petra, Petra, Petra, Petra. Instead they were…

I didn't love Petra the way I love you.

When Hazin had said *love* had he perhaps meant want?

Or had Hazin just told her he loved her?

And if he had, what on earth was she doing, walking away?

Flo could feel his eyes on her as she entered her

room. She wanted to get away from his gaze so she wouldn't break down and cry and instead could clarify things to herself and think.

But then Flo opened the door and she simply stopped thinking. In fact, she was stunned, because suddenly it had turned into Christmas.

There was a gorgeous pine tree with twinkling lights and all the presents she had wrapped were under it, as well as some she hadn't.

It was bewildering.

Flo stood and breathed in the scent of pine. She looked up at the gold streamers lacing the ceiling. Everywhere she looked it was Christmas—there was even fake snow on the balcony doors.

'Happy Christmas,' Hazin said, and he came up behind her and snaked his hand around her waist, and Flo just leant back on him.

'You did this.'

'No,' he said. 'The staff have been busy.'

'You arranged it, though.'

'With difficulty. When you declined to change rooms I had to think on my feet and somehow get you over to mine so the staff could decorate the room. I filled your stocking, though.'

Flo looked over towards her bed and sure enough there was a red velvet stocking hanging there.

'I believe you're supposed to open your stocking first?' Hazin prompted.

'Absolutely,'

Shaken, Flo walked over to the bed and undid a velvet bow and the stocking dropped into her hand.

'I didn't do the decorations, but I wrapped each gift myself,' Hazin said. 'Well, except for the fruit and nuts.'

He really had! There was a lipstick and a nail varnish and… 'False eyelashes?'

'I had to look up gift suggestions,' Hazin explained.

'Oh, well, thank you very much.'

'There's more,' Hazin said.

Flo smiled as she weighed the stocking in her hand. But then tears filled her eyes because what he had done was beautiful, but the hours before had hurt so very much.

He knew how much he had hurt her, so he took her in his arms and just held her as she tried to work out how it was possible to be so sad and so happy all at the very same time. How to swear never again in one moment, while knowing you were about to dive right back in the next.

'I don't understand what happened, Hazin.'

'Flo, I messed up…' he admitted. It had been the story of his life and Hazin was certain that no apology this time, however heartfelt, could fix it.

'You, really, really did,' Flo said.

'I won't do it again.'

'You might.' She giggled.

For Hazin, it was the most magical sound on earth, so much so that he peeled himself from her embrace and held her as he gazed upon forgiveness.

The right kind.

He just looked at her—and marvelled that she could smile after what he had done. The hint that there would be more chances of getting things wrong helped too.

'I am in love with you,' he told her.

It was so new to them both, such a naked honesty that neither really knew how to deal with a love so exposed.

And so they attempted normality, on a Christmas Day in Zayrinia that had not existed until now.

'The presents under the tree are from your family,' he told her. 'They were delivered last week.'

'So Kumu was lying.'

'On my orders.'

And though usually Flo would be diving under the tree and tearing paper, in bliss to open presents from home, instead she just stood there, those words he'd said still on repeat.

The *I love you* ones.

It was time for Flo to be brave.

She went to the tree and her hand hovered over the two gifts she had bought for him.

'I got something for you too.'

She went for the first, the safe option, yet as she handed it to him there was a flutter of hope in her heart.

He looked at the little card with his name on and opened the parcel carefully.

'Chocolate gingers?' he frowned as he read the box and opened them up. 'I've never heard of them.'

'*Dark* chocolate gingers. They really are the best.'

He bit into one and his smile grew wide. 'They are amazing.'

'I know, I know.'

'They seriously are. Thank you.'

'Once you know how good they are, it's sort of a tradition to eat them every year.'

'I think I can manage that.'

Then she looked at the pile of presents. There was even one from his parents addressed to her. Had they listened to his speech? Had kindness been sown? She looked at the labels on the presents from her family.

To Flo
With Love

Those words were such an unquestionable presence in her life, yet one Hazin had lived entirely without.

It *was* time to be brave.

And so she handed him another present—a slim package. Just an envelope dressed in silver and tied with a bow.

But within it lay her heart.

'This is for you,' Flo said.

He looked at thc little card, again with his name upon it, and he undid the bow and then peeled open the silver envelope.

Inside was a ticket to a West End show.

'I've got the other ticket,' Flo told him.

'But it's not until spring?'

'It was the earliest I could get weekend tickets,' Flo said, and then she took a breath. 'And it would give you time to think. If by then you'd missed me…' Then she said the hardest part. 'When I first thought about what to buy you, I was in a department store and decided on some sexy underwear. Something fun and light that could be kept for me, but it wasn't what I wanted…' She looked at Hazin and admitted a truth she had recently learnt. 'I don't speak up enough. I do at work, but in my personal life I'm the queen of pretending that everything's fine and not stating my wants. I've decided it's time that stopped.'

'I agree,' Hazin said. 'So what are your wants?'

'That if we see each other again I want it to be about more than just sex.'

'Such as?'

'I want to go out on a date.'

A first date.

A proper one.

'I would love to go out on a date with you,' Hazin

said, and he looked down at the ticket. It meant so much to be asked for a night out with Flo. 'Perhaps I could take you to dinner beforehand?'

'I'd like that,' Flo said. 'Very much.' But then, at the mention of dinner, her stomach cramped. 'I hate to ruin the romance but I'm so hungry, Hazin, I haven't eaten since…' Flo could honestly not remember when.

It had been her own fault. There had been refreshments discreetly delivered throughout the night, but the knot in her stomach had been placated by endless tea.

Well, no more.

And so, as unsexy as they were, Flo stated her wants. 'I need something to eat.'

'Then I'll call Kumu.'

'But then she'll know you're in here.'

'Flo,' Hazin said, 'I don't care who knows about us. Now, if you are truly starving, open your stocking.'

'It will take more than fruit and nuts…'

'It's not a mandarin,' he said, and picked up the discarded stocking and handed it back.

It felt like it was.

Well, satsuma was her choice of fruit for Christmas Day, but to pick him up on his naming of citrus would be rather splitting hairs when he'd gone to so much effort.

It felt like a heavy fruit for it was soft and round but when she pushed it up through the stocking, Flo found it was, in fact, a squishy, burnt orange velvet ball. Like a luxurious stress ball, it was a work of art, with tiny gold tacks all around and an intricate gold catch.

It was a box of sorts.

Flo did not want to get this wrong.

She did not want to get her hopes up only to be told they were Petra's earrings that he had long kept in a drawer and had hastily wrapped at the last moment so that he could give her a gift on Christmas Day.

She giggled at the chaos of her own mind for she could not quite believe that this moment was hers.

'Why are you laughing?' Hazin said.

'I have a very dark sense of humour.'

'I know you do,' he said. 'Are you going to open it?'

'I'm nervous.'

'Don't ever be nervous with me.'

Hazin wasn't nervous.

Doubt and uncertainty belonged to days prior—delivering a speech while knowing a ring was being made by the royal jeweller, and trying to politely accept commiserations while your heart was soaring for the first time in a decade.

Hazin hadn't just been looking up stocking filler ideas on the Internet, or Christmas decorations either.

He really wanted to get this right, and so when Flo didn't open it he took the box and got down on one knee. 'Florence, will you do me the honour—?'

'Hazin!' Flo screeched, embarrassed, laughing and happy, so happy, all at the very same time. 'Get up!'

'Not till you say that you'll marry me.' He smiled.

'Yes!'

Oh, yes.

And, oh, what a ring.

A diamond that, now she had a Christmas tree, could possibly have been hung on string, or even placed at the top as a star for it was so huge and sparkly.

'See the band…'

She couldn't see, for her eyes were filled with tears, but when she wiped them there were tiny intricate flakes of frost and snow engraved on the white gold band.

She had her white Christmas after all.

It really was the little things.

'I love you,' he told her. 'I have been planning this for a while, and I guess I felt guilty for all that Petra missed out on.'

Now she could see just how the guilt must have played on his mind.

'How do you think her family will react?'

'They were thrilled,' Hazin said, and he smiled at her startled look. 'When I went to dinner the first night, I apologised and they said they wanted me to be happy. That it was time to be.'

'It is.'

'I never intended to tell them about you, but I went over again yesterday. I didn't want them to hear it in an announcement.'

He was, for all his wild ways, the very kindest of men.

'And I had to inform Ilyas too.'

'Am I the only one who didn't know?'

'Pretty much.' He nodded.

'Maggie didn't know.' Flo shook her head as she thought back, because she was certain something would have been said last night, but then she realised what must have happened—Ilyas would have come back from the meeting with Hazin to find Maggie in labour. 'What did Ilyas say?' she asked.

'That he could not be happier for me, as long as you said yes. Flo, I know there is a lot to work out—my brother wants me here but I have told him that I love London too. It is also my home…'

'We'll work it out,' Flo said, for she knew that they would.

'I was going to tell him that for our residence here I

wanted a new area, but now, since you have been there a few times, it is starting to feel like home too.'

There was so much to think about, and so many changes to come for them both, but with the constant of love they would sort it all out, Flo knew.

'I'd better call my parents,' she said, 'given everyone else knows.'

'Why not call them after lunch?' Hazin suggested, as there was a soft knock at the door.

Kumu, with two maids, came in wheeling a huge trolley and they set up the meal at a table.

'Your meal is ready,' Kumu said, and it was clear to Flo that she expected them to come to the table and eat.

'I was just…' Flo started, and then halted, for she could hardly tell Kumu she intended to take her meal to bed.

As well as Hazin!

So she duly took a seat and so too did Hazin. Smiling, Kumu removed the silver cloche covering her plate and Flo stared in disbelief at her meal.

It was a true Christmas dinner.

There was succulent turkey and the trimmings, about which Flo was extremely particular, were perfect.

There were golden Yorkshire puddings and pigs in blankets with a side of bread sauce. Brussels sprouts had been roasted and crisped just as she liked them and there was a glistening cranberry sauce. There were parsnips loaded with butter and what looked like her favourite chestnut stuffing.

Hazin could *not* know all her trimmings.

'Did you speak to Maggie?' Flo asked shaking her head, because although Maggie had joined Flo and her family at Christmas a couple of times, surely she could not have so specifically remembered how things were done.

This was perfect, right down to the willow-pattern-print plate her mum used at Christmas.

Flo was bemused.

Confused.

She took up a fork and tasted the stuffing, and it melted on her tongue.

'That's *just* like my mum's stuffing.'

'Because it *is* your mum's stuffing.'

'Did you ask for the recipe?' Flo said, and then looked at Kumu, imagining the palace chefs trying to get it right, but, no, no one ever could.

For this was perfect.

'Enjoy,' Kumu said, and she left with the maids.

Flo sat facing Hazin and he took her hand.

'I spoke to your father,' Hazin said, 'to ask for his permission to marry you. And then I spoke with your mother and she said she would be delighted to cook dinner a little earlier…'

'This *is* my mum's dinner.' Flo could not take it in, then she remembered her mother on the phone, all tense and too busy to speak—no wonder! 'You had it flown all this way for me?'

'I've been planning this for…' He had been about to say days. About to say how, when the sun had streamed into the cave, he had known this was love.

It had been earlier than that, though.

Hazin thought back to the deserted beach in the Caribbean, knowing she was at the Palace and aching to return, yet wanting the anniversary out of the way first.

And then he thought of the night they had met and how his heart *had* beat faster.

'I've been planning this for quite some time,' Hazin

admitted. 'I got it into my head that I wanted the anniversary over and done with before you and I got together, but I couldn't last. I had Kumu discreetly find out your parents' phone number and on the morning of the anniversary I spoke with them.'

'Kumu knew then?'

Hazin nodded.

She remembered then Kumu standing beside her and translating the speech. How, of late, Kumu had been looking after her that bit more.

'Is that why she asked me to sleep in the west wing? So they could decorate my room?'

Hazin nodded. 'Had you just said yes, we could have avoided—'

'I don't want to avoid anything with you, Hazin. We can face anything. And I loved last night.' She smiled. 'Well, most of it.'

'Call your family…'

She needed to eat but she also needed to speak, so he fed her perfect roast potatoes as she called home.

'Thank you!' the conversation started. 'Yes!' it was all a bit garbled.

Hazin could hear the shouts and congratulations and then they somehow had dinner with her family and ate together across the miles.

And then one of Flo's sisters-in-law asked a question. 'I'm not sure.' She looked over at Hazin. 'Will I be a princess?'

'You'll be a sheikha princess.'

'Oh!' She relayed the information back to her family. 'Apparently I'll be a sheikha princess.'

Hazin loved it that she hadn't particularly cared or known.

For she loved him, he knew.

Then the call ended and they ate the last of their dinner. Flo needed bed, though not to lie down.

'Come here, my bride-to-be,' he said the second she put down her fork.

And suddenly Flo wasn't tired and they tumbled to the bed and kissed. A deep, tender kiss as they peeled their clothes away. Just so utterly thrilled to have found each other. And when they made love, he said her name over and over and over.

'I love you,' Hazin said. It felt so good to say it and deeply mean it.

'I love you back.'

And then, as they lay there in bliss, the oddest thing happened—a large cheer went up outside and they both laughed.

'For a second there,' Flo admitted, 'I thought they were celebrating us.'

'And me. They must have just announced the birth.' And then he looked at Flo, the love of his life. 'As of today, I'm third in line.'

'You've been demoted!'

'It doesn't feel like it.'

Flo looked at her shiny new ring and then at him. 'It's the best Christmas ever.'

He had made it so.

EPILOGUE

STOOD UP!

Hazin had sat alone in Dion's, where they were supposed to be meeting for their long-awaited date, but Flo had not shown.

Now he stood in the theatre foyer as the last call for patrons to take their seats sounded.

He glanced at his phone.

Ten minutes

Flo had sent that text twenty minutes ago!

To the chagrin of her fellow passengers, Flo did her lipstick and make-up on the tube and then ran up the escalators, changing into her heels when she got to the top. Once out on the street she ran a brush through her hair as she raced to get to the theatre.

It was supposed to be a hand-holding romantic night—their official first date!

And yet she was so late they'd missed dinner and would now have to be one of those wretched couples who were shown to their seats late with a torch as everyone pulled in their knees and silently tutted.

But then, there he was, and the world clicked into place with his easy, welcoming smile.

He was wearing a suit and just as stunning to her eyes as he had been on that first night.

'I'm sorry I'm so late.' Flo had been all primed to leave on time, but births worked to their own timeline and at the end of the day she had chosen to stay. 'I couldn't leave her…'

'It's fine. All I ask,' Hazin added as he gave her a kiss, 'is that you're a little more punctual for our wedding.'

The wedding was next week.

It was to be a huge white wedding in London in spring, with all the trimmings and the complication of royal guests too.

Flo could not wait to see Maggie and little Bassam.

Tomorrow was her final day at work and then there was her leaving do to squeeze in.

It was bliss to take their seats and be entertained for a couple of hours.

Except Flo couldn't switch her mind off.

She had just found something out.

It wouldn't be that much of a shock. She had come off the Pill after all, for this very reason.

Flo wanted to work, even after she married Hazin. He had not liked what was happening under his father's rule and had stepped back. Now that the leadership was transitioning toward Ilyas, Hazin wanted to step up.

With conditions, though.

They would have two homes. Flo loved London and her family and that wasn't going to ever change.

But, as Hazin said, it didn't have to. He had practically been raised there too and loved it as much as Flo.

They had found a stunning apartment that would be

their London base, and the rest of the time would be spent in Zayrina.

Flo could still do the job she loved while in London, and just as he pushed for her to follow her path, she pushed for him to follow his.

Ilyas had raised an eyebrow when his younger brother had told him that he would be commencing studying part time.

'We have a lot of ancient heritage,' Hazin had told him. 'I want to better understand it.'

They had decided that while juggling so many balls, yes, they both wanted a baby, so why not throw caution to the wind and see what happened?

She had just found out that it had.

Happened.

They sat in the dark and watched the performance unfold. The show was very good, so very good that the momentous news she had to share suddenly slipped backstage.

His hand was in hers and she loved his easy laugh.

When she had bought the tickets, Flo had thought she might sit through this performance alone.

She well recalled collecting the tickets for a performance that was months away, thinking that she might be the one standing in the foyer, waiting for him to show; that she might sit alone in the dark in the knowledge he did not want her love.

Yet Hazin did want it.

And over and over he showed her that.

It was there in all the little things he did.

The squeeze of his hand at a funny part.

The easy sharing of smiles and chocolate treats.

His love was there waiting, even when she was late.

And she was not nervous to tell him she was pregnant. Simply impatient, for she wanted the world gone, and then to be alone with him at home so she could share the news.

Yet it was only the interval.

'I love intervals,' Hazin suddenly said.

'Why?'

'I get restless.' He smiled that sexy smile. 'I start to smell your perfume. I start thinking of things that I shouldn't.'

'Like what?' Flo asked, assuming he would start the seduction now.

'You're late.'

'I told you, I had a mother who was stressed…' And then she halted as she realised he wasn't referring to her delayed arrival tonight.

In the dark, as her mind had been racing, his had been too.

'How late are you?' he asked.

'Enough for me to take a test at work.'

'And?' he asked.

She nodded.

Just a little nod was all it took.

A little nod that conveyed a huge message and then she felt his arms wrap around her.

It was bliss to be there, wrapped in his arms and breathing in his familiar scent, and to share the happy news.

'Do you know when it's due?' he asked.

It was early days yet, of course, but Flo had naturally worked it out. 'Around Christmas.'

'Well, then, we'd better make sure we have Christmas here,' Hazin said, and all the little flutters of nerves about where the baby would be born were laid quickly to rest. 'It's the best news, Flo.'

'It's not too soon?' she checked, albeit a little to late.

'Not at all,' Hazin said. 'You've been keeping me up all night.'

'You loved every minute,' Flo said. 'And we don't stop just because I'm pregnant.'

'That's very good to know.'

Now there was a choice to be made. They could celebrate the news in the way they did best or answer the call of the bell that was sending them back to their seats.

'Do you want to go back for the second half?' Hazin asked.

She thought for a moment and Flo decided that she did.

'It's our first official date!' she reminded him.

'Do you generally sleep with men on first dates?' Hazin asked, and as always he made her smile.

'Certainly not!' Flo said as they walked back to their seats. 'I'm offended that you asked.'

'Pity,' Hazin said as the lights dimmed. 'Because I've asked for the same table at Dion's and I've booked my old suite in the hope that you're easy.'

It was the very best of first dates.

For love was already sorted. They had the rest of their lives together now.

* * * * *